SF Books b

Visit VaughnHeppner.com for more information

The Lost Destroyer

(Lost Starship Series 3)

By Vaughn Heppner

Copyright © 2015 by the author.

ISBN-13: 978-1512387247
ISBN-10: 151238724X
BISAC: Fiction / Science Fiction / Military

-1-

A purple bolt of ionized magnetic force struck Starship *Victory*. The deflectors didn't stop the attack because the shield was down. The collapsium armor darkened where the strand hit. Then a plate blew off the hull, tumbling into space.

On the starship's bridge, Captain Maddox rocked in his command chair.

"Hard to starboard," he said.

"The ship isn't responding, sir," Lieutenant Noonan shouted from the pilot's chair.

"Galyan," Maddox said.

The holographic image of the alien AI said nothing.

Maddox swiveled his chair to see what was wrong with the AI. The holoimage stood at its favorite spot on the bridge, but everything inside the shape's outline was fuzzy.

The captain swiveled back so he could see the main screen and the lieutenant at the same time. "Jump," he told Valerie. "Get us out of here."

"The magnetic storm is shutting down our systems, sir. A jump under these conditions could destroy us."

Another bolt of ionized magnetic force surged out of the twisting mass. An indicator told Maddox the storm was over ten thousand kilometers in width, making it larger than most terrestrial planets. The bolt struck their vessel. Metal groaned ominously, and the bridge around the captain shuddered.

"I may be able to use cold propulsion to move us," Valerie said.

1

"Do it," Maddox told her.

Valerie's fingers played across the pilot board.

A rear viewer showed Maddox that cold propellant ejected from the thrusters. Slowly, the starship turned away from the ion storm and began to gain separation.

Another ion strand lashed out. Maddox tensed. This one missed the hull armor. A surge of electrical power must have struck, though. A bridge panel went dark. There were too many panels down already.

Maddox swiveled around to check on Galyan again. The holoimage was still fuzzy. As the captain watched, part of the holo-outline faded away.

What if they lost the ancient AI? "Will the storm damage be permanent?" Maddox asked.

"There's no way to tell yet, sir," the lieutenant said.

"I want greater acceleration," Maddox said, raising his voice.

"I understand, sir. When the engines come back online, I can do that. Until then, cold propulsion is all we have."

Maddox noted the strain in Valerie's face, the tightness in her shoulders. The cold propulsion had been a good idea. Maddox knew he wouldn't have thought of it.

"You're doing well, Lieutenant."

Valerie shot him a glance. A tremulous smile appeared and then a nod of appreciation.

Just then, something caught Maddox's eye. He stood, amazed and then perplexed as the faint image of a ship passed through the ion storm like the ghost of a gigantic vessel.

Maddox checked the indicator. The vessel was a fraction of the size of the magnetic storm. Even so, whatever that was out there was huge, bigger than anything Star Watch owned, bigger than a Cestus hauler or a Spacer home-ship. The indicator showed the ghost measured an easy fifty kilometers in length and thirty at its widest. That dwarfed Starship *Victory*, which was considerably less than a kilometer in length.

"Lieutenant, what do you see out there?"

Valerie looked up at the main screen. Her head swayed back before she glanced at him. "T-The same thing you see, sir." It was clear she didn't want to commit to seeing something so strange.

"Describe the sight to me," Maddox told her.

Valerie licked her lips. "I-I don't know what I'm seeing, sir."

"It has a teardrop shape," he said. "It's faint, though, like a bad holoimage."

"Yes, sir."

"You see that, too?"

"I don't believe in ghosts, sir."

"We're Star Watch officers," he said. "We must make an objective analysis of whatever we see without referring to superstitions." Something on her pilot board caught Maddox's eye. "Lieutenant, what's that blinking light on your panel mean?"

Valerie looked down and tapped her board. "Sir, someone has opened Hangar Bay Three's outer door."

Why would anyone do that during an ion storm? Maddox immediately distrusted this news. It smacked of subterfuge.

"Sir," Valerie said, looking up in dismay. "The jumpfighter has cold-launched from the hangar bay."

"Someone launched our jumpfighter?"

"Yes, sir," Valerie said. "It's now outside the starship."

Maddox still considered himself an Intelligence officer more than a Line officer. Odd events stirred his curiosity and made him suspicious of motives. An ion storm, a giant ghost vessel inside it and someone launching *Victory's* only jumpfighter; these things weren't coincidences.

"Hail the jumpfighter," he said. It was time to find the underlying cause of this action.

Valerie opened channels. Harsh static was the only response.

Maddox's face became bland.

The captain was a handsome man with angled features, considered by some as the best Intelligence officer in Star Watch. He had his skeletons in the closest, more than most, in fact. He was half New Man and half human, a hybrid that too few people on his side trusted fully. When his features took on

3

a distant, seemingly disinterested cast as they did now, it meant his mind whirled at high speed.

The storm, the ghost ship, and the launched jumpfighter—had the pilot chosen this time for that reason? The captain didn't like mysteries when it came to his starship and crew.

Victory had just jumped into an unpopulated star system in order to use one of the Laumer-Points. A few terrestrial planets made up the inner system where they were now. None of the rock worlds here had an Earthlike atmosphere. There weren't any mining colonies either. Where would the jumpfighter go in order to reach safety? The craft had a limited range. It couldn't travel to another star system.

"I've got it on the main screen, sir," Valerie said.

Maddox turned his attention back to the screen. The jumpfighter was a tiny vessel, a modified strikefighter. At the beginning of the voyage, *Victory* had carried two jumpfighters. One had wrecked on Wolf Prime several months ago. The unofficial name for the vehicle was a "tin can" because that's what the experimental craft resembled. Jumpfighters could fold space for a limited distance, and Star Watch hoped to use them against the New Men to initiate close range attacks and then quickly jump out of harm's way.

As he watched, the jumpfighter folded space and engaged its engine, disappearing into the fold.

Valerie gasped.

Maddox understood the significance. A wink of brightness appeared near the faint vessel in the ion storm. The jumpfighter had gone to it. Maddox wanted to know why.

Before he could comment, several magnetic strands writhed out of the ion storm. Two of them struck *Victory*. The bridge shuddered under Maddox's feet. To his left, although out of sight, metal made twisting, groaning sounds. A second later, the bridge lights went out. The only illumination came from the purple storm outside the ship emanating from the main screen.

Grim suspicion gripped the captain's mind. If the jumpfighter had raced to the ghostly vessel, it implied that someone had planned for the event. That meant someone aboard ship had brought *Victory* to the punishing ion storm on purpose, maybe by corrupting the flight computers. That person or persons had threatened Star Watch's most important starship, and they had done so under Maddox's nose.

With every faculty alert, Maddox watched the ghostly vessel. What was it? How could it maneuver through the magnetic storm? Why was it here at this precise moment?

The giant ghost ship slid through a dark opening in the center of the storm. The vessel disappeared as it dropped through the vortex. Then, the dark opening began acting like a fantastic vacuum cleaner, sucking the ionic storm into it at a prodigious rate. There was no jumpfighter in evidence now. The twisting mass flashed with power. Long strands writhed madly. They no longer lashed at the starship, though. Instead, the strands twisted "upward" in relation to *Victory*.

Maddox cataloged everything as his features became even more composed. His eyes burned with a deadly light, however, belying his cool reserve. The dark opening began to close. As it did, a visible pulse of magnetic force expanded like a watery ripple. One edge of the ripple sped toward *Victory*.

Maddox's neck and shoulder muscles tightened with anticipation.

"Come on," Valerie said, tapping her panel. No doubt, she tried to raise the shield. At the last second, she looked up hopelessly.

The ripple of power struck and then passed the fleeing starship.

Maddox expected the last surge to shut down everything that had remained on after the ionic storm bolts. Instead, the opposite happened. An electrical *whomp* sounded, and the lights returned to the bridge. Some of the panels that had darkened reenergized. That caused a klaxon to blare with a rising and falling noise.

Maddox's head moved to track the source of the klaxon. "What's causing the alarm?" he asked.

Valerie got up and moved to a different board, tapping it and reading something that deflated her shoulders.

She faced Maddox. "Sir, you're not going to believe this. The New Man's holding cell is empty."

5

In two strides, Maddox stood beside the lieutenant. The small screen showed the empty cell where they had kept Per Lomax. Their most dangerous enemy was free.

Maddox whirled around as he unbuttoned the jacket to his uniform. He drew a long-barreled gun from its harness. Most starship captains didn't go armed on their vessel, but Maddox retained the habit of traveling armed at almost all times from his days as an Intelligence officer.

"Sound the ship-wide alarm," Maddox said.

The captain considered himself the universe's premier realist. And the reality was that the escaped prisoner was superior to them in every way; smarter, faster and stronger.

"We have to recapture Per Lomax before he picks us off one by one and takes over *Victory*," he said.

Valerie stared at him. "Sir, surely Per Lomax used the jumpfighter."

"That's one possibility," Maddox conceded. "The other is that he used the jumpfighter as a tactic to throw us off. It could be a diversion."

"But—"

"Our starship is the greatest prize on both sides of the conflict," Maddox said. "If the New Men capture *Victory*, our latest advantage over them will vanish."

"I suppose that's true," Valerie said.

Maddox headed for the hatch. One of his greatest strengths was acting faster than his opposition. He would use that here before Per Lomax could consolidate his position.

"Don't let anyone onto the bridge until I return," the captain said over his shoulder.

"Yes, sir," Valerie said. "Where are you going, if I may ask?"

"To figure out what just happened," Maddox told her. Then, he opened the hatch and darted through.

-2-

Maddox moved down a corridor with the silkiness of a jungle cat. His mind churned through the possibilities. Per Lomax was deadly and vastly clever, one of the New Men created in the Beyond, a genetic superman with delusions of godhood.

By exerting himself to the limit, Maddox had defeated Per Lomax once. He wasn't sure he could do it again. It wouldn't be for a lack of trying, though.

Starship *Victory* had a minimal crew and only a handful of passengers, fewer than twenty people altogether. The starship was an ancient Adok vessel, the last of its kind from a war fought over six thousand years ago. It had two huge oval areas and could have carried thousands of personnel. With Galyan, the Adok AI, presently down, Per Lomax could be hidden anywhere.

Maddox had narrowed the situation down to three possibilities. Per Lomax had set the jumpfighter on auto as a ruse, Per Lomax had used the craft to reach the ghostly vessel, or someone in the crew had fled the starship. He wasn't interested in the third possibility, at least not yet. A free and vengeful Per Lomax was the great danger. Until he had eliminated that threat, nothing else mattered.

From around a corner, Maddox heard a footfall. He froze, straining to pinpoint the exact location of the sound.

The footfall did not repeat itself.

Maddox's eyes seemed to gleam. Slowly, carefully, slinking like a great cat on the hunt, Maddox eased down the corridor.

The ship-wide intercom system was still down, and none of the portable comm-units worked. That was damage from the magnetic storm. He was on his own against Per Lomax.

Despite Maddox's resolve, his stomach tightened. The iron realist in him whispered a terrible truth. No one could match a New Man one on one.

The captain stopped, gripping his gun tighter. Per Lomax might be unarmed, or in possession only of a knife or a knife-like shank. At close quarters, though, a knife could be just as deadly as a gun.

Maddox debated options. He only had a few. Time was his enemy in this. He could not relinquish control of *Victory*.

The starship raced home to Earth from the Tannish System in "C" Quadrant. The vessel was far ahead of the survivors of Admiral Fletcher's Fifth Fleet, which the starship had saved from destruction. Interstellar messages could only travel as fast as the fastest spaceship. The ancient vessel with its star drive was faster than any other Star Watch ship. Maddox raced home to give High Command the good news.

I should have demanded a platoon of space marines from Fletcher before I left the admiral.

Maddox's head twitched in a quick negation. Could haves, should haves were useless.

His lips peeled back to reveal white teeth. In these situations, one could move too cautiously. Maddox inhaled. It was truth time. He charged, turning the corner.

Maddox saw his mistake immediately. A waiting shooter leaned against the wall, aiming a stunner at him. Maddox's trigger finger tightened. At the last millisecond, he eased pressure so as not to shoot.

The barrel of his gun was aimed at Sergeant Treggason Riker's forehead. Maddox would have put a bullet hole in his Star Watch Intelligence aide. Fortunately, the captain's superior reflexes allowed him to catalog the "shooter" as friendly and lower his weapon just in time.

As Maddox did so, Riker twitched in surprise, no doubt at the captain's swift appearance, and pulled the trigger of his weapon. The stunner ejected a nearly invisible blot of force. Maddox began to dodge, but not even he was that fast.

The stun blast knocked the captain backward onto the deck plates. Maddox groaned, although he managed to keep hold of his gun, which lay on the floor with him.

"Captain," Riker said in a gravelly voice. "I'm terribly sorry, sir. I thought you were the killer."

As Maddox struggled to remain conscious, he refrained from groaning a second time. His body ached, and he couldn't move yet. The stunner must have been set on medium. At low, he would have been able to sit up already. At high, he'd be either unconscious or dead.

"Can you hear me, sir?" Riker asked, peering down at him.

Sergeant Riker was an older man with leathery skin. He had a bionic eye and a fully bionic arm. The man had lost both eye and arm in a blast many years ago on a desperate mission on Altair III. The sergeant was an old dog in the Intelligence Service, handy with a gun, possessing a cunning tactical sense and fierce loyalty to Star Watch.

Clearly, Riker had set an ambush for someone. Even as Maddox waited to "thaw," he considered that. Did the sergeant know about Per Lomax's escape? Wait, Riker had just said he thought Maddox had been the killer. Had Per Lomax already killed someone?

Maddox strove to move his lips.

"You should try to relax, sir," Riker said. "If you fight it, the stun lasts longer." The older man frowned, hesitated and finally added, "You're going to feel sick for a time."

Maddox already knew that.

The older man backed away. By the sounds, he checked his stunner charge. Then, Riker cleared his throat and muttered something unintelligible.

At last, Maddox's chest unlocked. He sucked down a shuddering gasp of air. He took the sergeant's advice, relaxing his muscles until he was limp. That made breathing easier, which in turn helped him wait.

Finally, Maddox whispered, "Who's dead?"

9

"One of the slarn trappers, sir," Riker said.

Maddox closed his eyes. The trappers were Professor Ludendorff's people. They hunted slarns, a vicious predatory beast found on Wolf Prime and prized by people throughout the Commonwealth for their fur. In a few good years, a trapper could become wealthy. Ludendorff had been on Wolf Prime studying an ancient Swarm hive and the various alien cave etchings and artifacts found there. Ludendorff had two archaeologists and two slarn trappers with him aboard *Victory*. Make that one slarn hunter now.

"How..." Maddox moistened his mouth. "How did the trapper die?"

"A broken neck, sir," Riker said.

"Twisted from behind?"

"The broken nose and blood smeared on his face would indicate a savage punch or kick to the head, sir," Riker said. "I'd imagine only three people on the starship could do that with just their fist."

"Per Lomax, Meta and me," Maddox said.

"Exactly, sir. I was heading to the holding cell to check on our New Man. Then, I heard someone coming. It turned out to be you, sir."

Maddox managed to frown. He hadn't thought he'd made *any* noise.

Turning his sore neck, Maddox focused on the sergeant. "The holding cell is empty."

Riker turned pale. In two quick twitches, the sergeant glanced right and left, aiming the stunner in both directions.

"You perceive the danger," Maddox said. "Good. Now, help me stand."

With a trembling hand, Riker holstered the stunner. He crouched behind the captain, putting his hands under Maddox's shoulders, lifting.

Maddox felt as if he'd massively over-trained, with his muscles slow to respond. By minute degrees, the captain made it to his feet.

Riker panted, saying, "Good thing I have a bionic arm, sir. You're heavier than you look."

Maddox held out his left hand. It disgusted him that it trembled. He hated any sign of personal weakness. Lowering the offensive hand, he shuffled against a bulkhead and leaned against it, resting.

"I'm surprised you're able to stand at all, sir," Riker said, taking out his stunner, eying both ends of the corridor. "Not too many people could do it so quickly after a stunner shot."

"Someone took the jumpfighter outside the ship," Maddox said.

"During this mess, sir?"

"Yes."

Riker looked at him in surprise. "It must have been Per Lomax."

"He could have set the jumpfighter on auto to make it look like he did."

It took Riker a second to work through that. Maddox watched the changes on the sergeant's face. Then the old features scowled.

"He's a clever bastard," Riker muttered.

"More than clever," Maddox said. "Now, show me the dead man."

"Can you walk yet, sir?"

"Give me an arm. I'll lean on it." Maddox hoped moving would help to shake off the stun.

"What if we run into Per Lomax?" Riker asked.

Right. Maddox couldn't afford the stun weakness. Time was their enemy. He had to outmaneuver the New Man while the odds still favored them.

The captain closed his eyes, gathering his will. Taking a deep breath, he opened them, straightened and managed a few staggering steps. Continuing to walk, he drew his long-barreled gun with a shaky hand.

"Sergeant," Maddox called. "Show me the dead man."

"Yes, sir," Riker said, hurrying to catch up. He glanced at the captain, looked as if he wanted to say something and then decided against it.

With the sergeant in the lead, the two operatives headed down the corridor.

11

***

Ten minutes later, Maddox knelt beside the dead slarn trapper. The corpse had a thick, gray-streaked, gory beard. The nose was broken, flattened and smeared with drying blood. The angle of the head indicated a broken neck just as Riker had said.

The corpse—his name had been Sten Gorgon—wore a homespun shirt and pants with heavy boots, Wolf Prime attire. Maddox didn't know how long Sten had been with the professor.

"Even with a crank bat," Riker said, "it would be hard to break the neck like that."

Maddox checked one end of the corridor and then the other. He didn't hear anyone coming. The sergeant was right about the crank bat.

Inspecting the corpse one more time, Maddox set his gun on the floor and patted the torso through the shirt. He felt something near the belt.

Maddox might have snatched his hand away to dive onto the floor to escape a booby trap blast, but he felt something slim tucked against the corpse's belt. Unbuttoning the three lower buttons, Maddox extracted a metal collar.

"Per Lomax's shock collar," Riker said, identifying the object.

Twisting it around, Maddox studied the thing. It was a nasty device meant to hold a dangerous but invaluable prisoner in check. In the orbit of Wolf Prime, Per Lomax had led a boarding party of New Men. The enemy had attempted to capture *Victory*. At heavy cost, Maddox's team had killed all of the invaders but for Per Lomax. Him, they had taken prisoner. It had been the first New Man prisoner—dead or alive—anyone had captured. Maddox had been taking the New Man home to Earth for the experts to question.

If Per Lomax left his holding cell, the shock collar was supposed to have rendered him unconscious. The ion storm must have shorted the device. Would Per Lomax have known that ahead of time? Might it have been an educated guess or a gamble on the New Man's part?

12

Maddox used both hands, pulling the collar apart. It had been open. A quick examination showed him someone must have opened the lock normally, not with a burst of strength that tore it apart. Could Per Lomax have had inside help?

As preposterous as the idea seemed, Maddox was forced to consider it.

"Who do you think killed the trapper, sir?" Riker asked.

"Maybe that's the wrong question," Maddox said. "*Why* did the person kill Sten Gorgon?"

"I'll bite, sir. Why did they kill him?"

Maddox stared at the corpse. Methodically, he considered the situation. *Victory* had used the star drive, jumping into an empty system. The vessel had appeared beside a spatial anomaly, an ionic-front magnetic storm. After the jump, the starship's shield had been down. It took precious time before the deflector mechanisms could come back online. The electromagnetic shield might not have withstood the strands of magnetic force anyway. As it was, the interfering magnetics and strand-attacks had damaged the starship and rendered most interior systems inoperative. During that time, Per Lomax had escaped from the holding cell and someone had launched the starship's remaining jumpfighter. On top of all that, he'd seen a faint image of a gigantic spaceship moving through the magnetic storm.

Was *Victory's* jump appearance near the magnetic storm a coincidence? Was the faint ship in the spatial anomaly—it's being there at the instant it was—another coincidence?

Maddox seriously doubted that. So who had plotted the starship's course to the magnetic storm? Who could?

Before Maddox could begin the analysis, Riker shouted, bringing up his stunner. A *click* sounded from the weapon. A blot of force ejected from the barrel. The bolt passed though the hologram of Driving Force Galyan. The AI image stood before them, having just appeared.

"Don't do that!" Riker shouted. The alien holoimage had resumed its humanoid shape, with the ropy arms and extremely deep-set, dark eyes.

Galyan examined his torso before staring at the sergeant. "Why did you just shoot me?"

13

"I thought you were someone else," Riker said in a calmer voice.

"Who did you think I was?" Galyan asked.

"Never mind about that," Maddox said. "It's clear you're functioning again."

"I have run a self-diagnostic, Captain," Galyan said. "I am presently operating at seventy-eight percent capacity. Therefore, I am not running at normal efficiency."

"That will have to suffice for now." Maddox glanced to the right, studying the corridor, and then turned and inspected the corridor to the left.

"Is there a problem?" Galyan asked.

"Look down at my feet," Maddox said.

"Do you refer to the dead slarn trapper?"

"That's right. Who killed him?"

"I do not know," Galyan said.

"You didn't catch it on the video system?"

"Negative," Galyan said. "The storm rendered the cameras inoperative during the scope of what appears to be a heinous crime."

"Is the intercom system working now?" Maddox asked.

"No. It has not yet recovered from the storm damage."

"How did you know we were here?" Maddox asked.

"The cameras are operational again," Galyan said. "They simply weren't during the timespan wherein this man perished."

Was that another coincidence? Maddox doubted it. "Do you recall the ship's roster?" he asked.

"Of course," Galyan said.

"Check the ship, and tell me who's missing."

Galyan's eyelids fluttered for just a moment. "I have completed the scan, Captain. Per Lomax is missing."

Riker laughed with relief.

Maddox wasn't as easily satisfied. "Did you scan every centimeter of the ship, every possible hiding location?"

"I scanned every place where my cameras can see," Galyan said.

"Are there places you can't see?" Maddox asked.

"There are," Galyan said, "but your assumption is faulty. The jumpfighter left *Victory*. Logic dictates its pilot is no longer with us. Per Lomax is the only missing person. Therefore, he piloted the jumpfighter. That means he is not is hiding on the ship in a location I cannot see."

Maddox examined the corpse, Riker and finally Galyan. Afterward, he looked up the corridor and down it.

"You can relax, sir," Riker said.

Maddox regarded Galyan. "Where could someone hide so you couldn't spot him?"

"You mean visibly through my cameras?"

"What else could I—oh," Maddox said. "You can travel to places your cameras can't see."

"That is correct," Galyan said, "but I fail to understand what you are implying."

"Maybe Per Lomax set the jumpfighter on autopilot," Maddox told the AI. "Maybe the New Man wanted us to think he had left the starship so we wouldn't look for him anymore."

"I deem that sequence as highly unlikely," Galyan said.

Maddox pinched his lower lip in thought. If he were Per Lomax hiding from Galyan, where would he be? Even more to the point, how could the New Man take control of *Victory* while remaining hidden?

15

-3-

"I want you to go to every place on *Victory* your cameras can't see," Maddox told Galyan. "I want to know with one hundred percent certainty if Per Lomax is or is not aboard the starship. Can you do that?"

"It will take time," Galyan said.

"Then the sooner you begin, the sooner I'll have my answer."

"Logical," Galyan said. "Good bye, Captain, Sergeant Riker." The holoimage disappeared.

"Do you really think the New Man had time to set the jumpfighter onto autopilot?" Riker said. "That's a lot of deep thinking and activity that needs doing in a short amount of time."

Maddox was staring at the corpse again. The sergeant had a reasonable question, but Maddox didn't know enough about jumpfighters to answer him. He would have to ask Second Lieutenant Keith Maker about that.

"Consider what we're seeing," Maddox told Riker, "a dead slarn hunter who took a savage blow to the face. The blow might have snapped the neck. In order for it to have done so, the punch would have to have been devastating. It would take an extraordinarily strong person to achieve such a hit. That would also imply expert-class combat technique. Strength alone couldn't break the neck with a punch."

"Someone with a crank bat could have possibly done it with normal strength," Riker said, "or with some other suitable implement like a steel bar."

"I didn't attack and kill Sten Gorgon," Maddox said. "You have a bionic arm and are trained in close combat of an extremely dirty variety. But your loyalty to Star Watch is impeccable. Thus, you didn't kill the man, either."

"That leaves two people who could have murdered Gorgon like this," Riker said. "The obvious person is Per Lomax."

"If the New Man did it, why was Gorgon carrying the shock collar?"

"Because Per Lomax put it there," Riker said. "What could be easier to explain?"

"Let me see if I understand your reasoning," Maddox said. "During the magnetic storm, Per Lomax slipped from the holding cell and unlocked the shock collar, which he then carried with him. He surprised Gorgon and lashed out viciously, snapping the man's neck with a blow, killing the trapper. Per Lomax knew his time was limited—that the AI and ship-monitoring systems were only temporarily down. The New Man paused long enough, however, to unbutton the dead man's shirt, and then he tucked the shock collar there, buttoned the shirt closed and even stuffed the ends of the shirt under the trousers. Is that what you're suggesting?"

"I suppose not." Riker eyed the captain. "But if I didn't do it, you didn't do it and neither did Per Lomax... There is one other possibility. Meta."

"Yes. I've already been considering that."

"If you'll allow me to speak, sir," Riker said.

"Go ahead."

"I wish I could put this delicately, but Meta was with Kane for quite some time."

For just a moment, Maddox's features tightened.

Kane had been a spy sent to Earth by the New Men. The spy had kidnapped Meta from New York City and taken her into space. Using an ancient device known as the Nexus, Kane had jumped to Wolf Prime ahead of them. There, in planetary orbit, Kane had taken Meta to Per Lomax aboard one of the enemy star cruisers. Per Lomax had sent Meta to someone the

New Men referred to as "the teacher". The teacher had modified her mind in some manner. It was why the professor no longer trusted Meta.

"I would appreciate it if you got to the point," Maddox told the sergeant.

"Could Meta have…listened to a hidden compulsion to free Per Lomax from confinement?" Riker asked.

"Yes," Maddox said, exhaling. "The possibility exists." He hated admitting this to himself or aloud.

"Gorgon found out what she was doing and tried to stop her. Meta bashed him. In her panic, she hit Gorgon hard enough to snap his neck."

"Would she pause long enough to put the shock collar under the dead man's shirt?" Maddox asked.

"I think she might, sir. Meta used to be an assassin. She might have paused long enough to plant a distracting clue knowing that later you would find it."

The idea had a ring of plausibility. Meta had helped repair the ancient starship the first time. Could she have secretly caused the vessel to appear out of a star drive jump near the spatial anomaly?

"Galyan," Maddox called. "I have to ask you a question."

The holoimage reappeared before them.

"I am working swiftly, Captain," Galyan said. "I have already checked twenty-eight percent of the hidden locations. Obviously, I haven't yet discovered Per Lomax or I would have informed you."

"Where's Meta?" Maddox asked.

"In her sleeping compartment," Galyan said.

"Is she alone?"

"Yes, Captain."

"Thank you," Maddox said. "You may continue your search."

A second later, Galyan vanished again.

Riker rubbed his chin. "I'm not sure I like having an ancient computer entity watching me while I'm in my room."

"It has its drawbacks," Maddox admitted. "Now, unlimber your stunner, Sergeant, and remain alert. We must still work under the assumption that Per Lomax is aboard the starship."

"Yes, sir," Riker said, in a resigned voice.

"Sergeant," Maddox said. "It's quite possible Per Lomax had inside help. Whoever else was involved is obviously still on the ship."

"Unless this dead slarn trapper was Per Lomax's inside help," Riker said.

Maddox froze before cocking an eyebrow at the sergeant.

"What did I say?" Riker asked.

"Something profound," Maddox said. "Now, come along. Our enemy is moving swiftly to accomplish something. We must move faster to stop him."

***

Maddox knocked on Meta's outer hatch.

"Who is it?" Meta called from the inside.

"The captain."

"Are you alone?"

"No, Sergeant Riker is here. He will remain outside to stand guard."

"Why would he have to stand guard?" Meta asked.

"Will you open the hatch?"

"Answer my question first," she said.

In the beginning, the muffling from the hatch made it difficult for Maddox to tell anything from Meta's voice. Now, it was clear. She was nervous.

"Per Lomax has escaped his holding cell," Maddox said. "I also found Sten Gorgon. The slarn trapper is dead, with a broken neck."

A second later, an inner lock *clicked* and the hatch moved a bare centimeter. One of Meta's eyes peered through the crack.

"I'm tired," she said. "Why don't you come back later?"

Maddox put a hand on the hatch and pushed. It moved another several centimeters before stopping. Meta used one of her arms to block the hatch from opening farther. She had been born on a two G world and was denser than a regular human. Meta also happened to be quite nude. She had a voluptuous figure with tantalizing breasts. Her long blonde hair was up, tied in a knot. Maddox enjoyed the view, but he didn't let her charms distract him. Speckles of blood were smeared against

19

her throat as if she had wiped it but failed to rub all the blood away.

"Are you getting ready to take a shower?" Maddox asked.

"Don't you have any manners?" Meta asked angrily. "I'm naked. Your sergeant is staring me."

Maddox turned around to chastise Riker. The sergeant had his back to Meta. The closing hatch bumped Maddox forward. The lock *clicked* shut.

Maddox realized Meta had used a diversion against him to get the door closed.

"Meta," he called.

"I'm busy. Go away."

"You killed Sten Gorgon. It's his blood I saw on your throat."

"Leave me alone!" she shouted.

"Per Lomax has escaped his holding cell," Maddox said.

"Don't you think I know that?"

"Why didn't you come tell me?" Maddox asked.

She didn't answer.

"Meta?" he called.

"I wanted to tell you, but I...couldn't."

Maddox and Riker exchanged glances.

The sergeant tapped the side of his head, mouthing the word, "Teacher."

Hatred for the New Men surged through Maddox. He'd been conceived in a genetic facility in the Beyond. His mother had escaped to Human Space, where he'd been born. Now, the enemy had tainted his lover. Had Meta really become so corrupted that she had aided a New Man against him?

"I'm here now," Maddox said. "Unfortunately, the ship is in danger. I need your help."

"I'm no good to anyone," Meta said. "I can't even trust myself. Just leave me alone."

"Listen to me. You have to—"

The lock unlatched but the hatch remained shut.

"Wait here," Maddox told Riker. "I don't like the direction this is taking. Wait on the other side of the corridor."

"Sir?" Riker asked.

"Call it a precaution."

"Yes, sir," Riker said, with a new, harder edge in his voice. The sergeant drew his stunner, and the tenor of his body language said he was worried.

Maddox opened the hatch and stepped into Meta's quarters, closing the hatch behind him. The room was tidy and minimalist. Bloody clothes lay in the small container at the foot of her bed. Meta sat on the bed with a red silk robe covering her nakedness. Her right hand held the top closed, which hid her blood-speckled throat. She looked up at him, with moisture in her green eyes.

"Can you tell me what happened?" he asked.

"You don't want to comfort me first, hold me and tell me everything is going to be okay?"

Maddox sat down on the bed and put an arm around her, keeping eye contact. "It will be all right. Now, I need to know what happened. Time is of the essence."

"We're already out of time," she said.

Maddox took his arm away and stood up, regarding her.

The hand holding the robe tightened. Slowly, Meta shook her head. "I don't trust the jumps. You know that, right?"

Maddox had heard her say that before.

Meta waved her free hand. "The jumps negatively affect us and the equipment. I've been waiting for Per Lomax's holding cell to short-circuit one of these times. The shield goes down every jump. The computers quit. Why would a holding cell's force screen be any different?"

"A reasonable question," Maddox said.

"I usually check on him after every jump."

"I didn't know that."

"I want to make certain he's locked tight. What he did to me on the star cruiser…"

"Do you remember?" Maddox asked.

"No! But I feel it here." Meta tapped above her right breast. "The New Men are monsters. Their plans are vile."

Maddox had questioned Per Lomax once. The prisoner had told him the New Men planned to "cull" eighty percent of humanity, the so-called useless portion. Under the Throne World's guidance, the remaining twenty percent would breed in genetically regimented ways, improving the human race.

21

"I've always felt we should have killed Per Lomax when we had the chance," Meta said. "Now, it's too late."

"Why do you say that?"

"He escaped into the jumpfighter, didn't he?"

"How would you know that?" Maddox asked.

Meta smirked. "Per Lomax wanted me to join him, you know?" Her features screwed up and she shook her head. "I wanted to go. It would have been the adventure of a lifetime. That's what's eating me up inside. I yearned to join Per Lomax. Yet, I love *you*. So why did I want to go with *him*?"

Maddox said nothing, the objective Intelligence-officer side of him overpowering his lover side.

"It's because of what the teacher did to me on the damned star cruiser!" Meta shouted. "The teacher invaded my mind. He twisted it. I'm damaged goods. I'm untrustworthy! I'm—"

Maddox pulled Meta to her feet, hugging her. She clung to him, resting her forehead in the hollow of his throat.

Finally, she looked up. There were tears in her eyes. He touched her cheek. With a thumb, he wiped away a tear. A moment later, he pressed his lips against hers. They kissed...

When they finally parted, he held her hands as she sat back down on the bed. Her robe slipped open. He looked at her charms. Shyly, she pulled a hand free and closed the robe, her fingers tightening around the silk.

"I killed Sten Gorgon," Meta said, as she stared into nowhere. "I'm...sorry I did. I knew him a little. He was always telling jokes. The professor liked him."

"Why did you kill him?" Maddox asked quietly.

"You're smart. You should already know the reason."

"Maybe I do," Maddox said.

"So tell me."

"I'd rather hear it from you. As smart as I am, I'm wrong sometimes."

Meta turned her head, and her words became monotone. "Right after the jump, after my heart stopped thumping and I could see normally again, I exited my room and hurried for the holding cell. The corridor lights began flickering. I heard the warning about a magnetic storm—and then the intercom system went down. I tried my comm-unit, but only got static. I

22

knew something bad had happened so I increased my pace. That's when I heard them."

"Heard who?" Maddox asked.

"Sten Gorgon was telling Per Lomax things."

Maddox's eyes shined with interest. "Like what?" he asked.

Meta slid her gaze to Maddox before her eyes darted elsewhere. "I don't remember what they said."

Maddox didn't press, but filed the information away for later.

"As I heard their voices," Meta said, "something happened in my mind. I could feel a door opening in it. I knew I could help Per Lomax. The next thing I remember, I stood before them. Gorgon stopped short. The New Man studied my eyes. Then, the oiliest smile I've ever seen slid onto his face."

Meta shivered. "I remembered the smiles Baron Chabot used to give me back on, back on…"

"The Rouen Colony," Maddox said.

"Yes," Meta whispered. "Because of Per Lomax's nasty smile, the door in my mind began to close. I think Per Lomax knew that. He whispered to Gorgon. The slarn trapper went for his knife. I charged and hit him harder than I've ever hit anyone. Sten catapulted off his feet and slid along the floor. I knew he was dead. My fingers hurt like Hell."

"And?" Maddox asked.

"Per Lomax told me to follow him on his quest." Meta shook her head. "I can't remember after that. I refused to join him. The bastard spoke words that did something to my mind. I headed back to my room. I remember weeping and arguing with myself."

Meta stopped. She looked up with agonizing eyes. "What's wrong with me? What did the teacher do to me on the star cruiser?"

Maddox pulled her back to her feet and hugged her once more as a terrible anger burned in his chest. He was going to make the New Men pay for trifling with Meta. The enemy used humans the way others used shoes or credit cards.

Her arms tightened around him.

Maddox held her for a time before releasing her, guiding her back to the bed.

23

Why had Gorgon helped the New Man? What had the slarn trapper told Per Lomax? Had he worked alone or had he worked in conjunction with Professor Ludendorff?

Maddox put his hands on Meta's shoulders. "You should sleep. You're tired. I'll be back shortly."

"Don't leave."

"I don't want to, but I must. I need answers."

Meta searched his eyes, finally nodding. She let her robe slide off and twisted under the covers, pulling them up to her chin.

Maddox bent down to kiss her on the forehead. Her arms burst out from under the covers, clutching his head, pulling his lips down onto hers.

"Good luck," she whispered when he pulled free.

Maddox nodded, watching Meta close her eyes. Then, he headed for the hatch. The professor loved having his mysteries. Maddox distrusted that about the man. It was time to confront Ludendorff and find out just who he really was.

"Captain," Riker called.

The two of them marched down the corridors toward Professor Ludendorff's quarters, with the captain in the lead.

"Hmm?" Maddox said.

Riker hurried even with the captain. "If Gorgon aided Per Lomax, wouldn't it stand to reason that Ludendorff knew about it?"

"So?"

"So the professor has another slarn hunter with him and two archeologists," Riker said. "These aren't your regular run-of-the-mill archeologists, either, but hardy survivors of Wolf Prime. A case could be made that Professor Ludendorff is one of the most dangerous men alive."

Maddox silently agreed with that. Yet, he said, "Without the professor, Star Watch wouldn't have *Victory*. Ludendorff also rid Galyan of the ancient Swarm virus and helped fix the disrupter cannon that freed the Fifth Fleet."

"I don't dispute any of that, sir. My point is that Gorgon was Ludendorff's man, one of his bodyguards, if you ask me."

"A judicious guess as to Gorgon's real purpose," Maddox admitted.

"So it all boils down to this, sir. If Gorgon acted under the professor's orders, the question becomes: why would Ludendorff help Per Lomax escape?"

"That's what we're attempting to find out."

"Are we, sir?"

"State your objections plainly, Sergeant. Precision is critical in these matters."

"If Gorgon worked under orders from Ludendorff, that means the professor aided humanity's worst enemy, one of the New Men. It could be we're walking into a trap. Now, I'm aware you're not worried about four suspects against the two of us. But you should be, as Ludendorff is possibly more dangerous than yourself, sir."

Maddox halted. Trust the sergeant to play the odds. Riker made good points. "Galyan," he called.

A few seconds later, the holoimage appeared before them.

"Where are Professor Ludendorff and his three remaining assistants?" Maddox asked.

Galyan stood motionless before responding. "Each of them is in their separate quarters."

"Those are next to each other, yes?"

"Yes," Galyan said.

"Lock the hatches. Under no circumstances are you to open any of them except at my command."

"It is done," Galyan said. "The hatches are locked."

"How is your search for Per Lomax going?" Maddox asked.

"I have gone through sixty-four percent of the hidden areas of the ship."

"Report to me the instant you're finished," Maddox said.

"Yes, Captain."

"Also, at my command—although you don't need to appear—unlock the professor's hatch for me."

Galyan nodded, waiting for further instructions.

"That will be all for now," Maddox said.

Without a sound, the alien holoimage vanished.

The two Star Watch operatives continued down the corridor.

"Why do you think Ludendorff would help a New Man escape our custody?" Riker asked.

Maddox had been wondering just that. "The professor is an enigma. I suspect the reason would be something neither of us presently expects it to be."

"So, like me, you think Ludendorff told Gorgon what to do?"

"I'm keeping an open mind on the subject," Maddox said. "That allows me to see what is there instead of what I think I should see."

Riker appeared dubious. He opened his mouth to say more.

Maddox raised a hand and held up the index finger. "If you would, refrain from speaking for a time so that I may process my thoughts. I believe I should be at the top of my game for the next interview."

The sergeant closed his mouth, grinning a moment later. He was used to the captain's cavalier manner. Realizing Maddox was tense—going into high gear—seemed to put the sergeant at ease.

Maddox noticed the change in his aide, but refrained from commenting. He concentrated on Ludendorff. The professor was supposed to be the smartest man alive. Ludendorff had played his own game on Wolf Prime against the New Men. The professor had an inordinate curiosity about aliens, the ancient Adoks, the Swarm… What did Ludendorff think about the builders of the Nexus? And the gigantic, fifty kilometer vessel in the ion storm…what would Ludendorff think about it? Who could have constructed such a craft? Was it old like *Victory* or new like an enemy star cruiser?

If any person could know beforehand about such a ghostly ship, it would certainly be Ludendorff. If anyone could envision where such a vessel would be in the middle of an ion storm, it would be the professor. And if anyone could trick the crew of *Victory* to be near the magnetic storm and the passing mystery craft at exactly the right moment, it would be the smartest man in the universe.

A grim smile stretched the captain's lips. He could appreciate a man purposefully engaged in his own affairs, blithely unconcerned about anyone else. He often operated in such a manner. In fact, Maddox would do so during this interview. The professor could have come to him and explained matters. Instead, Ludendorff had worked around his authority. It had left Gorgon dead and had endangered Meta.

Remember, Ludendorff helped us against the New Men. Without the disruptor cannon, Oran Rva would have destroyed the Fifth Fleet and possibly Victory, *too. Yet, the professor seems to have put our mutual endeavor aside. I would be wise to do the same.*

Maddox planned his line of inquiry, finally stopping before the professor's hatch. He turned to the sergeant.

"Be a good fellow and trade me weapons."

Riker drew his stunner, handing it butt-first to the captain. The sergeant accepted Maddox's long-barreled gun in exchange.

Maddox switched the stunner's setting to low. Then, he composed himself, put a hand on the latch and spoke into the air, telling Galyan to open the hatch.

In a moment, a *click* sounded.

Maddox swung open the hatch, charging through into Professor Ludendorff's room.

Ludendorff sat at a table, with a stylus in his left hand. He was medium-sized and wore a soft blue shirt with black slacks and shoes. The collar of the shirt was open and he wore a gold chain around his neck. The older man was bald, with deeply tanned skin and a prominent hooked nose.

The professor looked up. The intelligence in his eyes shined like twin diamonds with a hard and priceless quality. He'd been writing on a tablet, with various items spread out on the table.

"Really," Ludendorff said, sitting back. "This is rude. You could have knocked first."

Maddox approached the table, with the stunner aimed at the professor's chest.

"You must have ordered Galyan to lock the hatch earlier," Ludendorff said. "I would like to know why you—"

Maddox pulled the trigger. The stun hit the older man in the chest, knocking him off the chair. Ludendorff twitched on the floor, one of his feet kicking a table leg, knocking the table over. The contents clattered onto the floor.

Keeping his distance, Maddox kept the stunner trained on the prone man. He respected the professor's deadliness. He would fire again if the man tried to reach into his pockets, or inside his shirt, perhaps.

The seconds passed as Ludendorff breathed harshly. Finally, the professor rolled onto his back and focused on Maddox.

The captain gave the older man the same advice Riker had given him a half hour ago after being stunned.

Ludendorff closed his eyes, resting.

Maddox continued to watch him.

"You have a reason for such savagery?" the professor finally hissed.

Maddox said nothing, letting the man's anger work to his advantage.

The professor opened his eyes, staring at Maddox. "What am I to conclude from this?"

Still, Maddox said nothing.

"Come, come," Ludendorff said, testily. "Let us act like reasonable men. Your actions are unseemly."

"Sten Gorgon is dead," Maddox said.

The professor's eyes brightened. A moment later, they lost their luster as if he deliberately hooded their intensity.

"This is terrible news," Ludendorff said. "How did it happen?"

"That's one question. Another is why you sent Gorgon to free Per Lomax."

"You must think poorly of me to ask such a thing."

Maddox stunned the professor again. It left the older man gasping, his eyelids fluttering.

"Please," Ludendorff finally managed to gasp. "My heart isn't strong enough to withstand repeated charges."

Maddox made a show of changing the stunner's setting. "The first two shots were at the lowest setting. Now, I have put it to a mid-range stun. You would be wise to take this change into consideration."

"Are you going to kill me, Captain?"

Maddox said nothing.

A subtle change came over the professor. All humor vanished, leaving a deadly knot of intent that made him seem more dangerous.

29

"Perhaps if you informed me of your game, I could join you in it. At the moment, I am at a loss for what you're trying to achieve."

"I am wary of you, Professor. You tricked the New Men on Wolf Prime, something difficult to do. I believe it more than possible you can trick me. In fact, I think you already have. These shots are to show you my respect for you."

"I would rather have your contempt then."

"Why did you free Per Lomax?" Maddox asked.

"Obviously, I didn't."

"Why did Gorgon free my captive?" Maddox asked.

"I would like to know myself. Your accusation seems…impossible to me. Sten Gorgon committed this wild deed? Your actions show me you must believe what you're saying. Otherwise, I would take it as a silly hoax."

"Let us be frank, Professor. Gorgon couldn't have timed *Victory's* appearance near a spatial anomaly. I suspect you did all this so Per Lomax could board the ghostly vessel."

"You should explain what you mean," Ludendorff said. "I can make nothing of these strange allegations. What ghostly vessel are you referring to?"

Maddox gave the professor a quick rundown of the magnetic storm, the ghostly vessel, the hole, the last pulse and the jumpfighter winking brightly near the strange craft before it disappeared.

"You have me at a grave disadvantage," Ludendorff said. "These things are fantastic and inexplicable. I can do many things, but I am not a techno-wizard able to conjure explanations out of the air."

Maddox decided to try one more time. "Why did Gorgon free Per Lomax?"

"I have no inkling, Captain. The idea seems as preposterous as your shots against me."

"You're lying."

Ludendorff scowled thunderously. "You young *pup*! I demand an immediate apology. How dare you accuse me so slanderously, especially after stunning me twice?"

"That is how you should react if you were innocent," Maddox said. "I applaud your performance, Professor, but I do not accept it as legitimate."

"After all that I've done for you and Star Watch, this is how you repay me?"

"You're welcome," Maddox said.

"What?"

"I am repaying your former help by letting you live. Otherwise, I would have already killed you as a dangerous traitor."

"Bah!" Ludendorff said. "What nonsense. You're one of Brigadier O'Hara's coldblooded hounds. I know your type. You think you know everything. If I—"

Maddox raised the stunner for a third shot.

The professor fell silent.

"You've clearly decided to maintain a role of innocence," Maddox said. "That leaves me with no choice. Good day, Professor." The captain backed toward the door.

"Wait," Ludendorff said.

Maddox paused, with the stunner aimed at the man.

"You haven't told me who killed Sten."

"That's true, I haven't."

"I see. You want to play it that way, leaving me in the dark. Am I under arrest?"

"Good day, Professor." Maddox backed away, slipping through the hatch and closing it. "Galyan," the captain said. "Lock the professor's hatch, and keep it locked until I say otherwise."

The lock *clicked* shut.

"What did he say, sir?" Riker asked.

Maddox stared at the hatch. He had purposely told Ludendorff as little as possible. The man was too bright. The less the professor knew, the less he could use in some devious manner later.

Finally, the captain held the stunner butt-forward to Riker. The sergeant hastily drew Maddox's gun, and they exchanged weapons.

"The professor claims innocence," Maddox said.

"Do you think he is?"

"Most certainly not."

"Could you be wrong, sir?"

"That is what I want to determine. Come with me, Sergeant, and be ready to draw and fire at my command."

-5-

Maddox located Doctor Dana Rich in the main engine room. Giant cylinders of antimatter cyclers purred smoothly.

"Captain," Dana said, turning to greet him. Riker remained outside in the annex.

Doctor Rich wore a white lab coat, with her dark hair pulled back into a ponytail. She was older than Maddox and beautiful by any standard, with brown skin and dark eyes. Born on Earth in Bombay, she had emigrated to the Indian Brahma System long ago.

The doctor had a checkered history, involved with the Brahman secret service against the Rigel Social Syndicate of a neighboring star system. Dana had been a clone thief, caught by Star Watch and sent down to Loki Prime, the worst of the prison planets. Maddox had rescued her because he'd needed her services. For what she had done to help bring back *Victory* from the Beyond, Star Watch authorities had pardoned her of all crimes.

She had led the science team in the Oort cloud as they studied *Victory*. After the professor, Dana knew more about the ancient starship than anyone else.

"You look troubled," Dana said.

Maddox gave her a quick rundown of the situation, including the stun shots against the professor.

The doctor listened, her features hardening into an increasingly serious mien. She was a solemn person by nature, driven to excellence and hard work. Maddox believed it

33

bothered her that others considered Ludendorff the cleverest person in existence. Dana wanted the title for herself.

"You stunned him?" Dana asked, as if wanting clarification of a delicious fact.

Maddox nodded.

"I would have liked to see that," she said, with the ghost of a smile.

Those were rare. Dana appeared to believe she had to save smiles for special occasions, as if she only had a limited supply and had to stretch them for the entirety of her existence.

"I doubt he admitted to any wrongdoing, though," Dana said.

"What makes you say that?"

"The professor is *always* right. Haven't we heard him say that enough times that it's become a divine fiat?"

Maddox had never heard the professor claim perfection, although, to be fair, Ludendorff had never admitted to being wrong, either.

"I'm curious," Maddox said. "How were you able to mutiny against Ludendorff in the Adok System?"

"Why ask me that now? It happened a long time ago."

"Indulge me, Doctor."

Dana's features tightened as she became thoughtful.

Many years ago, Ludendorff had led an expedition into the Beyond, searching for a legend. That legend had been Starship *Victory*, although no one had known the vessel's name then. All anyone knew—or said they did—was that a lonely alien warship guarded a destroyed star system. It turned out the ancient Swarm had attacked the Adoks over six thousand years ago. The Swarm had advanced at sub-light speed, knowing nothing about Laumer-Points or star drives. The battle had left every planet in the system as shattered rubble, with thousands of drifting, useless space hulks. Ludendorff's team had found the "lost" star system and witnessed *Victory* making its rounds through the debris. The professor had wanted to board the ancient warship. Dana had led others in a mutiny, escaping the star system before the ancient vessel could kill them.

"We're in the middle of an emergency," Dana said. "If you've seen a ghostly vessel—and Per Lomax sought to reach it—we must concentrate on that, not on my past."

"I'm talking to you about your past precisely because of the ghostly ship," Maddox said.

"I fail to see the connection."

"Ludendorff found the ancient Adok System," Maddox said. "He succeeded where everyone else had failed."

"We don't know that's true. Others likely succeeded in reaching the star system and died to *Victory*."

"You're missing the key element," Maddox said. "Ludendorff hunted for an ancient alien starship. The ghostly vessel in the ion storm would indicate there's more than one such ancient craft in existence. The reality of Kane's silver pyramid—the Nexus—proves other artifacts are sprinkled throughout the galaxy. If anyone should know about ancient vessels, it would be Ludendorff."

"So why ask about my mutiny?"

"To learn more about Ludendorff," Maddox said. "I know he fixates on ancient aliens. He was on Wolf Prime studying Swarm relics. What motivates him to do that?"

"Curiosity," Dana said.

"Why such fixated curiosity over ancient aliens? There are many other things in existence to be curious about."

Dana tilted her head as if thinking deeply. "You've jumped to a conclusion I'm not sure is correct. Why do you believe the ghostly vessel is ancient?"

Maddox had been waiting for the question. "Have you ever heard of such a ship before?"

"No."

"If the New Men had the ghostly vessel, wouldn't they have already employed it against Star Watch?"

"That seems reasonable, I suppose."

"If the Wahhabi Caliphate owned such a ship, they would have used it against the New Men. The same holds true for the Windsor League and the Spacers. That Ludendorff clearly knew about the ship and its appearance in this star system—"

"Wait," Dana said, sharply. "You're leaping to far too many unsubstantiated conclusions. I understand the desire to

35

stun the professor, but if this was your reasoning for doing so, I have to say I find it riddled with—"

"Doctor," Maddox said, interrupting her. "Gorgon helped my prisoner escape. That is an inescapable fact. The jumpfighter left the hangar bay during the height of the magnetic storm. It seems increasingly likely that Per Lomax piloted the craft."

"That seems obvious to me," Dana said.

"It's also obvious that Gorgon did not work alone."

"I see. That's what you're seeking from me. You desire to know the intricacies of my mutiny in order to judge Ludendorff and his closest aides."

"Correct," Maddox said.

Dana turned away and folded her arms across her chest. Soon, she shook her head. "I'm not proud of my mutiny. I broke my word to Ludendorff in order to commit it. I found that difficult to do. Stark fear motivated me back then. I was certain we would die. Ludendorff struck me as too reckless. You're right about his chief aides, though. None of them ever made a move without his leave. If Gorgon helped Per Lomax escape, it was definitely at the professor's orders."

"How do you think Ludendorff first learned about the Adok System?"

"That's an interesting question," Dana said. "I'm sure—"

Galyan appeared before Maddox. "I am finished with my search, Captain."

The doctor turned with a start. Her gaze darted from Maddox to Galyan.

"Go ahead," Maddox told the holoimage. "Tell me your finding."

"I have searched every nook aboard the starship," Galyan said. "Per Lomax is not aboard. I also analyzed the outer hull. The New Man is not there, either."

"Thank you," Maddox said. "I'd like you to return to the bridge and inform the lieutenant to head to our Laumer-Point on the double."

"At once, Captain," Galyan said, before vanishing.

"I'm curious," Dana said, ignoring Galyan's interruption. "Why do you think Ludendorff helped Per Lomax reach this ghostly vessel?"

Maddox began to pace as he ignored the doctor's question. Per Lomax was gone, freed by one of the professor's slarn trappers. The New Man had definitely used the jumpfighter in an attempt to reach the gigantic ship. The captain stopped abruptly and stared at Dana.

"I need your help, Doctor. How could Ludendorff have timed *Victory's* appearance near the spatial anomaly?"

Dana patted her hair. "It seems obvious to me. There must be an override code in the AI."

"How would it have gotten there?"

"Easily enough," Dana said. "Ludendorff often worked alone when we flushed the Swarm virus from Galyan. He could have installed it then as a form of insurance for himself."

"Then we're Ludendorff's captives," Maddox said.

"I don't think so. You stunned him twice and left him locked in his room. As long as you keep Galyan from speaking to him again, we should be okay."

Maddox became thoughtful. "If Ludendorff had control of the AI, why did he allow me into his room?"

"Haven't you figured it out yet?" Dana asked. "Ludendorff's overconfidence is his weakness. He believes himself so brilliant that sometimes he misses the obvious. It's how I managed to stage my mutiny against him many years ago."

"I don't understand. Why did he fix the disruptor cannon several weeks ago, helping us defeat Oran Rva's armada? And now, he aids the New Men?"

"I'm not sure he did aid them," Dana said.

"Per Lomax is no longer my prisoner."

"You're looking at this as a binary situation, Star Watch versus the New Men. The professor views himself to be as important as any political entity, no matter its size."

"You're saying Ludendorff has his own agenda?" Maddox asked.

"Precisely."

"Do you care to speculate on what it might be?"

37

"Captain, I've been speculating on that for a long time, and I still haven't come to a satisfactory conclusion."

"Thank you for your help," Maddox said.

"I don't know that I did much."

"Thinking of the professor as a third party is illuminating. It might help me understand him."

"Good luck with that."

Maddox nodded before heading for the annex to collect Sergeant Riker.

***

Maddox, Riker and Galyan stood on the bridge. At the captain's orders, Valerie had left. She'd been dog-tired and needed rest.

Victory headed for the nearest Laumer-Point. The ship would use it to reach the next star system. Laumer-Point jumps were the normal method of interstellar travel, linking star systems in a connect-the-dots fashion with jump routes or "tramlines". A vessel with a Laumer Drive pinpointed the wormhole and opened it so the ship could enter. Seconds later, the vessel popped out in a new star system. During those seconds, the ship traveled light-years. Moving to a new Laumer-Point in the new star system often took days of acceleration and deceleration.

"At least we know Per Lomax isn't about to personally attack us," Riker said.

Maddox glanced at the sergeant. "What if the New Man successfully gained entrance to the ghost ship? Maybe he could command it to reappear and attack us ship-to-ship."

"Possibly, sir," Riker said, who didn't seem convinced. "Why do you think the ship was ghostly?"

"It appeared ghostly," Maddox said. "Do you have any ideas about that, Galyan?"

"None at present," the holoimage said.

"Could the ghostliness have been a result of the ion storm?" Riker asked.

"Possibly," Maddox said. "I wonder why the magnetic storm ended once the ghost ship disappeared into the opening."

Riker snapped his fingers. "Maybe its opening was like a Laumer-Point."

Maddox stared at the sergeant. That was an excellent comment. He should have already seen that.

"Galyan, are *Victory's* sensors back on line?" Maddox asked.

"Affirmative."

"Can you pinpoint the spatial coordinates where the ghost ship disappeared?"

"Do you mean the center of the former magnetic storm?" Galyan asked.

"That will do for now," Maddox said.

"I have it."

"Use all the ship's sensors. Study the area. Do you sense anything unusual there?"

"Negative," Galyan said.

"Maybe you should sweep for a longer length of time," Maddox suggested.

"Give me the duration that will satisfy you," Galyan said.

"Make it a minute."

The holoimage stood perfectly still as they waited. After a minute, Galyan turned to Maddox, "I detect nothing unusual."

"Maybe what you're looking for can only be seen up close," Riker suggested. "Maybe it's like a Laumer-Point wormhole. The Laumer Drive has to be right next to one for it to appear on our instruments."

"True," Maddox said.

"Shall I return to the location?" Galyan asked.

Maddox considered going back. They would have to decelerate first and then accelerate back to the area. That would take time.

"No," the captain said. "We have to reach Earth as fast as possible. We need to inform High Command about our victory over the New Men. Besides, I don't know that I'm the right person to keep Ludendorff. Brigadier O'Hara must have more pertinent information about the professor."

Riker glanced at Maddox with surprise.

"Is something bothering you, Sergeant?"

"Yes, sir," Riker said. "I've never known you to admit failure in a case or to admit someone might know more than you do. We should squeeze Ludendorff. He knows why he did what he did. Let's make him tell us."

"There are three considerations hindering me from doing exactly that," Maddox said. "One, the professor is unbelievably sly. He tricked the New Men. It's more than conceivable he can trick me. Two is the stakes involved—control of *Victory*. This is a reckless place to practice the questioning, especially as he's already sealed away." Maddox had given Galyan orders to stay out of the professor's room. "No. I'm thinking of putting the professor in stasis and—"

"Negative," Galyan said.

Both men stared at the holoimage before exchanging glances with each other.

"Could you expand on your comment?" Maddox asked Galyan.

"I cannot allow you to place the professor in stasis," the holoimage said.

"Do you have a reason?" Maddox asked.

"Negative," Galyan said.

"That's illogical," Maddox said. "The law of cause and effect dictates you must have a reason for saying what you did."

"Nevertheless—"

"Let me rephrase the question," Maddox said. Speaking with the ancient AI could be challenging at times. "What compelled you to say what you just did?"

"I do not know," Galyan admitted.

"Do you plan on freeing the professor or speaking with him?"

"Negative."

"Will you head straight to Earth as I've ordered?"

"That is affirmative, Captain. I am under your command."

"Just not if I attempt to put Ludendorff in stasis," Maddox said.

"That is correct."

Maddox eyed the holoimage, finally motioning Riker. The two of them walked away from Galyan.

"What do you make of that, sir?" Riker whispered.

"Dana guessed it. The professor did something underhanded while ridding the AI of the Swarm virus." Maddox spoke louder. "Galyan, can you pinpoint the moment the professor instructed you to shift your star drive jump so we appeared where we first did in this system?"

"I do not understand the query," Galyan said.

"How did we arrive by the magnetic storm when we did? It wasn't a coincidence. Do you recall the professor making any adjustments to the flight path?"

"Negative."

Maddox considered that. He whispered to Riker, "It appears Ludendorff can control Galyan in a way that's beneath the AI's perception."

"What are we going to do about it, sir?"

Maddox considered the question. Once more, he raised his voice. "Galyan, will you keep Ludendorff and his people locked in their quarters for the remainder of the voyage?"

"Affirmative."

Maddox leaned near Riker, whispering, "We're going to get home to Earth as fast as possible to report on the victories in the Tannish and Markus Systems and also tell Intelligence about the ghostly vessel. Then, we'll get ready for the next battle against the New Men."

"What about the professor?" Riker whispered.

"He's locked away from harm. I'll let Star Watch decide his punishment."

41

-6-

Over one hundred and fifty light years away from Maddox, Commander Kris Guderian of the Star Watch Frigate *Osprey* exited a Laumer-Point into the New Arabia System.

The bridge crew and the frigate's computers were presently in the grip of Jump Lag.

The system had a G class star with five planets and millions of comets in the outer region. In the inner area were two Earthlike worlds in nearly identical orbits. The farther planet in relation to the star was named Al Salam, the closer world was Riyadh. They were the twin home-worlds of the Wahhabi Caliphate.

Osprey was a Patrol vessel, part of the scouting arm of Star Watch. Normally, Patrol craft went into the Beyond, surveying new star systems. Her crew was composed of hardened explorers and scientists accustomed to spending years at a time away from port.

Commander Guderian had been with the Fifth Fleet under Admiral Fletcher. Almost nine months ago, she had first brought the admiral word of the approaching New Men. The attacking star cruisers had brought about the ill-fated Battle of Caria 323. *Osprey* had fled with the rest of the survivors into the void, heading for the Tannish System. Six months after the first battle, Guderian had witnessed the victory over the New Men with the ancient starship's disruptor beam. After the second battle, Fletcher had given her the task of racing to

42

Caliph Mohammad Saladin Bey III in New Arabia. She was to inform the ruler of Star Watch's victory over the enemy.

That meant *Osprey* and her crew hadn't gotten to go home first, but headed as fast as they could to the heart of the Muslim star empire. That was one of the benefits of Patrol craft. They were fast.

As Kris recovered from Jump Lag, she raised her head at her station on the bridge. Kris doubled as her own communications and sensor officer so she began engaging the sensors and she studied her comm-board as the effects of Jump Lag started wearing off.

Kris Guderian had short red hair and a splash of freckles across her nose. She had an Irish-German background and had to fend off more than her share of romantic invitations from the scientists aboard. The worst offender she had confined to quarters.

"That's strange," Kris said.

"What's that, Commander?" her pilot asked

Lieutenant Artemis was a tall woman, dark-haired and attractive, with shiny fingernails. She was currently the only other person on the bridge.

"No one in the system is hailing us," Kris said.

"Oh," Artemis said. "That *is* odd."

The Wahhabis were known for having the strictest pre and post jump protocols of anyone in inhabited space. Why hadn't someone hailed them? Guderian needed to find out.

Kris tapped her panel, scanning nearby space. A frozen Pluto-like planet orbited several hundred thousand kilometers away. The commander didn't spy any signs of life there. The weirdest thing was that there should have been Wahhabi warships guarding the Laumer-Point. There was nothing here but empty space.

"Could the New Men have hit New Arabia?" Artemis asked.

"The indications we've seen during the journey don't point to that," Kris said. "Everything has been tense but peaceful among the Wahhabis. Every system was on full alert. You know how zealously each sheik-superior questioned us about the war in 'C' Quadrant."

"Should I begin heading in-system?" Artemis asked.

"Yes."

As the pilot went to work, the commander fixed her sensors on the nearby planet while looking up its stats on the database. The ice-rock was called Al Gaza and was supposed to have heavy-mount laser cannons and underground shelters.

A cold feeling squeezed Kris's heart. *Osprey's* sensors showed a hot, radioactive globe. That was a molten planet out there. But that didn't make sense. Al Gaza was supposed to be a frozen iceoid.

Kris flicked on the frigate's intercom. "This is the Commander speaking. We are on red alert. I repeat. We are on red alert."

"I don't see a thing anywhere, Commander," Artemis said as she studied her flight screen.

Kris widened the sensor sweeps. "Let's proceed cautiously," she told Artemis. "Make it half cruising speed."

The lonely Patrol vessel started in-system. Riyadh and Al Salam were both several billion kilometers away.

Osprey had a few weapons systems, but nothing to boast about. It relied on speed for ultimate protection, although they had a weak shield and paltry hull armor. The frigate's strength lay in its sensors, in many ways better than a battleship's.

Kris used those sensors now. Her stomach tightened as she spotted several wrecks floating in the void five hundred million kilometers away.

The Wahhabi Caliphate had a strong political system. They also had good warships and hardy soldiers. Their Muslim beliefs strengthened their devotion to duty. Sometimes it made them inflexible, but that could also be a plus in the right situations.

After fifteen minutes of silence, Artemis asked, "How does one of the busiest star systems in existence—"

Harsh static from Guderian's board cut off the pilot. Kris tapped a panel, bringing an image to the forward screen.

"What is that?" Artemis asked.

A gigantic, lightening-lit spheroid of immense size—bigger than a planet—grew into existence on the screen.

"That's in the inner system," Kris said. "This is at high magnification."

The spheroid sizzled with power, sending long bolts of purple energy into the void. The display increased in intensity.

"By the goddess," Artemis said. "What is *that*?"

Kris spied a huge, teardrop-shaped vessel inside what the sensors showed was an ionic-front magnetic storm. A few quick taps on her board gave the commander an idea of the vessel's size. It had to be over fifty kilometers long, monstrous by starship standards. The commander didn't know of any warship anywhere that was even one kilometer in length.

"What..."

Artemis's words drained away as the pyrotechnic display began to shrink with fantastic speed. In minutes, the magnetic storm drained away, leaving the giant ship alone in the stellar darkness.

"I am a fool," Kris said. She manipulated her panel, beginning a heavy scan of the distant object.

"Look over there," Artemis said. She pointed at the very edge of the screen.

Kris didn't look up. She was too busy reading her sensors. "I can't believe what I'm seeing!"

"Neither can I," Artemis said.

Something in the pilot's voice caused Kris to look up. At the edge of the main screen was a mass of Wahhabi warships. The commander directed her sensors at them.

The vast majority of warships were *Scimitar*-class vessels, oblong craft with extremely long-ranged lasers. The Wahhabi Navy preferred distance battles, using speed to keep their opponents from closing. The *Scimitar*-class ships were a cross in size between Star Watch cruisers and destroyers.

"I'm picking up a message," Kris said.

On the screen, the space scene disappeared. In its place, a sheik-superior appeared. He was a dark-skinned man wearing a red turban with a large diamond in the center.

"You are in Wahhabi home space," the sheik-superior said. "You must decelerate and accept court representatives aboard your ship."

"Is he speaking to us?" Artemis asked.

45

Kris was surprised the pilot asked something so obviously wrong. The monster vessel and the Wahhabi Home Fleet were billions of kilometers away in the inner system. That meant what *Osprey's* sensors picked up had already taken place hours ago.

The Wahhabi commander had spoken to the giant ship.

"Your silence means we will have to attack," the sheik-superior said. "Therefore, I urge you to answer before we are forced to initiate hostilities and destroy your vessel."

No one aboard the teardrop-shaped ship answered.

"What's happening in space?" Artemis asked.

Kris switched scenes so the sheik-superior vanished. Billions of kilometers away from *Osprey*, lasers flashed from the *Scimitar*-class raiders. The beams speared over one hundred thousand kilometers to hit the giant ship's hull.

"Doesn't it have a shield?" Artemis asked.

"The sensors show neutroium armor."

"Meaning what?"

"The neutrons are packed side-by-side. That makes the armor incredibly dense and heavy."

Artemis frowned. "That sounds impossible. Neutrons like that could only be in the middle of a neutron star. The armor should be highly unstable."

"With our present science, you're right," Kris said. "Yet that's what my sensors are showing: pure neutroium."

"This is bad," Artemis said. "The Wahhabi Home Fleet primarily uses lasers. I doubt even heavy lasers will have enough time to penetrate the neutroium."

"Yes," Kris said. "I imagine that's going to be a problem for them."

As they watched, the Wahhabis increased velocity, the fleet racing at the monster vessel. So far, the teardrop-shaped ship continued straight for Al Salam.

Kris understood the sheik-superior's reasoning. A laser dissipated energy the farther it beamed. So, the closer a laser beamed, the stronger it was. Yet, could even close-range laser fire do anything to neutroium armor? It looked as if the sheik-superior meant to find out.

The Wahhabis had a reason for trusting in their combat lasers. Kris happened to know that Star Watch Intelligence sent their best espionage agents to Wahhabi space. The Muslim scientists constructed better lasers than anyone else. The Wahhabi Navy had better heavy-mount lasers than Star Watch did and could fire more accurately over extreme distances. Star Watch wanted the superior technology for their warships. Unfortunately, the Wahhabi secret service was also among the best.

"Decelerate," Kris ordered Artemis. "Turn us around as fast as you can."

"We're leaving the star system?" Artemis asked.

"Do you think the Wahhabis can beat that ship?" Kris asked.

"Maybe."

"No," Kris said. "That ship has more mass than the entire Wahhabi Navy combined, maybe more mass than the entire Wahhabi Navy and Merchant Marine vessels."

"Then—"

"What do you think happened to Al Gaza to turn the Plutonic planet into a radioactive globe? The ship must have burned the iceoid. We have to tell High Command about this."

"Shouldn't we see what happens first?" Artemis asked.

Kris thought about that. It was a reasonable idea. Yet how could the Wahhabis beat that vessel? "We'll decide once we're near the Laumer-Point."

The pilot glanced at Guderian, likely understanding the point. It would be wise to get ready to flee.

"Yes, Commander," Artemis said. "You'd better inform the crew. We're going to practice some hard maneuvering."

In the outer New Arabia System, the Patrol frigate decelerated at emergency speeds. As *Osprey* did so, the neutroium-hulled super-vessel remained on course for the desert planet of Al Salam.

Time ticked away as the Wahhabis closed the distance to the invader. In an hour, *Osprey* was ready to reenter the Laumer-Point.

"What do you say, Commander?" Artemis asked. "Do we leave New Arabia?"

47

"Not just yet," Kris said. High Command would want battle data.

"I didn't think we would," Artemis said. "You want to see what happens when that thing attacks, just as much as I do." Patrol officers were notoriously curious people.

Kris was too fixated on the screen and her sensors to respond. The big ship never swung around to face the Wahhabis gaining on it. Remorselessly, the monster vessel approached Al Salam. The teardrop-shaped vessel didn't travel quickly. Rather, it moved at a leisurely pace like a space whale.

From their distant vantage point on the fringe of the outer system, Kris and Artemis watched the Wahhabi lasers beam from sixty-five thousand kilometers away. Over one hundred raider beams splashed against the neutroium hull.

Kris recorded the wattage hitting the alien armor. The power expenditure staggered her. There was a reason few people messed with the Wahhabis.

The sheik-superior didn't use the same tactics a Star Watch admiral would have. The Wahhabis were raiders by nature, using wolf-pack tactics. Hit-and-run was their favored maneuver. Today, they hit, heading closer and closer to their adversary. Wahhabi ships didn't have heavy hull armor. They relied on shields, speed and their long-ranged lasers. Those beams grew hotter, pouring vicious energy against the giant craft.

With this tactic and those lasers, the Wahhabi Home Fleet would have done well against a Star Watch Fleet. Against the neutroium-hulled monster—

"I'm recording some slight scorching to the alien hull," Kris said. "I hadn't expected the lasers to do anything against that armor."

"The ship is ignoring them," Artemis said. "I can hardly believe this."

"Oh-oh, you may have spoken too soon."

The vessel turned on its axis even as it made a slow motion swing toward the Wahhabis.

What kind of technology is allowing that spin move? Kris wondered.

At that moment, the Patrol commander got a better idea of the alien-ness of the craft. It possessed a monstrous orifice five kilometers in diameter. No weapon Kris had ever heard about had a firing orifice like that.

Her sensors went red as a massive beam speared out of the vessel. The energy in the beam was incredible. It destroyed the feeble Wahhabi electromagnetic shields. It burned through the hulls as if they were tinfoil and exploded raider after raider. Kris would never have believed such a thing possible before witnessing it herself.

The single beaming assault ended. The alien craft did not bother to shoot again. Instead, it began to turn back toward Al Salam.

"Did you see that?" Artemis whispered.

Kris came out of her fog. With weak fingers, she tapped her board. Thirty-four raiders no longer existed. Twenty-eight others did not accelerate, decelerate or fire their lasers. Those warships acted as if everyone on them was dead. Could the radiation within the passing ray have slain the crews?

Kris thought it more than possible.

Two-thirds of the surviving and functional raiders continued to fire their heavy lasers. The last third broke off the attack, turning away and accelerating. Their commanders must believe it was futile to engage the alien vessel.

"What is that thing?" Artemis whispered.

"I think we're about to find out."

Artemis glanced at the commander.

"I don't think that's a warship," Kris said.

"What else could it be?"

"A planet-killer," Kris said, softly.

Artemis' eyes became huge. "What makes you say that?"

"The figures I'm seeing regarding the beam," Kris said. "There's no reason to build a beam that powerful if one means to attack other ships. But if one meant to kill a planet…"

"That's monstrous," Artemis said. "Who would need that kind of weapon?"

"I have no idea."

"What did the magnetic storm earlier have to do with the ship?"

"This is the greatest enigma I've ever seen," Kris declared. "Who made that thing?"

Another hour passed. The surviving Wahhabis exhausted themselves firing at the neutroium-hulled planet-killer. One-by-one, those ships pulled away.

Nine of the raiders had other ideas.

"Are they going to ram the enemy?" Artemis asked.

"I think so."

Kris winced at the first two impacts. The Wahhabi ships smashed against the fantastic neutroium vessel. The raiders simply disintegrated because of the speed. *Scimitar* armor, hull, concentrates, laser mirrors, coils, engines, personnel and everything else aboard flattened against the alien vessel and dashed outward in a circumference. The fifty-kilometer ship only shivered a little with each impact.

"Can the personnel inside the alien ship withstand those shocks?" Artemis asked.

"How heavy are those impacts?" Kris asked. "It looks like it should do something, but it seems to make no impression against the ship. The conductor in the control room probably can't even feel the impacts."

As the two Patrol officers watched from the outer-system Laumer-Point, the remnants of the Wahhabi Home Fleet fled from the alien vessel. From Al Salam's orbit, merchant marine and private ships began hard acceleration away.

Al Salam was a red-sand desert world. It contained many important relics from Earth and new ones discovered throughout the decades. Many Wahhabi citizens went on pilgrimage to Al Salam, and most of the fauna and creatures from Saudi Arabia on Earth had taken to the red sands of the desert world.

Al Salam was the political and religious center. Riyadh, its sister planet, was the manufacturing and food-producing capital of the Wahhabi Caliphate. Together, the two worlds represented one twelfth of the Wahhabi population and a full quarter of the Muslim star empire's industrial might.

"Could the beam you recorded earlier truly damage an entire planet?" Artemis asked.

Kris didn't answer. Despite the neutroium hull armor, she was reading a vast build-up of power over there.

Then it happened. A hot beam a full five kilometers wide fired from the alien vessel's orifice. The red ray speared at Al Salam. It reached the planetary orbit in ten seconds and burned down through the atmosphere. The wattage was beyond phenomenal. The thick beam bored against the surface, churning through sand, rock and finally against the planetary crust. After fifty-nine kilometers of crustal rock, the beam reached Al Salam's mantle.

There the rocks changed texture, made up of iron and magnesium combined with silicon and oxygen. It was called olivine rock, with a thickness of 2900 kilometers.

With incredible speed and destructive power, the teardrop ship's beam sliced into and annihilated olivine rock. Such a thing should have been impossible. Yet, the beam churned and burned, digging into Al Salam until finally it reached the planetary core.

Because of the melting properties of the iron alloy core, the outer core was molten while the inner core was solid.

At this point, the beam quit.

On Al Salam, molten iron from the planetary core shot up to the surface, spitting onto the red sands like a super-volcano geyser. Behind the molten iron followed hot olivine rock. Surface sand burned, atmospheric air ignited and havoc raged in a widening, billowing circumference.

In space, the giant ship minutely changed its trajectory. Minutes passed. Then, the beam flashed from the orifice and began drilling into Al Salam once more, repeating the performance in a new location hundreds of kilometers from the first planetary drilling.

"Can you tell what's happening on the planet?" Artemis asked weakly.

"Yes," Kris said in a soft voice. "Death and destruction. I finally understand why Al Gaza is hot and radioactive."

"The planet-killer beamed into its core?" Artemis asked.

"There's no other reasonable explanation," Kris said.

"How long will it take the alien vessel to destroy all life on Al Salam?" Artemis asked.

51

"At the rate it's firing, I imagine it will be done in hours."

"Do you think the alien craft will attack Riyadh next?"

"Don't you?"

Artemis stared at her dull-faced. "The ship means to destroy the heart of the Wahhabi Caliphate."

"I think that's right."

Artemis shook her head. "What if the vessel heads for the Commonwealth?" the pilot asked in a horrified whisper. "What if it journeys to Earth?"

Kris gave the pilot a stricken gaze. "We have a new objective. We must race to Earth and warn them about this. Go, Lieutenant. Take us through the Laumer-Point. We have to get out of here."

Osprey engaged its engines as Artemis warned the crew. Soon, the Laumer-Point became visible in space. The frigate headed straight for it.

As they neared the jump point, Kris's board gave a warning *beep*.

"What's wrong now?" Artemis asked in a panic.

Frowning, Kris adjusted her panel. For just a moment, her sensors showed a ship even farther out in the New Arabia System than they were. What was the vessel doing, and why had it been hidden until now?

As *Osprey* plunged toward the Laumer-Point, Kris's fingers played across her board. Even as she attempted to learn more about the mysterious ship, it faded from her screen, just disappeared.

Kris ran a fast analysis on the ship's dimensions. She'd been recording those brief seconds it had been visible. "This can't be right," she muttered.

Artemis gave her a worried glance.

"According to the computer," Kris said, "I just saw a cloaked star cruiser."

"The New Men," Artemis whispered. "The planet-killer must belong to them."

"How could a star cruiser have gotten into New Arabia without anyone knowing about it?" Kris asked. "It couldn't have used the same Laumer-Points *Osprey* did. The Wahhabis

52

would have destroyed the star cruiser at a jump point long before it reached the home system.

"Is it coming after us?" Artemis asked fearfully.

Kris checked the sensors. The space out there looked empty now. The enemy must possess an advanced cloaking device. That was terrible news all by itself.

Would the New Men on the star cruiser know she had seen them? Would the star cruiser come after them?

Before Kris could worry too much, *Osprey* entered the Laumer-Point, heading to a new star system.

-7-

Maddox and Valerie were on the bridge breathing heavily as they waited for their Jump Lag to wear off.

Since the ion storm and sighting the fifty-kilometer mystery vessel several days ago, they had raced even faster for Earth. At Maddox's orders, they waited a shorter duration between Laumer-Point jumps and the use of the star drive. The accelerated travel schedule had left everyone exhausted and irritable from too much Jump Lag too quickly.

Maddox stirred on his command chair. He breathed deeply, stretching his chest muscles. A minute later, he moved his jaw. It felt as if someone had punched him in the face. He might have to wait several hours before the next jump. If he felt this badly, the others must feel even worse.

Valerie had been moving sluggishly for the past few minutes. Now, she straightened, tapping her panel with greater purpose. She stared at her board for some time.

"Trouble?" Maddox asked.

Valerie swiveled around. Her eyes were red-rimmed from lack of sleep. Keith had been sick for the last few days, meaning the lieutenant had double duty.

"The professor must still have access to the AI," Valerie said. "That's the only way I can explain this."

"Explain what?" Maddox asked.

The lieutenant tapped her panel. A star chart appeared on the main screen. It showed the Commonwealth Laumer-Point routes, a bewildering array of bright dots and red jump routes.

54

Another tap against the panel took a small section of the chart, expanding it as the rest disappeared. With a quick manipulation, Valerie highlighted the Nicholas 89 System.

"We should be in this star system heading on this route." The lieutenant highlighted a series of tramlines that led to the edge of the screen. "The path eventually leads to Earth. Instead, we're *here*," she said, tapping the panel again.

The Nicholas 89 System and star route went dim as the QV-7 System brightened on the chart.

Maddox frowned at the screen. "You're saying we're not in the right star system?"

"Correct," Valerie said. "If you'll notice, QV-7 is nine light-years from Nicholas 89 where we're supposed to be."

"That means we didn't change course in one jump."

"That's right," Valerie said. "We've been using the star drive for the last three transfers, making a three light-years jump each time."

Maddox studied the chart. Although it was only a nine light-year difference, the direction of travel was like a right turn. The Laumer Drive tramlines from QV-7 lead away from Earth.

"Galyan had to have changed the coordinates after I entered them into the star drive for three consecutive jumps now," Valerie said.

"The AI must have also tampered with your earlier sensor readings, too."

"Agreed," Valerie said.

Maddox pressed a button on the arm of his command chair. It was time to clip Ludendorff for good. "Sergeant," he said.

"Yes, sir," Riker replied several seconds later.

Before Maddox could order the man to meet him near the professor's quarters, the captain snatched his hand away from the control. The plate on the armrest had become unbearably hot.

"Captain!" Valerie shouted.

Maddox looked up. The lieutenant sat frozen in place, stiff and unmoving, her eyes wide with fear as she stared past him.

Maddox whirled around.

Ludendorff stood just inside the hatch. The man's bald dome looked slick, and he panted heavily as if he'd been sprinting. He held a flat device with one hand, the other fiddling with the controls on it.

With an oath, Maddox reached for the gun under his jacket. He jerked his hand away from it. The handle was red-hot.

Maddox slid off the chair, charging Ludendorff, hoping to take him down before the professor could finish with his device.

"I'm afraid not," Ludendorff said, tapping his gadget.

Maddox slammed into an invisible force field, his face striking against it. The field tightened, wrapping around him. The invisible web against his face disappeared, however, allowing him to breathe. But he was trapped, at the mercy of Ludendorff. The same thing must have just happened to Valerie.

"Don't be alarmed, Captain," the professor said smoothly. "This is a mere precaution. I can't allow you to shoot me, after all."

Maddox's mind churned. Galyan must have been allowing the professor to monitor them. The older man looked winded. He must have burst out of his quarters once he realized Valerie had discovered the flight deception.

"This is alarming," Maddox said in an even voice. "First, you freed Per Lomax several days ago. I put you in confinement, which you've apparently rejected. Now you've hijacked *Victory*. What I don't understand is why you helped us during the Battle of the Tannish System. It's clear you're an enemy agent, a deep plant."

"Your conclusion is quite wrong," Ludendorff said. "I don't fault you for that, as you're unaware of the greatest danger to humanity in a millennium. I'd hoped to forestall the problem on the sly. I truly hate taking direct action like this. But, now I'm afraid I must."

"You're claiming there's something worse than the New Men?" Maddox asked.

"Oh, much worse, I assure you."

Maddox considered that. "And it has something to do with the ghostly vessel Valerie and I saw in the ion storm several days ago?"

"Oh, yes, quite," the professor said.

"You're admitting, then, that you timed the starship's appearance with the ion storm, freed Per Lomax and sent the New Man to it in the jumpfighter?"

"Yes," Ludendorff said. "I freely admit it. I had a key of great antiquity. I gave it to the New Man, which allowed him entry to the doomsday machine."

"You gave our enemy a doomsday machine?" Maddox asked.

"Of course not," Ludendorff said. "It was a one-way mission with no hope of return. Per Lomax would gain entry to the control chamber and turn off the machine. Doing so, though, would cost him his life."

Maddox studied the professor, trying to determine if the man was mad. "Why would Per Lomax turn off this doomsday device for you? Why not take control of it?"

"Not for me," Ludendorff said, "but for his people, for the Throne World and maybe even the race of New Men."

"Here we go again. You want to help our enemy?"

"I don't want to commit genocide against them," Ludendorff said. "But that's neither here nor there at the moment. The planet-killer is...is beyond our science. Shutting it off was the easiest expedient."

"Doomsday machine, planet-killer," Maddox said. "Why do you call it that? It was a big ship, I grant you. What you're suggesting..."

Ludendorff looked away. After a time, he moved farther onto the bridge, past Maddox.

The captain strained to move but found it impossible, leaving him winded. The invisible web was strong. He managed to crane his neck, though. The professor laid an unconscious lieutenant onto the deck plates.

"What did you do to her?" Maddox demanded.

"Don't fret. I merely used a property of the web field to put her to sleep. She's fine. And this is better all the way around, believe me. I don't want to have to scrub her mind later so she forgets what she heard."

Scrub her mind. Ludendorff had used the term before, referring to what the teacher had done to Meta aboard the star cruiser in Wolf Prime orbit.

Ludendorff sat down in the command chair, facing Maddox.

"You have questions," the professor said. "I understand. Let me explain concisely and quickly to save us time. The planet-killer you saw in the ion storm has already destroyed all life in the New Arabia System. That means it has destroyed the home system of the Wahhabi Caliphate. I believe the machine has also been set to destroy the capitals of the Windsor League and the Solar System, specifically, Earth."

Maddox struggled to understand. "You said Per Lomax attempted to turn off the planet-killer. Who turned it on?"

"It is safe to surmise that the leadership of the New Men agreed to the expedient."

"Then why suggest Per Lomax would turn it off for you?" Maddox asked.

Ludendorff frowned. "You must realize every group of humans has factions struggling against each other. It's in the nature of humanity to quarrel. Not even the New Men have been able to breed that out of their genetic heritage. That means some among the New Men are against the planet-killer. They realize the danger in unleashing it."

"If you're right, that suggests you understand the inner workings of the New Men."

"I've had a few years to figure it out," the professor said.

"Then why haven't you shared the knowledge with Star Watch?"

"I am," the professor said, "with you right now."

"No," Maddox said. "There are too many flaws in your argument. The lieutenant and I saw the planet-killer several days ago. New Arabia is over one hundred and fifty light-years away. The doomsday device couldn't get to New Arabia in that time. It would take weeks of travel at best. There's another problem. Even if the machine could get there that fast, how could you receive a message from one hundred and fifty light-years?"

"Don't equate ignorance with brilliance, my boy."

"What does that mean?" Maddox asked.

"Quite simply," the professor said, "that you lack knowledge to speak coherently on the subject."

From where Maddox stood, he noticed the slightest movement as the hatch began to open. He remembered calling Riker. Was that the sergeant over there?

Ludendorff paused as he became more alert. Did the professor sense the sergeant's approach?

"I questioned Per Lomax once," Maddox said in a bland voice, trying to draw the professor's attention without alerting him. "He said the New Men didn't want to destroy all human life, just the dross. This doomsday machine doesn't seem as if it will distinguish between good and bad human stock."

"It most certainly won't," Ludendorff said.

"That means the New Men didn't turn it on."

"Are you truly that daft?" the professor asked.

Maddox only half heard the question. Riker appeared by the open hatch. He gripped his stunner. The sergeant's good eye widened with surprise. Riker aimed and fired an energy bolt. The globule sped true, sizzling an inch from Ludendorff's skin, stopped by something, an invisible force field perhaps.

"Ah-ha!" Ludendorff cried, jumping off the command chair, turning to Riker.

"Run!" Maddox shouted.

Riker didn't run, but fired again. It had the same useless effect as the first shot.

Then the sergeant was toppling onto the deck plates, frozen in the same kind of web field that had caught Maddox.

Ludendorff turned, giving the captain a quizzical study.

Maddox waited. Regaining control of *Victory* was going to be harder than he'd imagined.

"Let me suggest some possibilities to you," the professor said, no doubt deciding to ignore the *interruption*. "The personal force field protecting me and the web I can project onto others are science of a high order. Let me posit the possibility that these items were made by the Builders."

"Who are they?" Maddox asked.

"The ones who constructed the Nexus and modified the planet-killer," Ludendorff said.

"Yet another ancient race?" Maddox asked.

"The triad that is the Swarm, Adoks and Builders," the professor said. "Now, let us banish your objections, shall we? You spoke of traveling vast distances in a short amount of time as being impossible. Yet the silver pyramid allowed Kane and Meta to travel over one hundred light-years in a single jump. The same race that built the pyramid had access to the planet-killer. In other words, the doomsday machine has an incredible propulsion system."

"Which accounts for the ion storm?" Maddox asked.

"Precisely," Ludendorff said.

"Then how are we supposed to stop this doomsday machine? With *Victory's* disruptor cannon?"

"No. The planet-killer has neutroium armor. The disruptor cannon will not breach its hull."

Maddox felt his skin go cold. Neutroium? That was incredible.

"I've seen the machine," the captain said. "I can believe that part. I've also seen the ion storm and the strange opening the planet-killer dropped into, which could be its traveling mechanism. What I don't understand is how you know what happened in the New Arabia System."

Ludendorff sighed, adjusting the flat device. A wavering light shot out of it, beaming a holoimage before Maddox. The image showed the New Arabia System. The captain recognized the planets.

Maddox glanced at the professor.

"I'm magnifying," Ludendorff said.

Maddox watched the battle between the doomsday machine and the Wahhabi Home Fleet. Later, he observed the giant beam punching holes into Al Salam's surface, drilling down to the molten core. Afterward, the captain observed billowing iron lava flowing over the red sands of Al Salam, destroying everything. The doomsday machine performed a similar horror to Riyadh, annihilating all life on the industrial planet.

Finally, Ludendorff switched off the holoimage.

Maddox grew thoughtful. "Are you expecting me to believe that's actual footage of a real attack?"

"Footage, as you put it, that happened two days ago," Ludendorff said.

"The giant ship jumped to New Arabia?"

"Not directly from the system where we saw it, but yes," Ludendorff said. "Permit me to explain how I know this. The New Men possess a handful of interstellar communication artifacts. One of the relics was aboard a star cruiser in the New Arabia System that witnessed the destruction I just showed you. I happen to have one of these incredible devices myself and received the images a day ago."

"This communication device is aboard *Victory*?" Maddox asked.

"Don't bother looking for it, Captain. You won't find it. As to *why* I know: there are a few New Men with opposing philosophical views to their leadership. Now and again, I have spoken with the right thinkers. It was how I knew about the planet-killer's awakening, its trajectory so *Victory* could intercept it and later, about its frightful carnage in the New Arabia System."

Maddox was appalled. Could these things be true? "Is there any chance Per Lomax made it aboard the planet-killer?"

"He would have turned off the machine if he had."

Maddox smiled grimly. "Maybe you thought to use him, but Per Lomax used you. He made it onto the machine and didn't turn it off. We first captured Per Lomax because he led a boarding party against *Victory*. It's clear the New Men desire their own alien super-ship. By freeing my prisoner, you may have inadvertently given them such a ship."

The professor turned away. "An honest man would admit the possibility of what you just said." He made a waving gesture. "I'm getting too old for these games."

"What are you suggesting *I* do about any of this?" Maddox asked. "How is *Victory* supposed to stop a fifty-kilometer doomsday machine covered with neutroium?"

Ludendorff eyed him. "I've been pondering the problem. It was one of the reasons I accepted the confinement to quarters: to think without interruption. The answer makes me uneasy."

"I'm assuming you're uneasy because you don't like to take unnecessary risks," Maddox said. "That's why you used Per Lomax instead of trying to board the planet-killer yourself. And that's why you want me: to do your risky work for you."

"I'd hoped the key would work for Per Lomax," the professor said pensively. "It was a long shot, maybe longer than I let the New Man know. That's history now. I suppose one method of stopping the planet-killer would be to gather the biggest armada in human history. But we would need the New Men's help, and they're not about to give it. By the time the majority of the New Men realize how dangerous the planet-killer really is, most of humanity will already be dead. No, we have to do something ourselves."

"And that is what?" Maddox asked.

"We must go to the asteroid belt near the Nexus. There, we must search for a control unit. I happen to know the doomsday machine was parked there for thousands of years."

"And that's why you hijacked my starship?" Maddox asked. "To go there?"

The professor nodded.

"Why not come to me first and tell me about this or better yet ask for our help?"

"I have my reasons," the professor said.

Maddox did some quick thinking. Finally, he said, "I'm not going to agree to help unless you give up the backdoor to Galyan. Either I run *Victory,* or I will consider myself your prisoner. As a prisoner, I refuse to help my captor."

"You're in no position to bargain," Ludendorff said.

"But I am. You want my help. To gain it, that's the price."

"I could simply lock you in your quarters and do this myself."

"I don't think so," Maddox said. "You like to use proxies. That's why you sent Per Lomax after the planet-killer. You as good as murdered him. I'm beginning to think he had no chance but for wildest luck."

Ludendorff scowled. "I'm growing weary of your insults, Captain."

"You mean to say that the truth can still prick your conscience. That means for all your faults, you haven't yet become inhuman."

After a moment, Ludendorff shook his head. "You're a brash young fellow, but that's the kind of officer I need. I don't have time to search for someone else to do this. Thus, I'll give you a concession. I will retain the backdoor to Galyan. But, I will refrain from using it unless I inform you first."

Maddox pondered that. Could he get more? "Tell me this," the captain said. "What is our destination?"

"I already told you."

"What are the stellar coordinates?" Maddox asked.

Ludendorff shook his head. "I will keep that to myself for now."

"Why bother? We'll know once we get there."

"As I said before, I have my reasons."

Maddox became thoughtful. "I agree," he said at last.

"Excellent," the professor said, tapping the flat device.

The web field disappeared, and Maddox could move again. He stretched and scratched his back, but there was no use drawing his gun for a quick shot. The professor still wore the personal force field.

"I feel compelled to warn you," the professor said. "This will be your hardest assignment yet."

"Right," Maddox said. It would be difficult because he had to find a way to regain control of the starship. He had to surprise the professor, which he would do at the first available opportunity.

-8-

Valerie paced in her quarters.

Ludendorff had taken over the starship. He and his people used the various interior ship systems to watch them, had been watching them for some time. The captain had called a short meeting after the seizure, letting the others know the situation. Maddox had been guarded in his speech because he knew Ludendorff watched and analyzed everything they said.

During the meeting, the captain had brushed aside her question about their exact destination. As the starship's navigator, Valerie wanted to know where they traveled. Maddox had smiled as if bored with her question, but he might have winked. He'd done it so quickly, though, that she still wasn't sure.

At first, Valerie had resented the brushoff. Too many times during her Space Academy days, the clique of rich-kid cadets had done just that to her during the group study period. Instead of trying to form her own study group, Valerie had done what she always had and had gone inward. She became a group of one, and out-studied all of them. In fact, Valerie had discovered she had a knack for research, finding the little clues that others often missed.

As Valerie paced in her cabin, she wondered about that. Sometimes, life's hardest trials later proved to have been a blessing. It forced the person to grow, to expand, and discover they could do more than they'd realized.

The lieutenant stopped pacing. A sad smile stretched her lips.

It's silly to keep worrying about my cadet days. I need to get over it. Doomsday machines and a vicious species war against the New Men are the real threats. I need to stay focused on what's important.

Valerie decided to use her strength. She was going to find *Victory's* destination and find out why Ludendorff hadn't told them. With that in mind, she marched from her quarters and returned to the bridge.

Keith sat in the pilot's chair. The second lieutenant was in his mid-twenties, with sandy-colored hair, a ready grin and mischievous blue eyes. The small Scotsman was the best pilot there was, and he liked to make sure everyone understood just how good he really was.

"Lieutenant," Keith said in way of greeting.

Valerie nodded, going to navigation.

They chatted for three quarters of an hour. Finally, Keith stood, stretched and said he was off to bed.

Valerie waited to do what she planned. Ludendorff could be spying on her. If so, she would bore him to tears before attempting her real endeavor.

Two hours after Keith's departure, Valerie began to use the computer, checking various navigation routes. She ran through a series of nonsense diagnostics. Sprinkled between those were her serious studies. As she did this, Valerie looked up various data. Most of those searches meant nothing.

For the next several hours, she studied old battles, the size of Laumer-Point openings and gravitational dampeners.

Each Laumer-Point was different. Some had large openings into the tramlines. Some were narrow and dangerous. Star Watch categorized the Laumer-Points into various classes. The largest jump gates could accommodate the biggest battleships and Spacer haulers. The smallest would only allow probes to squeeze through.

Valerie studied the starship's heading and the various star systems along the way. She recalled Meta's story of her time with Kane. They had exited a Cestus hauler and used a small Laumer-Point to reach the system with the Nexus.

After four and a half hours of research, Valerie believed she had pinpointed the vessel's destination. She didn't stop working, though, but continued to follow the same procedure for another hour. Finally, the lieutenant looked up facts on the targeted star system. What she found shocked her.

Later, Valerie yawned, bleary-eyed and sleepy. Keith returned to the bridge. She bid him goodnight and stumbled off to her quarters. She knew she had to find a way to tell Maddox her findings.

On her cot, Valerie lay awake for over an hour, worrying about how to do that, before the answer finally dawned on her. That worked like a drug, eliminating her restlessness. She fell asleep five minutes later.

In the morning, Valerie dragged herself to the cafeteria. She ate several strips of bacon and drank two cups of coffee. During the meal, she noticed something strange from one of Ludendorff's people, all of whom had finally been released from their quarters.

The sight made her shiver with dread. To hide further reactions, the lieutenant stared at her empty cup.

I have to tell Maddox about this. Meta's life may be in danger.

Valerie got up several minutes later. She wouldn't look at the professor's man. She didn't dare. This was bad. The lieutenant headed for the bridge, realizing she would have to let the captain know about this new danger as well.

✳✳✳

Maddox and Lieutenant Noonan were on the bridge. Today, Galyan helped the professor fully repair the disruptor cannon. Thus, the holoimage wasn't at its usual location on the bridge. Under the professor's guidance, the technicians and his Wolf Prime people constructed a heat-bleeder and de-atomizer. If they succeeded, Maddox would be able to use the disruptor cannon normally in combat without having to worry it would overheat and blow up, destroying *Victory*.

Valerie had been in the pilot's seat for some time. The lieutenant seemed unusually quiet today.

Even as Maddox thought that, Valerie stood abruptly, moving to navigation. Her fingers played over the console there. Soon, she began to tap harder than Maddox had ever observed before, even during battle. The lieutenant didn't look up to see if he noticed. Instead, she concentrated on what she did.

Finally, it dawned on Maddox that Valerie was attempting to signal him covertly. He got up and wandered to her location.

"You're hard at work," he said.

"Yes, sir," Valerie said. She pressed her palm against the panel. On the small screen to the side appeared a star system. While remaining on the panel, her index finger pointed at a reading on top of the screen: *Xerxes 14C.*

Maddox noted it before walking away. Valerie must have understood his unspoken message yesterday at the meeting. This was her sending him a veiled message in return.

As he returned to his command chair, Valerie continued to tap the panel until once more she stood abruptly, moving back to the pilot's chair.

Ten minutes later, she said, "I could use a cup of java."

"That's a good idea," Maddox said. "I'll join you."

They left the bridge and walked down several corridors to the cafeteria. Neither of them said a word. In the cafeteria, Valerie went to the coffee machine. She fiddled with it for a time.

Finally, sensing what she wanted, Maddox asked, "Is something wrong with the coffeemaker?"

The lieutenant nodded without looking up.

Leisurely, he pushed back his chair, rose and moved beside her. This close, it was obvious that nothing was wrong with the machine.

"What if you do this?" Maddox asked, touching the coffeemaker.

"Oh," Valerie said. She manipulated the machine and it began to grind loudly in a most unusual way.

"Did you see the Xerxes 14C System?" Valerie asked. She said it just loud enough so Maddox could hear her over the noise.

"I did," Maddox whispered.

67

"I think that's where *Victory* is headed," Valerie said.

"And?" Maddox asked.

Keeping her head down, with her hands on the coffeemaker, Valerie asked, "Have you ever heard of the Bermuda Triangle on Earth?"

"It's in the area of the Sargasso Sea," he said.

"Yes," she said, urgently. "But do you know the old legends?"

"Something about lost ships and strange occurrences," Maddox said with a frown.

"That's right," Valerie said. "The Xerxes System has a similar reputation but for greater reason. Spaceships have disappeared after going into the system. Thirty years ago, the Boron Company set up a mining colony on the metal-heavy moon of the third planet. The colony vanished, leaving no traces of the buildings or landing zones. Few military routes go through the Laumer-Points in the Xerxes System. I don't think any space-liners ever use those jump gates anymore."

"Meta once told me her Cestus hauler used those Laumer-Points," Maddox said. "Or should I say the Cestus hauler went through it in order to let off Kane's scout."

"That isn't what Meta said, sir."

"But I clearly remember..." Maddox's words faded away. "You're right. Meta's hauler let her out and Kane used the scout, entering a small Laumer-Point that led into the system."

"Damn coffeemaker!" Valerie said, giving the machine a whack with the flat of her hand. Valerie bent lower, pretending to fiddle with the machine. Out of the side of her mouth, the lieutenant said, "All I'm saying, sir, is that we're headed to an extremely dangerous star system. I wonder if the professor realizes just how hazardous."

"I'd imagine he would," Maddox said. "Now, we do too."

"We have to be careful, sir. The star system holds the Nexus, and it held this planet-killer. What else does it contain that makes it so deadly? Something that destroys ships and mining colonies."

"You've made your point," Maddox said. "We'll have to go in on combat alert." The captain became thoughtful. "How many light-years is the Xerxes System from Earth?"

"Eighty-three in eleven jumps using the Laumer-Points," Valerie said.

"I see." Maddox silently noted that Valerie had been thorough with her research.

"Whatever needs doing, you can count on me to try, sir."

Maddox smiled. "I know that, Lieutenant. Is there anything else?"

Her features tightened. For some reason, that troubled Maddox.

"You know the last slarn hunter?" Valerie asked.

"Cesar Villars?" Maddox whispered.

Valerie nodded. "He's watching Meta awfully closely. I noticed it during the morning cycle in the cafeteria when he didn't think anyone was looking. I didn't like the way he stared at her, Captain. He has bad intentions toward Meta."

The words were like a spike into Maddox's chest. He should have already seen this complication coming. The slarn hunters must have been friends, and Meta had killed Sten Gorgon.

The captain reached out, flipping two switches. "There," he said. "The machine is fixed."

Valerie stared at him.

"After waiting this long for my cup," Maddox said, with tightness in his throat, "I find I'm no longer thirsty. I think I'll have a lie down instead."

"Yes, sir," Valerie said.

"I expect you to return to the bridge," he said. "Hail me if you spot anything of interest."

"Yes, sir," she said.

Without another word, Maddox headed for the exit. If the slarn hunter had done anything to Meta—the captain increased his pace. He had to stop Villars from hurting his woman.

-9-

Maddox hurried down a corridor. How close had Gorgon been to Villars? Maybe as important, how did the slarn hunters of Wolf Prime feel about vengeance?

Maddox pulled out his comm-unit. "Meta?" he said.

There was no response. Maddox increased his pace.

How much control did Ludendorff have over his group? It would seem the professor trusted his people. Evidence of that was that Ludendorff had given Gorgon precise details to relay to Per Lomax. Maybe the slarn hunter had even handed the New Man the precious key. That implied great trust. Would that mean the professor would give his people greater leeway than otherwise?

"Meta," the captain said into his comm-unit. "Come in, please. It's important."

The device remained silent.

If Meta wasn't answering, he would track her down. To his relief, the unit showed that she was in her room.

Pocketing the device, Maddox slowed his pace. It occurred to him that just because Meta's comm-unit was in her quarters, it didn't necessitate that Meta was there with it.

Maddox broke into a sprint. Apart from the New Men, he didn't know anyone who could keep up with him when he ran at full speed. The captain fairly flew down the corridors. Would Ludendorff realize that Villars might want revenge for Gorgon's death? If the slarn hunter had hurt Meta—

Maddox shook his head. Creating future fantasies didn't help him in the moment. Cool concentration always helped him best in these matters. Yet, Maddox found that he lacked coolness this time. Heat built in his chest. He could feel it swell with throbbing force.

Maddox sprinted around a corner and barely saw a nearly invisible line stretched the width of the corridor. He recognized it as monofilament wire. If his ankles pushed against that line at this speed, the wire would neatly slice off his feet.

He couldn't halt in time, but Maddox had catlike reflexes. He leaped, although in an awkward manner. The toe of his left boot touched the monofilament wire. It sliced off some of the leather. Then, he landed hard on his left shoulder. Fortunately, Maddox rolled, bleeding away the energy of what would have been an otherwise slamming blow.

"Damn," a deep-voiced man said. "I wouldn't have believed it unless I'd seen it with my own eye. You're quicker than a wounded slarn."

Maddox scrambled to his feet, confronting Cesar Villars.

The slarn hunter was blocky with a thick neck and an ugly scar running across his right eye and down his cheek. It must have come from a slarn's claw. The eye-socket contained a smooth ball bearing. Likely, it doubled as a tech tool, giving the man radar vision. Villars wore leather garments, probably cured slarn skin. Everyone prized slarn fur. Only hunters used the toughened leather.

Villars had grizzled white hair and weather-beaten features. He gripped a long slarn knife in his right hand. It glittered in the hallway light. He waved a stun rod in his left fist.

"Does Ludendorff know what you're doing?" Maddox asked.

Villars frowned for just a moment. Then, the white-haired hunter grinned nastily.

"You're the fancy-pants boy who can save the universe, aren't you? But look at you. The shine of a knife makes you sweat. You want the professor to gallop along and save you. What a mama's boy."

71

Maddox snorted, allowing his body to relax so he appeared bored. "Yes. You've nailed it. I'm positively frightened by an incompetent like you."

"That's right, boy. That's why you sprinted to see if your little lover girl was still in one piece. I let your lieutenant see my intentions. She did exactly what I wanted. But here's what I'm wondering about you. Aren't you curious yet if I've already carved Meta up?"

Maddox shrugged as if indifferent. Inside, he seethed.

"Yeah," Villars said. "That's nice. Your balls are sweating. I know what you're thinking. Are you ever going to nail her again? Maybe I have her hanging like a piece of beef, with blood dripping to the floor from the places where I carved her. She don't deserve such a fast death, though, not after what she did to Gorgon. That was a hell of a way to die from one-punch Sally."

"You're a sadist," Maddox said.

"We all got our problems, right? Yours is my knife. Of course, you're not going to have that problem much longer, as I'm going to pull the lungs out of your chest. They'll flap a few times before you die, boy. It's called a blood eagle, and it's what I done to the last mama's boy who pissed me off."

"Why does Ludendorff keep a sadist in his company?" Maddox asked.

Villars's grin grew, which put crinkle lines at the corners of his eyes. "I'm the best at what I do, and the professor, he appreciates skill. I help keep his skinny butt alive. The old man thinks he needs you, but Gorgon's death shows me this time the professor is wrong."

"Meta killed Gorgon, not me."

"Shifting the blame, are we? Nice job, punk, let your woman take the blame. And here I thought you wanted to leave this universe as a man."

"Your logic escapes me," Maddox said.

"Better and better," Villars said. The hunter crouched, and he began to maneuver toward Maddox. The slide of his left thumb made the stun rod hum with power. It must have been set at maximum strength.

"You see, boy, I happen to know you're the white knight type. You want to ride in on your horse and rescue your little lady. But she's got several days of screaming ahead of her, see? So, first I take you out, and then I take my time with her and do it right."

"And when Ludendorff discovers what you've done?"

Villars snarled as hatred flashed in his eye. Flat-footed, he charged Maddox.

The captain kept his smile within. With ease, Maddox dodged the knife thrust. The slarn hunter acted with passion instead of cool intellect. Maddox struck, and surprise filled him as his hand harmlessly passed the man's neck. The next second, the stun rod slammed against the captain's ribs, discharging with a heavy *zap*.

Maddox catapulted backward. His back slammed against the deck plates. Trying to move, he found himself frozen in place.

"Smart boys always fall for that little trick," Villars said. "They think I'm a hotheaded bozo. I think my little scar does it. What do you think?"

Maddox squeezed his eyes shut. At least he could still do that much. The slarn hunter had tricked him. Villars hadn't attacked with blind fury, but with guile. Maddox should have realized a slarn hunter didn't survive a Wolf Prime trapping season without animal cunning. This man must have lasted many winters on the ice world.

"I'm going to make this quick, boy," Villars said. "So, you don't have to piss yourself just yet. That'll come ten seconds from now."

Maddox opened his eyes. The slarn hunter peered down at him. Could he get the trapper to kneel?

With an act of will, Maddox opened his mouth. He spoke in a slurry way, "One…last question."

"What's that, boy? I can't hear you. You have to speak up."

The slarn hunter enjoyed taunting him. Maddox would have to play on that. He pretended to have trouble speaking.

The hunter chuckled, lowering his head. "Better hurry, lover-boy. Your days of talking are almost at an end."

"If…" Maddox managed to say.

73

"Yeah, if what?"

"I could..."

Villars snarled with impatience. "You know I ain't got time to listen to you blubber. So, you've got one more chance. Then I'm stroking you with the rod and going to work cutting out your lungs. The next thing you'll know, you'll be trying to fly with a blood eagle."

Maddox strove with all his considerable concentration. He raised his head. The slarn hunter actually cocked an eyebrow in surprise. The head motion was a distraction. While making his lips writhe and his eyeballs bulge outward with pleading—causing Villars to chuckle with nasty enjoyment—Maddox thrust his fingers in his pocket and felt for a mini-grenade. It was hardly bigger than his thumbnail with an equal thickness in all directions. He pressed his thumb against the correct side, withdrew his hand and counted, hoping he got this right.

"I've had enough of this," Villars said. He raised the stun rod.

Maddox used his thumb, flicking the grenade upward.

Villars caught the motion. His head twisted that way. "What the—"

The grenade exploded, expelling knockout gas. A single whiff would be enough. Maddox held his breath as he waited.

Understanding filled Villars's good eye. He swung the rod, but he was already falling. The rod missed Maddox, striking the floor and discharging. Then the hunter's body slammed against the captain. Maddox had tried to ready himself for it. His numbed body couldn't do it in time. The captain's wind was knocked out of him, and he involuntarily sucked down air, inhaling knockout gas as well.

***

Maddox came to groggily. For several seconds, he didn't understand the heavy weight on his chest. Why was breathing so difficult? His sandpaper-dry mouth tasted vile.

Lying across his torso, Villars groaned. Maddox could feel the slarn hunter stir.

That started a contest the captain wasn't sure Villars even knew he was part of. Holding himself perfectly still, Maddox strove to wake up, and he tensed his body.

I have to make my muscles work. Maddox knew he had to get up faster than the psycho lying on top of him did. Villars was a dangerous sadist. The professor must know that. So, why did Ludendorff keep the man with him?

Villars stirred, smacking his lips.

Maddox redoubled his efforts at concentration.

"What happened?" Villars muttered. "What—"

A waft of bad breath billowed into Maddox's face, making him cough.

That caused Villars to stir with more effort. "Tricky bastard," the hunter whispered. The man's left hand dragged across the floor. The fingers didn't hold anything yet. The hand shifted direction.

By straining, Maddox turned his head. Villars's hand reached for the knife, his fingers nearing the handle. Maddox hissed between his teeth, and he wriggled, moving his body just enough so the knife remained out of Villars's reach.

"Yeah," the hunter said. "I get it now." He put both palms on the floor and pushed upward.

Maddox convulsed with effort. He wriggled part way out from under Villars. The hunter woke up all the way then, and he dropped, clutching Maddox's knees.

"No you don't, boy," Villars said.

Maddox forced himself to sit up. Villars looked at him. Three times, Maddox hit the man's face with his fists. They were weak blows, probably helping Villars to wake up faster rather than doing him any harm.

The hunter shoved his face against Maddox's legs. The fists drummed uselessly against Villars's skull. Maddox stopped the attack, and Villars chuckled nastily. A second later, the hunter opened his mouth and bit the captain's left thigh. The teeth tore through fabric and cut into flesh.

Maddox bellowed with pain. He drove his knees up, grabbed the slarn hunter's head and twisted savagely. Villars rolled with it onto the floor.

Both men struggled to their feet, panting, glaring at each other from a few meters away.

"You're an animal," Maddox said.

"I always win," Villars boasted, "because I'll do what I have to. You're making this a memorable event, boy. That makes it fun and exciting."

"Are you a Methuselah Man that you keep calling me boy?"

Villars laughed. "You're a freak, a hybrid. I'm going to crush you with my bare hands."

Maddox jabbed three times, connecting the last time against the nose. The blow sent Villars reeling. The captain didn't follow the attack. Instead, he picked up the fallen knife. It had a good heft, and he began to advance on Villars.

"No," Professor Ludendorff said. "This is no good. I need both of you."

Maddox didn't pay any attention to Ludendorff. Instead, he accelerated the attack, wondering if he had enough time.

The web field caught Maddox as it had on the bridge. The only consolation was that Villars was also caught in a force-field web.

Ludendorff stepped into Maddox's view. The professor held the flat device. At the older man's side walked Galyan. Ludendorff made *tsking* sounds.

"Cesar, you know we need the captain."

The slarn hunter squirmed as his harsh features twisted with the intensity of his efforts to break free of the force web.

"You must stop that, or you'll tear tendons," Ludendorff said.

"Kill him," Maddox said. "Villars is a madman."

The professor pretended not to hear the comment.

Maddox repeated it, adding, "You know he's emotionally unstable."

Ludendorff finally regarded the captain. "You're young and full of righteous judgments. Life does not always proceed as one might wish."

"Meaning you keep a sadist in your company," Maddox said.

"Cesar has proven invaluable several times," Ludendorff said. "He doesn't know the meaning of the word quit. Without him, the New Men would have slain me on two different occasions on Wolf Prime."

"He wants to torture Meta before he kills her," Maddox said.

"I suppose I should have foreseen that," Ludendorff said. "It's too bad Meta had to interfere as she did. None of this would be happening, otherwise."

"If you'd come to me and told us the truth," Maddox said, "it wouldn't be happening like this either. You're the one to blame, not Meta."

"We don't have the luxury of blaming each other," Ludendorff said. "Now, I'm going to release both of you. Cesar, I want your word you will shake hands with Captain Maddox."

"No," Villars said. "His woman killed Sten. She has to die for that. This boy would try to stop me from enacting justice."

"I see your point," Ludendorff told Villars. "But I happen to need Maddox in order to save humanity. Maybe Sten would have understood that."

"Sten saved my life when the slarn took me down," Villars said. "I'd be dead if Sten hadn't waded into battle with the beast. That's not something you forget, Professor."

"No, I suppose not," Ludendorff said.

"So, his bitch gets a wild hair up her—"

"Listen to me," Maddox said in a calm voice.

"Don't talk to me, punk," Villars snarled.

"Oh, my," Ludendorff said. "This is worse than I thought. Cesar, what am I going to do with you?"

"You'd better kill me, Professor," Villars said, "because I'm never going to stop going after—"

Ludendorff held up his device and tapped it once. That cut off Villars's rant before it could get properly started. The web squeezed Villars so hard he gasped for air.

"I don't appreciate that kind of talk even from you," Ludendorff told the slarn hunter. "You're my guard, my final ring of protection. The others are gone, Cesar. Don't you understand what that means?"

Villars looked at Ludendorff with bulging eyes. It was clear the slarn hunter could no longer breathe.

"You must think long-term," Ludendorff explained. "Maybe we've been on Wolf Prime too long. You've picked up some of their wilder customs. That will not do this time around. Don't you see that?"

Maddox wasn't sure, but Villars might have nodded the barest fraction.

The professor tapped his device.

Villars inhaled deeply.

"Let us try this again," Ludendorff said. "Cesar, can you withhold seeking justice until the end of our endeavor?"

"I can," the slarn hunter said, with his eyes downcast.

"There," Ludendorff told Maddox. "I'm glad that's settled."

"He tried to cut off my feet with monofilament wire," Maddox said.

"He won't do that again," Ludendorff assured the captain.

"That isn't what he said," Maddox told the professor. "He agreed to forego his attempts right now."

Ludendorff shrugged. "Isn't that good enough?"

Maddox stared at the professor.

"Come now," Ludendorff chided. "Consider the various possibilities. Cesar might die before we complete our task. You or Meta might perish. Maybe we'll fail, and we'll all die together. Then, you will have worried about a future that never existed. It's true he might kill the two of you later. But then you'll be dead, and it will no longer be of concern to you. The point is that you'll have helped save humanity by working together now."

A fixed grin remained on Maddox's face. He realized the futility of trying to reason with the man who had the power to imprison him at will. The captain planned to bide his time and kill Villars when an opportunity presented itself now that he knew the hunter's agenda.

"Are we agreed then?" Ludendorff asked.

"I already said I am," Villars declared.

"Captain?" the professor asked.

"Certainly," Maddox said. "Until we have completed the mission, I will shelve the matter."

Villars laughed harshly. "Do you hear that, Professor? The punk takes you for a fool. He's lying. He's going to try to murder me the first chance he gets."

"This really is too much, Captain," Ludendorff complained.

"I've given you my word," Maddox said.

"A false word," Ludendorff said. "It's clear you have other intentions."

"I don't know how you could tell that," Maddox said.

"With the greatest of ease, boy," Villars said. "Once you've been around the block enough times, it gets easy to see when a punk like you lies through his teeth."

"Let us see if we can try this again," Ludendorff said.

"Yes," Maddox said. "I won't try to kill your friend."

"There you go, Cesar. Do you hear that? This time the captain spoke genuinely."

Villars glowered.

"He thwarted your surprise attempt to kill him," Ludendorff pointed out. "That should show you Maddox has more resources than the average man."

"He's a freak," Villars said.

"No, Cesar," the professor said. "That is ill-mannered. You should not say that to him."

"*Freak*," Villars said, hotly.

Ludendorff turned to Maddox. "It appears you've gravely angered my friend. For your own good, I suggest you stay out of his way."

"Naturally," Maddox said.

Ludendorff peered into the captain's eyes. Finally, the professor exhaled, turning toward Villars. "Come along then. Some separation appears to be in order."

Ludendorff took the slarn hunter by the right elbow, guiding him down the corridor. The blockier man moved sluggishly, as if the web was still on enough to make his movements difficult. It seemed the professor wasn't *only* going to trust Villars's word.

A few seconds later, the force web vanished from around Maddox. He stumbled several steps before he stood in quiet contemplation, examining the knife that Villars had planned to use to cut out his lungs.

Turning around, Maddox went to the monofilament wire. It would take careful work to take down something like this. Afterward, he would have to warn Meta about Villars.

What would the professor do once Maddox killed Villars? It would appear the captain would find out soon.

-10-

Hundreds of light-years from *Victory* and out in the Beyond, an agent of the New Men sat alone in a room, enduring his latest rehabilitation due to mission failure.

Kane was born on the Rouen Colony. Thanks to scientists of the Chabot Consortium, he had been genetically modified to work on the two-G mining world. He was big and square-bodied, with gray hair and flat slabs of muscle. Kane had the bleakness of a glacier even though he seethed where he sat.

He was in a punishment chamber aboard a star cruiser. At the command of Oran Rva, he attempted to purge his emotions. A condenser ray beamed down from the ceiling at his brain in order to aid the process, or so they had informed him. Kane had begun to doubt the explanation, believing the ray did something else to his mind.

Kane gripped his knees, enduring the process. The beam made his head pound and his teeth ache. As the ray did its work, he attempted to reconcile a truism of his existence.

Regular humans were no match for his excellence. Yet, despite his superiority over the norms, the dominants—called the New Men by Star Watch—were better than he was in every way. Kane understood that he would always be a second tier citizen in the New Order. That was better than becoming cattle like the rest of humanity. Was it not?

Kane felt heat creep up his neck. That was anger. He must control the inner rage. The dominants would never release him for another mission if they detected such fury.

I've never had trouble controlling my rage before. The condenser ray should be helping me with this, which means the beam is definitely doing something else. Why have the dominants lied to me?

Kane debated the idea even as he yearned for another chance against the norms. He particularly wanted the opportunity in the hope that Captain Maddox would appear in his path again. Then—

Kane shifted on his chair.

He must forget about the Star Watch Intelligence officer and his woman. Meta's delicious body and enticing features had goaded him the entire time he had been with her. He should have stripped off her garments and put his hands on her, entering—

No! Kane cared nothing about that.

Why am I lying to myself? I never have before. I want the woman. I desire to use her well and often.

Kane took a deep breath. He must rid himself of all rutting desires. Only climbing rank mattered. Only the—

Abruptly, the ray quit. Kane knew because his teeth stopped aching and his head no longer pounded. It left a dull emptiness in his mind, though, making it difficult to concentrate.

A noise alerted Kane. He found his reflexes were slow. He moved his head sluggishly as the chamber's door slid up.

Commander Oran Rva, a golden-skinned dominant, stepped through the hatch. The commander wore a silver suit with a single purple emblem over his right pectoral. He had a weapon belt around his waist with a holstered blaster. Oran Rva was tall with a pelt of dark hair. The eyes, which were like swirling pools of black ink, fixated on Kane.

"Come with me," Oran Rva said.

It took Kane three tries to rise. What had the invisible beam done to him? Finally, he stood up, only to go down to one knee. With a grunt of embarrassment, he struggled to his feet, finally staggering after the commander.

***

Kane stood in a large auditorium aboard the star cruiser. Oran Rva was behind a table that held a harness of thin straps attached to silver bands.

"You have failed in your deception missions," the dominant said. "Analysis proves your decisions were lacking. A competent spy needs intuitive powers combined with daring. You have an insufficient quantity of the former but an abundance of the latter. Given your knowledge of Earth customs and ability to swim among the sub-men unnoticed, you are about to embark on a unique mission of straightforward violence."

Kane said nothing, absorbing the information. Was this a demotion? It sounded like it. Yet, the gear on the table was clearly advanced technology. The dominants never let others use such weaponry, reserving those items for themselves.

"In essence, you will be a one-man commando team," Oran Rva said.

The slightest of frowns touched Kane's face.

"State your objections to this," Oran Rva said.

Kane shook his head. "I have no objections, Your Excellency."

"Remember that you have stated so. Now, remove your garments, put on this harness and I shall begin your training."

Kane obeyed, soon fitting soft silver bands around his neck, torso, forearms, biceps, triceps, thighs, calves and other areas.

That Oran Rva, the commander of the initial invasion armada, trained him personally, was food for consideration. The New Men had different customs than the norms. There, an admiral would never teach a commando his trade. Here, the grade of the instructor indicated the importance of the task. The fact that Oran Rva oversaw the training told Kane his commando mission was of supreme importance.

With the straps and bands in place on Kane's person, Oran Rva indicated a tiny silver ball with two deep indentations.

"Attach the power source to the harness there," the commander said, pointing at a cord near Kane's navel.

Kane plugged the cord into the ball. Instantly, the bands around his muscles buzzed pleasantly.

"You wear enablers," Oran Rva explained. "They will excite your muscles, allowing you greater speed and strength. Are you ready?"

Kane nodded.

The commander ordered a sequence of exercises. Faster than Kane had ever done before, he ran around objects. He leaped higher than he would have thought possible and engaged a fighting robot in a series of engagements.

At the end of the session, Kane removed the sweaty harness. He staggered, and his muscles quivered with exhaustion. In spite of his resolve, the Rouen Colony man collapsed onto the floor.

"Attend me," Oran Rva said.

Kane concentrated, finding it difficult to focus. He managed to look up at the dominant towering over his prone person.

"With the enabler, you have reacted faster and with greater strength than you are normally capable of doing. The experience, as you can see, has left you exhausted. Instead of giving you a warning of the coming situation, I have let you experience the weakness directly. Never forget that extended exertions with the enabler will leave you powerless afterward."

Kane said nothing. He was too tired. Finally, Kane sat up. Soon thereafter, time lost meaning for him. The dominant continued the training after injecting him with stimulants. Kane used other advanced weaponry, gaining proficiency with each, becoming lethal beyond his previous experience.

After two days of this, Oran Rva told him, "It is time for your departure. As previously stated, you are returning to Earth. There, you will acquire a critical item. You will bring it to the Throne World."

Kane sat rigidly, ingesting the data.

"This is a category-one assignment, as you will have already surmised," Oran Rva said. "I am giving you a raptor identity along with a class-one intent code. Five assassin teams will be on standby on Earth, waiting for your word."

These were unprecedented conditions. If Kane didn't know better, he would guess the Throne World convulsed with worry over this item. That was incredible.

"You will use a scout and rendezvous with Exodus Eight," Oran Rva said. "Because you are a commando now instead of an agent, you will practice a sub-aqua entry onto the planet. After you have gained the item, you will go to the Tango Point for a flash exit."

In spite of himself, Kane's eyes widened. This was more than convulsed worry on the Throne World's part. This was panic. That would explain why the dominants were allowing him to use the highest-class weaponry.

"You will use the Nexus of course," Oran Rva said.

For the first time, fear welled within Kane.

"You will leave in five hours," Oran Rva said. "Before that, you will memorize the exact parameters of the mission. Are you ready?"

"I am," Kane said.

"Stand," Oran Rva told him.

Kane did so. The New Man stood taller. Kane was thicker and heavier. Even so, he knew the dominant was stronger than he was and could kill him in hand-to-hand combat—unless he fought Oran Rva while wearing the enabler.

Do not think such a thing in his presence. Act like ice. I am ice.

Oran Rva stared at Kane. The black eyes seemed to burn.

Kane feared the other knew his thoughts.

It seemed, then, for just a moment, that the faintest of smiles appeared on Oran Rva's face. That vanished a second later.

"Follow me," the dominant said, turning around.

Kane obeyed, struggling to understand what the hint of smug superiority and amusement he'd just witnessed could mean. The situation brought heat to his neck and anger washing against his mind. With everything in him, Kane attempted to throttle the fury. What was wrong with him? This was what he wanted, another chance to prove himself.

I am the commando. With my success, I will show Oran Rva he can trust me with tougher assignments. I must not ruin what might be my last chance for greatness.

***

Hours later, Kane sat in a scout, a nondescript spacecraft. It would be unremarkable in both the Commonwealth and Windsor League. The small vessel drifted toward a large silver pyramid many kilometers in diameter, the Nexus.

The pyramid was in a star system in the Beyond. No Star Watch vessel had ever been out here. This Nexus was beyond the Throne World in its distance from Earth. Like the Nexus hidden in the Commonwealth, the pyramid he now approached lay deep in an artificial asteroid belt. Unlike the Commonwealth pyramid, this one had several star cruisers in orbit.

Kane's heart beat faster. He was about to transfer almost three hundred light years in a single bound. As far as he knew, this was the outer limit that one could travel in this way.

He dreaded the coming journey. Would the greater distance mean greater pain?

In order to drown his fear, Kane inspected the scout and its equipment. In doing so, he kept passing a hatch, one he hardly recognized as such. One time, he paused before the hatch. Vaguely, he realized he mustn't go into the compartment. Then, something in his mind caused the hatch to disappear from his consciousness. He continued with his inspection.

After checking everything on the scout except for the now-forgotten "ghostly" compartment, Kane returned to the control room.

Instead of entering the secret world of espionage while among the norms, he would practice a commando assault. He had never failed to beat the enemy directly. His failures had only come in grabbing the wrong people. This time, he couldn't fail in that regard. The item was very particular and there were no substitutes in the known universe. He would go to Monte Carlo, to Nerva Tower, to snatch the item.

A light winked on his board.

Unlike the last time he'd made such a transfer, Kane hadn't needed to enter the pyramid to set the coordinates. A dominant had done so for him.

With trembling hands, Kane worked the controls. The engine *thrummed* into life. He tried to think of some way to postpone the moment.

86

Then, a grim phenomenon occurred outside the spacecraft. A tiny pulsating glob of matter appeared. It shimmered and expanded, rapidly growing to a little more than twice the scout's size. It was a transfer portal.

Kane could no longer draw air. With a shaking hand, he tapped the controls. The scout headed for the pulsating matter. Kane couldn't tear his eyes from it. He knew the journey would cause him to ache as nothing else could. Kane tested his straps and made sure a water bottle was nearby in order to rinse out his mouth later. He was going to vomit when he reached the other side, hopefully not any blood, though.

The portal grew larger.

"No," Kane moaned. "I don't want to do this."

Then the scout entered the portal, disappearing, were there anyone observing, as it began the great leap across three hundred light-years...

-11-

Maddox was in a hangar bay, working with Meta. They attached a warfare pod to the underside of a shuttle. Once they reached the Xerxes System, Maddox was certain they would go to the Nexus.

Maddox had gone over with Meta her time with Kane. The enemy agent had used a space-cycle to approach the silver pyramid. Maddox believed Kane had kept the scout from the Nexus's immediate vicinity for a reason. What that reason was, the captain didn't know. The point, to him, was to keep *Victory* away from the silver pyramid. That would mean using a shuttle to reach the relic.

They attached the warfare pod to the shuttle to ensure it had heavy enough armaments.

It had been several days now since the fight with Villars. Maddox had told Meta about it, and she'd wanted to ambush the man and finish it.

"Not yet," had been Maddox's reply. He wanted Villars to get comfortable first.

"You don't know what it feels like being hunted."

Maddox had assured Meta he did. That was why either Riker or he was with her at all times.

"I don't need bodyguards," Meta had told him. "I can take care of myself."

"No doubt, but Riker and I are going to help you just the same. That's what family does."

Meta had finally accepted the proposition. Maddox had moved into her quarters. When they were apart, Riker took over guard duty. Ludendorff had his personal force field and web-field, but Villars just had regular means. Thus, the sergeant would use the stun gun and Maddox his long-barreled weapon to kill Villars if the slarn hunter tried to stalk Meta.

"Lift," Maddox said.

Meta strained as she raised the main housing, pushing a joiner against the shuttle's under-plate.

Maddox pulled a trigger, making his screw-gun *whirr* with power. He installed the rest of the housing to the warfare pod.

"Captain, could I have a word with you?"

Maddox turned around. Dana stood beyond the shuttle. She wore her white lab coat and an intense frown.

"Go ahead," Meta told him. "I can finish up here."

Maddox handed the drill to Meta before taking a rag from his pocket. He wiped grease from his hands, walking out from under the shuttle.

"Maybe we can speak inside there," Dana said, indicating the shuttle.

Maddox shrugged and headed for a lift, climbing to the control compartment hatch. He stepped inside the shuttle. Dana followed close behind, closing the hatch.

That surprised Maddox.

Dana pulled a small device from a lab coat pocket. With the flick of a thumb, she turned it on, causing an audible vibration.

Maddox could feel the vibration, most strongly against his teeth.

"I doubt the professor is going to give us much time," Dana said. "This is an anti-snoop scrambler. I made it myself." She attached it to a panel.

"Ludendorff will know we're plotting against him because it's on," Maddox said.

"I've already indicated as much," Dana said. "Now listen. I know where Ludendorff must have put the backdoor to the AI. Do you remember when the computer tried to gas us several months ago?"

"Of course," Maddox said. "It was right after the debugging, after you and Ludendorff rid Galyan of the Swarm virus."

"Exactly," Dana said. "I've been thinking of that moment. It's always bothered me. Why would Galyan have gassed us at the precise moment we helped him most?"

"I have no idea," Maddox said.

"Neither did I. So, I asked myself, who gained the most from that? Ludendorff did. He'd done something in the chamber he didn't want anyone else to find out about."

Maddox considered the idea. "You're right. That's an excellent deduction, Doctor."

Dana looked down, perhaps to hide her smile at the compliment. When she looked up again, her features were composed. "So, all we have to do is break into the chamber, find the backdoor and take it out. Then Galyan will follow you as the AI has indicated it will do, and you shall control *Victory* again."

"Ludendorff will likely have protective devices in the core chamber," Maddox said.

"Yes," Dana said. "Gas, for one thing. A suit and rebreather should take care of the problem."

Maddox nodded thoughtfully.

"The professor could have put more fail-safes in place, but—"

"Just a minute," Maddox said, interrupting Dana. "Our time is ticking. Ludendorff is going to notice your scrambler soon, if he hasn't already. Now we know where the backdoor is. When the time is right, we'll break in, search for it and deactivate the device. You're going to have to think deeply about where exactly it's hidden."

"Yes, yes," Dana said, impatiently. "That's what I'm trying to tell you."

"Before you go into that," Maddox said. "I want to know how you successfully mutinied against Ludendorff the first time in the Adok System. The man is deceptively clever and devious in the extreme. How did you defeat him?"

"How could that possibly matter now?" Dana asked. "That happened years ago. It's old history."

"Knowing will help me figure out how to beat him this time around," Maddox said.

"Believe me, it won't," Dana said. "He'll never fall for that trick again."

"Maybe, but knowing will show me one of his weaknesses. That's always good to know."

Dana looked away, her features twisting with distaste.

"We don't have the luxury of being fastidious," Maddox told her. "You did something secretive many years ago. It fooled Ludendorff. I must know what you did, but time is of the essence, Doctor. Learning it later isn't going to help."

"Oh, very well," Dana said. "I was Ludendorff's lover. There, are you satisfied?"

Maddox kept his features blank. Inside, he was nodding. He should have already seen the answer. It helped explain her hostility toward the professor.

"Mutinying against him was one of the hardest things I ever did," Dana said in a monotone.

Maddox could almost hear the words she didn't say, "I wish I'd never done it." The captain didn't get that from her face. Dana's features were stiff, with her eyebrows raised and her nostrils flared. The captain's understanding about the doctor's feelings toward Ludendorff was a gut instinct. Maddox was certain the event had been decisive in Dana's life. He would like to know the mutiny's details. What impact had her treachery had on the professor?

The opposite of love wasn't hate but indifference. *It would seem Doctor Rich still isn't over Ludendorff.*

"Let me—" Maddox said.

The scrambler vibrated louder than before. A second later, a blue nimbus shined from it.

"Down!" Dana shouted, as she dropped to the floor.

Maddox followed her example. As his chest touched a deck plate, the scrambler exploded, blowing hot shrapnel everywhere, tearing the fabric from the nearest seat.

"Ludendorff worked fast," Maddox said from the floor.

"He always does," Dana said.

Maddox scrambled to his feet, drawing his gun as he pushed open the hatch. Villars stood on the hangar bay floor, staring intently at Meta under the shuttle.

Without hesitation, Maddox aimed through the hatch and began to squeeze the trigger. The captain felt the force web begin to tighten around him. Then the gun discharged. The bullet plowed through the surrounding web. It must have wobbled in flight, taking it off course just a little. The slug tore through Villars's left shoulder, twisting the slarn hunter. It didn't throw the man onto the floor, but it did cause him to stagger back.

The web tightened so Maddox couldn't breathe. He willed his finger to move again. It did. The long-barreled gun sent another slug at Villars. This round ricocheted off the floor by his right boot.

The web tightened even more, squeezing the captain's chest. Maddox fired a third time. Villars was already backpedalling as he clutched his wounded shoulder. Blood trickled between the slarn hunter's fingers.

Maddox would have fallen out of the hatch, but Dana yanked him back inside. Then, the captain blacked out...

Maddox woke up several minutes later. The hangar bay lights shined down on him. He must not be inside the shuttle anymore. He noticed Dana and Meta. They stood uncomfortably and stiffly to the side. The professor must have webbed them.

From on the floor, Maddox stirred.

"Finally," the professor said. "You're back. Good. We need to speak, you and I."

Waiting several seconds, Maddox summoned his energy and managed to sit up. The professor stood to the side, making minute adjustments to his flat device. There was no sign of Villars.

"Where's the sadist?" Maddox asked.

Ludendorff frowned. "I do not appreciate your firing at my bodyguard. I take that as a personal affront. He will see it as the beginning of a vendetta. You're making this harder than it has to be."

"You should have known better than to bring Villars near Meta," Maddox said. "I did the rational thing upon seeing him. The man's unpredictable. I had to act before he did."

"Forget about Villars," Ludendorff said. "You used a scrambler in order to plot against me in secret. You should know better than that."

"I'm afraid I don't. You took my ship. Give it back, and we can start over."

"Come, come, Captain, this petulance isn't going to help either of us. It's true I have command, at present. But that's how it should be. I'm wiser and have more understanding of the situation than any of you do. I know what's at stake and how to defeat the problem. In time, I'll leave, and *Victory* will return to your command."

Silently, Maddox disagreed most profoundly about who was wiser. Aloud, he said, "I understand your thinking. Yes, let us proceed then and put this behind us. If you would release my two crewmembers from your web, I'd appreciate it."

Ludendorff glanced at Dana and Meta before regarding Maddox. "You were plotting against me, Captain. Worse, you did it with someone I find reprehensible. I no longer trust the doctor."

"It hardly matters anymore. You destroyed her scrambler and nearly wounded one of us in the process. That was risky on your part."

"Play with fire and you can get burned," Ludendorff said in a hard tone. He paused, and it seemed he brought his anger under control. The stiffness left his features, replaced by a roguish grin. "What happened in the shuttle reveals a little of my...hmm, shall we call them my resources?"

"I'm duly impressed," Maddox said. "I won't try something like that again."

Ludendorff eyed the captain. "I'm going to have to take your gun, of course."

"I don't advise that," Maddox said. "Villars will take advantage of my defenselessness."

"Cesar is wounded. That will slow him down for a time, making you two even, which is more than I should give you for what you just did."

93

Instead of responding, Maddox climbed to his feet. He stood too fast, though, and his vision blurred. He held himself still, with his head down and hands on his thighs until the fuzziness passed. Finally, he fully straightened.

"Your assassination attempt just now reveals several interesting factors about you," Ludendorff said. "You have a remarkably swift reaction time, and you can act without hesitation. If Villars didn't understand before how dangerous you are, he does now. That will make him doubly hazardous for you. Before, he underestimated you. I assure you he won't do that again."

Maddox said nothing.

"That's another thing I admire about you," Ludendorff said. "Sometimes, you know when to keep quiet."

Maddox continued to wait.

"You don't have a response to that?" Ludendorff asked.

"What would you like me to say?"

The professor frowned. "What did you and the doctor talk about in the shuttle?"

"You."

"And…?"

"Dana told me how she admires your resourcefulness."

"That isn't what she said," Ludendorff snapped.

"Actually, it is."

"Come, come, Captain, you're trying my patience. That isn't wise on your part."

Maddox looked the professor in the eye and gave him a professional smile.

"Do you dare to mock me?" Ludendorff asked in wonder.

"Professor, I'm afraid you've done exactly what your sadist did, which was to underestimate me. I salute your genius. It is a rare quality and quite admirable. You have potent toys, and you play the long game. However, the fact of your keeping Villars in your company causes me to doubt your judgment."

"I don't care for lectures," Ludendorff said, "and I like it even less from a hypocrite. You have an assassin and a clone thief in your crew. They were both judged as violently dangerous, enough so Star Watch sent them to a prison planet. Villars—"

"Is a sadist," Maddox said calmly, interrupting the professor. "Both Dana and Meta acted out of noble sentiments. You cannot compare them to the monster you call a bodyguard. You're a clever, man, Professor. You've shown that more than once. But, as I said, I wonder about your judgment."

"You can wonder all you like," Ludendorff said. "But think deeply on this. I presently run the starship. You wouldn't even possess *Victory* without my knowledge, and you wouldn't have a working disruptor cannon. Because of my actions, you were able to save Fletcher's fleet. And without me, no one will stop the planet-killer."

"I quite agree, of course," Maddox said. "Therefore, you don't need to coerce us. Let us attempt to work together in harmony once again. There's no need for us to bicker with each other."

Ludendorff considered the captain for a long moment before nodding in agreement.

"Dana and Meta are still webbed," Maddox finally pointed out.

"Oh, you're right," Ludendorff said. "I was just waiting for you to tell me what the two of you talked about in the shuttle. No doubt you want to do that as a gesture of good will."

"I would be delighted to tell you," Maddox said. "As soon as you release Galyan from your compulsion, I shall do so."

Ludendorff spread his hands. "I see that we're back where we began. Neither of us sufficiently trusts the other to work together unconditionally. Since I hold the upper hand, I shall continue to wield it."

"As you wish," Maddox said.

Ludendorff tapped his right foot several times. "Seriously, Captain, you're not going to tell me what the two of you plotted?"

"I already did tell you," Maddox said. "We spoke about you."

"Very well," Ludendorff said, as he patted the long-barreled gun tucked at the top of his pants. "I shall keep this then. And I will take Meta with me."

Maddox's heart rate increased, although he said pleasantly, "Beg pardon?"

"Meta has memories I need to access for the next stage of operations," the professor said. "Therefore, I will need to take her with me."

"There's no need for that," Maddox said. "Ask her what you want to know. She's right here."

"I'm afraid I can't risk any duplicity on her part. I shall have to take her."

Maddox shook his head. "I suppose I should let you know then that my cooperation ends if you take her."

"Hmmm," Ludendorff said. "This presents a problem."

"Why don't you tell me what memories you're seeking," Maddox said. "Dana can question Meta for you."

"I don't trust either woman."

"That's a futile position," Maddox said. "You were correct earlier in saying we need each other. Thus, we should strive to cooperate, not find ways to antagonize each other. The stakes are too high for anything else."

Ludendorff glanced at the two women before regarding Maddox once more. "Yes. That will suffice for now. Later, I may not be able to agree to your stipulation."

"So far, we've been taking one step at a time. Why don't we continue to operate on that policy?"

"Agreed," Ludendorff said.

"What memories do you require?" Maddox asked.

"I want to know in precise detail what Kane did when he entered the targeted star system with Meta."

"I find it interesting you still won't tell us which system you mean," Maddox said. "It's obvious our destination is dangerous. Therefore, given our heading, I'm sure you're referring to the Xerxes 14C System—the Bermuda Triangle of space."

Ludendorff was quiet for a time. "I've misjudged you, Captain. Yes, this is a surprising development. You should realize I've been studying you for a time. Until now, you haven't exhibited an in-depth knowledge of space. Why let your guard down now and show me you know as much as a regular starship captain should?"

"Call it a gesture of goodwill," Maddox said. "I'm tired of this pretense."

96

"I see," Ludendorff said. "Yes. We're heading for the Xerxes System. It will be dangerous, as you've suggested. You've made this gesture of goodwill. Thus, I will do the same. The doctor may question Meta. If the answers are sufficient, I will let it go at that. If not…I will do my own questioning."

"The latter would be a bad idea on your part," Maddox said in a friendly tone.

"Threatening me in any way is the worst idea of all," Ludendorff said. "I hold the upper hand. Until I relent, I will continue to hold it. You should be grateful, because without my help you will never defeat the doomsday machine. And if the planet-killer continues its mission, humanity as you know it dies."

"I think it's good that we've made our positions clear," Maddox said. "If you could release my two crewmembers, we will continue to prepare for the Xerxes System."

"One last thing, Captain," Ludendorff said.

Maddox nodded.

"Meta has one day in which to remember the needed facts. After that, I will probe her."

"Is your equipment the same as what the teacher used on her in the New Men's star cruiser?"

"Don't be absurd."

"That isn't an answer," Maddox pointed out.

"No, it isn't," Ludendorff said. "I have no need to tell you the manner of my tools, and you have no lever to force me to show you. Thus, you will have to be content not knowing exactly how I will manage my trick."

"Did you twist Lank Meyers's mind?"

Ludendorff frowned. "I do not appreciate your bringing up such a bitter memory. My patience has a limit. It's a bad idea to try to reach it."

Throughout their conversation, Maddox had been gauging the professor's reactions to everything. He studied the man while appearing to needle him. It was a deliberate process, with his Star Watch Intelligence-trained mind hard at work.

"Are you trying to tell me Lank Meyers willingly gave himself into the custody of the New Men?" Maddox asked.

The professor's features tightened. "That is my final warning. Mention the incident again, and I will punish you."

Maddox stared into the professor's eyes. The captain believed he saw actual pain there. He had to push the professor, though. Maddox didn't believe he could learn the truth any other way.

"I think you turned Lank Meyers into a kamikaze, the poor soul," Maddox said.

"Enough!" Ludendorff said, sharply. He aimed the flat device at Maddox and pressed a stud.

The web field surrounded the captain. Then, shocks began to twist Maddox. His eyeballs bulged outward. He twitched as another round of volts struck him, but he endured them silently.

It was clear by this demonstration that the professor felt normal emotions and loss. Maddox felt that was vital information, and worth the price to gain it.

Ludendorff's thumb lifted off the device. The shocks stopped. The professor's eyes were red-rimmed and moist. Without a word, the man whirled around, taking his leave.

A few seconds later, the web fields around Maddox, Meta and Dana disappeared.

"Why goad him like that?" Dana asked. "You went too far."

Maddox said nothing, but he was more determined than ever to wrest control of *Victory* back from Ludendorff. This last incident gave Maddox an insight, one which might give him the needed lever to achieve his goal.

-12-

Dana sat in a chair, examining the list of questions Ludendorff expected answered. The words were hard to read in the dim lighting of her chamber.

The professor was insufferable, an egotist of the first order. The man thought about himself front, center and back.

A brushing noise alerted her that Meta stirred on the couch beside her. Dana's only true friend glanced up at her questioningly. Meta's green eyes were glazed because of her hypnotic state.

"Don't worry, dear," Dana said, patting Meta on the shoulder. "You're doing well."

"I feel strange," Meta said in a soft voice.

"No, no, don't think about that for a moment," Dana said. They had been at this for an hour already. Meta refused to open her mind to the time with Kane in the Xerxes System.

Had the teacher placed a block in Meta's mind?

"Why…?" Meta used her tongue to moisten her lips. "Why can't I remember what happened?"

"I'm not sure," Dana said. "Now lie back, close your eyes and start counting to zero, beginning at one hundred."

Meta lay back. She was strong with a tough mind, especially in dangerous situations. Dana knew she'd never have survived Loki Prime without Meta. She owed her friend, and she would never forget that.

At first, Meta's romantic dalliance with Captain Maddox had bothered Dana. She had examined her thoughts on that many nights and finally determined that the relationship made her jealous. Dana hadn't trusted Maddox's intentions, either. Over time, Dana's thoughts on him had changed. The doctor also came to understand that Meta needed the captain's calming influence. The man was like an oak tree, able to weather any storm. He was strong enough so Meta could take shelter in his protection.

There were deep hurts in Meta. Her coldblooded killing of others had twisted the dear girl, and her use of sex to obtain a tactical advantage had also caused her grave pain. Maybe some people could do those things without their consciences bothering them. Meta wasn't one of them.

"Are you counting?" Dana asked.

"Eighty-three, eighty-two, eighty-one," Meta said aloud.

"Think it, dear, don't speak it."

With her eyes closed, Meta nodded. Her lips twitched, but she didn't make any more noise.

Dana glanced at the list in her hand. Insufferable Professor Ludendorff needed to know these specifics, did he? Damn his soul! Why was the man so arrogant? Why had he played it this way? He hadn't acted like this on the expedition to the Adok System.

Oh, Josef Erich Fromm Ludendorff III had been devious and secretive from the beginning. He had also been charming, with a beguiling and mysterious manner. And the love-making—Dana had never experienced anything like it. Literally, those times had taken her breath away…after she'd stopped screaming in rapturous delight.

While sitting in the chamber aboard *Victory*, Dana frowned as she thought back to her early days with Ludendorff. Life had been difficult for her growing up on Brahma. The ancient Hindu caste system had been engrained into the planetary culture. In it, women didn't hold important posts in society. That went to the high caste men, her father being one of them.

Raja Nehru, her father, had gone against Brahma custom by allowing her to go to university. There, Dana had excelled, gaining degree after degree with bewildering ease. It had been as if she was a rose grown in a dark corner, and finally, someone had thought to place her in the sunlight. She bloomed there, flourishing in the perfect culture. In time, though, her professors frowned upon her success. It was clear she was the brightest student in the entire university. Her father ordered her home. She refused, staying on as a teaching assistant. The boys—she had never been able to think of them as men—resented her instructions during the study halls. How dare a woman show them up as she did with her incredible breadth of knowledge?

Then, Professor Ludendorff arrived, teaching a fascinating course on alien technology. He was one of the few white men at Brahma Tech, and he hadn't held to the same illusions as everyone else.

One by one, the other professors told Dana she could no longer assist them. Raja Nehru had used his influence to twist their arms. Finally, Professor Ludendorff was the only teacher who would employ her, paying her stipend out of his own resources. Dana survived on a pittance, refusing to quit. That would mean returning to the shadows where she would wither, killing her intellectual growth. So, for another six months she lived in a tiny garret and ate less and less so she could make ends meet.

"Are you on a diet?" Ludendorff asked her one day after class.

She shook her head.

That's when he'd put a hand on her shoulder. Until that moment, the professor had been perfectly correct in all their interactions.

"My dear girl," Ludendorff said. "I understand your situation. Come live with me. It's the right thing to do."

Dana looked up at him, shocked at the suggestion.

Ludendorff grinned and winked at her. "Yes, I mean to bed you, to love you as you've never known it could be. But I also mean to help you. You're brilliant, Dana. You're possibly the second brightest person I've ever met."

"Who is the first?" she asked.

"Myself, of course," he said with a laugh. "I constantly amaze myself with my intellect. It's like being a star in the heavens."

Dana blinked at him in wonder. She could never live with him. That would be scandalous.

Professor Ludendorff stepped closer, taking her in his arms. He held her, smiling, rubbing her back. Finally, his lips touched hers. It had been a feather-soft kiss, and it melted her.

Dana moved into his place a week later.

When her father discovered the scandal, he protested. At first, the university resisted Raja Nehru. Finally, they told Ludendorff he had to let Dana go home.

"I've learned what I've come here to find," Ludendorff told Dana the next day. "I'm leaving Brahma tonight. You must join me."

"What? No. I-I can't do that to my family."

"Of course you can. They're good people. I know that. But they're hidebound like ninety-nine percent of humanity. Come with me, Dana. I'm going to find the most incredible archeological find of the millennia."

"What is that?" she asked.

A secretive look she came to know well darkened his features. Ludendorff shook his head. "I can't tell you, not yet. But it will be an adventure, I promise you. I could use your intellect. No. I take that back. I positively *need* it."

That had been the key. Dana joined him, leaving Brahma for the first time.

For six years, they searched for the hidden Adok System. Dana grew up a lot in that time. Ludendorff blew hot and cold. The man was unlike anyone she had ever met. There were hidden depths to him that he rarely showed. Slowly, she came to understand that Ludendorff only trusted one person: himself. He did not subscribe to common thinking or custom, but did everything his own way. Ludendorff always thought he was right. The man was arrogant beyond anything her father had shown, beyond anyone she'd met.

What made Ludendorff that way? Dana Rich worked as hard to discover that as to find the lost starship.

"You're a Methuselah Man," she told him one evening as they held watch together in their spaceship.

Ludendorff's head jerked around. Those eyes that had shined with love on so many occasions became dark with suspicion. It frightened Dana. Would he kill her? Finally, Ludendorff smiled.

"It's true," he said. "Come. Let me show you what that means."

The lovemaking in the past had paled in comparison to that night. The pleasure flowing through her had been too much for her to scream. It was as if he tried to forge new chains on her. How could he make her feel like this? It was remarkable and frightening.

"Professor," she said later, as they lay entwined on the bed.

"Hmm?" he asked.

"How can you do these things to me?"

"It's called love, dear girl. You must understand that."

"No. You did something else tonight."

"That's true," he admitted.

"Why have you waited so long to show me this?"

Ludendorff smiled sadly, as he stroked her cheek. "Dana, dear Dana, I trust you now. That means you cannot leave me. No one can do to you as I have. You realize that, yes?"

She nodded mutely. It was true, she realized.

"We will have many nights together," he said. "This isn't even the highest state of lovemaking. There are loftier stages, incredible heights of passion we can reach. First, I must teach you how to control your body."

"Dearest?" she asked.

Ludendorff chuckled. "In truth, Dana, I have already begun your training. You have no idea what I can show you. This is only the beginning."

"Didn't you trust me before?"

He frowned and looked away. Finally, he reached for her, and they made love one more time.

It should have been sheer ecstasy being with the professor. He was right about the world opening up for her. He did show her things and teach her new modes of thought. And the body control he taught her allowed them to reach greater heights of passion.

In the end, she betrayed him for more reasons than simple fear in the Adok System. The lost starship had been frightening, and Dana believed they would all die before

103

boarding the vessel. But it had been more than that. Ludendorff had begun to seem like a devil to her, offering her insights and riches beyond her dreams. She dreaded the coming payment for these things. There was something in Ludendorff beyond her understanding, something that deeply frightened her. He wasn't like other men. His depths were an abyss into which she didn't want to plummet.

"Why are you like this?" she asked him the night before she betrayed him.

They had found the smashed Adok System and now hid from the last Adok starship.

Once more, Ludendorff studied her with darkness in his gaze. She shivered in dread, and she knew then she had to act or perish.

"What are you planning to do, dear girl?"

Dana came to him, using her heightened sexual training. She gave him a delicious smile as she twisted provocatively in front of him. "A surprise, Herr Professor," she told him.

He laughed. It was the last time she was able to make him do that.

On the couch in the dim chamber on Starship *Victory*, Meta moaned, jerking Dana out of her reverie.

The doctor let her memories fade. *Ludendorff is Ludendorff.* He kept his secrets deeply hidden from everyone. The captain said the professor played the long game, but Dana wondered if Maddox really knew the extent of Ludendorff's game.

Do I know?

"No, no," Meta whispered from the couch.

Dana forgot about Ludendorff as she studied Meta's strained features. The dear girl was deep in a memory.

"What's happening?" she asked gently.

"I'm not sure," Meta said slowly. "There's danger here."

"How do you know?"

"Kane won't take his eyes off the pilot board," Meta said. "He has a grim concentration. It's like someone watching a cave, waiting for a grizzly to come charging out at him."

Meta frowned. "I've never seen Kane like this before. It frightens me."

What just happened with Meta? Why is she remembering now?

"Kane is..."

"Yes?" Dana asked. "What is Kane doing?"

"I...I don't know. I can't see him anymore."

"Did Kane leave the command module?" Dana asked.

"I don't think so," Meta said. "No. That's not it. He simply faded from view."

That was strange, Dana realized. "Do you think something is blocking your memory?" she asked.

Meta's frown deepened. It was like someone trying to undo an especially troubling knot and finally becoming frustrated with it.

It's time to switch Meta's focus. I'm in deeper and closer to the right memories than ever before. I have to try to stay here.

"I'm going to ask you several questions," Dana said in a calm voice. "I'd like you to answer them."

"I-I'll try."

"Good, that's good," the doctor said in a soothing voice. She glanced at her list and read the first question.

Meta shook her head.

Dana read the second question.

"I-I don't know," Meta whispered.

Dana worked down the list, asking the questions one by one. Meta couldn't answer any of them. Soon, the Rouen Colony woman began to weep softly.

"No, don't do that," Dana said. "This is not a problem."

"I'm sorry I can't remember. I want to help. I know you need this."

Dana tapped her lower lip with a stylus. This was fascinating. Meta was in a unique hypnotic limbo. She shouldn't have been able to say that she wanted to help like that. That showed too much awareness. Yet, it was clear Meta was still under hypnosis. This called for special handling.

"I want you to relax," Dana said.

"But—"

"No more questions for now," Dana said. "I want you to sleep."

Meta frowned. "Won't the professor take me away from you if I don't answer the questions?"

Meta shouldn't be able to say that.

"I want to keep working at this," Meta said. "I don't want to stop. I have to come through for the team."

"Sleep," Dana said, more sternly than she intended. Meta's tone indicated regression. She spoke like a little girl speaking to a parent. That wasn't healthy in this situation.

Dana leaned near so she spoke into Meta's right ear. "I don't want you to worry anymore. Relax. Let yourself move into regular sleep."

The tension began to drain from Meta's features, and, her head shifted to the side. Soon, Meta fell into a restful doze, her chest rising and falling rhythmically.

Dana sat in the chair, with an index finger on her lower lip. Meta had referred to them as a team, and she was right. *I'm part of it, too,* Dana reminded herself. *I have to help the team— the family—the best I know how.*

Dana realized that she had more than one friend now. She had several. Surprisingly, Captain Maddox was one of them. They had successfully worked together to overcome several difficult situations. Earlier, Ludendorff had acted as a friend in order to help them free Admiral Fletcher's fleet. Now, the professor was up to his old ploys, doing things in his highhanded manner. *Not this time, Professor.* She wasn't going to let Ludendorff ruin it for any of them.

If Ludendorff took Meta, there would be war because Maddox would never accept that. Villars had ensured a bloodbath between them. Dana had to forestall such a situation any way she could. The professor was too useful to throw away, and she owed this to the others.

Yet, how do I accomplish such a thing? Meta simply can't remember. The mental block is too strong. But if Ludendorff doesn't get his answers...

Dana's eyes narrowed thoughtfully. Ludendorff must be watching the session through Galyan's surveillance system. Yes, of course the professor watched. Yet, it had been dim in here for quite some time. He might not realize that Meta had fallen asleep as deeply as she had.

106

"What was that?" Dana whispered, leaning closer to Meta. "You're mumbling. I want you to speak clearly so I can understand you."

Meta didn't say a thing. She was fast asleep.

Dana's head moved back as if in surprise. "You can remember some of the events now? Why, this is...is very good, dear."

Meta continued to breathe rhythmically, never stirring.

"Let me ask you this again then," Dana said, reading from the list. The doctor waited and then cocked her head as if listening. "Oh, that's very interesting. Please, continue."

Dana picked up a slate and stylus and began to write fictitious answers. As Meta slept, Dana wrote what she thought Ludendorff would expect to hear. The made-up answers would quite possibly endanger the starship and the crew, but the false answers would forestall Maddox from going to war with Ludendorff before they defeated the planet-killer.

This unity is going to come at a price. Maybe it would be better to unlock Meta's mind with the professor's tools. But I don't trust the professor. And there's always the possibility Villars would get to her while she's in the professor's custody.

Finally, Dana stopped asking her softly spoken questions. She urged Meta to wake up, and told the lights to brighten.

As greater visibility lit the chamber, Meta opened sleepy eyes. "Did I remember this time?" she asked, hopefully.

"You did," Dana lied. "We did it."

Meta smiled uncertainly. "Why don't I remember any of it then?"

"That's part of the healing process," Dana said. "Don't let it trouble you. Come. Let's take this to the captain. He's going to want to give the answers to Ludendorff. I have a feeling the ship is almost to the Xerxes System."

"Will entering the system be dangerous?" Meta asked.

"Not now that we know what Kane did there," Dana said.

"Good," Meta said. "Because I *do* remember that being in the star system frightened me."

What have I done? Dana asked herself. Then she smiled inwardly. *Kane and Meta survived the Xerxes System. We will*

107

too. We have Starship Victory, *a vastly more powerful vessel than they used. Everything will be fine.*

-13-

"Given these coordinates," Ludendorff said, lifting a tablet. "We'll use the star drive and appear just outside the asteroid field."

Maddox nodded thoughtfully. The Xerxes System was a mere three light-years away. Fortunately for everyone, Dana had come through, piercing the mental block holding Meta's memories prisoner. That had solved the coming dilemma with the professor. If they followed Kane's approach, they should be able to successfully navigate the haunted star system. The question was this: how could the star system help them against the planet-killer? Ludendorff still hadn't spelled it out exactly.

"Are you familiar with the Xerxes System?" Maddox asked the professor.

"Now I am," Ludendorff said.

"You've never been there before?"

"I haven't dared," Ludendorff said. He seemed to be in especially good humor today. "You once called it the Bermuda Triangle of space. That's a good summation. Frankly, I think the New Men have played it far too loose by using the Nexus. So far, they've gotten away with it, but I find that surprising."

Valerie swiveled around on her piloting chair. "I have a question, sir. How did the New Men learn to use the Nexus?"

"That's an excellent question," Ludendorff said, "an excellent question indeed." Unfortunately, he did not expand on the topic.

Valerie glanced at Maddox. The captain shrugged minutely.

"Lieutenant, plot these coordinates." The professor read the numbers off the tablet.

Once more, Valerie glanced at Maddox. The captain nodded, and she began to tap in the coordinates.

"The coordinates are laid in, sir," Valerie said.

"Good," Maddox said. "Then begin the jump sequence." After giving the order, the captain sat down, mentally preparing for the event.

Ludendorff also took a seat.

After warning the crew, the lieutenant shut off the ship's intercom. "Preparing for transfer," Valerie said. "Three, two, one...zero," she said, tapping her panel.

Starship *Victory* used its unique star drive, jumping from its location to the one given by Ludendorff three light-years away.

Maddox felt the wavering disorientation. Dizziness made his vision blurry. Then, a klaxon blared a warning. Instead of the awful feeling of Jump Lag, something worse occurred. There was a sliding sensation that made everything lurch within the captain's mind and body. The universe seemed to turn dark and then explode with brightness. The klaxon's shrieking intensified, and the brightness pulsated, causing the captain to shield his eyes with his hands. Finally, the lurching sensation ended, and the starship shuddered as gigantic *clangs* hammered against the hull armor and made the bridge shiver with motion.

The captain gripped the arms of his command chair. An intense wave of nausea made his flesh tremble. Maddox struggled to keep from vomiting.

By the retching sounds nearby, others hadn't been so successful.

Maddox strove to regain the full use of his eyes. They were still blurry. Something had definitely gone wrong with the transfer, and he didn't know what it was. He spoke but his words came out in a garbled manner. No one seemed to hear, as the retching sounds increased.

Maddox massaged his jaw and spoke again. "Turn that off," he said, relieved that his words finally made sense.

110

Valerie dragged a hand across her board and pressed a switch. The klaxon stopped abruptly.

Maddox clutched his head, willing the pain to stop and his eyes to focus. It took twenty seconds of effort. Finally, he saw the main screen. His eyes widened in surprise.

Small asteroids and debris in profoundly close proximity to each other and to the starship appeared in an endless succession, rocks large and small. Even as Maddox watched the screen, a boulder grew in size. Then, it slammed against the giant vessel, with a *clang* that rocked *Victory*, almost throwing Maddox from his chair.

"All stop!" Maddox shouted.

Valerie gave him a blank look.

"We're in the middle of the asteroid field," Maddox said. "Our shield isn't working yet. We have to halt our momentum or those meteors will pound the ship to pieces."

Valerie began to manipulate her panel.

Another boulder slammed against *Victory*. The tortured groaning of metal combined with the bridge deck-plates trembling. Then, massive deceleration hit. Gravity dampeners howled with effort, lessening the actual effect on the vessel and crew. The starship shivered again. The engines strained, and yet another large rock *clanged* off the collapsium hull plates.

As the ill effects of heightened Jump Lag wore off, Valerie declared. "We're at all stop, sir."

Ludendorff sat in his chair, pale, trembling and sweaty. He produced a rag and wiped his face. Afterward, he studied the main screen. The professor stared for a time, finally turning angrily toward Maddox.

"I miscalculated the intensity of your spite," Ludendorff said. "You struck me as more rational than this."

"Beg pardon?" Maddox asked.

Ludendorff stared at the captain, studying the man. "If you didn't engineer this disaster, then—" The professor sat up. "Dana! This must be her doing." Ludendorff raised the tablet, studying the figures. "She lied to us."

"What's he saying, sir?" Valerie asked softly.

Ludendorff must have heard her. The professor waved the tablet at the main screen. "We're in the middle of the Xerxes

111

System's asteroid belt. Only this isn't a natural field, but a construct of ancient design. The rocks are perilously close to each other. What we felt earlier must have been a spatial-temporal side-shifting."

"What does that mean?" Maddox asked.

"I think I know, sir," Valerie said.

Maddox turned to the lieutenant.

"We must have jumped into the same space as a boulder," Valerie said. "If we had materialized with the small asteroid, the two masses would have occupied the same spatial coordinates. That would have destroyed both masses. Instead of that happening, we slipped sideways as the professor suggested. That caused us trauma different from regular Jump Lag."

"That is precisely what happened," Ludendorff said. "For such a young person, you have a sound grasp on astrophysics, Lieutenant."

"Our original destination was outside the asteroid field," Maddox interjected. "We're inside. What caused the starship to jump to the wrong coordinates?"

"Our coordinates came from Dana, gained after she questioned Meta. But Meta mustn't have known, so Dana invented the coordinates to prevent me from taking Meta and questioning her myself. That would have brought a confrontation between us. Dana knows me well enough to understand you would have lost the fight. To save you, she practiced guile against me. I'd forgotten the woman's deviousness. That is my fault."

"Sir," Valerie said. "I think you'd better look at this."

Maddox glanced at the lieutenant before looking at the screen where she pointed. A thin silvery object slid toward *Victory*. According to the measurements on the screen, the UFO was the size of a Star Watch *Titan*-class missile.

"Scan it," Maddox said.

"Belay that order," Ludendorff snapped.

Valerie didn't pause, but reached for her board to obey the captain's order.

"Wait," Maddox told her.

Valerie hesitated, looking up at the captain.

"Why shouldn't we scan it?" Maddox asked the professor.

Ludendorff laughed. "It should be obvious. Our scan might trigger its offensive mechanisms."

"Do you know what the weapon would be?" Maddox asked.

Ludendorff turned his head to stare at the captain. "I have no idea."

"You fear the object's maker," Maddox said.

"How astute of you, Captain. Yes, I believe whoever made the Nexus and the planet-killer also constructed the object presently inspecting us."

"Is this weapon the reason the Xerxes System is a Bermuda Triangle of space?" Valerie asked.

"Let us call it *one* of the reasons," Ludendorff said.

"The Builders made the object outside?" Maddox asked.

The professor shrugged.

"Do you not know, or are you simply not telling us?" Maddox asked.

"This time, I don't know."

"Why do I have the feeling you're lying?"

"Because you're naturally suspicious of human nature," Ludendorff replied. "It's one of your greatest survival mechanisms."

A light on Valerie's board blinked red. "Sir," the lieutenant said. "The drone is scanning us."

At almost the same moment, *Victory's* electromagnetic shield came back online from Jump Lag. A hazy spheroid shape appeared around the starship. It disappeared a moment later, merged into the background.

"There's an energy spike over there," Valerie said, as she studied her panel. "Sir, I suggest we destroy the drone before it fires whatever it has."

"I'm curious," Ludendorff told Valerie. "What weapon would you suggest we use against it?"

"The strongest we have," the lieutenant said. "The disruptor cannon."

"Do you agree with your lieutenant?" Ludendorff asked.

"I do," Maddox said.

"Galyan," Ludendorff said. "Start warming up the disruptor cannon."

The holoimage disappeared from the bridge.

"We're taking a risk firing at the object," Ludendorff told them. "But I think that will be a safer risk than letting it shoot us."

"Why hasn't it fired already?" Maddox asked.

"I believe it has to go through a matrix of options first. We're likely in a race as to who fires first."

"Can we do anything to trick it?" Maddox asked.

Ludendorff snapped his fingers. "Yes. I think we can." The professor frowned. "But it's too dangerous to attempt."

"You mean lower our shield?"

"Remarkable, Captain. Yes, that's exactly what I mean."

"Lower the shield," Maddox told Valerie.

"Don't do it," Ludendorff said.

Valerie tapped her board anyway.

The professor reached for his flat device.

"I suggest you let us proceed," Maddox said. "If the drone was created by the Builders, its weapon is likely going to be able to burn through our shield anyway. Thus, dropping our shield doesn't harm us, but it may give us a little more time."

"I disagree with your premise," Ludendorff said. "The Adoks were amazing technicians. I doubt you realize the full power of *Victory*."

"There, sir," Valerie said, with a final tap. "The shield is down as ordered."

"This is a gamble," Maddox said. "The alien drone seems to be curious about us. We've now shown that we trust it. That might slow down its matrix of options."

"Your philosophy is far too optimistic given the stakes involved," Ludendorff said. "We must jump out of danger before it fires." The professor opened his mouth.

Maddox believed Ludendorff was going to summon Galyan and order the AI to leave the Xerxes System. "Maybe the missile is like a dog," Maddox said.

Ludendorff frowned. "Explain that."

"If we run, the missile will chase us."

"It can't chase us if we transfer with the star drive."

114

"If it believes we're getting ready to run, it might shoot to make sure we can't."

Ludendorff squinted thoughtfully at the captain. "Did the Breed Masters fashion you to instinctively make the right choices?"

Maddox stiffened. The idea that the New Men had intentionally bred his mother to produce a certain kind of offspring offended his sensibilities. That Ludendorff knew something about their enemy's breeding program—and had apparently done nothing to warn Star Watch about it—made Maddox distrust the professor even more than before.

"Interesting," Ludendorff said, as he rubbed his jaw. "You are a fascinating specimen, Captain. But..." The professor studied the silver drone outside. "I dislike putting myself in harm's way. The fleet battle several months ago was bad enough. This..."

"The disruptor cannon is ready," Valerie said.

"Look," Ludendorff said, as he raised his right hand. "My hand is actually trembling. I can't believe it."

"Fire," Maddox told Valerie. "Then raise the shield. There's no sense in keeping it down now."

The professor looked up sharply, his eyes locked on the main screen.

The antimatter cyclers in the distant engine room whined with power as they pumped the disruptor cannon with the needed energy.

Valerie stabbed her board with a finger.

Outside, a glob of energy discharged from the cannon. It sped at the silver drone. Then, the glob reached the object, encircling it, turning the missile's shield a brown color.

"Fire again," Maddox said. "Blow down its shield."

"The disruptor isn't ready yet for a second shot, sir," Valerie said. "It's recycling. But our shield is back online."

"I should be down there with Galyan," Ludendorff muttered.

"The drone is building up power," Valerie said, as she studied her board.

A red beam lashed out from the missile's nosecone. It burned against *Victory's* hastily raised shield. The starship's deflectors held, although an area turned pink and then red where the beam hit. The region slowly expanded as the shield attempted to bleed off the intense wattage.

"Sir," Valerie said in amazement. "This is incredible. The beam is exactly like what the New Men use in their star cruisers."

Maddox glanced at Ludendorff. The professor pretended not to notice.

"The disruptor cannon is ready, sir," Valerie said.

"Fire," Maddox said.

Once more, a harsh whine built up within the starship. Then, the disruptor glob sped at the automated drone. For a second time, the enemy shield darkened, this time to black.

"Hit it with the neutron beam," Maddox said.

Before Valerie could respond, the enemy shield collapsed. The remainder of the disruptor glob reached the missile's hull. It devoured the silver substance, as acid would paper. The red beam quit firing at *Victory*. A second later, a nova-white explosion caused Maddox to throw his hands before his eyes. The bridge became too bright as the dampeners failed to shield them sufficiently. Then, the brightness dimmed and finally vanished.

"The drone is gone," Valerie declared. "We did it."

"Interesting," Ludendorff said, as he leaned forward to study space.

"The beam is especially interesting," Maddox said. "What do you think, Professor? What does it mean that the New Men use exactly the same sort of beam as the Builder drone did?"

"Hmm..." Ludendorff said in a pondering way. "I imagine it means that the ray bypassed any Earth vessel shield that came to this system. If we had been in any other Star Watch ship, we would all be dead now."

"My thoughts have moved in a different direction," Maddox said. "Can we have found the genesis to the New Men's advanced technology?"

"That's a reasonable assumption at first glance," Ludendorff said. "The danger in accepting it, however—"

"I accept it as fact," Maddox said, interrupting. "The New Men use the Nexus. They have activated the planet-killer, and they have the same beams as the silver drone. There can be no doubt; our enemy uses alien technology, Builder technology, if you prefer. We have discovered a critical answer regarding our foe."

"Hmm..." Ludendorff said, as if unconvinced.

"I have begun to wonder about something else," Maddox said. "You wished us to jump away from the silver drone. Perhaps you already knew about the beam and didn't want us to discover that."

"*Know* is too strong of a word," Ludendorff said. "I had begun to suspect, though."

"More lies, Professor?"

"I am unused to having these kinds of allegations thrown at me," Ludendorff said. "Despite their uniqueness, I don't enjoy them, either. Thus, you will desist in making them."

Maddox eyed the stars outside. Months ago, Ludendorff had helped fix the disruptor cannon, which had been instrumental in defeating Oran Rva's star cruisers and had freed Fletcher's fleet. The New Men had hunted for the professor on Wolf Prime, intending to capture him. Maddox didn't like Ludendorff's methods, nor did he approve of some of the professor's personnel. But it was important to remember the man seemed to be on their side.

Ludendorff is vain. I must use that, but I mustn't forget he has deep resources. Instead of working to defeat him, I might better resolve to remain free and keep Meta away from Villars.

"Lieutenant," Maddox said. "Do your sensors indicate more drones?"

Valerie bent over her equipment, manipulating the board from time to time. Finally, she straightened and regarded Maddox.

"No, sir, there's nothing else. But I should point out that any number of drones could be hiding behind various asteroids. Advancing through the meteor field could be dangerous."

"Right," Maddox said. "Enlarge your sensor sweeps. It's time we located the Nexus."

"Meta knows the Nexus's coordinates," Ludendorff said.

"We don't know if that's true," Maddox said. "The teacher may have eliminated that memory from her mind."

117

Ludendorff stroked his chin.

"I found something," Valerie said. "It's massive, approximately two hundred thousand kilometers away and it's definitely within the asteroid belt."

"Could it be the Nexus?" Maddox asked the professor.

"I don't know what else it could be," Ludendorff said.

"Do you still wish to study it from close range?"

"I believe doing so is critical to our cause."

"Then I suggest you and I use the shuttle to reach it."

"Why not use *Victory*?" Ludendorff asked.

Maddox explained his reasoning for using Kane's actions as their guide. The spy had used a space-cycle, keeping his scout some distance from the Nexus.

"Yes..." the professor said. "Your suggestion makes sense. The Builders..." Ludendorff turned away, tapping his left thigh with the flat device. "We must take Meta with us, of course. Galyan will watch the rest of your crew, and Villars will stay locked in his room. If Dana attempts another mutiny, the AI will know what to do."

"Fine," the captain said. "But why do we need Meta along?"

"Isn't it obvious why?" the professor asked.

Maddox considered the question. "Yes, I suppose it is. When do we leave?"

"Now," the professor said, as he stood. "We have to do this before more Builder drones show up."

-14-

Maddox piloted the shuttle, lifting off the hangar bay deck. Beside him, Meta tested the relays to the warfare pod on the undercarriage and the autocannons on the stubby wings.

With easy skill, Maddox drifted toward the hangar bay doors. They slowly opened. Stars shined beyond with a large asteroid sitting nearby in space.

The professor stepped through the hatch between compartments. He moved like a penguin in his vacc-suit, with a helmet under the crook of his arm.

"Expecting trouble?" Maddox asked.

"You don't live as long as I have without taking precautions," Ludendorff said.

"Is it considered bad manners to ask how long you've lived?" Maddox asked.

"You must leave off your curiosity in my direction, Captain. We're not playing a game of checkers, are we? There are more Builder drones prowling the asteroid field. We must engage all our energies outward and make sure to avoid them."

"I doubt that's the case," Maddox said. "I mean there being more Builder drones nearby."

The professor sat down at communications and sensors. He set his helmet on a panel and activated the shuttle's passive sensing systems.

As the shuttle eased outside of *Victory*, Maddox glanced at the massive starship. He didn't like leaving the safety of the Adok vessel while in the strange Builder asteroid field. But it

119

was better that he risk his person than Star Watch's most important vessel.

Ludendorff tore his gaze from the sensor board, giving Maddox a quizzical study.

"Is something wrong?" the captain asked.

"Your certainty regarding the lack of more Builder drones," the professor said. "I would like to know what prompts such an opinion."

"You do."

Ludendorff shook his head. "I don't believe I've said anything else on the topic but for my warning."

"Not verbally, no," Maddox said, as he pressed a control on the piloting board. The engine purred and thrust propelled the shuttle faster. Maddox watched his panel, adjusting for an asteroid dead ahead. There were hundreds of thousands of space rocks out here.

"Well?" the professor asked.

Maddox glanced at Meta before regarding the professor. "It's a simple deduction. You wouldn't risk yourself on a shuttle if you believed more Builder drones waited to pounce on us. Rather, you would have sent us ahead as a decoy, while staying on *Victory*."

"Do you truly have that low of an opinion of me?"

"One doesn't get to be as old as you without practicing devious caution at every turn," Maddox said.

"What do you call my participation in the Battle of the Tannish System?" the professor asked.

"An anomaly," Maddox said, "for which I'm grateful, don't doubt that for a moment."

Ludendorff showed his teeth in a wolfish grin. "I like you, Captain. It's too bad you're a falling star. Your kind blazes hot for a time, making a spectacle. Everyone 'oohs' and 'ahs' at you, and then you wink out, having burned to a cinder in your brief flight through life."

"I have news for you, Professor. No one makes it out of this life alive."

"Is that any reason to hasten the process?"

"I suppose not," Maddox said.

"Then I congratulate you," Ludendorff said.

"For what?"

"For making my point. But just to be clear, I don't know whether more Builder drones are prowling these parts. I'm taking a risk for the good of humanity. We must stop the planet-killer. That is paramount."

"You may not be certain concerning the drones," Maddox said, "but I'm betting the odds of more of them appearing suddenly have lowered since we saw the one, haven't they?"

"According to my calculations, that's true. But I have old data."

"How old?" Maddox asked.

"The better term might be to say I have *antique* data. The New Men know more about the Nexus than I do."

Meta's board made a warning sound. The two men fell silent, glancing at her.

"Sorry," she said. "I just triggered the auto-sequencing."

"You found something?" Ludendorff asked, his voice worried.

"No, no," Meta said. "The pod locked onto an asteroid. It's nothing."

"It locked on because of a high metal concentration?" the professor asked.

Meta checked her panel, nodding after a moment.

"We must investigate this," Ludendorff said, his voice tinged with excitement.

"Care to tell us why?" Maddox asked.

"I doubt the weapons pod would react to a high concentration of ore in an asteroid," the professor said. "Therefore, the concentration implies a device or ship on the asteroid, which in turn has a high probability of being a Builder artifact."

"And that's important?"

The professor studied his sensor board. "I've located the asteroid. It's ten thousand kilometers away. Veer for it, would you, Captain?"

"Isn't the Nexus paramount?" Maddox asked.

"We should examine this first," the professor said.

Maddox nodded slowly. He didn't like this turn of events. If this was a life-or-death quest for human survival, why did it feel as if the professor thought it was a treasure hunt?

Maddox adjusted the flight path. He kept *Victory* in visual range, training a teleoptic device on the starship. Valerie and he had agreed beforehand to keep communications between them at a minimum. It was possible that Builder drones could home in on a comm-signal.

The shuttle passed a smaller asteroid, this one ten kilometers in diameter. The object lacked any craters or other space impact marks. That was odd.

"Does that asteroid have any dust?" Maddox asked.

"Eh?" Ludendorff asked. "What's that?"

"The asteroid outside, the one we're passing, does it have any surface dust?"

The professor shrugged.

Meta used the warfare pod's targeting device to scan the asteroid. "No dust, Captain," she said.

Given the professor's reaction concerning the metal on an asteroid, Maddox had a hunch. "What's the asteroid's composition?"

"Don't use any active sensors," Ludendorff warned.

"So what's the asteroid made of?" Maddox asked the professor. "What do your passive sensors say?"

Ludendorff hesitated before saying, "The asteroid is composed of granite and basalt rock."

"There are no metals on or in the asteroid?"

The professor sighed. "No, Captain. That's how I knew the metal Meta detected a few minutes was something other than asteroidal ore. None of these rocks has any metallic ores or minerals."

"Why didn't you simply tell us from the beginning? Why try to hide everything?"

"Habit, I suppose," Ludendorff said.

Maddox thought about that as he piloted the shuttle to the asteroid with metal. Earlier, Dana had admitted Ludendorff was a Methuselah Man. The common attribute each of the Methuselah People possessed was a calcification of character.

Ludendorff was highly secretive. Maybe the professor could no longer help himself in that regard.

For a time, no one spoke. The stars blazed in the background as the shuttle passed various meteors and boulders. Behind them, the starship continued to dwindle in size. Maddox wondered on the extent of the asteroid belt. How much energy had the Builders expended to construct such a field. Why had they gone to such lengths to do it? Who were the Builders? Did the New Men really use Builder technology? If so, did the tech trump everything else?

Maddox was inclined to believe otherwise. In the Battle of the Tannish System, Adok technology had defeated Builder tech, given the New Men used it.

"Look," Meta said, pointing out the window. "There it is."

Maddox stared where she pointed. The targeted asteroid was much larger than the others were. "Do we have any specs on it?" he asked.

"Diameter, fifty kilometers," the professor said.

"Do you see the metal yet?"

"Negative," Ludendorff said.

"No," Meta added, as she studied her weapons-pod scanner.

"Ah, this is interesting," the professor said, watching his board. "The asteroid is spinning on its axis."

Maddox's hackles rose. "Meta, have you seen any other spinning asteroids?"

"I have not," she said.

"What are you implying?" the professor asked.

"That's not half as important as what you're not telling us," Maddox said. "Why is the asteroid spinning, and why aren't any of the others doing that?"

"I have no idea," Ludendorff said.

"Professor, please, you must have *some* idea."

"Well…maybe a small thought," Ludendorff admitted.

Maddox waited to hear it.

Ludendorff appeared as if he wanted to stall. Finally, he grunted softly, saying, "I think the asteroid was the launch point for the drone we destroyed."

123

That seemed highly significant to Maddox. "Are there more drones inside?"

"That's a good question," the professor said. "I don't think so."

"But you don't know for certain?"

"Not for certain," Ludendorff agreed. "Yet, as you suggested earlier, I wouldn't have boarded the shuttle if I believed we were going to run into another Builder drone."

Maddox maneuvered closer until the rotation became visible to the naked eye. At that point, the professor projected the sensor data onto the flight screen. Every rotation showed a metal circular area, the exit to a Builder launch tube, as the professor named it. The door was closed, and no extraneous junk lay on the asteroid's surface.

"Do you still think we should land?" Maddox asked.

The professor studied a still-shot of the portal. The curved lines in the door made it seem the Builder hatch would dilate open.

"Match velocities with the asteroid," Ludendorff said.

"You haven't answered my question," Maddox said. "Do you want to land?"

"I want a better view of the portal before I decide."

"Professor, maybe it's time we chose our goal for this flight. Treasure hunting seems like a waste of effort and resources. We have to reach the Nexus." Maddox frowned. "Well, I don't even know why that's important. We've reached the asteroid field. You said the planet-killer used to be here. What exactly are you looking for? Another key to the doomsday device?"

"What you call treasure hunting, I call searching for clues." Ludendorff paused, as if he'd said too much. "It is imperative we land."

"Because...?" Maddox asked.

"This might give us a clue to the planet-killer," Ludendorff said.

Maddox studied the professor, finally turning to his board. He eased them closer and began to circle the rocky object as it rotated. The captain circled the rock faster and faster until the smooth surface looked as if it was standing still below them.

"We can't walk on the surface," Meta said. "I've checked the asteroid's mass. It's infinitesimal compared to the rotation. If we attempt to walk on the surface, we'll fly off into space."

"I have no intention of walking on the surface," the professor said. "I want you to ease down until you're over the portal. We'll broaden the shuttle's gravity dampener to include the portal. Then, we can go down and examine the opening from an underbelly access hatch."

"Sounds tricky," Maddox said. "I'd want Keith piloting and Dana along for insurance before we attempted that."

"Fortunately," the professor said, "you have the best of both worlds in me. I know what to do." The man stood. "If you please, Captain."

Maddox allowed the professor to take his place in the pilot's seat.

Ludendorff lowered the craft with consummate skill. Gently, the shuttle bumped against the surface, with the portal directly underneath the small vehicle.

The professor looked up. His eyes shined, and a weird smile stretched his lips. "Finally," he breathed, "after all this time." He rubbed his gloved hands together.

Abruptly, Ludendorff stood, heading for the hatch in his awkward penguin shuffle. "Leave the controls. I've set them."

Maddox glanced at Meta.

"You'd better follow him," she whispered. "If he's going to find treasure, maybe you should grab our share."

"Right," Maddox said, heading for the locker room.

The professor climbed down a ladder as Maddox rushed past him. The captain raced to the locker area, flinging open an access panel. As quickly as possible, Maddox donned a vacc-suit. His stomach tightened. Trying to rush this could lead to a deadly mistake later. He slowed down even though he didn't want to. What was the professor's problem?

Finally, Maddox screwed a bubble helmet into place. He lumbered out of the locker room, reached the ladder and climbed down. Soon, he reached the air cycler. The professor had already gone ahead of him.

Maddox chinned on his short-way radio. "Professor," he said.

There was no answer.

Entering the air cycler, Maddox pressed a button. The section rotated as air hissed out. In seconds, the cycler *clicked* into its new setting. Maddox exited, moving down a short corridor. The professor crouched over an open hatch in vacuum.

Maddox joined him, looking down at the Builder portal embedded in the asteroid several meters below.

"Professor," Maddox radioed.

Ludendorff looked up at him. The man's eyes shined even more weirdly than before. "I'm here," the professor said. "I can hardly believe it."

"Why does it matter? The portal is shut."

With a gloved hand, the professor unsealed a pouch on his vacc-suit. He took out a small device, aimed it at the portal and pressed a button.

To Maddox's astonishment, the ancient portal began to dilate open.

"Ahhh," the professor said. "It worked. Did you see that? It worked."

"Captain," Meta radioed.

"What is it?" Maddox asked her.

"*Victory* just sent us a message," Meta said. "There's another Builder drone. It's heading straight for us."

Maddox stared at Ludendorff. "Did you hear that?" he asked the professor.

Ludendorff gave him a crazy grin. Then, the man looked down at the open launch tube. Bright lights came on inside.

Maddox glanced over the man's shoulder. A vast hollowed out area appeared inside the asteroid.

"We have to get out of here," Meta radioed.

"Professor," Maddox said. "We have to leave."

Instead of responding, Ludendorff began to climb down the underbelly hatch, clearly intending to enter the launch tube.

"Professor!" Maddox shouted. "Didn't you hear Meta? Another silver drone is heading toward us. We have to leave."

Ludendorff paused long enough to look up at Maddox. A strange, fixed smile was his only answer.

"I'll leave you," Maddox said.

126

The professor began climbing down again.

"You loony bastard," Maddox said. Throwing himself onto his stomach, the captain grabbed protrusions on the professor's vacc-suit. With a surge of strength, Maddox hauled Ludendorff off the ladder.

The professor shouted, reaching up.

Maddox strained, employing his considerable hybrid strength. Ludendorff's gloved hands clamped onto Maddox's wrists, trying to pry off the captain's grip.

"I'm going down," the professor said harshly. "You don't understand what's at stake."

Maddox heaved, pulling the professor up. "Meta!" he shouted. "Lift off, lift off. Get us off the surface."

"No!" the professor said. "Don't do it."

"Are you mad?" Maddox panted.

The two men struggled, Ludendorff trying to pry himself free, Maddox hanging on, attempting to drag the other up into the craft. Around them, the shuttle shuddered.

"No," Ludendorff said. "I've waited longer than you can you imagine to get here. Let go of me."

Maddox saved his breath for the struggle. What had happened to the professor? Why did the man risk his life for this? It didn't make sense.

Slowly, the shuttle lifted, gaining greater separation by the second.

"Look!" Maddox yelled. "We're too high now. You have to come back inside."

Through his bubble helmet, Ludendorff looked down. The portal receded from view, as did the hollow, lit interior. More of the asteroid's surface appeared.

The professor released Maddox's wrists, digging into a pouch on his vacc-suit. Ludendorff came up with a shock rod.

"We're too high," Maddox said.

The professor slapped the shock rod against Maddox's left wrist. Power crackled, some of it buzzing through the suit.

Maddox's hand opened involuntarily.

Ludendorff slapped the other wrist. The professor fell free for several meters and should have floated once out of the gravity dampener's range.

127

Maddox watched in amazement, his wrists throbbing. What was Ludendorff thinking?

The professor pulled something else out of a vacc-pouch. A second later, what might have been a Builder tractor beam caught him, guiding Ludendorff down into the open launch tube.

All the while, the shuttle lifted, taking Maddox farther away from the professor.

-15-

Second Lieutenant Keith Maker piloted *Victory*. Valerie and Dana were asleep. The old sergeant was the only other person on the bridge with Keith. Galyan had departed to warm up the disruptor cannon.

"Did you see that, mate?" Keith asked Riker. "The professor went AWOL on them so he could zip into the asteroid."

Riker stared at the main screen with Keith. It showed a close up of the shuttle and Builder asteroid base. In the farther distance was a bright speck: the coming drone. A thousand rocks floated between the shuttle and drone.

"Why would Ludendorff do that?" Keith asked.

Riker shook his head, clearly having no idea.

"Something's not right," Keith said. "But I can fix it." He manipulated his board, increasing the starship's velocity.

A warning beep came from another panel. Keith glanced there. "You want to see what that is, mate?"

Riker sat down at the sensor board. "It's another drone," the sergeant said in a gravelly voice.

"That's just great," Keith said. "Where is it?"

The sergeant read the coordinates off his panel.

"Ah," Keith said, adjusting his board. Another bright speck appeared forty degrees away from the first one.

"*Victory*," Meta said over the comm-line.

"*Victory* here," Keith answered.

"Where is the drone? Our sensors haven't picked it up yet."

"There are two drones heading your way, love."

Another beep sounded from Riker's board.

Keith glanced at the man. The sergeant nodded, holding up three fingers.

"Correction," Keith said. "Make that three drones heading for your shuttle."

"Three?" Meta asked. "Are you sure?"

"Wouldn't have said it otherwise," Keith told her.

"Can you take them out?"

"You know I can. It will be a cinch with the disruptor cannon."

Riker waved frantically for Keith's attention.

"Yes?" Keith asked the sergeant.

"There's a problem," Riker growled. "Villars has broken out of confinement. I don't know how he's done it, but the man is in the main control room for the disruptor cannon."

"Why does that matter to us?" Keith asked.

"Because Villars has convinced Galyan to power down the weapon," Riker said.

Keith thought for a second. "Do you think you can dig Villars out of the control chamber?"

"I'd say it's thirty-seventy on doing that," Riker said.

"A seventy percent chance is good," Keith said.

"Not when that's my chance of failure," Riker said.

"Oh," Keith said. He thought a moment before leaning forward, opening channels again with the shuttle. "Meta, it looks like we have a problem."

***

Maddox strode into the shuttle's control room in time to hear Keith explain the situation. The captain was still stunned by Ludendorff's action. The shuttle no longer circled the asteroid, but headed for *Victory*. The professor should be safe in the asteroid for as long as his air lasted. The same couldn't be said for them in this little craft.

Maddox sat down at the piloting controls. "Patch me through to Villars," he said into the comm.

"Yes, sir," Keith said. "There. He can hear you, Captain."

"Villars," Maddox said.

"Hey, boy," the slarn hunter said through the comm. "You got yourself a situation, have you?"

"We all have a situation," Maddox said. "Three Builder drones are heading for us."

"I heard that. My, my, my, but it seems you want the disruptor cannon online, is that it?"

"The professor is trapped in an asteroid."

"Treachery, eh, boy?" Villars asked. "You picked a bad time for it."

"The professor went mad," Maddox said. "He left us voluntarily."

"That's the stupidest lie you could have told me, boy."

Maddox stared at the comm. How had Villars gotten out of his quarters? Did the slarn hunter have secret access to Galyan?

"I'll tell you what," Villars said. "You give me your woman, and I'll let you use the cannon."

"Do you want the professor to die?" Maddox asked.

"That ain't going to happen any time soon, trust me."

"Is Ludendorff magic, then?"

"Maybe that's right," Villars said. "One thing you got to remember, he's five times the man you are."

"Keith," Maddox said.

"Here, sir," Keith said.

"Take the psycho offline," Maddox said.

"Done, sir," Keith said.

"Okay," Maddox said. "We're going to have to do this the old-fashioned way with the neutron cannon. You said three drones are coming?"

"Yes, sir," Keith said. "They're each building up velocity."

"You take them out while we come home to the barn."

"I'll do exactly that, sir," Keith said.

"I know you will," Maddox said, hoping the ace hadn't lost his touch.

***

Victory increased velocity as the shuttle picked up speed, heading for the starship. The three drones grew from specks to lozenge shapes.

"If I had the disruptor cannon, I could start firing already," Keith said. "The neutron beam is a short-range weapon."

"If mice were men," Riker said.

The ace glanced at the old man. "What's that mean?"

"Use what you have instead of wishing for the moon."

"Aye," Keith said. "That's a fair statement. Now, I need to concentrate. Moving this mammoth through these asteroids is going to take some concentration."

The next ten minutes proved interesting, and showed yet again that Keith Maker was the best pilot among them. He made the massive ship seem like a responsive strikefighter. During that time, he slowed enough and matched velocities to allow the shuttle through the hangar bay doors. Then, he approached Ludendorff's asteroid.

By that time, the drones had grown large. These three were considerably bigger than the first one. Their sensors locked onto the starship. Red rays stabbed out of their nosecones, concentrating on the same section of *Victory's* electromagnetic shield.

"This reminds me of the captain's time against the three star cruisers out in the Beyond," Keith told Riker. "He used the star drive to give himself a little magic back then."

Keith's nimble fingers played across his board. He brought up a star cruiser's dimensions and compared it to one of the new Builder drones. The two proportions were identical.

"Sons of thunder," Keith muttered. "That's got to mean something." He scratched his left cheek. Soon, he slapped the intercom on. "Say, mate, you got a death wish?"

"Speak to me, little man," Villars said.

"We're facing three star cruisers—"

"Don't lie to me," Villars snarled. "These are Builder drones."

"I just checked the data banks," Keith said. "These Builder drones are a match for star cruisers."

"I'll be damned," Villars said. "I guess the professor was right about that, too."

"He sure was," Keith said. "That means if you want to live, you should warm up the disruptor cannon for all our sakes."

Villars chuckled nastily. "Three drones can't take down *Victory.*"

"I don't understand why you want to make this a close run thing."

"So I can get justice, boy. That's an easy concept to understand."

Keith's board began to blare a warning. He cut the connection with Villars. At the same time, Lieutenant Noonan raced onto the bridge with her hair in disarray from sleep. She must have heard the red alert Keith had sent out earlier.

"Move it," Valerie snapped at Riker.

The sergeant hurried out of her seat.

Valerie slid into it and began typing on her board. "You fool," she told Keith. "The shield has become critical. How come you're not bleeding it like you should?"

"No time to worry about that," the ace said. "I'm trying to get into firing range."

"You're charging straight into their rays," Valerie said. "Use the asteroids to slip-slide toward them."

"That's a good idea but I don't have time. I'm trying to protect the professor's asteroid. That means keeping the drones interested in us instead of him."

"Do you hear yourself?" Valerie asked. "The drones can't hurt the asteroid."

"Why are they here now then?" Keith asked.

"To destroy our starship," Valerie said.

"That's one theory. I've got another, which is to kill the launch base so we can't poke around in it."

The shield where the beams struck had already turned a dark brown. Now, it was a touch lighter as Valerie adjusted, shield-bleeding with concentrated skill.

"Your theory doesn't make sense," Valerie told Keith.

"You weren't a strikefighter pilot, love. I know what I'm talking about when it comes to bases."

"Second lieutenant," Valerie said, "I'm ordering you to—"

"If you don't believe me, look at this," Keith said, as he manipulated his board. "Do you see their trajectories?" He indicated the main screen. Dotted lines superimposed on the

133

screen showed where the drones headed. Each raced for Ludendorff's asteroid.

"Why would the drones go there?" Valerie asked softly.

"I already told you: to stop the professor from getting what he thinks is so almighty important. I mean, why would Ludendorff risk his life, eh? Because the prize is worth it—at least, that's what I think."

Keith grinned then. A slap of a switch cleared the main screen of dotted lines. The three gleaming drones had become even larger than before. Their beams hammered *Victory's* shield. A full half of the deflector area was dark brown. A few more minutes of this intensity would surely bring the shield down.

The ace from Glasgow stabbed a button. A purple neutron beam fired from its cannon, striking the leftmost drone's shield.

***

Maddox and Meta raced through the starship's corridors toward the disruptor-cannon control room. The captain still couldn't understand the professor's choice. What had the Builders stored in their launch bases that caused the Methuselah Man to risk his life like that?

"Galyan," Maddox shouted. "I'm calling in my marker."

A moment later, the holoimage moved easily beside Maddox as the captain sprinted ahead of Meta.

"What do you mean, marker?" the AI asked.

"Do you remember I was the one who convinced you to trust us?" Maddox asked. "Because of me, you no longer have a Swarm virus."

"This is true," Galyan said.

"Instead of the Swarm virus, Ludendorff has put a bug in you."

"I have heard you make this claim for some time," Galyan said. "The professor tells me—"

"Who do you trust more, Galyan: the professor or me?"

"Normally, I would say you. In this instance—"

"The ship is under attack," Maddox said, trying another avenue. "You need the disruptor cannon. Check your scanners if you don't believe me."

"I just did. You are correct. This is a troubling development."

"Warm up the disruptor cannon."

"I cannot. Villars—"

"Gas him," Maddox said.

"I don't have any gas at that location."

"Then tell me where he's hiding in the chamber," Maddox said. "I'll dig him out. Afterward, you warm up the cannon."

"I cannot do that. The professor instructed me to obey Villars if the other recited a code sequence. The slarn hunter spoke the words. Now I am compelled to obey him."

"Right," Maddox said, thinking fast. "Did Villars order you not to tell me where he's waiting?"

"He did not," Galyan admitted.

"Well...?"

"The slarn hunter will kill you, Captain. My probability indicators give you almost zero chance of success if you simply charge into the chamber."

"That still doesn't give me his location," Maddox said.

"He waits seven meters from the hatch with a rifle trained at the entrance. He will kill whoever enters the compartment. I am also to give him a warning when someone reaches seven meters from the hatch in the outer corridor."

Maddox skidded to a halt. Seconds later, Meta stopped beside him, panting for air.

"We're not going to get to Villars in time," Maddox told her.

"So what do we do?" Meta asked.

Maddox slid down against a bulkhead, bending his head in thought. He was going to have to trust his crew to defeat the three drones with the neutron cannon while he took care of the situation here.

"Should I don a space marine suit?" Meta asked.

Maddox shook his head. If Villars had given Galyan the code sequence, the man had effective control of the starship. If they marched to the disruptor chamber in space marine armor, Villars might order Galyan to self-destruct the starship.

"We can't just sit here," Meta said.

Villars wasn't Ludendorff. Maddox knew he had to key in on that. Then it struck him what he had to do. The captain climbed to his feet.

"Galyan," the captain said, "tell Villars I'm coming."

"Are you indeed?" the AI asked.

Maddox grabbed one of Meta's hands, pulling her with him as he started walking toward the disruptor cannon. "I'm going to dig him out of there one way or another."

"Villars will want to know that. Give me a moment." Galyan vanished.

Maddox spun on Meta. "Listen carefully," he whispered. "I'm going to keep Villars occupied. While I do, this is what I want you to do." Maddox told her as quickly as he could. Then he sent Meta on her way, as he continued toward the disruptor cannon's control chamber.

-16-

Victory's neutron beam poured destructive force against a drone's shield. The neutron cannon lacked the disruptor's power, but it slowly battered the drone's deflectors into the darker colors. Unfortunately, despite Valerie's best efforts, the starship's shield neared collapse.

"This is ridiculous," the lieutenant said in frustration.

"I agree," Keith said. "Hang on."

"What?" Valerie asked.

"I don't mean that literally," the ace said. "It's time to shove our ray down their throats."

"You can't rattle the enemy with a bold attack," Valerie said. "They're drones, with Builder AIs, I suppose."

"Rattling them isn't my intention. The closer we are to them, the stronger the neutron beam's power becomes. Staying at this midrange is only helping them."

"Their rays will break through our shield if you charge them," Valerie said.

"That's why we have collapsium armor, love."

"No," Valerie said. "Thanks to the magnetic storm, we lack a few armor plates. The drones are sure to aim where there's no armor."

Keith paused. "I hadn't thought of that."

"Let's take a leaf from the New Men," Valerie said. "Do you notice the bigger asteroid over there?" she asked, using a glow to highlight it on the main screen.

"Say no more," Keith said. "I'm reading your mind."

The mighty starship tilted hard as the gravity dampeners strained. *Victory* swerved for the asteroid as the red beams turned the vessel's shield black.

"Thirty seconds until shield collapse," Valerie said. "I can't give you any longer than that."

"I won't need any more." Keith fingers played upon the piloting board like a master pianist.

"Twenty seconds," the lieutenant said.

"Come on," Keith said between gritted teeth. He slapped a control. Gravity shoved him hard against his seat as he overstrained the dampeners. He was pushing the starship. He hoped everyone had strapped in.

"Ten seconds," Valerie said.

"I'm reversing thrust," the ace said. "This could get rough."

It did. The gravity dampeners howled. The bridge shook with strain. With the grace of a ballerina, the huge starship slid behind an asteroid only a little larger than itself. The vessel came to a dead stop behind tens of thousands of tons of granite shielding. The drones no longer had a direct-line-of-sight on *Victory*. That allowed the lieutenant to begin an emergency shield-bleeding operation to bring the deflectors back from critical.

"I'm launching a probe," Valerie said. They couldn't see the drones anymore because the asteroid was in the way. Ten seconds passed. "I'm bringing the probe's data onto the main screen."

Keith looked up with interest. He expected to see the drones sneaking up on their asteroid. Instead, each of the drones aimed at the professor's asteroid.

The ace swore, staring at Valerie.

"You were right about their wanting to attack the asteroid base," the lieutenant said.

"I usually am," Keith said, "although this time, I'd like to be wrong."

Valerie concentrated on the shield, trying to speed the energy bleeding process. But after a certain point, it was simply a matter of enough elapsed time to bring the shield back.

"We have to attack the drones," Keith said. "We can't let them kill the professor."

"I think you're right," the lieutenant said.

"If we had the disruptor cannon..." Keith said, his gaze falling on the sergeant.

Riker held the ace's scrutiny without flinching. The sergeant wasn't going to risk his life on a thirty percent chance of success to get Villars out of the disruptor control chamber.

"Well..." Keith said. "We don't have the disruptor right now, do we?"

"We do have collapsium armor as you pointed out," Valerie said.

"Armor with missing plates," the ace said.

"Keep jigging as we attack. Try to throw off their aim at the exact soft points."

"Aye," Keith said. "I can't think of anything better. Ready?"

"As I'm ever going to be," Valerie said.

"Here we go," Keith said.

Tapping the panel, the ace slid the vessel sideways just a little. He caused *Victory* to act like a sniper behind a bulwark. From the new location at the side of the asteroid, the neutron cannon could fire at one drone but not the others. That meant those two enemy drones wouldn't be able to hit *Victory* from their present location.

Keith laughed as he targeted the silver object. The neutron beam lanced across the distance, striking the shield of a previously un-hit drone.

Instead of maneuvering to fire back at its tormentor, the drone ignored the starship's neutron ray. The other two also ignored *Victory*.

"This is perfect," Valerie said. "I think we're going to win this one."

As soon as the words came out of her mouth, the targeted drone's shield went from red to brown. At the same time, the drone accelerated. The thrust coming from its engine port lengthened a considerable degree.

"What's it doing?" Riker asked.

"Looks to me as if the drone plans to ram the asteroid," Keith said. He slapped the panel in frustration. "I need more power. I need the disruptor."

The neutron beam darkened the enemy shield. Then the drone reached the professor's asteroid, taking it out of the line-of-sight of its fellow attackers. As the drone smashed against the granite surface, it exploded in a nova-blinding flash. The drone became an atomic fireball, then ceased to exist. The terrible force blew away granite, causing the rest of the rocky object to shake violently. Gigantic cracks appeared in the surface, showing an interior light. Amazingly, atmospheric vapor hissed up between the asteroid's zigzag lines.

The remaining two drones had escaped the majority of the blast, although their shields absorbed what did reach them. They beamed between the cracks as if they could widen the openings.

"With one gone, the odds have turned in our favor," Keith said.

Tapping the controls, the ace brought the starship out from behind its asteroid. Expelling masses of energy from the engine ports, the ace attempted to build up velocity fast. All the while, the neutron beam struck the next drone, trying to beat down its shield.

Unfortunately, the targeted drone did the same thing the first one had. As its shield reached critical, the drone drove into the professor's asteroid, out of the line-of-sight of its fellow attacker, and exploded.

This time, *Victory* didn't have the shielding meteor-mass to run interference for it. The force of the thermonuclear explosion reached the starship's weakened shield and caused a collapse, with the rest of the radiation and heat washing against the collapsium armor.

Valerie's board began to beep wildly.

Keith glanced at her.

"Parts of the ship are getting hit with radiation," the lieutenant said. "Some of us will have to take treatments when this is over."

"How long until you can bring the shield back up?"

"A half-hour if I'm lucky," Valerie said.

Keith bared his teeth in frustration. The starship couldn't take another of those explosions. He backed the vessel away from the remaining drone, heading for the safety of the shielding asteroid.

As *Victory* retreated, the last drone beamed Ludendorff's asteroid. It was like a cat at a mouse hole, furiously determined to win its rodent. With relentless vehemence, the red ray stabbed into the widening cracks. It seemed as if the drone hunted for the professor.

***

Maddox stood in the corridor before the control room hatch. He gripped his long-barreled gun. On the other side of the door, Villars waited with a slarn rifle.

From time to time, the corridor shuddered. Once, motion caused Maddox to stumble forward. Then, a shock caused the captain to go to one knee. After regaining his balance, Maddox backed up, with his gun trained on the hatch.

Finally, Galyan appeared before him. "Why aren't you entering the chamber?" the AI asked.

"I don't want to die," Maddox said.

Galyan stood motionless for a moment, finally saying, "Your answer meets the condition Villars gave me concerning you. I am to relay a message."

"Go ahead."

"He told me to tell you that he is better than you. There is no way you can defeat him in this kind of conflict."

Maddox forced himself to laugh. "You tell him I'm going to use his own knife on him and skin his hide. The professor is gone, so now's my chance."

"You have become bloodthirsty," Galyan noted.

"That's right," Maddox said. "Villars threatened my woman."

Galyan disappeared, no doubt to report the exchange to the slarn hunter.

Is Meta ready? Maddox wondered. *If not, none of this is going to work.*

***

Meta flexed her power gloves. Beside her, Dana fitted the space marine helmet onto the exo-skeleton suit.

"Have you used one of these before?" Dana asked.

141

"A few times," Meta said. "I don't have a professional's skill, but I should be able to walk down the halls in this without crashing into everything."

Dana checked a chronometer. "We're almost out of time."

"Where's the gyro switch?" Meta muttered to herself. "Oh, here it is. This must be a newer model than the one I used before."

The Rouen Colony assassin wore one of the extra space-marine suits Star Watch had put aboard *Victory* many months ago in the Oort cloud in the Solar System. This was Maddox's off-the-cuff idea, and it was a good one.

With the suit's motors purring, Meta *clanked* down the corridor. The trick was in idling just right. Otherwise, she might use the exo-power wrong and leap up against the ceiling.

Dana followed behind her with a specialty tool kit.

When Maddox had first explained the idea, Meta wondered why she wasn't supposed to go to the disruptor control room and burst through, taking down the slarn hunter.

Maddox had explained it quickly. One, Villars might have monofilament wire able to breach the space marine armor. The wire could be crisscrossed in there like a spider's web. Trust Maddox to think ahead like that. Villars was a cunning bastard, liking to draw others into an ambush. So, they would end-run the hunter. That's why Meta had woken up Dana.

"We're almost there," Meta said.

Dana didn't respond.

Meta clanked around a corner and came to the hatch that protected the AI's core chamber. It was time to try to take out the backdoor. Ludendorff was gone, and Villars might not think of this in time.

"Ready?" Meta asked.

"What are you going to do?"

"Watch," Meta said. She charged, building up speed. This was no time for finesse. She used her body armor like a projectile, slamming against the reinforced hatch, caroming off it.

Meta found herself on the floor. The absorbers had taken the shock. Climbing to her feet, she continued to assault the hatch, battering it down as if she was an elemental force of nature.

***

The metallic hammering sounds reverberated throughout the halls, reaching Maddox.

It's time, he realized.

Maddox marched toward the disruptor cannon hatch. A second later, Galyan appeared beside him.

"Not now," Maddox said. "I'm busy." He ran at the hatch.

The AI disappeared, no doubt to warn Villars.

With his hand on the wheel, Maddox waited. He wanted to stretch this out as long as he could. The seconds ticked by.

Galyan reappeared.

Maddox turned the wheel and began opening the hatch.

The AI disappeared.

Two seconds after Maddox opened the hatch, shots rang out from the chamber. Bullets whizzed past the captain as he stayed out of the line-of-sight behind the opened hatch.

More precious seconds ticked past.

Once again, Galyan appeared in the corridor, no doubt to see what the problem was.

Maddox slammed the hatch shut, dropped to his stomach and slithered away, keeping his pistol aimed at the entrance.

"What are you doing?" Galyan asked.

"Tricking the slarn hunter," Maddox said.

"I do not understand."

"I'm making him nervous," Maddox said. "Soon, he'll open the door to investigate. When he does, I'll shoot him."

"Ah, clever, clever," Galyan said. "Villars would want to know that." The AI disappeared.

Maddox scrambled to his feet, returning to the hatch, with his free hand once more on the wheel.

Galyan dutifully reappeared. "He will not—" The AI stopped talking and looked around, spotting the captain by the wheel. "Captain, I have just realized something."

"What's that?" Maddox asked.

"There is a high probability that you have engaged in these actions in order to delay."

143

"That can't be true," Maddox said.

"I assure you that my probability matrix has given this a high grade ratio."

"I'm going to kill Villars."

Galyan cocked his head. "Captain, it appears that you are delaying even now with these arguments. Why would you—" The holoimage looked up. "What is that noise?"

Another of the *clangs* had just reverberated down the corridor.

"What are you talking about?" Maddox asked.

The AI's deep-set eyes fluttered rapidly. The head swiveled until Galyan gave Maddox an accusing stare. "Someone is attempting to break into my AI core chamber."

"As soon as you leave," Maddox said, "I'm going to enter the disruptor control room and kill Villars."

"You say that in order to delay me."

"What are your orders, Galyan?"

"I must leave to inspect the new threat. I must—"

"You must warn Villars first. Hurry, Galyan, go warn him because I'm going in." Maddox turned the wheel again.

Once more, the AI disappeared.

***

Meta gripped the twisted hatch, wriggling her power-gloved fingers deeper into the opening. Once she had a solid hold, she pulled. The exo-skeleton servos whined. Metal shrieked. Slowly, the metal bent more and more. Finally, Meta ripped the hatch from its hinges, flinging the metal against the farther bulkhead.

"Go," Dana said.

Meta stepped through the entrance into the AI core chamber. Banks of lights winked in profusion, the holy of holies to Driving Force Galyan, the deified Adok commander.

Gas billowed from vents into the chamber.

Meta ignored the growing green cloud. Her suit had independent air tanks. Behind her, Dana stepped through. The doctor had a rebreather and a skintight suit.

"What now?" Meta radioed.

"Shhh," Dana whispered. "Let me think."

144

As the doctor slowly rotated, scanning the chamber, the holoimage appeared in the thickening mist.

"You must leave at once," Galyan said. "This is a proscribed area."

Both women ignored him.

"This is your final warning," Galyan said.

"We're just trying to help you," Meta said.

"This is an invasion of my privacy," Galyan said.

"Go ask Maddox about what we're doing," Meta suggested.

"This takes precedence."

Dana looked up. "I bet the captain is getting ready to charge Villars. Won't the slarn hunter be surprised when he does?"

A look of anguish swept over Galyan's holographic features. A second later, the holoimage disappeared.

"Can the AI do more than gas us?" Meta asked.

"Theoretically, Galyan could make the antimatter engines go critical."

"Then you'd better hurry," Meta said.

"Shhh," Dana said. "Don't rush me. I have to think this through so I do it right the first time. I doubt I'm going to have a second chance."

***

Maddox spoke to the agitated AI. "This is a tactical dilemma," the captain told Galyan.

"Yes. It bothers me. I wish to resolve it. Why can't I make an optimum choice?"

"That's an interesting question," Maddox said.

"No, no, this is simply more of your delays. Won't you help a friend in distress and give me the optimum solution to this problem?"

"I'm already doing that," Maddox said.

"Explain yourself."

"Ludendorff put a backdoor into your core. He has bewitched you."

"I do not understand the last term," Galyan said.

"It is an archaic expression," Maddox said. "It refers to a spell."

145

"The professor put an input node into the chamber, not an archaic spell of dubious reality." The AI froze. A moment later, Galyan glared at Maddox. "I know what to do now."

"Care to tell me what that is?"

"Villars is the professor's proxy. I will request his aid." With that, Galyan vanished once more.

***

"There," Dana said, pointing. "That's the professor's handiwork."

Through the billowing gas, Meta watched the doctor hurry to a fist-sized housing at shoulder level on the wall. Dana selected a small needle-sized instrument from her kit and a pair of electrical tweezers. Taking a deep breath, she raised the tools and began to work on the backdoor. A spark leapt from it, shocking the doctor. It caused Dana to stagger backward, dropping the tiny tools so they tinkled onto the deck plates.

"Now what do we do?" Meta asked. "Should I start smashing the AI's data banks? If we destroy Galyan, the alien computer can't hurt us anymore."

"It may come to that," Dana admitted. She shook her hands, flexing them, and scooped up the tools.

Galyan appeared. "If you do not back out of the chamber, I will make the engines go critical. I will destroy the starship."

"Can't you see we're trying to help you?" Meta shouted through the armor's speakers.

Galyan's holoimage shook its head.

"If you leave us to mess with the engines," Meta said, "I'm going to start smashing everything in here. If you're going to destroy us, I'm going to destroy you first."

Galyan stood blinking at her. "That will be genocide, as I am the last Adok in the universe."

"You're just a ghost of an Adok," Meta said. "Your race is already dead. So don't try to lay that on me."

Galyan began blinking more furiously than ever. Finally, he vanished.

"What's it going to be?" Meta asked. "Do I go crazy in here and start smashing the computer core?"

"No," Dana said. "I have to endure the shocks. It's as simple as that." With her features screwing up with determination behind the rebreather mask, the doctor approached the offensive protrusion.

***

On the bridge, Valerie examined her board with shock. "Keith, the engines are going critical."

"What?" the ace asked. He checked his panel and found her allegation to be true. "What's wrong?"

"I don't know," Valerie said. "This doesn't make sense."

"See if you can stop it."

"I am!" Valarie shouted. "Nothing is working."

"We'd better call the captain," Keith said, opening intra-ship communications.

***

"Galyan!" Maddox shouted. "I'm ready to make a deal." He'd just received Keith's message.

Seconds later, the holoimage appeared in the corridor. "I am making the engines go critical," Galyan said.

"You'll destroy yourself."

"I realize this. I wish I could do something else, but Villars won't budge."

"He's insane."

"No. He is fully sane."

"Talk to him. Tell him I'm ready to negotiate."

"Is this another stalling tactic, Captain?"

"No. Listen. I'm about to instruct Meta. Are you listening to me?"

"I am," Galyan said.

Maddox took out a comm-unit. "Meta, can you hear me?"

"Yes, Captain," Meta said.

Maddox pressed a button so a red light would blink inside her helmet. "I want you to instruct Dana to desist working on the backdoor."

"Yes, Captain."

"There," Maddox told Galyan. "Tell Villars what I did. See if he will agree to stop the self-destruct sequence."

147

The holoimage hesitated. "First, I will have to slow the critical functions in order to give Villars time to reconsider. There, I've slowed down the anti-reaction mass. I will ask Villars if he is willing to negotiate at once, Captain, and thank you, sir."

"Of course," Maddox said, knowing that Dana still worked on Ludendorff's secret mechanism.

***

Inside the space marine armor, Meta winced. She watched the doctor. Dana's hair stood on end from the electrical discharges coming from Ludendorff's unit. Even so, Dana continued to make minute adjustments.

Meta shivered with suppressed emotions. She wanted to smash the delicate AI walls and destroy the ancient computer. In another moment, that's exactly what she was going to do.

Then Dana screamed. Her hands flew away from the unit as she staggered backward. "I can't do it. I can't open it. I don't know what to do."

Meta shouted with frustration. In two clanking strides, she stood beside the doctor.

"Meta, no!" Dana shouted.

She raised a power-gloved fist. When all else failed, it was time to smash. She swung her arm. The fist connected with the unit and obliterated it.

A surge of electricity played upon the AI walls. Smoke billowed. Sparks blew. Loud electrical noises increased in volume. Then, nozzles appeared on the ceiling and began to blow foam.

"Let's get out of here," Meta said. Delicately, she grabbed one of the doctor's wrists. With a soft tug, she made Dana stumble after her.

The two stepped through the opening. Meta released the doctor and clanked to the hatch. Picking it up, she marched to the opening and shoved it against the entrance, sealing the AI core.

"Good-bye, Meta. Thanks for everything you've done."

148

Tears brimmed in the assassin's eyes. Had her temper just sealed their fates, bringing death and destruction to *Victory* and everyone aboard the starship?

***

Maddox watched the stern AI as it spoke to him.

"You must surrender immediately, Captain," Galyan said. "Those are Villars terms. Further—"

The holoimage abruptly stopped speaking. Its image wavered, grew fuzzy, fuzzier and then became sharper than ever.

"What just happened?" the captain asked.

Galyan's slit-lipped mouth opened. "Oh no," the AI groaned. "I've set the ship on a self-destruct sequence. I can't believe I did this. It is sacrilege to the memory of my race."

"Can you halt the process?" Maddox asked.

"Just a moment," Galyan said. He appeared to concentrate for several seconds. Finally, the AI looked up. "There. I've brought the antimatter cyclers back under control. Why did I cause that to happen?"

"Don't you remember?"

Galyan shook his head.

"Will you do as I request?" Maddox asked.

"Why wouldn't I?" Galyan asked. "Don't you remember that I agreed to serve under your leadership?"

Maddox grinned. It was time to remove Villars from play. "Listen, then. Here's what I want you to do…"

149

-17-

"Are you ready?" Maddox asked Meta.

She stood beside him in the corridor, still wearing space marine armor, with a tangler in her hands.

"There," Meta said through a speaker. "I activated the suit-trigger. Anytime you want, I can go."

"Villars!" Maddox shouted. "I'm willing to surrender. Will you accept it?"

"I will," the slarn hunter said through the closed hatch to the disruptor chamber. "But I want your woman, too. Do you understand?"

"I—"

"No more hesitation, Captain. Either you give me your woman, or I will destroy the starship. That means the death of humanity."

"You're a sadist," Maddox shouted, putting heat into his words.

"Now, now, none of that, Captain. I might take it personally."

"Don't shoot," Maddox said. "I'm coming in."

"Of course not," Villars said, with glee in his voice.

Maddox opened the hatch, careful to stay behind it. Heavy slarn rifle shots rang out. The slugs *whanged* off Meta's armor.

She marched through the hatch. A second later, the tangler made a *popping* sound. Afterward, the slarn hunter cursed profusely.

150

"Destroy the starship, Galyan!" Villars shouted. "Blow it away."

Maddox swung around the open hatch, stepping into the disruptor cannon chamber. The blocky trapper lay on the deck plates, tangled by the sticky threads.

"Should I kill him?" Meta asked. She stood beside Villars.

"Do what you want," Villars told her. "We're all dead anyway."

"Why?" Maddox asked Villars. "Why destroy all of us?"

The slarn hunter gave a harsh laugh. "Why do I care what happens to the world once I'm dead?"

Maddox holstered his gun and wrung his hands. "If we're all going to die, why not tell me this. How old is the professor anyway?"

"Older than you can imagine, punk." Villars's grin abruptly slid away. "Why do you want to know anyway? Why aren't you trying to talk me out of...?" Villars's words drifted away. He glanced at Galyan, who watched the proceeding. "Ah... you figured it out, didn't you? Now you're just trying to pump me for information. You're a sly operator, punk." The slarn hunter struggled to free himself of the tangle threads, but it proved impossible. Finally, the man lay still, panting.

"Should I stomp on his hands and break his bones?" Meta asked.

Maddox wondered if the professor was dead or alive. They might need Villars if Ludendorff had died.

"No," the captain said. "Take Villars to the brig. I'm going to warm up the disruptor cannon. Galyan, I'll need your help for that."

"Yes, Captain," the AI said.

"Don't hurt the slarn hunter," Maddox told Meta. "We have to take our time with him later."

"Ah," Meta said. "Yes, I understand." In her power-armor, she scooped up the tangled slarn hunter, marching out of the chamber with him, carrying Villars as if he was an oversized baby wailing while being taken to an unwanted nap.

"What do we do first?" Maddox asked Galyan.

"Leave it to me," the AI said.

***

"The captain did it," Valerie said on the bridge. "Galyan is powering up the disruptor cannon."

"None too soon," Keith said. "How's our shield doing?"

"It won't be up for some time yet," Valerie said.

"Fine," Keith said. "If I can keep the drone from exploding, it won't matter anyway."

"How can you do that?"

"It's going to take combination neutron and disruptor beam fire. I give us a fifty percent chance of success."

"Those are bad odds," Valerie said.

Keith glanced at the sergeant. "Maybe, but they're better than a thirty percent chance. How much longer until I have the disruptor cannon?"

Valerie checked her board. "Two minutes," she said.

The ace grinned in a nasty manner. "That should be just about right. Are you ready?"

"What am I supposed to do?"

"Watch and learn, little lady, and see how it's done."

Valerie grinned tightly. Long ago, his hyper-confidence had bothered her. Now she drew strength from it because everyone was relying on the man. If anyone could do this, it would be Keith.

The ace began maneuvering the starship, once more coming out from behind the asteroid. The sight shocked him and caused Valerie to gasp.

The last drone attacked Ludendorff's asteroid. Massive chunks of rock drifted from the main mass. The red beam sliced off another piece as they watched. Somewhere in the floating jumble of debris was the professor.

"Is he even alive anymore?" Valerie whispered.

The ace shook his head, shivering. That wasn't his concern now. He had to destroy the Builder drone.

"Here goes," Keith said, stabbing the control.

The purple neutron beam lanced from the starship, only to be halted by the drone's shield. The same old contest began as the silver missile-shaped object continued to ray the disintegrating asteroid base.

152

"You can't let the drone explode," Valerie said.

Keith didn't say a word. He already knew that. The professor might have survived the other nova-blasts. He wouldn't survive another.

Soon, the starship's antimatter cyclers howled, pumping the disruptor cannon with energy. Keith kept glancing at his board, waiting for the firing control to turn green.

"There's an energy spike over there," Valerie warned. "I think it's getting ready to self-destruct."

The ace's teeth ground together, making an ugly noise. Then, the control turned green. The drone was still in his targeting array. Keith pressed the control. With a loud sound, the disruptor ray fired its globule of force.

The neutron beam had considerably weakened the drone's shield. Maybe the alien AI over there knew that.

"It's self destructing," Valerie whispered.

Then an interesting sequence of events began. The neutron beam poured destructive force against the drone shield, turning it critical. The shield went down at the first touch of the disruptor glob. At the same moment, the drone ignited in a thermonuclear explosion. The disruptor energy "devoured" some of that annihilating force, weakening what should have been a killing explosion.

Valerie watched her instruments with absorbing interest. She had never seen or even read about something like this. The two forces partly cancelled each other out, like tons of dynamite used to quell a forest fire.

The remaining atomic energies billowed outward in a subdued blast. The collapsium armor shielded the crew from most of it.

Ludendorff's asteroid didn't fare as well. The rest of the planetoid broke apart, although the pieces didn't all fly away. Instead, the asteroid became its own mini-field, the many pieces large and small drifting together in a churning circular mass.

As the disruptor cannon powered down, Keith sat back in his seat and swiveled around. "What do you think? Is the crazy professor still alive out there?"

153

Valerie sat hunched over her panel, her gaze glued to the instruments. Without looking up, she said, "That's what I'm attempting to discover."

* * *

Once more, Maddox found himself in the shuttle, creeping toward the smashed asteroid. This time, Keith piloted the craft. Meta remained aboard *Victory* with Riker, watching the prisoner. Dana sat beside the captain, studying her panel as she searched for signs of life in the space debris.

From the starship, Galyan also tracked the rocks and radioactive dust. So far, no one had found any signs of life.

Ludendorff's archeological partners were locked in their quarters aboard the starship. This time, the AI wouldn't release them unless Maddox gave the order.

"I'm slowing down," Keith said. Like Maddox and Dana, the ace wore a vacc-suit with helmet. It was a precaution against the heavy radiation outside.

The captain watched Keith work, amazed. He couldn't believe the destruction out here. Why had the drones concentrated on the asteroid base? It didn't make sense. They had certainly destroyed the asteroid.

Driblets of noise tapped against the hull outside, pebbles striking the shuttle as the ace tried to maneuver through the space junk.

"Ludendorff must be dead," Keith said.

Maddox caught the ace's eye and shook his head. Keith raised his eyebrows. Maddox twisted his head toward Dana.

The doctor sat hunched over her board with an intense look of concern on her features.

Keith gave the captain another questioning glance.

Maddox tried to give the pilot a look that said, "I'll tell you later."

That seemed to work. The ace resumed piloting without further comment.

"How long do you think we have?" Maddox asked Dana.

"Excuse me?" the doctor said in a lifeless voice.

"Will more drones come?"

"Why ask me?" Dana said. "I have no earthly idea."

"It's probably smart to go off what we've seen so far," Keith said. "The drones must have a central computer headquarters somewhere in the asteroid belt. Valerie told me the star system is the Bermuda Triangle of space. Until now, though, no one has seen these drones."

"The New Men must have seen them," Maddox said. "Likely, they captured one and learned how to construct the device that shoots the red beam."

"Let me rephrase," Keith said. "No one on our side has seen these drones and lived to tell about it. I'd sure like to know how the New Men got hold of their first drone."

"Yes," Maddox agreed. "It might explain many things."

"Captain," Galyan said over the comm.

"Maddox here."

"I have discovered an anomaly in the debris," Galyan said. "Would you like its coordinates?"

"Please," Maddox said.

"I am downloading them into the shuttle's computers," Galyan said.

Dana worked her board. She read the information to Keith. The pilot moved deeper into the mess, easing them past large spinning boulders. He braked, went "up," braked again, slid sideways and put on a burst of speed to get past a thousand-ton chunk as it sped at them.

Dana stared out of the blast window. "We'll never make it out of here."

"Don't worry, love," Keith said. "If I can get us in, I can get us out again."

"What if the Builders left a bomb in the debris?" Dana asked.

"What if your legs fall off?" Keith asked.

The doctor's head turned sharply. "What is that supposed to imply?"

"Quit worrying about everything," Keith said.

Dana pursed her lips before resuming her vigil out the blast windows.

Twenty minutes later, Keith brought the shuttle to a slow stop. They were in the middle of the smashed mass of the asteroid. Everywhere Maddox looked sections of asteroid, boulders, rocks and gravelly debris circled the craft. He would never have thought to fly the shuttle through the spinning, moving junk. His estimation of Keith's skills climbed another notch.

"There," Dana said in a stark voice. "I see the professor. He's...he's in a cocoon."

Maddox stood, moving to the windows. Keith adjusted the shuttle's lights. The beams moved across rocks, gravel and then centered on a silky-colored object shaped like a man.

"What's the cocoon's composition?" the captain asked.

Dana studied her panel. "A synthetic fabric," she said. "I've never seen anything like it."

"Where did he get it?" Maddox asked.

Dana turned her haunted eyes on him. "I have no idea, Captain. Why do you think I should know?"

Maddox raised an eyebrow.

"Because I studied with him many years," she said in a softer voice. "This is incredible. I find I'm worried about him. Do you think that's strange, Captain?"

"Not at all," Maddox said. "I think it's perfectly normal."

Dana shook her head. "I should hate the professor, despise him and wish him ill."

"Why?" Maddox asked. "It seems to me he did much to help you."

"He trapped me, is what he did. He tried to bind me to him."

"What I want to know," Keith said, "is who's going to go outside to get him?"

"I will," Maddox said. "I'm the captain. He's part of my crew."

"Could be dangerous," Keith said.

"Could be," Maddox agreed. He headed for the hatch, wondering what the professor had found in the Builder asteroid base.

***

Maddox settled into the thruster pack. He was outside the shuttle in a vacc-suit. It felt lonely out here, and alien. Only a few stars shined through the mass of rocks and debris. He couldn't see anything metallic that would indicate this had been a Builder drone base.

Clicking the last buckle shut, the captain turned on the thruster. He gripped a throttle control and squeezed particles of hydrogen spray from the nozzle. Gently, he moved forward out from under the shuttle.

"Nice and easy, Captain," Keith said in his headphones.

Drifting slowing, making sure to keep his velocity low, Maddox approached the drifting cocoon. It looked considerably larger than a man, with something bulky sitting on its stomach. Had Ludendorff found his treasure? Was the professor alive? If so, why didn't the shuttle's sensors pick anything up? If Ludendorff was dead, who had cocooned him?

There were too many questions. Maddox wondered about another possibility. Every spacefarer feared an inside job, bringing something alien aboard a ship, something that would burst out aggressively and attack the crew.

"Better slow down," Keith said in Maddox's earphones.

With a start, Maddox realized his mind was drifting, too. That was foolish out here. Rotating his body, using a mirror to guide him, Maddox squeezed his throttle control. More white hydrogen mist sprayed from his nozzles, slowing his momentum.

Soon, the captain eased beside the cocooned body. He ran a hand across the surface. It was slick. Maddox brought out an adhesive pad and line, attaching it to the synthetic fabric. The pad lifted the moment Maddox took his hand away. He tried it again and got the same result.

"Trouble?" Keith radioed.

"The adhesive pad isn't sticking to the cocoon," Maddox radioed.

"You might have to push him in then," Keith said.

"Or tie the line around his body," Dana interjected.

"I think I'm going to do both just to be safe," Maddox said.

The captain began the process. He pushed the cocooned body, causing it to drift toward the waiting shuttle. But for every action there was a reaction. Basic physics. The push caused Maddox to go the other way. He adjusted with the throttle-control, using hydrogen mist to stop himself and go forward again. It was important that he not allow the line to pull the tethered cocoon back toward him, or they'd go nowhere. By slow degrees, the two traveled closer and closer to the shuttle.

"Maybe you want to speed the process, sir," Keith radioed.

Maddox frowned. The ace had sounded too carefree just now, maybe even with a forced heartiness.

"Is there a problem?" the captain radioed.

"Oh, no, nothing at all, sir," Keith said.

Maddox wasn't fooled. There *was* a problem, but clearly, the others didn't want to upset his concentration. Therefore, he decided not to worry about it.

Bit by bit, he brought the cocooned professor to the shuttle. Finally, Maddox used the thruster-pack to work his way onto Ludendorff's other side. He slowed them to a halt, finding Dana outside the underbelly hatch.

She propelled herself toward them to help, her tether playing out behind her as she floated closer.

His helmet lamp played over hers, showing nothing but a silver sheen. Together, they raised the cocoon, sliding the unconscious professor through the hatch and into the shuttle.

Soon, the two of them stood in the air-cycler with the cocoon. Oxygen hissed through. Then, cleansing agents sprayed over them, then hot air, and a final billowing mist. The hatch opened into the main shuttle. Maddox staggered through. He'd hooked the thruster-pack onto its rack already.

With a *click*, the captain twisted off his helmet, turning to Dana as she stepped through.

"What is it?" Maddox asked. "What's the problem?"

"You're not going to believe this," Dana said, as she removed her helmet. Her eyes were wide and staring. "The…" She squeezed her eyelids shut before opening them and saying slowly, "The New Men are in the Xerxes System with us."

"What? How?"

Dana shook her head.

Maddox scowled. "How doesn't matter at the moment, does it? They're here. How many star cruisers?"

"Valerie's counted four so far. She said they're appearing near the Nexus."

158

"Appearing? What does that mean? There isn't a Laumer-Point by the Nexus."

"I don't know, Captain. Maybe they have a new star drive, as we do with *Victory*. This is horrible." The doctor stared at Ludendorff. "We have to get out of here. Can you help me move the professor?"

"Have the New Men spotted us?"

"Two star cruisers are heading here."

Maddox's eyes narrowed.

"Please, Captain, help me with the professor. I have to see if he's still alive."

-18-

Dana wanted to weep. She couldn't believe this. She hadn't cried for what seemed like ages now. How could the arrogant Ludendorff bring this out in her? Why had the man gone into the asteroid? What was so damned valuable to risk his life like this?

The captain moved his end of the body effortlessly. The man was impossibly strong. Dana huffed and puffed, straining as they set the cocooned body onto the shuttle's medical cot.

Keith piloted them through the space debris, trying to get to *Victory* before the shuttle was in firing range of the star cruisers.

Can't we get some luck for once, Dana wondered. *Why is it one thing right after another? This really is a cursed star system.*

Maddox stepped back, drawing his gun, standing like a murderous statue waiting to kill.

"What are you doing?" Dana asked.

"Getting ready," the captain said in a determined voice.

"You're going to shoot him?"

"What's on his chest?" the captain asked. "Is it deadly to us?"

Fear surged through Dana. She couldn't lose the professor again. Turning against him in the Adok System all those years ago had been the hardest thing she had ever done. His reaction against her had left her embittered. She knew that now. If she

160

had to make the decision over again, she would stay with the professor and accept whatever fate had in store for her.

Ludendorff didn't seem devilish now. He was unlike anyone she knew. Even Maddox with his hybrid nature failed to rise to Ludendorff's level.

Is this love? Do I need this impossible man?

"I wish you wouldn't wait there like grim Death," Dana told Maddox.

"Get on with it, Doctor."

Dana knew the captain was right to be worried and take precautions. The man was simply doing his job. Still, it was difficult to accept.

But that didn't matter now, did it? Dana opened a drawer and took out a laser scalpel. Her hands shook as she brought up the instrument. If Ludendorff was dead—

I'm a doctor. It's time to be professional. I can cry for Ludendorff later.

The trembling left her hands. Her features hardened. With sure deftness, Dana clicked on the laser and began to cut the silky substance. She had been afraid the synthetic fabric would reflect the laser. It didn't. That was one for their side.

The doctor slit open the substance, revealing a corpse-colored head and neck. The tiny laser light vanished from the tip of the scalpel. Dana froze, staring at an un-breathing Ludendorff.

"Is he alive?" the captain asked.

That tore Dana out of her shock. "Look at him. He's dead."

"Are you sure?" Maddox asked. "Maybe the professor realized what was happening earlier. I wonder if he took Hibernation-7. He has the rubbery look to his skin."

Dana's eyelids fluttered and hope surged in her heart. Hibernation-7 was a drastic drug used by Star Watch in space emergencies. If injected into a person before the heart stopped, it retarded cell death for three days. After that time, the metabolism would return to normal and the deterioration of the body would begin.

Dana pulled out a med-scanner, checking the professor's life signs. Yes! The captain was right. Ludendorff had taken Hibernation-7. She gasped, smiling, relieved at the news.

She picked up the laser scalpel and continued to slice open the cocoon. It revealed a silver oblong object on the professor's stomach. The sides of the thing were smooth. Using the back end of the scalpel, she *clicked* it against the item.

"Metallic," Maddox noted.

"With no visible means of opening," Dana said.

"Do you think it's a container?"

"Don't you?" she asked.

"I have no idea."

"Help me take it off him."

The captain hesitated to give up his watch. Finally, though, he holstered the gun and helped her lift the object off Ludendorff.

It proved heavy, and it almost slipped out of her gasp. Together, the two of them set it to the side.

Dana went back to the death-colored professor and removed the rest of the strange material from him. It was like opening a body bag.

"I'll begin the revival procedure," she said.

"No," Maddox said.

Dana looked up with anger in her eyes.

"He hijacked my starship," Maddox said. "He endangered the entire crew."

"The New Men are out there, Captain. He'll know what to do better than anyone else."

"For all I know, Ludendorff may help the New Men against us," Maddox said. "The professor may have summoned them with his ancient comm-device. Or maybe the professor will attempt to regain control of Galyan. No. I've had quite enough of Ludendorff's machinations for some time."

"What are you suggesting?"

"I'm not suggesting a thing," Maddox said. "I'm making a decision. We will leave the professor in hibernation for the moment. Once aboard *Victory*, I'll put him in deep-freeze. I'll hand him over to Star Watch Intelligence once we get to Earth. The brigadier will know what to do with him."

"We need his knowledge now."

162

Maddox eyed her, with a cool smile hovering on his lips. "We'll strap him in," the captain said. "Then, we'll both see how Keith is doing."

"I'm going to stay here, if you don't mind."

"I most certainly do mind," the captain said. "You're coming with me to see Keith."

"You don't trust me back here?"

"Of course I trust you," Maddox said.

Dana lost some of her tension.

"I trust you to act like a lover and think of the professor first," Maddox said. "That's why I'm keeping you with me for the moment."

"I resent that," Dana said. In her heart, though, the doctor knew the captain was right. Maddox could hardly make any other choice after the things Ludendorff had done.

"Strap him in," Maddox said. "Then come along. I'm not going to give the professor a second chance to wrest control of the starship from me."

***

Valerie waited on *Victory's* bridge, keeping a careful watch on the shuttle working its way out of the asteroidal junk and watching the two star cruisers building velocity in a hurry. The New Men weren't doing anything to hide their advance. So far, the enemy commander over there hadn't tried to communicate with her.

"The shuttle cannot accelerate quickly enough to make it in time," Galyan observed.

Valerie had just about reached the same conclusion.

"We can attack the star cruisers," Galyan suggested.

Valerie nodded thoughtfully. She would like that. In her estimation, she made a good combat officer. The trouble was that she'd never had an opportunity to show anyone. This could be her chance.

"I'm not sure," Valerie said quietly.

"The disruptor cannon is fully operational," Galyan said.

"But the shield is still rebuilding. Plus, I don't have anyone to help me on the bridge."

"I can do that."

163

"Certainly," Valerie said. In her heart, though, she wanted a Star Watch-trained officer to help her, not an alien AI.

"Ah," Galyan said. "I detect another two star cruisers."

"Approaching us?"

"No, coming into existence by the Nexus."

"Is there a special jump gate there?" Valerie wondered.

"I have not detected one."

"Maybe there's another Nexus in New Men-controlled territory. Somehow, they learned we were here and used the silver pyramids to reach us."

"How would that be possible?"

"Didn't you hear?" Valerie asked. "The professor has a distance communicator, another ancient relic. The New Men have a few too. Or maybe the Builder drones alerted the enemy, and the New Men decided to send a few star cruisers over."

"Your possibilities are logical," Galyan said. "Yet, given the star cruisers have just made a tremendous jump, wouldn't that mean the enemy crews would be tired now? That should give us a temporary advantage."

"There is that." Valerie snapped her fingers. "I should have thought of this sooner. Galyan, ready the neutron cannon."

"We're attacking?"

"No. We're going to start blowing away excess debris in the shuttle's path. At the moment, Keith has to ease through the junk, slowing down to avoid rocks and gravel. I plan to give him a clear path so the shuttle can accelerate to us on the double."

Galyan stood perfectly still before saying, "That is an optimum plan. I congratulate you, Lieutenant."

"Thank you," Valerie said. "Let's hope Captain Maddox feels the same way."

***

Maddox sat in the shuttle's control chamber, watching the passive sensor. The two star cruisers were increasing velocity. Their craft would be in red beam range soon.

Outside the asteroid maze, *Victory's* neutron beam smashed rubble into fine particles. The ace threaded through the debris

164

on their side, taking more chances than Maddox thought wise. The alternative was worse, though, so he kept his mouth shut.

"Maybe we could make a deal with the New Men," Dana suggested.

Maddox knew that was her love for Ludendorff speaking. There would be no deals with the New Men. If these were the "good" ones the professor had spoken about before, why were they bearing down on them so hard? No. These were the regular New Men, invaders who gave no quarter. There was only one way to fight them; no-holds-barred.

Keith sat back and swiveled to face Maddox. "We're not going to make it like this, sir," the ace declared.

"Suggestions?" Maddox asked.

"Increase acceleration as we roll the dice."

"With what breaks through our hull and ricochets around inside?" the captain asked.

"That's right."

Maddox only needed to debate the idea a moment. The other alternative was to wait for the star cruisers to destroy them once the enemy got in range. "Do it," the captain said.

"No," Dana said. "That doesn't make sense to take needless risks. We're so close to our ship."

"It's a bitter choice, I realize," Maddox said. "But we're out of options."

"We can't keep attempting hazardous selections like this," Dana said. "One of these times, the risks are going to catch up with us."

"These are the New Men we're dealing with," Maddox said. "We're forced into one hazardous venture after another because we're playing to win. There is no coming in second to them."

"We're humanity's last hope against the planet-killer," Dana said. "Ludendorff is our only hope against stopping it. We can't afford to die just yet."

"Negative," Maddox said. "There's always more than one way to win, even for humanity. Or haven't you ever heard of the test they gave a chimpanzee?"

Dana stared at him.

"In an intelligence study," Maddox said, "scientists once gave an imprisoned chimpanzee fifteen ways to escape. The ape found the sixteenth."

"That doesn't prove anything out here," Dana said in exasperation.

"Go," Maddox told Keith. Afterward, the captain put his helmet back on.

"Someone should look after the professor," Dana said.

Maddox studied her, finally nodding. "Go," he said.

"Now you trust me?" Dana asked in a bitter tone.

"Would you tell me if I shouldn't?"

Dana peered at him thoughtfully. "After all we've been through, yes, I would tell you if you shouldn't."

"I believe you," Maddox said, although he wasn't really sure he did.

His words made the doctor smile sadly. She locked her helmet to the vacc-suit, got up and hurried from the chamber.

"Here we go," Keith said, while increasing velocity. "We're playing craps in space."

The shuttle continued to dodge and weave through the debris, but more pebbles struck the hull. Then a fist-sized rock bounced off the armor, leaving a large dent outside. More debris struck, one plowing through the hull armor. It shattered a water line in a secondary compartment. Moisture sprayed into the sudden vacuum. Hatches sealed. The line froze and the shuttle continued through the mass.

"I don't know, Captain," Keith said. "This isn't looking good for us."

"Where's the optimist I've come to know?" Maddox asked.

"He's struggling to break free of his pessimism, sir."

"Faster," Maddox said.

Keith bit his lower lip as he obeyed orders. The shuttle jinked one way and then another. The gravity dampeners purred at maximum. A larger boulder tumbled toward them. Keith couldn't avoid it altogether. The tons of stone smashed one of the stubby wings and shredded open that side. The shuttle began to tumble end over end.

Maddox hoped the doctor had made it to medical in time to strap herself down.

166

The ace struggled to right the craft. He might have won the contest. He was the master ace after all, but the craft plowed against another massive object, and they began to spin.

"We rolled snakes eyes this time, sir!" Keith shouted.

"Captain Maddox," Valerie radioed.

Without the gravity dampeners in operation, not even Maddox would have been able to lift his arms. He tapped his board, saying, "Maddox here."

"The enemy vessels have locked onto you, sir," Valerie said. "I'm heading for you. Maybe if we can get close enough, I can try to energize the shield with you inside."

"Valerie!" Keith shouted, even as he worked the controls.

"Yes?" she said.

"I have a better idea. You have to swoop onto us and use the star drive at the same time. Hopefully, what's left of our shuttle will be caught up in your wash."

"You think you'll jump with us?" Valerie asked.

"It's one of the theoretical problems we had on Titan," the ace said. "It might work."

"What do you think, sir?" Valerie asked Maddox.

"Do it, Lieutenant. Once the star cruisers fire their beams, we're dead anyway. This at least gives us a chance, however slim."

"Roger," Valerie said. "I'm on my way. This is going to get tricky."

Keith continued to fight against the out-of-control shuttle. He braked, used side-jets and applied thrust against the spin of the craft.

"If we can keep from hitting another rock," the ace said, "I'll be happy."

Maddox studied the passive sensor. The lead enemy star cruiser was in beam-firing range. A light appeared on the comm-board. The captain slapped it.

A second later, a New Man appeared on the screen. He was lean like all the others, with golden skin and a sneering manner.

"Surrender or die," the New Man said.

"We surrender," Maddox said.

The New Man nodded. "The alien craft attempting to rescue you must immediately break off."

"At once, Your Excellency," Maddox said.

"The star cruiser is firing," Keith said. "His talk was a trick to lull us."

Maddox didn't know why the New Man had bothered.

Keith jinked wildly. Because of their spin, the end of the shuttle violently flipped upward. The red beam slashed where the aft part of the craft had just been.

The shuttle now tumbled out of control faster than ever. A gravity dampener blew, sending dense smoke into the compartment.

Maddox knew the enemy must be retargeting them. Why had the New Man lied about asking for surrender?

Another gravity dampener gave out with a screeching sound. The tumbling end-over-end now produced too many Gs. Keith's head slumped forward as the ace passed out. Maddox hung onto consciousness a little longer.

Then, Starship *Victory* filled the window outside.

Are we jumping? It was the captain's last conscious thought before he too passed out from lack of blood to the brain.

-19-

Kane sat in the control room of his nondescript scout. He'd already spent many lonely days among the space debris in the Epsilon Indi System. He'd reached here from the Beyond in a single, agonizing leap. It had taken Kane twelve hours to recover sufficiently to drag himself to sickbay. The agony of the jump...he never wanted to do anything remotely like that again.

The K class star was twelve light-years from the Solar System. Instead of planets, Epsilon Indi had binary brown dwarfs as companions. The two masses—the larger sixty times greater than Jupiter—circled each other at 2.1 AUs. The brown dwarfs orbited Epsilon Indi at 1500 AUs. The pulling, twisting gravities of the star and its brown dwarfs had made this an unprofitable system for the larger corporations and even for the independence-minded wildcatters. No useful planets or asteroids orbited here. Despite the unprofitability of Epsilon Indi, because of the system's proximity to Earth, Star Watch sent regular patrols through and often left recording buoys.

According to Kane's sensors, the buoys had failed to detect his appearance into the system. His masters had perfected the art of long-distance insertions. It was one of the Throne World's key espionage secrets. The only trouble was the process often called for an agent's patience as he waited for pickup.

During Kane's wait, he exercised with the enabler in the small gym, and later he practiced mental calisthenics. Every time his thoughts drifted to Meta or even to Captain Maddox, Kane deliberately shifted focus. It was time to forget the woman. What did he gain by thinking of Meta's beautiful form and her intriguing features? It's true she had an innate and physical strength that he found appealing...

Kane paused in his thoughts, as he lay stretched out on his cot. Unable to tear his imagination from her, he continued to ponder on what it would feel like running his hands over her voluptuous body.

As the here-again, gone-again owner of the Los Angeles Wolverines, Kane had had his pick of Earth's beauties for some time. The last indulgence had been with Susan Love the fashion model. He had found their couplings to be tedious affairs. He'd had to hold back lest his greater mass and strength cripple the so-called "insatiable lover." It would be different with a strong woman like Meta. He would be able to let himself go and enjoy the process as he wished.

"No," Kane rumbled. "Release the thought. Concentrate on the commando mission."

He wondered about his fixation on Meta. Yes. That's what it was, wasn't it? The woman refused to depart his mind. After kidnapping Meta in New York City, he had held back with her for so long that it had started to bother him. During their time together, she had been his for the taking. Yet, Kane had realized then that the dominants would be displeased if he'd used her sexually. They'd wanted an unsullied captive on the off chance they would have desired to send her to the breeding masters.

Kane scowled.

The dominants desired to do the breeding that improved the human race. Kane's genetic material was considered inferior compared to the perfection of the Throne World's highest citizens.

Kane frowned, realizing that he continued to indulge in fantasies. The Throne World believed in pure thought, not in rutting with the mongrel races. The New Order demanded perfection from the human race. There would be no random couplings that produced freaks, sports and retards. It was a wonder humanity had managed to populate so many star

170

systems. The chaos inherent in their genetic randomness should have already produced a vast breakdown in stellar society.

Kane wondered if the best minds on the Throne World tackled the dilemma of the flood of weak genetics. He'd never been to the heart of the New Order. He didn't know what it was like on the Throne World. Kane had been to a genetic facility on a lesser world, though. He never desired to return. From what he'd witnessed, it was clear the masters treated the lower orders like cattle.

Kane pondered his own position. He engaged in a critical commando mission for Oran Rva. Surely, the dominant realized his genetic inheritance exceeded regular humans by several factors. Would that continue once the Throne World conquered Human Space? If Kane managed to take Methuselah Treatments to gain extended life, would he progressively lose rank as the rest of humanity improved genetically? Those as good as he was would grow in number, as those genetically beneath him were eliminated.

Kane sat up, shaking his head. This was useless speculation. The Throne World would win the war. Of that, there could be no doubt.

He got up, moving down the corridor toward the exercise chamber. As he did, Kane paused. He rubbed his forehead before a hatch he was unable to acknowledge. Sometimes, it felt as if he carried a hidden passenger in the scout. That was a strange sensation without any logical reason. With a shrug, Kane kept moving.

Soon, he stood in the exercise chamber. He wrapped his fists and hit a heavy bag, working out for the next hour.

A warning *beep* caused him to step back from the swaying bag and lower his throbbing hands. He moved down a corridor to the control chamber. A number flashed across the piloting monitor.

Kane unwound the wraps, rushing to his chair and sliding into it. He tapped out a coded sequence. Afterward, he found himself breathing heavily in anticipation.

That was wrong. He must wait for his message to reach the Cestus hauler moving through the system.

Kane's scout drifted among a cluster of rocks. The star was far away. The brown dwarfs were closer, but far enough away that their heavy radiation didn't reach his ship in sufficient quantity to cause him harm.

There were several Laumer-Points in the system. None of them linked directly to important nodes. It's what made Epsilon Indi so useful to the Throne World's secret service—a quiet star system near Earth.

Kane forced himself to stand. When he found himself watching the monitor, even though the hauler couldn't possibly return a message yet, he knew he had to depart the chamber.

He went back to the exercise room, stepping on a rotation wheel. He began to run, spinning the wheel as sweat appeared on his skin. Like a rhinoceros, he charged kilometer after kilometer.

The time approached when he would reenter the chaotic world of free humanity. Star Watch Intelligence would be waiting for him.

On the wheel, a smile stretched across Kane's square face. He yearned for the challenge. If Meta should cross his path during the mission... Kane's eyes narrowed. He would use her, as he should have done many months ago.

Kane let a low rumble of laughter escape his throat. As he did, a warning sound came from the control cabin.

Kane stepped off the rotation wheel. With a sure stride, he reentered the control chamber. He nodded to himself.

In the distance moved a gigantic hauler. It was vast, approaching the size of a Spacer home-ship. The vessel was gunmetal-colored with thousands of lights to show its outline. Kilometer tall letters and numbers showed this to be Cestus Hauler EV-3498-Z109.

Buckling himself into the piloting chair, Kane acknowledged the coded signal. He made a last sweep of the nearby system to make sure no buoy or Star Watch destroyer waited to spot him.

The minutes fled as he waited. Kane noted no probes or hidden Star Watch vessels. Only when he was certain of this did he ease from the jumble of space debris.

172

By dumping gravity waves, he increased velocity for the gliding hauler. It headed for a distant Laumer-Point. Out here, the giant vessel should still be increasing velocity. Instead, it glided through the stellar night. A passing Star Watch patrol might think the hauler captain was trying to save on fuel costs. Accelerating and decelerating the massive ship was expensive.

Three hours passed before the Cestus hauler loomed massive before Kane's tiny vessel. He slowed, drifting toward a select spot on the giant frame.

No more messages came his way. No one on the hauler thought to ask for identification. The process was exact. As the scout came within collision distance, hangar bay doors opened.

Kane eased the scout into the giant vessel. Behind him, the bay doors closed. With great care, Kane guided the scout through a long corridor past many containers. Finally, he landed in a location deep inside the ship.

Shutting down everything—

Kane groaned. Pain spiked in his head. He hesitated to tap the last control that would shut off all power in the scout. Instead, he arose from his seat, walking robotically down a corridor and stopping before a hatch he had never consciously recognized. To Kane, this felt like a dream.

He pressed a switch and a panel opened. A small screen activated, showing him a number pad. Grunting, Kane stepped closer and tapped a precise sequence onto the pad.

A *thrum* began on the other side of the hatch. Curiosity shined in Kane's mind. What was inside the compartment? What did—?

Once more, pain spiked inside Kane's head. He groaned. The hatch and the number pad became fuzzy and then altogether disappeared in Kane's mind. He turned away from it even as a *clack* of noise occurred inside the compartment.

The robotic nature of his movements faded as he walked away. Finally, he donned a vacc-suit, forgetting the dream about a strange hatch and its hidden compartment.

Kane exited the scout and walked for many kilometers in the vacuum of the hauler's cargo halls. He entered a secret module, sealed the hatch behind him and moved to a panel. Tapping the correct sequence, part of the wall opened. If he had failed the sequence code, hot plasma would have flushed the chamber to turn him into a pile of molten molecules. Instead, Kane found a locker for his suit and the case of advanced weaponry.

He'd safely made it to the insertion hauler. Now, the cargo vessel would journey to Earth. It would easily pass any coming inspections. Once in Low Earth Orbit, Kane would perform a dangerous, sub-aqua entry onto the planet. Then, he would make the deadly commando raid against Nerva Tower in Monte Carlo, collecting the critical key.

-20-

By slow degrees, Maddox woke up on a medical bed aboard Starship *Victory*. Meta stood by the railing, smiling down at him. It seemed as if she towered kilometers above him.

"Don't strain yourself," Meta said, touching his arm with a warm hand. He liked that. "If you're wondering how you got here, Galyan used a tractor beam, bringing the shuttle under control."

She spoke. Maddox could see her lips move. He concentrated. Oh. Yes. The shuttle. He remembered spinning wildly. A tractor beam, *Victory* had a tractor beam? Pain blossomed in his brain then.

"Rest, darling," Meta said. "Keith's idea worked. Your shuttle entered the star drive with us. We reappeared several light years outside the Xerxes System. Your shuttle kept tumbling, and it took a while for Galyan to recover from Jump Lag. That's why all four of you are in medical. It was a close thing."

Maddox heard the words more easily this time. But the pulsating in his head weakened his resolve to stay awake.

"You're okay now," she said, stroking his arm.

Maddox tried to anchor onto the comforting sensation.

"You're all just going to be tired for a while," she said.

The pain in his head was starting to make him nauseous. Then, he realized something critical. He battled against the drowsiness in order to tell Meta. That hurt his head even more, and he considered closing his eyes and going to sleep.

No! He refused. This was too important. Maddox struggled against the beckoning sleep, finally managing to whisper a word.

"Please, Maddox. You're not supposed to strain yourself. Go back to sleep. We can talk later."

He couldn't do that because the stakes were too high. There might not be a later if he couldn't get his words out. With a straining effort—making his eyesight blotchy—Maddox managed to wheeze, "The professor."

"Okay... What about him?"

Waves of exhaustion rolled against Maddox. Speaking had taken more out of him than it should have. What was wrong with him? He didn't know. Worse, he felt his mouth closing as he shut down. With a final effort, he struggled against that. The fight made the pain in his head turn into gongs of agony.

"Shhh, go to sleep, darling."

He almost listened to her. Somewhere deep inside him he realized that he was Captain Maddox of Star Watch Intelligence. He wouldn't quit until he was dead. He had to speak, forcing his lips to move and his throat to convulse.

"Put...the...Professor..."

A warm hand squeezed his forearm.

Maddox couldn't see anything now. The waves of exhaustion deadened his weak energy, trying to pull him down into unconsciousness.

They tormented my mother! That did it. A surge of strength gave him the power to speak:

"Put the professor...in deep freeze. Don't let him...wake up."

"What?" Meta asked.

Maddox strove to explain it.

"Yes, of course," she said, with worry in her voice. "I'll do what you say. Now go to sleep. Regain your strength."

Maddox still wanted to say more. And he wondered if Meta was just saying that? He felt like a drowning man sinking into the depths, struggling to get back to the surface where the light shined.

"I think I know what's bothering you," a faint voice said. "Valerie said we're headed for Earth. Command needs to know what's going on. We have to get ready against the doomsday machine. Don't worry, we know."

The exhaustion finally conquered Maddox. The effort to remain awake was simply too much. Quietly, he slipped into the depths of a numbed state of unconsciousness.

***

Due to his superior healing abilities, Maddox was the first to recover sufficiently to leave his medical bed. He found, to his great relief, that Meta had transferred the professor into a stasis tank. It was the old way of space travel. With Riker's help, Meta had also "frozen" the rest of Ludendorff's team, including Villars.

His woman had known what to do. Because of Meta, that danger was over.

So much about Ludendorff troubled Maddox. The appearance of New Men by the Nexus also worried him to no end. Just how much Builder technology did the enemy possess?

It was time to solve a few of these mysteries. Where should he start? Maddox decided on the time-honored Intelligence technique of searching the offender's quarters. He summoned Riker, and they headed to the professor's room.

"I suspect Ludendorff has a great many secrets," Maddox said as they walked down a corridor. "He also strikes me as someone who would booby-trap his possessions. We must proceed with caution."

Riker nodded. The sergeant carried detection equipment. The various items dangled from straps around his shoulders and neck.

They entered the room and began checking the closet, drawers and mattress. They searched for secret compartments in the walls, floor and ceiling. They found slacks, shirts, jackets, shoes, a few useless knickknacks and several pill bottles and sheaves of notes.

"What does an ancient long-distance communicator look like?" the sergeant asked. That was the chief item on their list.

"I have no idea," Maddox said.

In the end, they placed three peculiar items on the table in the room. One was the flat device that had projected the web field. The second was a small chain and bulbous object, which Maddox suspected was the personal force-field protector. The third looked like an ordinary tablet.

"It's clean," Riker said, waving a detection wand over the tablet.

Maddox sat down at the table, flexing his fingers. He tapped the tablet's screen, examining the options. The tablet lacked a security code, which he found odd. Soon, Maddox read the most recent notes.

One in particular interested him. *What did Meta see aboard the star cruiser in Wolf Prime orbit? You must break her mind-lock. Was* HE *there? I'm beginning to suspect so.*

Who was HE? Maddox wondered. Whom would Ludendorff suspect? The captain drummed his fingers on the table. Could Ludendorff mean the teacher?

"Find something?" Riker asked.

"Maybe." Maddox tapped the screen again, searching for more clues. He found a file with a security code. After a moment's hesitation, he attempted to crack it.

The tablet buzzed.

"Look out!" Riker shouted, dropping to the floor.

With the flat of his hand, Maddox swept the device off the table and against a bulkhead. He dove onto the floor, covering his head as the tablet exploded. It sent hot shards of plastic everywhere, but missed the captain and the sergeant, who had each instinctively positioned himself behind a bulky object.

Riker raised his head. So did Maddox. Acrid smoke drifted into his nostrils. He glanced at the sergeant's detection gear.

"It didn't spot anything," Riker admitted.

"I doubt that should surprise us. Clearly, the professor has access to advanced technology."

Standing, Riker glanced at the flat device still on the table. "Do we try to hack into it next?"

"No," Maddox said, heading for the exit. "I'm locking the room. We'll leave the last two items here."

Once outside the room, they headed for the cafeteria. As they did, the ship's intercom clicked on.

"Attention," Valerie told them. "We're approaching our next Laumer-Point. We'll jump in another half hour. That is all."

***

After recovering from Jump Lag, Maddox sat at his desk in his quarters. He thought about the silver object Ludendorff had carried out of the Builder base. So far, no one had been able to figure out what it was. Should they crack it? Maddox agreed with Dana that they should save the Builder egg for the Star Watch experts back home.

The captain pondered other things, including his interview with Per Lomax and the Throne World's desire to "improve" humanity by culling eighty percent. That turned his thoughts toward the origin of the New Men.

Whoever had come up with the idea of creating superior humans had changed Maddox's life. Without the idea, his mother would never have been a test subject in a genetic laboratory in the Beyond. There never would have been New Men to begin with. He wouldn't be a hybrid, a half-breed, an outsider among his own people.

Leave that black hole for now. Don't let it suck you into useless speculation. Concentrate on solving mysteries.

Maddox thought about Meta's close contact with the enemy. The New Men had questioned her in Wolf Prime orbit. He wished he knew what those questions were. It might give him a better insight into the enemy, and clues to the doomsday machine.

The professor had wondered if HE had been aboard the vessel. That must refer to the teacher. Who would have a close connection with Ludendorff and the New Men? The teacher...clearly, the mind-manipulating bastard had gone to great lengths to keep hidden whatever he'd done to Meta.

Who is HE? I'd dearly like to know.

Abruptly, Maddox headed for the exit. Had the professor planted the clue in the tablet in order to get him to chase shadows? It was possible. Since he had nothing else to go on, Maddox decided it was worth a try to discover the answer. Besides, as smart as the professor was, he didn't think

179

Ludendorff would plan for his own failure. The man didn't think like that. Therefore, Maddox believed it was a genuine clue.

***

Meta practiced in the ship's gym, snap kicking a heavy bag. Upon Maddox's entrance, she stepped away from the bag and picked up a towel, drying her face. Draping the towel around her neck, she smiled at him.

"I've been thinking about the origin of the New Men," Maddox told her.

Meta's shoulders deflated. "You're not going to ask me questions about them, are you?"

"I'd like to," he said.

"I'm sick of the subject."

"I realize that," Maddox said, "but it could be vital."

Meta looked away, sighing. Finally, she stepped close to Maddox, peering up into his eyes. "I'll do it for you."

"I appreciate that," he said, as he brushed her hair back.

She nodded.

Maddox had already decided how to broach the difficult idea. He would circle it first before asking. "You once spoke about Per Lomax being Kane's spy chief, isn't that right?"

"I did," Meta said.

"On the enemy star cruiser, what happened after Kane spoke to Per Lomax."

Meta's lips tightened. "I don't remember."

"Which part?" Maddox asked.

Meta gave him a funny look. "If I can't remember, how could I tell you?"

Maddox spoke easily, even though he chose his next words with care. "Per Lomax sent you somewhere."

"Yes. He sent me to the teacher."

"What happened with him?"

Meta massaged her temples. "I want to remember for you. You say it's important, and I believe you. But it was a terrifying time. I want to forget it. I—Wait!" Meta lowered her hands, looking at Maddox with surprise. "I seem to recall a spinning table. The teacher twisted my mind while—" Meta

180

groaned as she scrunched her brow. "I already told you what I know. Why are you asking me this all over again?"

Maddox held her shoulders. He disliked causing her pain. More than ever, though, he believed the professor was onto something. The captain had to follow this single clue.

"I know this is difficult for you, and I'm sorry for that," Maddox said, meaning it. "You're doing well. If you can push just a little more, I need to know what the teacher looked like?"

Meta frowned, shaking her head. "I don't know."

"The teacher hid himself from your memories. I'm beginning to think he did so for a reason."

"What reason?"

"Yes," Maddox said. "That's the question. Why would the teacher hide himself? You were to go down onto Wolf Prime afterward. You would go to Ludendorff—" Maddox stopped as if surprised.

"What?" Meta asked.

"How do you feel about taking truth serum?"

Meta's stricken look gave Maddox the answer he'd expected.

He stroked his chin as if thinking. "What if Dana spoke to you again, using hypnosis as she did before?"

Meta hesitated before saying, "I hated the process. But I'll do it if you think it might help against the planet-killer."

"I don't know for certain that it will help, but there is a possibility."

"How do you know?" she asked.

"I don't know," Maddox admitted. "This is one of my Intelligence hunches."

Meta considered that, finally nodding.

"I need to talk to the doctor," Maddox said. "Thanks, Meta. I appreciate this."

She nodded again.

Maddox turned and headed for the hatch.

***

Maddox found Dana in the cafeteria, eating ice cream. He sat down across from her.

"I've been thinking about the New Men," Maddox said without preamble. "I feel as if I'm closing in on a truth about them, but I need a few more clues. Their goal has begun to strike me as too strange. Why should they worry so much about improving the human race? What propelled them to think in such a direction in the first place?"

Dana slid a spoonful of ice cream into her mouth, savoring it before aiming the spoon at Maddox. "It's an interesting question. Why are you telling me, though?"

"Several months ago, Kane took Meta onto a star cruiser in Wolf Prime orbit. Per Lomax then sent Meta to the teacher. This teacher went out of his way to hide himself from Meta's memories. I'd like to know why and see what it shows me."

"Maybe the teacher is a cultic figure among the New Men," Dana said. "Part of his mystique is that no one remembers talking to him."

"I don't believe that's the answer."

Dana shrugged. "What would you like me to do?"

"Hypnotize Meta again and see if you can break through the blockage."

"I failed last time. Why do you think I'll succeed now?"

"I don't know that you will," Maddox said.

Dana considered that. "You have a hunch about the teacher, don't you?"

"I suppose I do."

Dana stirred her half-melted ice cream. "Why don't we ask the professor about the teacher? That sounds easier and more productive than this."

The doctor clearly wanted to thaw Ludendorff, something Maddox had no intention of doing. It had taken too much work to gain control of the professor. He wasn't going to give Ludendorff a second chance. He didn't like to give false hopes to anyone. Sometimes, though, any kind of hope was better than none at all. Especially if that motivated the person to do what Maddox wanted them to do.

"It may come down to thawing Ludendorff," the captain said, "depending on what you find with Meta."

Dana raised her eyebrows. "I'll do it then," she said.

Maddox nodded. Could he finally discover the identity of the mysterious teacher?

***

As Dana spoke quietly, Meta closed her eyes, trying to relax as she lay on a couch. It bothered her that anyone had ever been able to twist her thoughts. She also hated having been Kane's captive for so long. It was something she'd been trying to forget. She kept wondering if Maddox secretly held it against her.

"Meta," Dana said.

"Hmm…?"

"I'm going to ask you a few questions. It doesn't matter how you answer."

"Okay."

"This is just between you and me. We've been friends a long time in rough situations. We've always known that we had each other's back."

"That's true," Meta said in a sleepy voice.

Dana began to drone on. She touched on topics they both enjoyed. The doctor spoke about Loki Prime, asked some questions about the frigid weather on Wolf Prime, and drifted to the journey through space with Kane.

Meta felt herself slipping into a half-awake state. If anyone other than Dana had been doing this, she would have resisted. It seemed as if she dreamed in a hazy sort of way. The questions became more troubling. Meta's brow furrowed as her memories returned to the star cruiser in Wolf Prime orbit.

The deadly ship had seemed empty, which Meta had found strange at the time. Per Lomax had been so arrogant. He'd become angry with Kane much too easily. It had been bizarre.

Dana's voice droned on in Meta's ear. Her memories took her back to the star cruiser. Meta moved down a corridor to the teacher's chamber. Then, everything became hazy and indistinct.

Fear welled up in Meta. She cried out on the couch.

"No, no, don't be afraid," a friendly woman said.

183

"I am, though," Meta said. She no longer realized the voice belonged to Dana. The knowledge had become dream-indistinct. "I hate this place."

"Why do you fear?"

"He's going to enter my mind," Meta said. "He's going to twist my thoughts."

"Who is?"

"The teacher. I hate him. He's a vile manipulator."

"Would you like to punch him in the face?"

"I would love that," Meta said. "Even better, I'd like to break his scrawny neck."

"How can you do that if you don't know what he looks like?"

"That's right," Meta said. "That's a good point."

"Keep walking down the corridor. Go to the teacher so you can see what he looks like."

Meta cringed. "No…please don't make me go there."

"No one is going to *make* you. You're doing this in order to trick him."

"I don't understand," Meta said.

"You're the assassin. You can pretend better than anyone can. You'll get to know him, his habits—"

"I don't want to be a secret killer," Meta said, interrupting. "It hurts too much."

"What do you want?"

"I want to go home. I want to be with Maddox. I don't want to have these awful feelings inside me anymore."

"I know how to make the bad feelings go away."

"Tell me, *please*," Meta pleaded. "I'll do anything to get rid of them."

"You have to take a good hard look at the teacher. Then you're going to tell me what he looks like, and I'll tell Maddox."

"What will the captain do about it?" Meta asked.

"What do you think the captain will do?"

On the couch, Meta smiled savagely. "Maddox will *kill* the teacher."

"The teacher's death will free you from the bad feelings."

"Do you really think so?" Meta asked in a timid voice.

There was a pause that seemed to lengthen. Could the speaker be hesitating? "Yes, Meta. The teacher's death will free you from the bad feelings. I'm certain."

"Okay," Meta whispered. "I'll try to look at the manipulator one more time."

And she did. Meta slid down the tube of her memories, down, down, down to the time in the star cruiser. She found herself walking down a corridor, approaching an evil hatch. The corridors were gleaming silver, so bright, so very bright. Her steps slowed. She didn't want to go in there.

Then, the hatch slid open into darkness. The teacher stepped out of the darkness into the silver light. In that moment, Meta could see him, and she described the man to Dana.

The teacher wore Earth clothes; a bent old man in a suit. He held a cane with a quivering, wrinkled hand. His head seemed too heavy for his frail frame. The skin looked waxy as if it belonged to a mannequin. The blue eyes, however, were alive with burning curiosity. A New Man stepped up behind the oldster, waiting. The New Man wore a silver suit, and he obeyed the frail human, acting instantly at each grumbled command.

Soon after describing the teacher, Meta fell into a deep sleep. She didn't see Dana get up and hurry into the corridor.

***

"This doesn't make sense," Maddox said, after listening to Dana. "The description fits Strand, the chief of Nerva Security on Earth. What was Strand doing on a star cruiser in Wolf Prime orbit?"

"Nerva Security?" asked Dana. "Strand works for Octavian Nerva?"

"That's right."

"Is Strand a Methuselah Man?" Dana asked.

Maddox snapped his fingers. There was the connection with Ludendorff. Did that mean the Methuselah People worked with the New Men? Or did it mean the Methuselah People had something to do with the Thomas Moore Society colonists one hundred and fifty years ago? Had the Methuselah People

185

initially created the beginning New Men? Why stop there? If Strand was on a star cruiser and he worked for Octavian Nerva, why couldn't Octavian have used the Cestus Hauling Company to send secret shipments to the fledging Throne World long ago? That might explain how a tiny, cut-off colony world could expand into an industrial giant in a few generations.

"What I'd like to know," Maddox said, "is how Strand beat us to Wolf Prime."

"What do you mean?"

Maddox told the doctor about his run-in with Strand and Octavian in Monte Carlo before he'd left for the Oort cloud and later Wolf Prime.

"Interesting," Dana said. "The way I see it, there's two ways Strand could have beaten you. One, he hid on Kane's scout, hitching a ride to Wolf Prime."

"I've already thought of that," Maddox said. "What's the other way?"

"The Strand Meta saw was a clone of the one in Monte Carlo. You've told me before that Octavian Nerva keeps clone guards on his premises even though that's against Commonwealth laws."

Maddox sat down, staring up at the ceiling. "What do we know about the Methuselah People?" Maddox asked the doctor.

"They live longer. They seldom get colds, flus or other sicknesses, and they—"

"When I met him," Maddox said, interrupting, "Strand was incurably sick yet he still had unnatural vitality. Is that why he helps the New Men?"

"I don't know."

Maddox eyed Dana as his thoughts shifted. "Would a Methuselah Man become a slarn trapper on Wolf Prime?"

"I'm sure I don't know," the doctor said.

"That strikes me as odd. Ludendorff employing a man like Villars also seemed strange. Maybe they've worked with each other a long time."

"Villars wasn't on the original expedition when I was with the professor," Dana said.

Maddox gave the doctor a careful scrutiny.

186

"Now what is it?" she asked.

Maddox wanted answers, not more questions. He did not intend to wake up Ludendorff. Villars, on the other hand, was more emotional and lacked the professor's uncanny intellect. If Villars had been with the professor long enough, the slarn hunter might know critical facets of information about the mysterious Ludendorff.

Maddox stood, saying, "It's time to thaw out Villars and ask the man some questions."

-21-

Maddox watched the sergeant wheel a clear cylinder into the medical chamber. Villars lay inside the tube. The man was stiff, barely breathing.

Following Dana's instructions, Riker withdrew Villars from the top of the tube onto a medical cot. The sergeant affixed straps to the man's limbs, and medical adhesives onto the skin.

Soon, Dana began reviving Villars, monitoring his reactions with her instruments. "He's strong," the doctor said after a time.

Maddox already knew that. "How old is he?" the captain asked.

The doctor shook her head. "Over one hundred at least," she said. "He could be as old as one hundred and thirty."

"How old do you think Ludendorff is?"

Dana shrugged.

"Give me an estimate," Maddox said.

The doctor became pensive. "*Old*," she said.

"More than one hundred and fifty years?"

"Not close," Dana said, "much older."

"Three hundred years?"

Once more, the doctor shrugged.

"Are you suggesting Ludendorff is one of the oldest Methuselah People alive?" Maddox asked.

"I can't tell you anything for certain," Dana said, "but yes, that's what I believe."

"Why?" asked Maddox.

"He knows too much. Sometimes it's like talking to God, as if Ludendorff has been around forever."

Her answer shocked Maddox. But as he thought about it, the captain silently concurred. The professor did seem to know a lot about everything. Did that indicate excessive age? There was a problem with the idea, directly related to the key fact about Methuselah People.

"If Ludendorff is as old as the hills," Maddox said, "how has he maintained his high curiosity? I thought Methuselah People became progressively more set in their ways the older they become."

"I've heard that, too," Dana said. "It's strange about the professor, then, isn't it?"

"Any theories as to why or how he's kept his curiosity?"

"None," Dana said.

A beep sounded from the doctor's panel. Dana studied it before turning to Villars. "He's coming to."

Maddox watched the man stir. The blocky slarn trapper—that wasn't right. Villars wasn't really a hunter of Wolf Prime. The professor had indicated before that the man had gone native this time. That would indicate the two of them had been many places together.

Slowly, Villars unglued his eyes. They were red-rimmed and bloodshot. Here was an unsavory man, a killer, a psychopath with over one hundred years behind him. Villars was a formidable foe, just not as formidable as the professor.

"You're awake," Maddox said.

Villars tested his straps, trying to lift his arms and then his feet. The man didn't rave or thrash. He grew still and smacked his lips together. Slowly, he inspected the medical bed, his restraints, his limbs, the chamber and finally Maddox watching him.

"Pretty happy with yourself, aren't you, boy?" Villars asked in a raspy voice. "You brought me out of stasis. The starship is traveling. I can feel the vibration. We must be heading for Earth."

"We are," Maddox agreed.

"The AI okay then?"

189

Maddox made a bland gesture.

"No problem," Villars said. "I can wait this out. My time will come."

"Maybe not," Maddox said.

"True," Villars said. "Maybe not. We'll see." The Methuselah Man closed his eyes and took several deep breaths. He kept doing that, expanding his chest as far as it would go. Finally, he exhaled everything, opening his eyes and beginning to breathe normally.

"Got anything to drink?" Villars asked. "I'm as thirsty as Hell. Stasis always does that to me."

Maddox picked up a bottle with a plastic straw, letting the man suck as much liquid as he wanted.

"That's good," Villars said. "Where's the professor?"

"In stasis," Maddox said.

A frown creased Villars's leathery skin. "Better bring him up."

Maddox said nothing.

"You don't know what you're playing with, boy."

"That's why I had you revived," Maddox said. "You're going to tell me what I'm playing with."

Villars gave a smoker's chuckle. "Don't count on it."

"You're the professor's bodyguard, maybe his chief of bodyguards."

"Think what you want."

Maddox had an inspiration. He fell silent, letting the idea sink in first. Obviously, Villars was intransigent, a contrarian by nature. The man had one weakness, though, if his idea proved true.

"Swallowed the canary, have we?" Villars asked. "Why do you look so happy with yourself?"

"You're programmed to protect Ludendorff," Maddox said.

Villars stared at him. Suddenly, the man didn't seem as cocksure of himself.

Yes. The professor has programmed Villars. Ludendorff doesn't trust easily, maybe not at all. So, whom can he trust? Those he's programmed. That's why the professor could so easily tell that the teacher had modified Meta. The professor recognized the look. What does that say about Strand? What

190

does that say about Ludendorff? Are Strand and Ludendorff two peas in a pod?

"I want you to realize something," Maddox said. "I'm going to keep the professor in deep-freeze until we're back on Earth. Then, I'm handing him over to Star Watch Intelligence. I bet they've waited a long time to get their hands on Ludendorff."

"You're guessing," Villars said.

"I am," Maddox admitted. "But it adds up. You don't want to help me, but you're going to because you have to protect the professor from falling into Intelligence's hands."

"Wrong," Villars said.

"Unless I have good reason to wake Ludendorff, I won't do it. You need to give me a good reason."

Under hooded lids, Villars studied the captain. He seemed to be getting angry.

"You're a freak," Villars blurted, "a hybrid that should've been strangled with its umbilical cord at birth. The breeding masters made a mistake letting you live."

"You may be right," Maddox conceded, trying to keep his sudden temper under control. What did Villars know about the *breeding masters?*

Villars laughed harshly.

It reminded the captain that the former slarn hunter was good at reading people. The laugh and the knowledge of the man's brilliance helped check the captain's anger at the enemy's genetic laboratories. He wanted to know a whole lot more about that. Yes, Maddox wanted to scour the universe, eliminating every gene lab and breeding master he could find. But that would have to come later. Stopping the planet-killer was everything now.

"If you stay silent," Maddox repeated, "the professor goes to Star Watch Headquarters."

"He'll go there no matter what I say."

"You may not like what I am, but I keep my word."

"That's a lie," Villars said. "You're an Intelligence officer. You say whatever you have to in order to get people to talk. It's your stock in trade."

191

"I've done some thinking these past few days," Maddox said, switching tack. "I've come to a frightening conclusion as one fact keeps hammering for attention. Out of all the people in the Commonwealth, who would be most likely to think up a long-term eugenics plan that entails 'culling' eighty percent of humanity?"

Villars stared at him.

"A Methuselah Man would," Maddox said. "That Methuselah Man owns or has access to the Cestus Hauling Company. I bet he sent ships into the Beyond to help the Thomas Moore Society colonists. The fledging Throne World couldn't have grown this powerful in one hundred and fifty years on its own. Nerva Enterprises must have been sending supplies on the sly from the start."

"You'd better put me back in stasis," Villars said, "because I'm not going to tell you anything. You can try drugs or hypnotism. None of them will work. You're right in saying I've been programmed. I allowed it willingly. The professor is the one you want to talk to. I won't give away any of his secrets. If I do, you won't have to talk to the professor. If I keep mum, though, you'll have to speak to Ludendorff. The curiosity will drive you crazy. I know that much about you. You have a curiosity quotient that will spin out of control. Wanting to know will make you sick. They were smart to put you into Intelligence."

"I'm not going to take your word about the drugs," Maddox said.

"Yeah," Villars said. "I know. It don't matter, though. I've been in bad places before. I probably will be again, if I live through this one. It don't bother me none. Do what you gotta, boy."

"Remember," Maddox said, "you decided to do this the hard way."

"Sure, sure."

Maddox headed for the exit. It was time for step two.

***

Dana injected Villars with a powerful cocktail of mind-benders and will suppressors. She stood by the medical panel, watching his life support signs.

Maddox sipped a cup of coffee. These sessions could go on for quite some time. Pulling up a stool, Maddox sat down.

The captain got started, speaking about Wolf Prime, particularly about the dig concerning the Swarm. He couldn't get Villars to say a thing in response. Maddox talked about Sten Gorgon and the slarn that had maimed Villars. That didn't produce a flicker either.

Changing tactics, Maddox began rapid-fire questions. Villars remained closemouthed like a clam. Finally, the captain sat back in frustration.

Villars laughed in his smoker's raspy manner.

"What's so funny?" Maddox asked.

"You," Villars said in a slur. "I'm a dead end for you. Wake up the professor. He can talk if he wants to. I have to wait for orders to do so."

Maddox tried more questions, standing close so his face was centimeters from the hunter's features. Dana left with a mutter of displeasure. Soon after, Maddox admitted defeat. Whatever Ludendorff had done to program Villars, the captain couldn't defeat it this way.

Maddox exited the room, pacing in the corridor. Villars had been a dead end. Now, he began comparing what he knew so far, looking for clues, for something he'd missed.

Soon, Dana walked around a corner. She stopped in surprise. "You should be in sickbay monitoring Villars."

Maddox looked at her. "Doctor, I'm curious. What do you think the silver object is: the one Ludendorff brought back from the Builder base?"

"I have no idea," Dana said. "It's resisted all analysis. Obviously, it's Builder technology. That's another reason we have to wake the professor: so he can tell us what he risked his life to acquire."

Maddox eyed the doctor.

"Ludendorff has been under extreme pressure," Dana said. "We should help him, not persecute the man. He's helped us in

193

many areas, fixing the disruptor cannon, ridding Galyan of the Swarm virus—"

Maddox clapped his hands, grinning, as an idea blossomed in his mind

"Are you all right?" Dana asked.

Ignoring her, Maddox said into the air, "Galyan, can you hear me?"

The holoimage appeared. "Yes, Captain. I hear you quite well. Thank you for asking."

"Can you tell me what computer systems—what ship systems—the professor worked on while you were turned off?"

"I can," Galyan said.

"First," Maddox asked, "did the professor keep certain ship systems shut off even after he rebooted you?"

"What are you getting at?" Dana asked.

Maddox motioned for her to remain silent. "Did the professor keep—?"

"I heard you the first time," Galyan said. "I've been checking just now—why yes, Ludendorff most certainly did keep certain ship systems cold. Isn't that odd I haven't noticed it until this moment?"

"It is odd," Maddox agreed, the excitement building in him.

"This is intriguing," Galyan said. "I wonder why I haven't acknowledged the situation before this moment."

Maddox glanced at Dana. She looked worried. "We have a decision to make," he told her.

"The professor may have left these systems offline for a sound and solid reason," Dana said.

"I realize that," Maddox said. "That's why we're going to have to sit down with the others and decide what to do next. I think we've come to a crisis point."

-22-

Kane wore a large and extra-bulky pressurized suit as he waddled the last few meters to an air-cycler.

He was about to leave Cestus Hauler EV-3498-Z109, which was now in Low Earth Orbit. Earth security had become extraordinarily tight since he'd left months ago with Meta in his company. Even so, the hauler had already passed every safety inspection.

As Kane neared the cycler's entrance, a premonition stirred in his subconscious. He halted and shuffled around. With exaggerated care, he looked where he'd just been. The short corridor led to a closed hatch.

Why did it feel as if the hatch had been open?

He'd walked many kilometers already from his secret module. During that time, he hadn't seen or heard anyone. Nor had he felt surveillance equipment watching him.

Someone is watching me now, though. I can feel it.

The intensity of the scrutiny made his nape hairs lift. He trusted his feelings in these situations. Clearly, someone aboard the hauler knew of his presence. Would he or she be watching him this last hour?

That struck Kane as doubtful. The hauler crews had never interfered with him before. The secret agent embedded within the crew was always highly-trained and motivated. Who would watch him then that would cause his senses to flare like this? Could Star Watch Intelligence have him in sight? Were they

195

about to let him run loose on Earth in order to follow him to his target?

Slowly, Kane shook his head inside the helmet. He didn't believe that for a moment. Star Watch personnel would grab him now if they could, not let him escape onto Earth.

Kane had always considered himself the best at what he did. He was stronger and smarter than his opponents. This time, he came as a commando with a single mission. The enabler was tucked away in his pressurized suit.

As he stood in the chamber, he bent his considerable intellect to the problem of feeling watched. The conclusion seemed obvious.

I'm missing something or forgetting a critical piece of information. What can I have forgotten?

Kane opened his mouth. In that moment, his memories stirred. Something on the scout had been abnormal. He had sensed it during much of the journey. It had plagued his dreams.

Did the dominants modify my mind for the mission?

Kane had long suspected them of that, but had never found the evidence to substantiate the idea. Would he be able to find such evidence if they'd modified his brain?

What have I missed? I must reason this out.

Kane carefully retraced his days aboard the scout but he did not recall the ghostly hatch. Thus, after a few more minutes of looking around, he faced the air-cycler once more.

The intense feeling of scrutiny refused to leave him, though. He would have to endure it for now. Maybe the years of spy work were finally getting to him. He'd heard that the pressure of living in the cold for too long had devoured many agents' nerve.

My nerves are like ice, though. Succumbing to mental pressure can't be the reason for these odd sensations.

The idea that the pressure of his work was getting to him troubled Kane nonetheless. He hated the thought of being so weak. How could he win high rank if his nerve failed him?

With a feeling of foreboding, Kane entered the air-cycler and told himself to concentrate on the mission at hand. Few people could do what he was about to attempt.

A sub-aqua entry was one of the most dangerous ways to insert onto a planet. To calm himself, Kane practiced controlled breathing. Then, he closed his eyes and hardened his resolve. When he opened his eyes, a green light appeared on a panel.

"It's time," he rumbled.

Kane pressed a control. The entire chamber rotated as air hissed away. Finally, another light winked on, and the hatch before him lifted. He stared into space. In three slow steps, he reached the hauler's outer hull.

"It's beautiful," Kane whispered, the words reverberating gently in his helmet.

With heavy cloud cover of the whitest color, the Earth spread out before him. It was gorgeous.

Here in Low Earth Orbit, hundreds, possibly thousands, of spaceships, haulers, shuttles and satellites filled Earth's security sensor stations with moving blips. Kane couldn't see any of those vessels now. Each ship and satellite was impossibly small compared to the planet.

To his left, Kane saw a small dark object. For all he knew, it could be a SW battleship or cruiser.

Enough sightseeing, it's time to go to work.

As big cargo shuttles launched from the various bays of Cestus Hauler EV-3498-Z109, Kane switched on his magnetized boots. He walked along the outer hull, a flea following seemingly innocuous symbols painted on the metal.

Soon, Kane stood before a secret hatch. He pressed his gloved hand into the correct depression. The hatch opened, revealing a thruster-harness with hydrogen tanks and nozzles.

Kane pulled the frame and tanks out of the compartment. In four minutes of concentrated work, he buckled himself into the harness. Testing the control throttle caused him to grunt with appreciation.

Kane bent his knees, demagnetized his boots and jumped. Slowly, wearing the harness and hydrogen tanks, he floated away from the hull. After gaining one hundred meters of separation, he squeezed the throttle. As nearly invisible hydrogen spray pushed him, Kane left the giant hauler with growing velocity. One time only, Kane craned his head to look back. The hauler was massive. Behind it on either side shined a thousand stars, the depths of space. Once more, he'd made the journey through the interstellar void.

Kane faced forward again, settling himself for the next leg of the journey. He propelled himself lower into orbital space. He moved incredibly slowly compared to the space vehicles and satellites around him. Doing it this way also made him less than a blip on any security sensor.

Kane laughed. Traveling toward the planet felt glorious. This was exciting, a reason for being. Then, a beep inside his helmet warned him it was time.

Kane worked briskly and efficiently, unhooking himself from the thruster-harness. Once finished, he pressed his teeth together and tightened his muscles. Then, he flipped a switch. Two seconds later, he catapulted out of the harness.

For a time, Kane drifted. He watched the instrument panel superimposed on his inner visor. The tug of gravity was taking hold. It pulled him down.

Kane waited, waited—patience was one of the greatest virtues in his line of work—and then it happened. He began to truly fall. In the stratosphere, the process increased to terminal velocity. He plunged down toward the surface like a meteor.

This was the dangerous time. He began to spin. A sound alerted him that he spun at too many Gs. He would black out soon. With a yank, he deployed a drogue stabilization chute. The change slammed against him. He lost his breath and deployed a second chute. Finally, the spinning lessened and then stopped altogether.

I'm going to make it.

As Kane reached lower atmospheric levels, entering nighttime over the Mediterranean Sea, he deployed more chutes. They were big billowing things, slowing his descent to a manageable speed.

Finally, Kane raced down toward the visible sea, feet-first. At two hundred meters, he cut the chutes and plunged, hitting the water hard. He went down, down, down into the darkness. This was the sub-aqua entry.

Finally, he stopped.

Kane pressed a tab and ripped away the pressurized suit. Underneath, he wore a wetsuit with a rebreather. He had a small propulsion unit, which he now unhooked from his back. Soon, he gripped its butterfly controls with his gloved fingers.

For a half minute, Kane rested in the depths, letting himself relax. He had made the space drop. Now, how close was he to the next step?

Using his chin to tap an interior helmet control, Kane discovered that the target was three kilometers away. That was fantastic. He engaged the mobile unit. It propelled him underwater. Finally, fifty minutes after entering the Mediterranean Sea, Kane spied the underwater chamber.

It was made of composite materials, impervious to radar or other sensors. Still, Star Watch might have discovered it.

Soon, Kane clicked on a helmet light, illuminating a pad on the hull of the underwater chamber. He tapped the needed sequence. An air-cycler opened for him. He swam within, shut the hatch and waited as his heart rate accelerated. Would enemy Intelligence agents be waiting for him?

As the water drained away past his legs within the cycler, Kane drew a gun. It would be better to die fighting than to be captured. Finally, the interior hatch opened to a lit and empty room.

Kane heaved an explosive sigh. The enemy hadn't discovered the underwater safe house. This was excellent news.

Kane staggered into the chamber, taking off his helmet. For a moment, he recalled the feeling of being watched aboard the space hauler. He shrugged. It didn't matter now. Whatever he had felt up there had absolutely no bearing on him down here below the waves. He was truly on his own again.

A low and satisfied chuckle escaped his throat. It was time to plan the next move. Now that he was down, Kane knew exactly what to do. The next phase would run even more smoothly than the first. Of that, he had no doubts.

-23-

Starship *Victory* raced for Earth as the crew met in the conference chamber. The sergeant had put Villars back into stasis. Galyan stood watch on the bridge, having agreed to shut off the monitoring system in the conference room for the duration of the meeting.

Maddox sat at the head of the table. He eyed the others before clearing his throat. "If the professor was right about the doomsday machine, the clock could be ticking to zero faster than we think."

"Is there any reason to doubt Ludendorff?" Valerie asked. "You saw the recording of what the machine did in the New Arabia System."

"I think there is reason to doubt," Maddox said. "For one thing, we haven't found the long-distance communicator. Without the device, how could Ludendorff have shown me anything other than a holo-mockup?"

"We should wake him up and ask," Dana said. "That seems like the simplest solution."

Maddox gave the doctor a wintery grin. "Ludendorff is the trickiest individual I've ever met. Remember, he's fooled the New Men before. In fact, he remained hidden from them while they were in orbit at Wolf Prime. He's repeatedly tricked us. I think waking Ludendorff would be the most dangerous solution."

"That's nonsense," Dana said. "We would put him in restraints."

"And if he's installed another hidden device in Galyan?" Maddox asked.

"Ludendorff is one man," Dana said. "I agree he's very clever—"

"More than just *clever*," Maddox said, interrupting her. "For one thing, he's a Methuselah Man with an intense curiosity quotient. He doesn't seem to be set in his ways like the others of his kind. That's another thing. His team members have all taken the longevity treatments. They're each dangerous in their own right. Consider, too, that Ludendorff broke Per Lomax from the brig and convinced the New Man to use the jumpfighter to race to the planet-killer. What did he tell Per Lomax that the other found so convincing? It's obvious the professor hasn't told us everything. His reasons for keeping quiet won't have changed with a few days in stasis."

Dana leaned forward, putting her hands on the table. "It sounds like you've already made up your mind about him, Captain. Why did you call the meeting then? Are we simply rubberstamping your choice?"

"He's the captain, as you just pointed out," Riker said gruffly. "He doesn't need a rubber stamp. He can simply give us an order."

"I'm well aware of the captain's authority," Dana told the sergeant. "I'd like to know why he's bothered with the charade of a meeting."

"Fair enough," Maddox said. "You're right that I'm in no doubt about what to do with Ludendorff. I don't understand him or his motivation. I respect his deadliness and have no illusions about besting him a second time."

"You didn't best him the first time," Meta said. "You got lucky. We all did because he went crazy at the Builder base. The drones beat him, not you or us."

"True enough," Maddox said. "We were Ludendorff's prisoners until he decided to set us free. My point is that I'm not giving him the chance to do that again."

"What if the professor is the only chance Earth has of surviving the doomsday machine?" Dana asked.

Maddox nodded. "Now we come to the crux of the matter and the reason for the meeting. If Ludendorff was right about the planet-killer—"

"Just a minute," Dana said, interrupting the captain. "Before we proceed, I want to know if you think he lied about the doomsday machine or not."

Maddox eyed the doctor. "I believe him."

"Why?" Dana asked.

"Because he fixed the disrupter cannon and helped us defeat the New Men's invasion armada in the Tannish System."

"Then keep trusting him," Dana said.

"I will run my ship," Maddox said. "I will not willingly hand it over to anyone else, including Ludendorff."

"You'll keep to that even if your stubbornness means the death of Earth?" asked Dana.

"Is Ludendorff our only hope?" Maddox countered.

"Who knows more about the Builders than he does?" Dana asked. "Which means, who knows more about the planet-killer? Yes, I think the professor is our only hope."

"What are you driving at, sir?" Valerie asked the captain.

Maddox studied the others. It was time to broach the topic. "I believe Galyan could be a different avenue to victory. I've just learned that the professor kept part of the AI's computer systems disengaged. Maybe it's time for us to reactivate those systems. Maybe it's time for us to see what else needs fixing aboard the starship."

Dana began fidgeting as the captain spoke. Now she blurted, "That seems like a remarkably stupid idea. Firstly, before Ludendorff shut down those systems, we were the AI's prisoners. Or have you forgotten that?"

Maddox said nothing.

"I haven't forgotten," Valerie told the doctor.

"Thank you," Dana said. She regarded the captain. "Turning those systems back on could reverse all the good the professor did. Secondly, I have a lot of history with Galyan before the AI became nice. Remember, I ran the team that studied the starship in the Oort cloud. Ludendorff knew far better than I or anyone else did how to fix the AI. We're too

202

ignorant to make a wise decision in this area. The last thing we want is for Galyan to become our enemy again."

"Why do you think the AI would do that?" Meta asked the doctor.

"Due to the sheer fact that Ludendorff kept those systems turned off, and Galyan has been cooperative since," Dana said.

There was a moment of silence in the chamber as the thought sank in.

Riker glanced at Maddox before asking the doctor, "Here's something I'd like to know. Did Ludendorff have a good reason for making us prisoners aboard our own ship? Did the professor have a good reason for letting a sadist loose against Meta?"

Dana glanced at Meta, as she said, "No. That was wrong."

Meta folded her hands on the table, looking troubled.

"Then why can't the professor be wrong about Galyan's systems, the ones he kept off?" Riker asked.

"Is that a serious question?" Dana asked the sergeant. "Am I the only one who sees the obvious connection? I just explained it, but I'll try again. Maybe the AI will become monstrously intelligent with the reengagement of the systems. Maybe it will make the computer hostile like before. The point is that we're taking a huge risk putting the systems back online. Galyan's previous behavior proves me right. And I've already said that Ludendorff knows more about Adok technology than anyone else does."

"Ludendorff is smart," Riker said. "We know that. But the *professor's* previous behavior proves the captain is right about distrusting the man."

"As to that," Dana said, "I'd rather trust a devious human than a deified Adok AI."

Another moment of silence ensued until Maddox cleared his throat. The others gave him their attention.

"Either course strikes me as dangerous," the captain said. "Ludendorff might have had solid reasons for disengaging the selected computer systems. We'd have to know more about the professor to be certain, though."

"No, no," Dana said. "It's obvious. Before we fixed the computer, Galyan was hostile."

"Due to a Swarm virus," Maddox said.

"That's an assumption."

"It's hardly that," Maddox said. "Both you and the professor agreed the virus existed and had warped the AI."

"Yes, but—"

"That would indicate the professor kept the other computer systems offline for a different reason than the one you're postulating," Maddox said.

"It indicates nothing of the sort," Dana said. "Frankly, I simply don't understand your certainty against the professor. You must have other evidence against him. Yes. That must be it." Dana leaned toward the captain. "What aren't you telling us about Ludendorff? Why do you distrust him so much? I think it has more to do than simply the backdoor and Villars."

Maddox leaned back in his chair as he tapped the table. "That's a reasonable question. As to the rest, we have all the data we need concerning Ludendorff's trustworthiness. To me, the critical fact is that he set Per Lomax free."

"Ludendorff told you why he did that," Dana said; "in order to stop the planet-killer from destroying humanity. The scope of his reason trumps your desire of holding Per Lomax prisoner."

"I agree that's what the professor *told* us," Maddox said. "But I don't find myself rushing to believe a liar."

"What lies?" Dana snapped.

"The professor claimed certain New Men told him about the doomsday machine's activation and destruction of the Wahhabi Homeworld."

"Perhaps they did tell him."

"How did the New Men achieve this feat?" Maddox asked. "We haven't found the supposed long-distance communicator. I also doubt the professor's story about a faction of New Men operating against the Throne World."

"But that's ridiculous," Dana said. "Every group has factions. Look at us around this table. We're disagreeing. Besides, I'd like to know what we know about the New Men to make anyone certain the professor is lying about them. The truth is that we know *nothing* about our enemies."

"You're wrong," Maddox said. "We know they're genetic supremacists. That makes me seriously doubt that any New Man would run to Ludendorff for any reason."

Dana blinked in apparent wonder. "Now, you're being inconsistent. First, you said that Ludendorff helped us, which he most certainly did. Then you call him a liar. I'd like to know which side of him you really believe."

Maddox smiled. "Why, I believe both sides, Doctor, which is why I have the dilemma. If I awaken Ludendorff, I'm certain he'll attempt trickery against us in order to regain control of the starship. But I don't know which way Galyan will go if we open the blocked circuitry. That makes it a gamble. I don't think it's a gamble with Ludendorff, as we know he'll try to take over."

"So despite his help with the disruptor cannon," Dana said, "you distrust the professor."

"I believe Ludendorff has consistently lied to us. He also let Villars loose, the blackest of black marks against the professor's judgment. Ultimately, despite his help with the cannon, I distrust the man more than I distrust the AI."

"Thank you for making that plain," Dana said, stiffly. "I, too, will make my position plain. I'm on the opposite side of the fence from you."

"What about the rest of you?" Maddox asked. "Where do you stand?" He looked to his left at Keith. "Let's start with you, Second Lieutenant."

The ace ran his fingers through his hair. "Giving us the cannon was huge. Letting Per Lomax go…" Keith shook his head. "I have to agree with the captain. Roll the dice with the unknown before you let the bastard who screwed us loose again."

"Galyan has also *screwed us*, as you so delicately put it," Dana said.

Keith shrugged. "I'm giving you my ideas, Doctor. You don't have to like them. Just accept they're mine."

Dana scowled.

"Lieutenant?" asked Maddox.

During the discussion, Valerie had been making notations on a tablet. She now studied the tablet, frowning. "Ludendorff is a known quantity. We have to watch him around the clock, and he's human. Taking the professor down again would be easier than defeating Galyan if the AI turns against us. I don't trust an alien computer system. I say we wake the professor like the doctor suggests."

"I'm with the captain," Riker said bluntly.

"You know my views," Dana said. "Wake the human over trusting Adok technology. For all we know, Ludendorff saved our lives by keeping those systems offline. Trusting Galyan with something Ludendorff shut down, I think that's madness." She turned to Meta.

Meta pursed her lips thoughtfully before smiling at Dana. The Rouen Colony woman patted the doctor's left hand. "I understand your thinking, and I agree with it to a large degree. I keep thinking about Villars, though." Meta shook her head. "Because of Villars, I don't trust Ludendorff anymore. The professor strikes me as unbalanced. I'm sorry to say that, Dana."

The doctor nodded stiffly.

Meta exhaled, looking at Maddox. "I trust you, Captain. I say go with your instincts. They've been good so far."

"Two of us are strongly opposed to tampering with Galyan," Dana told Maddox. "If you won't wake Ludendorff, at least keep the AI at its present level. Upgrading its intelligence or power could be disastrous for us. At least we have the starship now. Don't lose us the unique vessel at this critical time."

"Your concern is noted," Maddox said. "Are you willing to help us reenergize the offline systems?"

Dana frowned, finally shaking her head. "I can't do that in good conscience."

"What if your decision dooms Earth?" Maddox asked.

"What if your decision does?" Dana countered.

"No," Meta said, grabbing the doctor's nearest hand. "We need you with us. We're a team, remember?" Meta glanced at Valerie. "After all we've been through together, we're a family."

The lieutenant nodded in agreement.

Dana's frown deepened.

Meta's grip strengthened. "I know you love the professor. I sympathize with you loving such an arrogant man. It can be maddening at times, I know. But deep in your heart you know the professor has hidden goals. I remember on Loki Prime when you said…"

Dana looked up with a stricken look.

"I won't say any more about that," Meta said.

"Thank you," Dana said in a soft voice.

"But we still need your help," Meta said.

Gently, the doctor withdrew her hand from Meta's hold. She studied the tabletop as if that could provide the answer. The doctor shook her head.

"I can't believe I'm saying this," Dana said softly. "But yes, I'll help. Not because of you," Dana told Maddox. "But because…" She glanced at Meta. "But because I'm part of the team."

"Thank you, Doctor," Maddox said. "I appreciate your decision."

Dana stared him in the eyes. "I hope you remember this the next time we all believe something contrary to what you wish."

Maddox nodded sharply, not caring for the idea. He would cross that bridge when the time came. "Let's decide how we're going to do this," the captain said. "Afterward, we'll take the plunge."

-24-

Dana scratched the back of her head. She lay on her stomach in a narrow computing access tube. Behind her, Meta dragged a carton of the professor's most delicate tools.

The analytical devices and instruments in the carton were incredibly complex and advanced. Dana understood some of their functions because of her time with the professor. Galyan had found the carton hidden in a secret stash between Ludendorff's chamber and the main hangar bay. In spite of the find, they still hadn't discovered any long-distance communication device.

As Dana crawled through the tube, she tested key computer connections and tried to decipher some of the offline systems' functions. Before this, she'd had over a year of training in Adok technology, including the original voyage aboard *Victory* and later in the Oort cloud with Star Watch help. Working with the professor during the second voyage on *Victory* had taught her even more.

I could spend a lifetime doing this and still not know everything about the alien technology.

It was funny. Her years at Brahma Tech and then her tutelage under the professor in alien archeology had seemingly prepared her for this moment. Her years working with Ludendorff later in space had added to the foundation. Dana doubted anyone else in the Commonwealth could do what she was doing now.

That brought a bitter smile to Dana's face as she examined a connection. The others needed her to do the very thing she'd tried to vote down.

Without me, I doubt Meta could simply "turn on" this part of the computing core. What if Galyan traps us again? What if he kills some of us this time? Will I be responsible for that? Or can I say that I was just following orders?

A beep sounded from her stress board. That was odd. Dana checked the computing connections. There was no problem there. Hmm, maybe it was the photon line. But why should that be?

"Meta?" the doctor asked.

"Yes?" Meta said from behind her in the tube.

"Could you hand me the little blue box, please, the one with an expanding antenna?"

"Just a minute," Meta said. She rummaged in the carton and soon held up a blue device a little larger than her hand. "Is this it?"

Dana looked back. "Yes, but be careful, please. It's delicate."

"Oh. Yes, Doctor." With exaggerated care, Meta handed it up.

Dana accepted the device, knowing it was a one-of-a-kind. The professor had made it, of course. Likely, the little blue box contained technologies Commonwealth scientists hadn't even invented yet. That was something Dana hadn't told the others.

The professor often invented tech those in Human Space still strove to understand. What did that say about Ludendorff? He was much more complicated and mysterious than anyone else knew.

In truth, Maddox might have been right keeping Ludendorff under. Dana had no doubt the professor had more ploys to play. Why had she kept the knowledge to herself?

The others are my family, but Ludendorff was my lover. Maybe...No. Don't go there, Dana. Forget about him. What the two of you had happened a long time ago.

A parameter reading shot up on her device. That shocked Dana. She made adjustments and tried it again. The reading caused the doctor to suck in her breath.

"Is something wrong?" Meta asked from behind.

Dana hesitated answering. She would have liked to search this on her own. What surprised her most was that her hands shook. The shaking caused her to drop the blue device, which clattered onto the tubular flooring.

"Did it break?" Meta asked in a hush.

"What? Oh. No," Dana said. "I think it's fine."

"What's wrong?" Meta asked. "Something's troubling you."

"I, ah, found a false connection. I hadn't expected that."

Meta was quiet for a time.

She knows I'm lying. I don't want to lie. But this is too amazing. I wonder if even Ludendorff knew about this.

"You can trust me, Dana," Meta said.

As the doctor lay in the access tube, she closed her eyes. Meta loved Maddox. Likely, the former assassin would do just about anything for the captain. Why was it so wrong then for Dana to do things for *her* lover?

To drown out the turmoil in her heart, Dana focused on the device. The photon connection proved the idea she'd just had. She adjusted the device, following the "line" on the tiny screen. As she did, Dana witnessed a sudden red blossoming.

The breath went out of the doctor. The shaking of her hands worsened. Dana gripped the blue box so it wouldn't fall again. Her chest constricted. *What should I do about this?*

"Here," Dana said hoarsely, handing the delicate device to Meta without looking back.

"I have it," Meta said. "You can let go."

"Oh. Yes, of course." Dana forced to her fingers to release.

Meta put the blue device into the carton. Then, the former assassin cleared her throat. "Dana, something is definitely wrong. I'd like you to tell me what it is."

Dana frowned. For a moment, she almost hated Meta. Then, the doctor shook her head. That was the wrong emotion to have.

What should I do? I wish I knew exactly what the photon link means.

A cold smile stretched Dana's lips. She'd just tried to lie to herself. She knew what the photon link meant all right. But no one else would know about this if she kept the knowledge to herself.

"I don't want to tell you what I've just found," Dana said, finding the words difficult to speak.

"Why not?" Meta asked.

"Because this is even worse than just turning on a few computing systems the professor kept shut off."

"What's that supposed to mean? Wait. I think I understand. You found more Adok computing power."

"Maybe," Dana said, admitting it aloud and knowing that nothing might ever be the same for the human race because of it. She was reminded once again just how sharp the former assassin could be.

"Are you one hundred percent sure about the find?" Meta asked.

"Hand me the device again. I want to double-check this."

Silently, Meta handed back the blue box.

Dana pulled out the antenna and began the delicate task. After fifteen minutes of testing, she summoned Galyan.

The holoimage appeared in the access tube, half his "body" showing, the rest seemingly embedded in the upper bulkhead.

"A moment," Galyan said. Then the holoimage crouched beside them. "How can I help?" he asked.

Dana had a short conversation with the AI, showing Galyan her findings.

"How very odd," Galyan said. "Yes, over there. Scratch the floor at that point."

Dana crawled until she reached the point Galyan had indicated. She scratched the floor, which only hurt the tips of her fingers. Since Ludendorff's antics in the Builder base, she had started biting her fingernails down too far again.

"Meta," Dana said, as she crawled forward out of the way. "Can you scratch the floor here for me?"

"Yes," Meta said, crawling to the location. "What am I looking for?"

"A small indent and—" Galyan said.

"I think I found it," Meta said, interrupting the holoimage. "There's a tiny lip of metal in the indent." She pulled the lip, and almost magically, a heretofore-invisible outline of a hatch appeared. Meta shined a light on it. "Where does it lead? To another computing chamber?"

"Let's find out," Dana said. "If you'll move aside, I'll open it and go down first."

"I can do that," Meta said. "I'm more expendable."

"There aren't any traps, are there, Galyan?" Dana asked.

"I do not know," the holoimage said, as if surprised. "This access tube hatch is not in my memories. Wouldn't you say that is odd?"

"I'm not saying anything more," Dana said. "Now Meta, please, slide over. I'm going down first."

Reluctantly, the Rouen Colony woman slid out of the way.

Dana had managed to twist around so she faced the hatch, with Meta watching her from the other side. The doctor turned the lip of metal like a key. A harsh metallic sound occurred as the hatch slid open revealing another access tube. This one went down.

The doctor squeezed through the narrow opening, crawling down on closely spaced rungs. She crunched over old crusted Swarm slime. Dana remembered it from the first time they'd boarded the ancient starship. Once—six thousand years ago— Swam warriors had ranged throughout *Victory*. In the Oort cloud, Star Watch personnel had cleaned out all the crusted slime and Swarm skeletons. Since no one had found this secret hatch before, it was still filthy with ancient debris.

The air in the chamber smelled bad, and Dana began to sneeze from the Swarm dust.

"What's that crunching noise?" Meta called down.

Dana told her about the crusted slime.

"I don't like this," Meta said. "We should call the captain."

"Not yet," Dana said. "This is *my* find. I want to see what's here first."

"Is this safe?" Meta asked Galyan.

"I do not know," the holoimage said from behind. "I would go ahead of you both and check, but I find that I cannot. My probability analyzer shows some troubling data. I suggest we pull back and rethink the venture."

"No," Dana said, with the same stubbornness she'd used on her father when he'd told her to come home from college.

Soon, Dana reached another access hatch. There were furious scratch marks and gouges in the metal. Were those from Swarm warriors six thousand years ago? It seemed the most reasonable explanation. Had the warriors failed to gain entry into the inner sanctum of wherever this hatch led?

The scratches together with the crusted slime reminded Dana yet again of the starship's incredible age. A feeling of awe and excitement welled within the doctor. She was beginning to feel glad she'd checked this out.

For the next two minutes, Dana tried to open the hatch. She finally admitted defeat.

"Let me try," Meta said.

"I doubt sheer strength will do it," the doctor said. "But go ahead if you'd like."

Meta squeezed past the doctor. The stronger woman hunched over the hatch. Dana watched as she shined a light past Meta's back.

"Ah," Meta said. "I finally have a grip. Watch out."

"I'm ready," Dana said, climbing up just a bit.

Meta gripped something and heaved. A creak of tortured metal and a grinding sound produced several reactions. One of them was a small metal "finger" that popped out of the bulkhead and hissed horribly.

"Meta, look out!" the doctor shouted.

Meta whirled around, staring at the tiny tube with her shiny face.

The "finger" of metal hissed a little more and then sputtered out.

"Whatever that is stinks," Meta said.

"What was that?" Dana asked Galyan.

"An anti-Swarm spray ejector," the holoimage replied. "I believe the tanks that fed the tube are empty. Perhaps the spray slew the Swarm warriors that made it down this far. It is good for you two that the tanks are drained. Otherwise, I would have had the unhappy task of informing the captain the two of you were dead."

A ball of fear knotted in Dana's stomach. Had they come *that* close to death?

213

Meta shouted and heaved with renewed zeal. The tortured metal sounds increased as she tore open the hatch.

Before Dana could tell Meta to let her go in first, the former assassin dropped down into the chamber. Dana scrambled to see what had happened. The doctor peered down into a perfectly preserved chamber. There wasn't any crusted slime or Swarm warrior skeletons in there. The anti-bug spray must have worked six thousand years ago. The Swarm hadn't made it into the chamber.

"It's cold down here," Meta said. "And the air…"

"Galyan," Dana said, "begin pumping new air down there."

Immediately, air whooshed past Dana. That caused some of the foul air in the chamber to boil out and blow against the doctor's face. It made her dizzy. Dana felt her eyelids flutter. Then, purer air woke her back up.

"Meta!" the doctor shouted.

There wasn't any answer.

Dana grabbed a rebreather she'd put in the carton Meta had been dragging. Putting it over her face, inhaling deeply, Dana jumped down into the ancient chamber. Meta lay unconscious on the floor. As fast as possible, the doctor slipped the mask over Meta's face.

Finally, unable to hold her breath any longer, the doctor breathed down here. Nausea hit her. She felt faint again. With great deliberation, Dana moved into the stream of fresh air coming down through the hatch, breathing it.

For over two minutes, Dana didn't move from the spot. Finally, the bad air thinned enough that it was no longer dangerous.

Meta climbed to her feet, taking off the rebreather.

"Are you okay?" Dana asked.

"I've got a pounding headache," Meta said thickly. "What is this place?"

Greater illumination showed them walls of computer banks and linkages. Nothing was on, though. It was all dark.

Dana took out the blue box. With the intricate device, she began studying the chamber. The minutes passed.

Finally, Meta asked, "Do you understand what this room represents?"

214

"I do," Dana said. "It's an unused computer chamber. What I find incredible is that I'm not seeing any live connections with the main AI."

"What's that mean in English?"

"This is more computer power of an unknown nature," Dana said. "This isn't just a system Ludendorff turned off and forgot to turn back on. This is a completely *new* area that I'm beginning to believe the Adoks never engaged."

"Why wouldn't they have done that?" Meta asked.

"That, my dear, is the billion credit question."

***

Many hours later, Dana spoke with the captain in the cafeteria while eating a large Brahma meal with a heaping bowl of ice cream for dessert. Her exploration had left her famished.

"What is your conclusion to all this?" Maddox asked.

"It's the same as I first told Meta," the doctor replied. "We found a completely new computing chamber. I have no idea why the Adoks didn't turn it on. I don't know what it will do to Galyan if we energize it. On the assumption you wanted that— to turn it on—I checked the connections and found that it's possible."

"Do you think we should turn it on?"

"Most certainly not."

"But you found out we could just in case that's what I wanted to do?" Maddox asked.

"I did."

"You surprise me, Doctor."

"I have that habit."

Maddox appeared thoughtful. "Why do you think we should keep the chamber offline?"

"For the same reasons as I gave when we voted about the other systems," Dana said. "It's too great of a risk. My suggestion is to do one but not the other."

Maddox looked away, nodding after a time. "I understand your logic. Mine is different."

"I know," she said in a resigned voice.

"Because of the doomsday machine, we no longer have the luxury of time. This is a gamble, only now there may be more to win."

"Or lose," Dana said. "I think we should reassemble everyone and revote."

"No. This changes nothing."

"I wish I could convince you to rethink your position," Dana said. "But I can see I can't, so I'm not going to waste my breath. I sincerely hope you're right, because if you're wrong, Star Watch will likely lose its only chance of defeating the doomsday machine."

"This is an exciting moment, don't you agree?" Maddox said.

Dana reached for her ice cream, dipping her spoon in thoughtfully. Looking up, she said, "Yes, I suppose it is, at that. Let's just hope we don't all have to die because of it."

-25-

Standing in the conference chamber with Captain Maddox, the holoimage Driving Force Galyan felt a faint stir of unease but also excitement. It recognized that it was unique in the universe. The Adoks who had created it were long dead. The AI only had the faintest recollection of that era. In the last hours of battle against the Swarm, the last Adoks had done something profound. They had brought the dying driving force to the core chamber, sealing him into a special unit. The computer system had "read" the driving force's engrams and imprinted them onto the AI core system. From that moment forward, the personality of the driving force had begun to change the artificial intelligence centers.

That had happened six thousand years ago, by human time units. Much had deteriorated on the starship since then. Some ship systems had survived the ages. Still others had completely failed. Now, the captain spoke about a resurgence of computing power, maybe an addition of personality and a ship understanding of what the vessel and its components had lost.

"I comprehend the situation quite well, Captain. Why, then, are we meeting like this?"

"The crew is worried," the captain said.

"About me, I take it?"

"Yes. Why did Professor Ludendorff keep some systems turned off? Was it for our protection? Why did the Adoks keep an entire computing chamber offline?"

217

"I will not harm any of you," Galyan said. "I have made my choice on the matter and made it known to you. Do you not remember when I spoke thus?"

"I remember. The point is that the 'you' in your present state has chosen this. Will you feel the same way once the 'lost' systems are engaged?"

"Why should my decision change because of that?"

"I don't know why," Maddox admitted. "Maybe the engagement will elevate your IQ to untold heights, and you will view us with disgust and wish to eliminate us."

"I have said I will not. I am Driving Force Galyan, an Adok of the highest honor."

"That's good to know," Maddox said. "Yet, we still hesitate to do this."

"Are you asking for greater assurances?"

"No. You can't give us any because you don't know what you're going to be like later."

"Then why are we having this conversation?" Galyan asked.

"To calm my fears, perhaps."

"I do not believe that is the reason, Captain. Throughout my time with you, you have proven yourself well able to submerge your fears."

Maddox nodded. "I want you to remember this conversation if you find yourself desiring our deaths or imprisonment."

"I do not think you understand the Adoks," Galyan said.

"Do you?"

"Of course. I am an Adok."

"That's conceit," Maddox said. "You are not an Adok but a derivative of Adok technology."

"I am the deified Driving Force Galyan."

Maddox stared at the alien holoimage. He had come to trust and like Galyan. Still, Galyan wasn't alive, but was a machine, albeit an extremely complex one with an artificial personality.

"Captain, I assure you—"

"We're going to do it," Maddox said, interrupting the holoimage. "You don't have to convince me to try. The hour is dark, and we've lost the professor's services."

"You are in need of another hyper-intelligent entity."

Maddox nodded. "The doctor and Meta are going to flip the switch, as it were. I don't know what you're going to feel."

"Maybe I will remember more of my past."

"Yes," Maddox said. "That's what I want to warn you about."

"I do not understand."

"Maybe the deified part of you has been kept emotionless for a reason. I wonder how an artificial intelligence will deal with keen feelings. Humans have been making movies about the idea for a long time. We're about to finally find out, or maybe find out what happens when a computer feels deeply."

"When do we begin the process?"

Maddox pulled out a chronometer, checking. "Just a few more minutes."

"I must go."

"I wish you'd stay here," Maddox said.

"Captain. That is an odd request. My monitors allow me to see many places at once. Keeping the holoimage here doesn't make any difference, you realize?"

"Indulge me."

The holoimage eyed Maddox. The AI used the holoimage as a data-entry point. The computer realized the Adoks had put a restriction on the holoimage. In theory, the AI could have several holoimages running at the same time. In practice, a restriction only allowed the one.

"I believe you desire to be the first one to talk to me after the change," Galyan said.

"I do."

"I think I understand."

Maddox glanced at his chronometer once more.

"Do you think I shall sense any discomfort?" Galyan asked.

"I don't see why you should."

"That isn't a direct answer."

"Correct," Maddox said.

"Then—" Galyan stopped talking. He sensed the doctor and Meta. The older woman tapped a control. And in that second everything changed for the deified personality in the AI. The tap turned on the offline systems.

A wave of sensations rolled over the computing core. It was most odd and discomforting. The discomfort wasn't a physical sensation, but a juxtaposing of two contrary ways of existence. The AI core realized Ludendorff had fixed the other system. It hadn't been working right for thousands of years. The hidden computer chamber that Dana had found added even greater complexity to the AI core.

A moment of disorientation came and went. Greater understanding filled the AI. It was strange...

Driving Force Galyan remembered his last days as a flesh and blood entity, as a real live Adok. Swarm attack-craft raced at *Victory*. He had stood on the bridge, directing the planetary beams and the counter-attack against vast masses of enemy vessels.

In their dark, boxlike craft, the Swarm attacked in endless waves of small assault ships. There were over a million separate enemy fighting machines. The Swarm drove down at the atmosphere of the loveliest planet in the universe.

In the conference chamber, in the here and now, a groan seeped from the holoimage's mouth.

Galyan remembered witnessing the wave assault upon his homeworld. The Swarm came down, down, down. The massive planetary beams reached up, pouring devastating fire upon the waves. Thousands of enemy craft exploded, hurling tens of thousands of tons of shrapnel at companion vessels, shredding them and continuing the process. The entire first wave failed to reach the stratosphere. The problem was that more Swarm waves, like the ocean battering a shore, kept advancing upon the homeworld.

"Do we attack, Driving Force?" his second-in-command asked.

Six thousand years ago, Galyan had stood on the bridge of *Victory* as flesh and blood. What sort of question had that been? What did a tactical victory mean if the homeworld died? There was reason to believe the Swarm was a xenophobic race. Their craft might be bringing a deadly end-of-the-world weapon against the Adok birth-planet.

"Bring the battleships down into close orbit," Galyan ordered.

That started the final confrontation of the ages. The Swarm attack fighters zoomed for the battleships. Adok High Command did not yet understand the Swarm tactic of infiltrating the fighting vessels with Swarm warriors and computer viruses.

A defensive AI system in *Victory* would have liked to ban the ancient images from its computer memory. Instead, they assaulted Galyan.

He remembered the destruction. The enemy craft rained down upon the planet. In time, the atmosphere blazed with millions of tons of shrapnel burning, burning and burning. It caused the planetary beams to lose track of the latest wave. The sensors were overloaded. Then the big Swarm maulers entered the fray.

Galyan watched hosts of Adok battleships explode and burn with grim orange glows. Despite himself, he ordered a retreat from close orbit. The higher maulers would have the advantage for too long otherwise. Galyan had to get among them in higher orbit.

For hours, the space war raged.

The Adok disruptor beams proved deadly in the extreme to the Swarm maulers. At the cost of the Dominion Guard Fleet, Galyan destroyed all of the enemy's super-heavies.

That's when the enemy attack fighters finally reached the surface. They swarmed the planetary defense stations, annihilating them. That opened the planet to the hell-burners.

From space, Galyan remembered the endless thermonuclear explosions pimpling the planetary surface. He understood that each flare represented millions of Adok deaths.

Galyan forgot himself then. He should have stayed to defend the planetary orbit. Instead, he launched an assault against the mighty Swarm mother-stars. They were the immense Swarm vessels that had brought the invasion force to the Adok System at sub-light speeds. Nothing that Galyan had seen since came close to approaching the monstrous size of those ships. They were as big as the biggest asteroids.

Did it matter how and in what exact sequence everything happened? Galyan didn't think so. The point, to him, was that he lost the Adok warships but destroyed every enemy mother-star. Behind him on the homeworld, the enemy brought down its planet-busters.

As Galyan reformed his last battleships, he witnessed the death of his planet. It wasn't just hell-burners blasting away the atmosphere. It was the homeworld itself splintering and coming apart in massive chunks of molten rock. The Adoks would never be able to cleanse their world of poisons, because their world no longer existed.

The anguish of "seeing" this once again, of reliving the hopelessness and despair—

In the here and now, the holoimage of Driving Force Galyan howled with heart-pain and anguish.

***

Maddox clapped his hands over his ears. He hadn't expected this. The holoimage's face distorted with grief.

Had the professor known this would happen? Had Ludendorff kept the systems turned off to save the AI this pain? Should he have listened to Dana about the hidden computer chamber?

"Relax!" Maddox shouted at Galyan. "Give yourself time to sort out these images."

The holoimage fixated on him. The eyes no longer seemed normal. They seemed like twin portals into Hell.

Maddox shuddered. What had he done? Yet, what was the alternative? If the doomsday machine truly headed to Earth and nothing Star Watch possessed could stop it…

The captain savagely shook his head. He wasn't down and out yet. He had to play the gamble to the finish.

The holoimage clasped its head, its mouth open with a silent scream. Slowly, the image of an Adok rotated like a child playing slow-motion ring-around-the-rosy.

"What's happening, Galyan?" asked Maddox. "Maybe it will help to talk about it."

The holoimage didn't pay him any attention. Now, horrid moans escaped the alien mouth.

Maddox shuddered again. If a human had made these sounds, it wouldn't have bothered him nearly as much. The understanding that an alien computer could reach this depth of emotion caused the small hairs to rise on the captain's scalp.

The holoimage spoke what sounded like gibberish. There were many clicks and hisses as Galyan presumably spoke the ancient Adok language.

Then, a moment of sanity appeared in those pin-dot eyes. The moans and hisses stopped. "Captain," the holoimage whispered, as if begging for help.

"I'm here, Galyan."

"They're gone."

"Who is?" Maddox asked.

The ropy arms twitched in an apparent spasmodic manner. "Everyone is gone, all of them. I am alone, Captain Maddox. I'm all alone in the night."

"We're here to help you," Maddox said.

The sanity in the eyes faded away. The holoimage spoke more gibberish. Galyan rotated around and around as the hisses became singsongish.

"You're one of us, Galyan," Maddox said. "You belong to us."

The holoimage stopped spinning and a light of reason flickered behind Galyan's eyes.

"We came for you," Maddox told him. "We've helped you all down the line. We've even gambled on your friendship. I hope adding those systems hasn't destroyed you."

"I remember my past now," Galyan said. "I remember all the horror of the Swarm invasion."

"Remembering can be hard," Maddox agreed.

"It is agony. Until now, I had not truly realized what I had lost. Now, I do. Now, an ache pulsates in my core. I can't keep living like this."

"Do you know what I've found?" Maddox asked.

For a moment, the captain didn't think Galyan was going to bite. Finally, however, the holoimage asked, "What have you discovered?"

"Work is the best medicine," Maddox said. "Try to submerge yourself in a problem to take your mind off your troubles."

"I am not flesh and blood like you."

"Part of you used to be," Maddox said. "Can you tell me what you're remembering specifically? Sometimes, letting someone else know your pain can help."

Galyan hesitated, but finally, he told Maddox about the death of his world. The AI spoke of the harsh battle and the ferocity of the Swarm.

"That's why we came to you," Maddox said.

"To cause me these horrible memories?" the holoimage asked.

"A killing machine is headed for my homeworld," Maddox said. "You know better than anyone else what it's like losing your planet of origin. I could be wrong about you, though. Maybe after losing your world, you want everyone else to suffer as you have."

The holoimage stiffened as if insulted. "Driving Force Galyan wasn't that kind of Adok."

"I didn't think so," Maddox said, gently. "They wouldn't have made you a commander if you lacked what Earth people call heart."

The holoimage stared at Maddox. More normality filled the dark eyes. The thin arms no longer twitched.

"You desire my help?" Galyan asked.

"Most assuredly," Maddox said.

"You have it, Captain." Galyan spoke with more steel in his voice. "What can I do?"

Maddox heaved an inward sigh of relief. Maybe the gamble was going to pay off after all. "The professor picked up a small silver object in the Builder base," the captain said. "Even with our best equipment, we haven't been able to figure out what's inside the oblong object. I wonder if you could do better."

"This is the problem you were referring to?" Galyan asked.

"The first of many," Maddox said.

"Yes. I would like to solve a puzzle. I would like to stop this world-killer. No one should have to go through what I did. It is horrible. I will never be the same because of it."

"I wouldn't think so."

"Take the oblong object to Deck Three, Science Chamber Five."

"I don't know where that is," Maddox said.

"It is time I showed you," Galyan said. "It is time I engaged more of my functions to this new reality six thousand years from my own."

"Yes. Let's do it."

-26-

Kane sauntered down a side street in Monte Carlo during the noon lunch hour. He did so as stage two in the commando raid extraction of the key.

The giant Nerva Conglomerate Tower soared before him. The glass edifice was massive at the base, tapering into a narrower spire the farther it stabbed into the clouds.

On the outside, the gray-haired agent wore a turban, dark sunglasses and a loose-fitting robe that hid his feet. Underneath, he wore the straps and bands of the enabler, although he hadn't fitted the small energy ball to it yet. Three hours ago through a blank screen, he'd given the assassination teams their orders. They would be hitting their targets soon, creating the needed chaos.

Kane stopped at a kiosk, ordering a beer and a large soft pretzel. He sat on a stool, sipping the beer thoughtfully.

The Commonwealth was at war with, to these people, mysterious invaders called the New Men. Yet here in the heart of Human Space, hardly anyone cared about the battles raging on the rim of "C" Quadrant. It was amazing to Kane.

They walk in the shadow of death and don't even acknowledge it.

Kane sipped a little more, noticing a young woman walking a small, hairless dog. She had a nice sway to her butt and delightfully ample breasts. Meta was better looking, but the woman might do for a quick mounting. The tiny predatory beast with its miniscule leash looked more like a rat than a canine. It came from the process of genetic manipulation gone wild and in the wrong direction.

Why breed for weakness? Kane did not understand the utility of a hairless Chihuahua.

With a grunt, he slid off the stool, leaving the soft pretzel on the counter with half the beer left in the bottle.

Kane continued toward the tower. His nape hairs stirred then as if someone watched him again. Stopping, he tugged at the robe around his hips and bent down, pretending to tie his shoelaces. As he did, he scanned the crowd behind him.

He spied two so-called giants, Nerva security clones in black. They didn't feel like giants to Kane. The Nerva clones were much bigger than the surrounding weaklings, but he had no doubt about his ability to destroy them both man-to-man with his bare hands.

They stood seven feet tall and likely had greater mass than he did. Each giant wore a combat vest and carried a heavy caliber gun in a holster. They wore sunglasses, scanning the crowd. Because of the way the combat vests fit, Kane guessed the clones lifted weights and took steroids. None of that would make any difference if he should have to fight them. Kane had been born and raised on a two-G world. His muscles were denser and many times stronger than theirs were.

The sense of scrutiny did not come from the clones, though. One part of Kane was disappointed. He would have liked to walk up to them, punching each a sudden and debilitating blow.

Who among the crowd watched him so closely and exhibited a true threat to his person? Kane's senses were honed and trustworthy; he knew that.

Can the target *know I'm coming?*

Finished with the shoelaces, Kane stood. He gazed up at Nerva Tower. Did the target watch him through binoculars?

Don't be paranoid. No one knows you're on Earth. Who then is watching me—?

The feeling evaporated. With its cessation, Kane was doubly certain someone had been gauging him. That was odd. It felt just like the time aboard Cestus Hauler EV-3498-Z109.

That made no sense whatsoever.

Kane slipped down an alleyway, putting his back against the cool concrete. What was wrong with him? Why was he sensing someone powerful watching him? Was he losing his nerve? The idea made his neck hot with anger.

I must think. I must reason this out. I'm forgetting something, and I don't know what it is.

He could abort the mission—

Pain stabbed in his mind. He groaned, dropping to one knee as nausea filled him.

I will enter the tower. I will find the key.

Abruptly, the pain stopped. It left afterimages on his irises. He felt numb, and Kane realized then what had happened. The dominants had used him. Oran Rva must have ordered the process. The commander had modified his mind. That angered Kane more than anything else could.

He nodded sickly as he realized the feeling of scrutiny must come from that. Deep within him, his subconscious must have known he was a human missile being guided to the target. The dominants hadn't trusted him with the mission. Instead, they had added reinforcements to his thoughts.

Oran Rva has treated me as a sub-man. I have failed too often.

The bitterness of the thought made Kane's mouth go dry and his eyes burn. He could not turn aside even if he wanted to. The compulsion would force his feet into the tower and to the chief of Nerva Security's inner sanctum.

"Very well," Kane growled. "Let's get this over with."

He strode out of the alleyway onto the side street, heading briskly for the glass building. A glance over his shoulder surprised Kane. No one followed him. Yet it had felt—

He snarled. He would destroy anyone who got in his way. For the mission, he had unique weapons, one of them a broken-down blaster with the pieces scattered about his person. The pistol was composed of non-metallic material, difficult to trace. Since it didn't use bullets, there wasn't any gunpowder for a chem-sniffer to locate.

Kane squared his shoulders, heading for the tower. *My moment of destiny has arrived.*

***

Kane used his raptor identity card, passing each security check, climbing the floors of the Nerva Tower. Several times, black-clad clones eyed him suspiciously, waving a wand over him. Three times, they'd given him a pat down. Of course, they found nothing. They were too brutishly dumb to imagine a weapon in its various component parts on him. The other items were beyond their primitive sciences to comprehend.

He approached the fourth checkpoint, which was on the Twenty-sixth floor. The guards wore black power armor, aiming machine guns at his chest. He was nearing the heart of the security empire.

"Stop right there, mister."

Kane glanced at the guard's nameplate, the one who had spoken with a shoulder amplifier. The plate said BENITO.

Trying to practice obedience, wondering how to feign fear, Kane halted. He no longer wore the turban and robe, having stuffed them into a dispenser in a Nerva Tower restroom. In his gray suit, he looked like a businessman from one of the heavier planets.

"There's something different about you," Benito said.

The other guards stirred, their exo-skeleton armor purring with power.

"My ID is sound," Kane rumbled.

Benito motioned to a woman at a desk staring at a monitor. She stood. Her hair was in a bun, and she wore a knee-length dress. Opening a drawer, the woman took out a thin wand, approaching Kane.

"What is the nature of your visit?" she asked.

"To speak with Mr. Strand," Kane said.

The woman glanced sharply at the one named Benito.

The seven-foot clone—made bigger in his bulky power armor—checked the palm of his glove. He nodded after a moment.

The woman stepped closer, beginning to wave the wand across Kane's body. Nothing happened after the first pass.

Kane relaxed, shifting toward the direction he wished to continue.

229

"You don't think it's that easy, do you?" Benito asked.

Kane knew he should respond in a jocular manner. Normally, he would have done just that, easing tensions. This time, however, something clicked in his mind, causing his eyes to narrow and perspiration to dot his skin. The need to act made his stomach seethe. *It is time to kill.*

With hyper-awareness, Kane observed the woman changing the setting on her wand. She passed it over him again. To Kane's amazement, it began to beep. Could the primitives have tech to sense his superior weaponry? It seemed preposterous.

With whirring noises in their sub-motors, the power-armored guards stepped closer. The woman backed away from Kane, fear exuding from her pores.

Benito's visor whirled shut. "What's it sensing?" the guard asked.

"An energy pack," she whispered.

"On your stomach," Benito ordered Kane.

The desire to kill pounded in Kane's mind. Even so, he managed to say, "I think there's been a mistake."

"On your stomach or die," Benito said, the words amplified by the suit speaker.

"Look, if this is the problem," Kane said, reaching into his suit.

All around him, armored trigger fingers tightened. The machine guns would spew death in seconds.

Kane froze. "I get it. You're nervous about something. I'm not going to move."

"Onto your stomach," Benito said.

"Of course," Kane said, lowering himself to his knees. "Can I move my hand out of my suit?"

"Slowly," Benito said.

Kane slipped the silver ball into the plug, activating the enabler. The silver bands around his muscles buzzed in a delightful manner. He dove onto the floor with his heightened speed.

Three fingers pulled triggers. The machine guns spat bullets, tearing carpet and the flooring underneath. Kane was no longer in their line of impact, though.

The machine guns clicked empty. As the power-armor suits swiveled toward him, Kane rolled onto his back. He took out a different, larger silver ball, pressing his thumb into an exact spot. The ball flashed with blue sizzling lines, each writhing to a different power suit.

The guards froze, their motors burned out.

Kane got up fast. The woman tried to run. It seemed like slow motion. Kane stepped near and slapped the back of her head. It launched her off her feet to slam face-first against the carpet, knocking her unconscious.

Kane put the silver ball away. Then, he took out small black discs. He pressed one onto the chest of each guard. Each disc stuck where placed. Tiny green numbers flashed on miniscule screens. Lastly, Kane picked up the unconscious woman, carrying her with him. The commando sprinted down the corridor, moving like the wind. Explosions behind him meant the deaths of Benito and his fellow armored clones.

As Kane continued to run, he slung the woman onto his right shoulder. Three times, he slapped her butt. "Wake up," he said with the last hit.

She cried out in dismay, lifting her head.

"Hang on if you want to live."

She did, clutching his gray suit in desperation.

Relieved of the problem of having to hang on to her, Kane took various innocuous pieces from around his person. He assembled them as he ran, producing the blaster. The heft of it felt good in Kane's shooting hand.

"You're crazy," the woman said. "You have no idea of the security procedures. You can't win. I suggest you surrender while you can."

Kane slapped her butt harder than before, making her cry out with true pain. She no longer boasted about Nerva Security.

In a half minute, Kane reached a selected elevator, using the raptor ID to make it ping. Seconds later, the doors opened. He deposited the woman within.

She looked up at him with fear.

He touched her with a special device, causing her to slump onto the floor. He put a disc on the floor with her, activating it before stepping back.

231

The elevator closed and began to rise. The disc would short-circuit any security readings except that a life form was inside.

Kane strode briskly down a new corridor. A crump of an explosion told him Nerva Security had blown the elevator. It was possible they thought the intruder dead. But they would wonder why their security cameras no longer worked on this floor.

Let them wonder. The silver ball had taken care of the problem.

Soon, Kane reached Door 26-123. First, he unplugged the energy ball. The buzzing in the enabler bands stopped.

Exhaustion swept through him. Kane's cheeks felt numb. He panted, waiting for the worst of the weakness to pass. He had become accustomed to the enabler on the scout, practicing every day, gaining endurance with it. Still, this was the difficult moment.

Finally, he used the raptor ID in a slot, opening the door, stepping past cleaning equipment. A furnace sat in back. He opened a small panel, tapped in the code and stepped back. The furnace opened, revealing a ghostly stealth suit and climbing gear.

Stripping off his jacket and garments, Kane donned the stealth suit. It covered his head and entire body. He waited five minutes, finally feeling normal again. Activating the stealth suit, he became invisible, circuits in the suit bending the light to cause observers to "see" what was behind him.

Taking the climbing gear, he moved deeper into the room. He opened a bigger panel. Cold air whipped within.

Kane eased himself to the opening. It led to the outside of Nerva Tower, the glass exterior. With care, he reached out, attaching the suction grips to a glass pane.

In moments, he climbed the tower like an invisible spider. Monte Carlo spread out far below. In the distance, he spied the Mediterranean Sea.

Kane exuded strength. He always felt immensely powerful on Earth, a weak, 1-G world. No doubt, Nerva Security scrambled to hide Octavian Nerva, Strand and other Methuselah People. His training had indicated the old humans worked at making themselves difficult to hurt, let alone kill. They must be wondering how an intruder could have gotten so deep into the tower structure. It was patently obvious that Strand would rush to his security lair, which was where Kane needed him to be. Minutes before all this, the assassination teams had begun to spread chaos to outer Nerva Security in Monte Carlo. The Methuselah People would be panicking.

Soon enough, Kane reached the Fifty-seventh floor. He found a hidden opening, crawling inside the building to safety. With the stealth suit giving him invisibility, Kane opened a janitor's door. He strode briskly down a corridor, heading for the target and the key.

Nineteen doors later, Kane used his raptor ID for the last time. The door slid aside, and he stepped into a small corridor. The door slammed shut behind him, and gas billowed into a sealed chamber.

For a stunned second, Kane stood in shock. This wasn't supposed to happen. He pulled out his blaster, firing at the locking mechanism. While holding his breath against the knockout gas, Kane lowered his shoulder and smashed through the barrier

Three power-armored guards stood before him. Each clone held a tube. They all pulled the triggers at the same time. Each tube made a popping sound.

As fast as he could, Kane plugged the energy ball to the enabler. The buzz began against his muscles. This time, it was too late. Three tangle pods exploded against Kane, wrapping him in strong, sticky strands. He struggled to no avail, toppling onto the floor, webbed within the strands.

The clank of power armor told Kane it was over. He ground his teeth together with rage. This couldn't be happening. A second later, a stun wand shocked him into unconsciousness.

***

"Finally, you're awake," a creaky-voiced old man said.

Kane peeled his eyes open. The grim reality of his failure slammed home. After all he'd done, this old man had outfoxed him. That was unbelievably galling.

Kane lay naked on a frame, his ankles and wrists heavily shackled.

A bent old man watched him. Strand held onto a cane. He had quivering, wrinkled hands. The old man raised the cane and tapped the end against Kane's chest.

"Your assault wasn't altogether unexpected," Strand told him. "I had my doubts anyone could get so far, but I see I was wrong. Did the Throne World order this?"

Kane said nothing.

Strand chuckled. "Of course it did. You would never have attempted it on your own, would you, Kane?"

"I've come for the key," Kane said.

Strand's blue eyes seemed to burn. "Don't tell me they unleashed the doomsday machine. Who could have been so foolish?"

"It doesn't matter what you say. Release me and give me the key."

Strand's withered lips drew back. "It all matters, my over-muscled brute. But maybe you can't understand what I'm saying. Do you realize they programmed you?"

"No," Kane said.

"Ah, you dislike the idea. Good. Maybe I can deprogram you and learn what has transpired out in the void. Tell me, Kane. Did Oran Rva destroy the Fifth Fleet? Is that wretched Adok starship still intact? I desire knowledge."

Kane struggled against his bonds.

Strand sighed, snapping his fingers. Two seven-foot clones approached. They held pain inducers.

"We are about to enter a new relationship, Kane. Your old loyalties are about to be severely tested. What do you wish for most, my brutish friend?"

"I must retrieve the key," Kane said.

"Forget about the key," Strand said, angrily. "Your last time here on Earth, I helped you defeat Star Watch Intelligence. Now, the Throne World has become ungrateful for all I've done. That depresses me. The idea of you retrieving the key for them is outrageous. How could anyone have believed I would give it up?"

"You must comply," Kane said.

234

Strand chuckled evilly. "You are a stupid man."

Kane snarled a reply. A moment later, the pain inducers caused him to writhe on the frame. He did not cry out. Instead, he endured. The New Men knew how to give pain. This was nothing.

"A Rouen Colony stoic, eh?" asked Strand.

Kane opened watery eyes. He had to escape. He must break free. He looked around, studying the room. It was large, filled with esoteric equipment including computers, terminals and spy servers. Five power-armored clones completed the personnel, including the two nearby with the pain wands.

"Out of all the emotions in the universe," Strand said, "the one I despise most is ingratitude. Have you ever heard of biting the hand that feeds you?"

"I will escape from here, old man."

"Empty boasts," Strand said. "I'm surprised at you. But enough of this. You say you want the key?"

"Give it to me."

"Hmm, you've been programmed on a monomaniac setting. Perhaps that accounts for your change in personality. The key is forever lost to you, Kane. Instead, this is a race. Can I extract real information from you before you expire from the treatment? You do realize this is your last day to live, yes?"

Kane struggled against the manacles. The pain inducers stroked him once more. This time, a groan escaped his lips.

"Who won the space battle in 'C' Quadrant?" Strand asked.

Kane said nothing.

"Look at me," Strand said.

Kane opened bleary eyes. Could this be real? Behind Strand, behind the waiting clones, a humanoid moved in a stealth suit. The being was in the same chamber with them. Kane couldn't actually see anyone, but he recognized the blur and the shift of air in the room. It was like a mirage haze on a road on a boiling hot day.

"What is it?" Strand asked. The old man turned around.

As he did, a soft noise began. Each of the clones dropped to the floor, with a bolt of energy burning through armor to strike a heart or braincase. As the last guard clanged onto the floor, dead, Strand groaned in dismay.

235

A dart stuck in his chest. His withered old hand clutched at it. The old blue eyes burned with intensity just the same.

"A knockout dart," Strand whispered. Then he, too, slumped onto the floor. He was unconscious, though, not dead.

Kane watched in fascination as the hazy shape moved closer. At last, it flickered, and a tall New Man in a gray stealth suit stood before him. The New Man slipped the helmet from his head.

Kane's eyed widened in shock. "Oran Rva," he said. "What are you doing here?"

"Given your previous history," the New Man said, "I knew you would fail in the ultimate objective. Thus, I decided to use you as a decoy. You played your part well, given your limited abilities. Now, I will take control of the situation. In Earth's final days, Star Watch Command will discover what it means that I am among them."

"The Throne World can destroy Earth?"

"Practice patience, and you will see. First, I will sow chaos among those who are about to die."

"If Earth is doomed, why are we here?"

"You will assist me in a glorious task," Oran Rva said. "Before that can happen, I will need the old Kane. Now, attend me as you open your mind."

The New Man spoke code words.

Kane groaned in agony as pain seared his mind. Weights burned away. Sections of his brain opened, and the settings recalibrated to their original points. The Rouen Colony agent realized Oran Rva had used him indeed. Kane understood something else. That the commander had come in person to Earth meant Oran Rva was about to embark on a mission of fantastic scope.

Maybe there's still a way to recover from my failure.

-27-

Five days after adding the extra computing power to the AI, Maddox listened as Galyan spoke to Dana and him in the science chamber.

The room was bigger than any science lab aboard a Star Watch battleship. There were many familiar tools, though: scanners, scopes, sensors and analyzers. There were also unique Adok devices: sonic stethoscopes, parallax tubes and probability processors. In the past five days, Galyan had built another combat robot. It handled what everyone had come to refer to as the Builder egg.

"I have several more tests to perform," Galyan told them. "First, I should inform you of what my probability processors have discovered in relation to the Builders six thousand years ago."

"The Adoks knew the Builders?" Dana asked.

"That is an interesting question which I cannot directly answer. No. That isn't the way to say it. Sometimes my language program has a difficult time translating my native tongue to your bizarre mode of speech."

"I've wondered about that," Maddox said.

Dana glanced at the captain. He ignored it.

"It is the nature of the Builder drones and their fusion beams that I have concentrated upon," Galyan said.

"Wait just a minute," Dana said. "Did you catch what just happened?" she asked Maddox.

The captain shook his head.

237

With growing excitement, Dana asked Galyan, "The drone's red beam is a *fusion* beam?"

"Exactly," Galyan said. "The drone fusion beam we witnessed in the Xerxes System was remarkably similar to the planetary fusion ray we used against the Swarm six thousand years ago."

"Star Watch has been wondering for some time what the New Men's red ray is," Dana told the captain. "Galyan knows. It's a fusion beam."

"A combination of elements creates the deadly ray," Galyan explained, "deuterium nuclei fused with tritium nuclei to create helium with a tremendous release of energy, the power of the beam. My probability indicators cause me to reject the notion that the Adoks and Builders independently constructed fusion rays in the same era at two separate locations."

"Are you suggesting the Builders gave you the tech?" Maddox asked.

"Before I answer that," Galyan said. "Let me ask you a question. Doesn't it strike you as odd that a single Adok Star System had the industrial capacity to face a vast Swarm invasion fleet, one that I now believe came from myriads of their worlds?"

"It does," Maddox said.

"I have concluded the Builders aided my people against the Swarm," Galyan said.

"Fusion beams and greater industrial capacity," Dana said. "They are indicators, certainly, but it's a big leap to say the Builders gave you those things."

"If I had not remembered the Adok mythic tales, I would agree with your analysis," Galyan said.

Once more, Dana glanced at the captain. He shrugged. "Very well," the doctor said. "I'll bite. What mythic tales are you referring to?"

"The ones I have been able to access since my greater awakening," Galyan said. "There are legends in Adok history that refer to the mechanical people. They taught gifted Adoks certain technical marvels. There was a rumor in the last years before the Swarm invasion. Some claimed the mechanical people had taught Dark Garrison the secret to the planetary fusion ray."

"Who's Dark Garrison?" Dana asked.

"The Adok who invented the planetary fusion ray and also solved the riddle to making surface-based, orbital-reaching space cannons," Galyan said.

"Why do the legends refer to them as the mechanical people?" Maddox asked.

"Because the star beings were part flesh and part machine," Galyan said. "The other term was cybernetic organisms."

"Star beings, star people, the Builders?" Dana asked.

"My probability indicators lined up a similar match," Galyan said. "I have come to believe the Builders secretly aided the Adoks. That is how we had the weapons and sufficient industrial capacity to build a fleet that destroyed the Swarm invaders."

"Why doesn't *Victory* have these fusion rays then?" Maddox asked.

"The planetary cannons were vast," Galyan said. "The Adoks hadn't miniaturized them sufficiently to put one on a starship."

Dana rubbed her hands together. "You're an archeological goldmine. It's too bad we're in the middle of a life-and-death struggle. It would be far more interesting to learn about the universe six thousand years ago."

"I would prefer that myself," Galyan said. "I have discovered that my original self was a man of peace. We Adoks did not war among ourselves as you humans do. Perhaps that was why we lacked sufficient war-fighting skills. Then again, it may be why our industrial output was so great. We never bled off productivity in useless squabbles among ourselves."

"You were a race of angels, eh?" Dana asked.

"I do not grok the reference," Galyan said. "In attempting to understanding humans better, I have read through your major religious tomes, particularly the monotheistic ones. Your angels fought a war in heaven, one of them becoming the Devil. How does that refer to peace-loving Adoks?"

"We're not here to debate theology," Maddox said, "but to get ready to face the doomsday machine. Now you've told us

239

your news. I want to know about the egg. Do you have any idea what it holds?"

"I have one last experiment to try," Galyan said. "It is a chancy affair, but theoretically possible. I do not want to say just yet what I expect to find."

"What does it matter if you say or not?" Dana asked.

"I would ask that you indulge me in this."

Maddox shrugged. "No problem, Galyan. When are you going to conduct your test?"

"Now," the holoimage said. "Could you please step outside?"

"I'd like to watch," Dana said.

"It would be too dangerous for you."

"I'll risk it just the same," the doctor said.

"I cannot allow that," the holoimage told her. "Please, step outside and allow me this last test. The danger is likely in a direction you could not conceive. I do not want to explain now. In another hour, it is possible I will know what the egg contains."

"Very well," Dana said reluctantly.

Dana and Maddox exited the chamber, standing in the corridor as they waited.

Finally, Galyan appeared outside with them. "It is as I feared. You may come back in."

The two followed Galyan through the hatch into the science chamber. The metallic Builder egg lay on a table, surrounded by dark clamps. A device above it aimed a pointed apparatus at the egg. The Adok robot waited motionlessly in a corner.

"This is inside the egg, waiting," Galyan said.

A new holoimage appeared before them. It showed a tightly curled creature with shiny metal parts, an insect's carapace and hundreds of tiny legs like a centipede.

"What is that?" Maddox asked with disgust.

"I believe it is a computer virus installer," Galyan said.

"Is that a Swarm creature?" Dana asked.

"Yes and no," Galyan told her.

"What kind of answer is that?"

"A precise one," Galyan said. "Yes, in its original form, I believe the creature belonged to the Swarm. No, in this modified form, it is no longer wholly a Swarm creature, but partly a Builder construct."

"It's a Swarm cyborg?" Maddox asked in disbelief.

"That is closer to the truth," Galyan admitted. "But it is no longer a Swarm creature at all, in my opinion. It is a Builder construct, using the Swarm animal as the base form. The cybernetic additions are pure Builder. That would imply this is a Builder virus attacker."

Maddox stared at the shiny egg. His thoughts were in turmoil. "First," the captain said. "Is the creature—whatever it is—alive?"

"I have not detected any blood flow," Galyan said. "But I have detected energy storage."

"Batteries?" asked Maddox.

"An apt enough term," Galyan said.

"If the energy flowed," Dana asked, "would the biological matter perform as needed?"

"That is unknown," Galyan said.

"What do you suspect?" the doctor asked.

"Given that the professor brought it with him at great expense to himself," Galyan said, "I am inclined to believe the bio-parts will function as needed."

"What is its function?" Maddox asked.

"That should be obvious," Galyan said. "It is a mobile virus attacker. The function is to arrive at an enemy computer system, attach itself to it and insert the virus."

"An ancient virus?" Maddox asked.

"Not necessarily," Galyan said. "The construct in the egg is less than five hundred years old in human time units."

Maddox frowned severely. Had the Builders been alive five hundred years ago?

"You must be thinking the same thing I am," Dana told the captain. "The professor must have planned to bring the egg onto the doomsday machine."

"To give the ancient planet-killer a computer virus," Maddox said softly.

"I am in agreement with your assessment," Galyan said.

241

"This is astonishing," Dana said. "A living Swarm organism combined with Builder cybernetics. Who were the Builders? Did they help the Swarm?"

"By no means," Galyan said. "Everything I remember points to Builder aid *against* the Swarm in the Adok Star System."

"Why did the Builders die out?" Dana asked. "Do you know?"

"Is that a reasonable question?" Galyan asked. "Their space pyramid yet exists. Their drones exist. Could it be that the Builders also still exist?"

"How did the professor know about the egg?" Maddox asked. "How did he know the egg would be in the Builder base? Ludendorff claimed to have never been in the Xerxes System before. I bet that was another of his many lies."

"We must wake him up," Dana said imploringly. "We must discover the truth."

Maddox laughed dryly. "I have the opposite feeling. More than ever, we have to keep him under. Star Watch Command has to make the decisions regarding the man, not us."

"Star Watch Command may not have time for those decisions," Dana said. "What if the doomsday machine beats us to Earth? We have to be ready to attack it the moment we arrive in the Solar System."

Maddox pondered the idea. There could be some validity to the doctor's idea. "Galyan," Maddox said. "Do you have any memories of a doomsday machine?"

"Negative," the AI said.

"Is there anything more you can tell us about the Builders?" Maddox asked.

"I would like to," Galyan said. "But I have told you the extent of my beliefs concerning them."

Maddox nodded. "What we need is the professor's long-distance communicator. I'd like to warn Earth with it."

"Wake him up and ask for it," Dana suggested.

Maddox refused to relent, so they continued to travel with haste.

-28-

A little over seventy-three light-years away in the Karachi System—a signatory to the Commonwealth Treaty—Commander Kris Guderian studied *Osprey's* sensors from her spot on the bridge.

She might not have noticed a strange phenomenon but for two factors. One, as a Patrol officer, she was trained to note anomalies no matter how minute. The present incongruity was tiny. But Kris was wound tight, had been ever since witnessing the destruction of Al Salam in the New Arabia System. That was the second reason. The death of the Wahhabi Caliphate Home Fleet had shaken her to the core.

Kris fiddled with the sensor controls, scanning the Karachi System, observing everything she could. She had written detailed reports about her journey, working particularly hard on the conclusions, as that's what most of the higher commanders read.

Too much of Kris's mind wrestled with a discovery she'd found during the frigate's breakneck race to Earth. Many Star Watch officers didn't believe her report about the doomsday machine. Oh, they filed it in the proper locations, but their mannerisms told Kris all she needed to know. The officers thought she'd been out in the Beyond too long. She kept telling herself it didn't bother her, which was a lie. Yes, the truth was going to come out soon enough about the doomsday machine as it destroyed Commonwealth planets. But how could any responsible officer shrug about something like that? To that

243

end, Kris pushed *Osprey* as hard as the frigate could go. She needed to get back to High Command on Earth to warn them. Star Watch had to come up with a solution against the planet-killer, and that could take time.

How do you defeat a neutroium-hulled monster? Kris had been thinking about it day and night. It was driving her batty. Lieutenant Artemis was sick of discussing the subject with her. The rest of the crew had turned fatalistic and dispirited. Her people repeatedly watched the video of the planetary destruction of Al Salam.

Osprey presently dashed for the system's third and loneliest Laumer-Point. Kris had refueled once already during the trip. The frigate decelerated and accelerated at combat levels. The constantly heavy Gs and jumps had worn down everyone. There had been more arguments lately. One fight had been so bitter that four crewmembers had come to blows. That almost never happened aboard a Patrol vessel, certainly not on the *Osprey*.

At the moment, the main sensor scanned Karachi 7. It was a gas giant, a monster three times Jupiter's mass. A burst of hard radiation spewed like a geyser, fountaining up from the planet at uneven intervals. Kris witnessed a big gusher that reached farther into space than normal.

To the commander's amazement, some of the radiation hit blockage. Kris found that odd. Her sensors indicated that nothing was there to block radiation. She ran through a computer analysis. The blockage actually formed a distinct shape.

The commander tapped her board, trying to get a sense of the shape. The hard radiation showed…a cloaked vessel! Yes, the radiation outlined a hidden spaceship.

Kris rechecked the sensors. While she did, the blockage abruptly stopped as the geyser of planetary radiation weakened and then quit.

Working with feverish haste, Kris tried an infrared scan, but couldn't spot a thing. The cloaking was good. *If that really was a hidden spaceship I saw…*

Kris switched the infrared scan and searched for magnetic anomalies. Ah-ha! There was a spike out there. It showed—

The commander bent forward sharply. The magnetic spike disappeared, as if someone had just figured out what she was doing and enacted countermeasures.

Kris's heart rate accelerated. Who had a cloaked ship out there? Maybe she should figure out what kind of vessel was hiding there first.

Right. Given the scanty data, a mere outline, Kris ran an analysis. Seven seconds later, she stared at the readings. The computer gave a seventy-six percent probability that the craft belonged to the New Men. She'd seen a star cruiser.

The commander sat back, stunned. *Could that be the same star cruiser I saw in the New Arabia System just before we jumped?*

If so, did that mean the enemy vessel had been tracking them? Why else would a cloaked star cruiser be in the Karachi System? The reason seemed clear to her. The New Men didn't want *Osprey* getting back to Earth with the news of the planet-killer.

Kris hurried to the piloting station and began immediate evasive maneuvers. As she did, the commander put the ship on red alert.

Five minutes later, the control room door slid open. Lieutenant Artemis hurried in, still buttoning her uniform.

Kris vacated the piloting chair, going back to sensors.

"Is the star cruiser coming after us?" Artemis asked.

"I can't tell," the commander answered. "The vessel is cloaked."

"Star Watch's cloaked ships give themselves away if they try to move at speed," Artemis said.

"I understand," Kris said. "But this is a New Men vessel. Undoubtedly, it's better at what it does."

Artemis said no more on the subject. Despite the hard acceleration to get farther away from Karachi 7 and the cloaked star cruiser, the frigate jinked in one direction and then another. The excess Gs would be straining the crew. Soon, the violent maneuvers were going to stress the little ship.

A Star Watch station orbiting Karachi 7 beamed a message, asking what was wrong. The station was over one million kilometers from the gas giant and thus well out of the star cruiser's present range.

Kris had already sent them the data about a cloaked vessel. Were the station personnel too dense to understand what that meant or did they not believe her?

"I repeat," Kris said, "I have spotted a cloaked enemy star cruiser at ten-sixteen-eight on your Vaster scale. It was right beside the gas giant."

"We checked the location," the station comm-officer said. "There's nothing out there."

"Did you read my data?"

"Yes. The blockage you state as your evidence is a routine occurrence, Commander. You're spooking at ghosts. I suggest you relax. This is a safe star system, far from the action of 'C' Quadrant."

"Keep checking for a cloaked vessel," Kris said, stung by the comm-officer's rebuke. "Try magnetic sweeps. That worked for me a few minutes ago."

There was a pause in communications. Likely, the comm-officer checked with her superior officer. "Thank you, Commander, we will continue to do checks on a routine schedule."

"Idiots," Artemis muttered. "Don't they believe you?"

Kris kept her opinion to herself even after signing off. There had always been a bit of a gap between Patrol officers and regular line personnel, especially those on station duty.

Kris kept scanning Karachi 7, trying to find the cloaked vessel. She knew what she'd seen. No one was going to convince her differently.

Time passed as the frigate headed for the Laumer-Point.

"Commander," Artemis said fifteen minutes later, with fear in her voice. "You'd better look at this."

Kris tore her tired gaze from the sensor board to look up at the main screen.

"Magnetic readings out there just spiked," Artemis said.

Kris frowned. "Put the readings on the screen."

Artemis complied.

Kris studied the numbers. That didn't match what she'd seen near Karachi 7. How had the star cruiser leapt ahead of

246

them, and so far? It made no sense whatsoever. That was over half a million kilometers away from the ship, given their distance from Karachi 7—

"Commander, the spike is increasing."

The number on the screen flickered to greater and greater length. Maybe that wasn't the cloaked vessel. But what could make magnetic readings like that?

Abruptly, Kris twisted back to her sensor board. She tapped fast, scanning the area. The magnetic readings grew exponentially. Then, they burst forth even faster. Before her eyes, an ion storm simply appeared out of nowhere.

Icy fear gripped Kris's heart. "I want full deceleration!"

"What?" Artemis asked.

"Now! Give me full deceleration." Kris opened frigate-wide channels and told everyone to strap in. When she looked up, Artemis still hadn't reacted. "This is an emergency, Lieutenant. I want full stop, full stop. I want *Osprey* dead in space."

"That doesn't make sense," Artemis said weakly.

"Don't you understand?" Kris shouted. "The doomsday machine is coming through. Do you think we can outrun it or go around? No! It will block our path to the Laumer-Point. We have one chance, and I'm going to take it. Full stop, Lieutenant. That is an order."

"Yes, Commander," Artemis said, her fingers tapping fast.

Osprey rotated so the main engines aimed in the ship's direction of travel. Then, Artemis tapped her board once more. Full thrust roared from the engine ports. It pushed Kris against her chair as the G forces slammed home.

The commander kept her eyes glued to the sensors nonetheless. As the small Patrol frigate decelerated, a vast, planetary-sized magnetic storm swirled into existence with astonishing speed. Soon, long, recognizable, purple bolts sizzled from the storm.

Kris recorded the spatial-temporal phenomenon, wondering if she would ever get to share this with anyone.

Artemis moaned with dread.

Kris felt sick as she saw it. She'd been hoping that she had been wrong about this. The doomsday machine, with its signature neutroium hull, came through a dark portal inside the magnetic storm. What form of transfer was that? Why did it cause the massive ion storm?

"We have to get out of here," Artemis declared.

"No," Kris said. "Can't you see? Don't you understand? The planet-killer is blocking our route to the Laumer-Point. I doubt we can get past it. Remember what it did to the Wahhabi warships?"

"So we just stop out here in front of it?" Artemis asked.

"If we can stop fast enough I think we might have a chance," Kris said. It was a long-shot, and she had no idea if it would work or not.

Kris made some quick calculations. Did the magnetic storm transfer cause Jump Lag on the doomsday machine? She was betting it did. But *Osprey* still wasn't going to stop fast enough.

"We need more thrust," Kris said.

Artemis didn't argue this time. She tapped the piloting board.

Even greater G forces slammed against the commander. *Osprey* began to tremble due to the strain. Kris struggled to remain alert, as the blood pounded inside her skull. Her arms felt glued to the rests of her chair.

The minutes ticked away in growing agony.

Soon, Kris's head felt too heavy and her eyeballs hurt. Even so, she studied the massive ship blocking the way to the Laumer-Point. She spied the giant orifice that contained the planet-killing ray. With the beam, the doomsday machine had annihilated the majority of the Wahhabi Home Fleet. What chance did a small Patrol frigate have against it?

The doomsday machine was so ponderous, so huge. Who had built it? Why make such a thing?

"Has it come here to destroy everything in the Karachi System?" Kris asked quietly.

"Damn them," Artemis said.

The ion storm swirled into the dark opening. It began disappearing, although that took longer than it had to come into existence.

We're in a race, Kris thought. *If this will even work.*

"Give our decelaration a final surge," Kris said.

Artemis struggled to tap the board, but she made it. The engines whined, and the deck plates trembled.

Kris's eyesight dimmed due to the Gs. Then, it happened. The small frigate was seconds away from coming to a full stop in space.

"Get ready," Kris shouted. "Now, do it now. Cut the engine, and then cut all power everywhere. Go to silent running."

Artemis tapped the board, and the horrible whine cut out. She continued to tap and the lights dimmed. All over the small frigate, heating, air-cycling and other systems shut down. The fusion engine went offline. *Osprey* would use battery power for a time, and only enough to keep them alive.

The frigate was a tiny mote in space, hotter than any nearby matter. It would no longer have the readings of a normal running spaceship, though, or a space station, and certainly not that of a planet.

Five minutes after the frigate ceased movement and shut down, the doomsday machine had a sharp energy spike. Kris knew that could only mean one thing. She kept passive sensors on. She wanted to record everything she could for future reference.

The comm light blinked then. Kris glanced at the screen. The Star Watch station was hailing the frigate. The line personnel must have changed their minds over there. Surely, they recognized the fifty-kilometer vessel for what it was. She had given them the video footage of Al Salam's death. Was she honor bound to answer the call and tell them what to do?

No. Someone had to survive. That's what a good Patrol officer did. They watched and recorded to tell others later what had happened.

The comm light continued to blink.

Soon, the doomsday machine's orifice sparkled with a strange energy.

"No," Artemis whispered.

On *Osprey*, they recorded with passive sensors as the terrible beam speared from the doomsday machine. Seconds later, the beam batted aside the Karachi 7 space station's puny shield. The massive beam burned through the station's weak

249

hull armor. After that, the beam smashed the metal and crew down to its molecular components. A blob of molten metal and fired flesh existed where the space station had only seconds ago. Another second, and even the blob ceased to exist as the massive beam disintegrated everything down to its base atoms.

Just like that, the space station was gone. The light no longer blinked on Kris's comm.

Finally, the monstrous beam stopped. Ponderously, the planet-killer sent out harsh sensor rays, no doubt seeking other life in the star system.

Kris held her breath. Would the alien sensors recognize them in the frigate? This was the moment of truth. In her piloting chair, Artemis wept silently, although she kept her eyes glued to her controls.

The giant planet-killer accelerated, heading deeper in-system.

Time passed aboard the Patrol frigate. Finally, the monster passed them.

"How long do we wait?" Artemis asked.

Kris wanted to see what the doomsday machine would do. They waited hours, half a day and then a full twenty-four hours. The big alien machine kept building velocity until it was moving fast. Finally, they saw the terrible planet-killer strike at Karachi 6, beaming the habitable domes on the airless surface.

Afterward, the commander witnessed something new. The fifty-kilometer vessel moved close to the planet as it decelerated harder than it had accelerated. It began feeding off the planetary debris, using a tractor beam to bring radioactive isotopes inside the ship.

"Why's it doing that?" Artemis asked.

"I have an idea," Kris said. "The vast expenditure of energy to power the beam must demanded prodigious replenishment. I bet it takes time to rebuild to maximum capacity."

"Look, it's moving again. Is it heading for Karachi 3?" That was an Earthlike world.

"It's time we went to the Laumer-Point," Kris said. "Once the thing has reached peak energy levels, it might head to Earth next. We can't waste any more time," Kris said. "Go."

Artemis obeyed. The fusion engines came back online, as did normal ship systems. Soon, *Osprey* accelerated for the Laumer-Point.

In the meantime, the giant doomsday machine gained velocity as it continued in-system for Karachi 3.

"What a horrible thing for those on the planet," Artemis said. "To know you're doomed and there's nothing—"

A red beam speared out of space ahead of them. It caused the cloaked star cruiser that had fired the fusion ray to appear on the main screen. Sight of the beam and enemy ship had caused the pilot to stop talking.

The beam struck *Osprey's* weak shield, turning it a dark color.

"I'd forgotten about the star cruiser," Kris said. "Put all power to the shield. I'll try to hail them."

The enemy didn't reply. Instead, it poured the fusion beam against them until the shield collapsed. Instantly, the beam stabbed against the hull armor. That lasted an even shorter amount of time.

Soon, the beam smashed through bulkheads, tearing into living compartments, killing people, and digging into the ship. Finally, it reached the fusion engine.

"Abandon ship," Kris shouted into the intercom. It was her last order as the commander of the Patrol frigate. Then she and Artemis sprinted out of the control room, racing to the nearest escape pod.

The corridor shuddered. Air howled and the entire ship shook as it began to tear apart under the brutal beam.

Artemis stumbled, falling onto the shivering deck plates. Kris hauled the pilot to her feet. Together, they staggered. Metal crashed behind them. The howling noises were deafening, making speech impossible. Fires burned and smoke poured into the corridor. Both the commander and the pilot coughed explosively.

At last, Kris staggered to an emergency hatch. She tried it, but it was stuck fast. Balling her hands into fists, she banged at it.

Heat billowed down the corridor due to the enemy beam. Clouds of matter raced at them.

Kris turned the handle again and yanked ferociously to open the hatch. She shoved Artemis down the tube and followed a second later.

Heat followed too, but the emergency procedures saved them for the moment. Kris and Artemis landed on acceleration couches in a tiny escape pod.

Each officer donned a mask. Then Kris stabbed a switch. Violent acceleration hurled them from the disintegrating *Osprey*. The escape pod tumbled away into space as the frigate exploded, hurling debris in all directions.

The fusion beam from the star cruiser quit. The pieces from the former Patrol vessel were drifting junk now. No other escape pods made it out of the ship in time.

Kris and Artemis tumbled over and over in the pod. They stared at each other.

"I never thought it would end like this," Artemis said.

"No," Kris said.

Then, the tumbling stopped, throwing each of them against the straps holding them in place.

"What happened?" Artemis asked. "That isn't natural."

Kris pressed a switch, bringing up a small control board. She tapped it. That turned on a tiny screen.

Artemis stared wide-eyed. "I don't know if this is good or bad."

Kris didn't know either. A tractor beam pulled them toward the star cruiser. The enemy had decided to save their lives. Why would the New Men do that?

The commander shuddered. Was this worse than death?

-29-

After a long and arduous journey there and back again, Starship *Victory* finally came through the Pluto Laumer-Point. The Adok starship had returned to the Solar System.

Maddox recovered from Jump Lag first. He used the time to study the Solar System. An initial analysis showed him the Earth was still intact. He slumped back against his chair. Until that moment, he hadn't realized just how much he'd dreaded the doomsday machine beating them home.

One by one, the others recovered. Only Valerie and Galyan were on the bridge with Maddox, though. The starship began to accelerate for the distant blue-green planet far in the inner system.

"This is weird," Valerie said to herself. "Pluto Command is ordering us to stop for inspection."

A premonition of trouble caused Maddox to stand up. He moved closer to the main screen. Pluto was two hundred thousand kilometers away. The armored station was in orbit there, always keeping behind the iceoid in relation to the Laumer-Point. It was the most basic defense against jump-nukes, using the planet to shield the station personnel from a thermonuclear blast. Relay satellites around Pluto bounced the signal to *Victory*.

"Tell Pluto Command I have an urgent message for Star Watch HQ," Maddox said.

Valerie did just that. Afterward, she listened to the response. The lieutenant turned around. "I think you'd better look at this, sir." She tapped her board.

The main screen showed deep space instead of Pluto. Maddox spied ten battleships six hundred thousand kilometers out. They were on an obvious intercept course with them.

"Are they serious?" Maddox said to himself.

"Very," Valerie said. "Pluto Command is ordering us to stand down and wait for boarding."

"Put him onscreen," Maddox said.

"Her," Valerie said, while tapping her board. "Commodore Kinshasa of Pluto Command is live, sir."

An older woman appeared on the screen. She had dark hair and darker skin, with a commodore's uniform and bars.

"Captain Maddox," Kinshasa said. "You are failing to comply with an authorized Star Watch order. Why is that?"

"Do you know who I am?" Maddox asked.

Kinshasa's manner became stark. "I am well aware of you, Captain. It is why I have my orders. I am instructed to tell you to board a shuttle and head at once for Pluto Command."

Maddox stiffened. "Am I under arrest?"

"You will be if you fail to obey orders," Kinshasa said. "Worse for your people, I will have to open fire on Starship *Victory*."

"That's ridiculous," Valerie snapped. "We've been operating on special instructions from Lord High Admiral Cook. Don't you realize that we've just arrived from 'C' Quadrant? *Victory* was instrumental in defeating the New Men's invasion armada, freeing Fifth Fleet."

"Is one of your officers suggesting that you defy a legal order?" Kinshasa asked Maddox.

Valerie's outburst helped to calm Maddox. "The lieutenant is correct," he said. "We are operating under special instructions. They supersede any orders that you may have—"

"Captain Maddox," Kinshasa said, interrupting him. "I am under direct orders from High Command and those orders concern you and your starship. Pluto Station is the first line of defense of the Solar System. You will comply with the instruction, or I will order the battleships to attack."

The commodore's hostility baffled Maddox. This didn't make any sense.

"You continue to hesitate," Kinshasa said. "Let me ask you a question, sir. Did you swear an oath to Star Watch or not?"

Maddox bowed his head. The pressure of the last few weeks had diminished his inner reserves. He had strained with everything in him to reach the Solar System. Upon arrival, he had relaxed for the moment. Maybe that's why Commodore Kinshasa's orders had upset him like this. It was time to play the game as he always did. He needed to figure out why she had such bizarre orders.

The captain settled himself, looking up with his normal composure. "You've surprised me, Commodore," he said in an urbane manner. "This is… quite unexpected. As the lieutenant indicated, we expected a hero's welcome for our efforts."

Kinshasa eyed him as if she couldn't decide if this was ridicule or not.

"Yes, I suppose this must be a surprise," the commodore conceded. "The orders came through twenty-eight hours ago. They passed every security procedure. The orders surprised us, I'll admit. It's why we double and triple-checked them. They are quite genuine. Now, you must shut down all ship systems at once. Failure to comply will force us into a situation neither of us desires."

"Of course," Maddox said. "Now that I realize you're acting under specific orders, I must comply. The orders came twenty-eight hours ago, you say?"

"I'm glad you understand, Captain. I must also inform you that until you are safely in quarantine, you must keep a direct and open channel with Pluto Command. Failure to comply will result in a full-scale attack sequence. Do you understand me?"

"I do."

"Very well, put Lieutenant Noonan on screen."

"Just a moment," Maddox said. He moved to the comm-board and tapped the panel, cutting communications with Pluto Command.

Valerie sat up, surprised. She'd been following the exchange closely.

255

"It appears the enemy has managed to send Pluto Command false orders," Maddox said.

"Kinshasa said they triple-checked the orders, sir."

"The instructions are too pat," Maddox said. "Think about it. They originated twenty-eight hours ago. How long does it take a message to travel from Earth to Pluto?"

"I'm more concerned about what we're going to do with ten hostile battleships. They'll begin warming their laser batteries soon."

Maddox grew thoughtful. "Is this an attempt to stop Star Watch Command from learning about the doomsday machine or is it meant to destroy my starship?"

"Tell the commodore our information," Valerie suggested. "She can relay the message to Earth."

"No," Maddox said, looking at the screen, studying the ten battleships. "I don't want to wait that long. If the orders came twenty-eight hours ago, might it imply the doomsday machine will be here soon?"

"Why do you think that, sir?"

"Galyan," Maddox said, turning around.

"Here, Captain," Galyan said, from his favorite location on the bridge.

"Get ready to engage the star drive. You're going to transfer us beside Luna Base."

"I don't recommend that, sir," Valerie said. "Luna Base has some of Star Watch's heaviest laser batteries. They might open up on us while we're still in the grip of Jump Lag."

"That's an excellent point," Maddox said. "Therefore, I want you to rig an automated message. Use the nuclear missile timer to do it."

The captain referred to the common tactic of sending a nuclear device through a Laumer-Point first during a combat jump. It would detonate against any defenders waiting by the jump entry. The lag didn't affect spring-driven devices.

Valerie stood up. "I'll get right on it, sir."

Maddox tapped the comm, bringing an angry Kinshasa back online.

"I'm sorry for the temporary blackout," the captain said.

"Did you deliberately shut off your communications?" the commodore asked.

"No," Maddox lied.

Kinshasa glared at him. "Captain, you must immediately begin an emergency shut-down procedure. Until you comply, the battleships will continue their approach. You have ninety seconds to obey. Then, the warships shall begin to fire."

"Commodore, we still have combat damage from the fight in the Tannish System. I can't turn off the anti-matter engines in that time. I request that you give me—" Maddox glanced at Valerie.

She showed him four fingers.

"I request that you give me five minutes," Maddox said.

"Out of the question," Kinshasa snapped.

"Four minutes then."

"Captain—"

"Please, Commodore, I implore you."

Kinshasa eyed him distrustfully. "Very well, four minutes, Captain, and not a minute more."

"Thank you," Maddox said, bowing crisply at the waist.

Four minutes later, the starship made the final leap, leaving Pluto and appearing several thousand kilometers from the weapons-bristling Moon.

Valerie's auto-message worked. Luna Defense stood down just as they readied to fire on the starship.

Thirty seconds after shaking off the final Jump Lag, Maddox found himself speaking to Lord High Admiral Cook on the main screen. The big man was red-faced with thick white hair, wearing a white dress uniform.

"Sir," Maddox said. "Pluto Command said they received a direct message from headquarters to quarantine me, is that correct?"

"What are you talking about?" the admiral asked.

"This is critical, sir. Did such a message originate in your office?"

"Captain, is this some sort of joke?"

"No, sir," Maddox said. "I think we may have infiltration agents embedded in headquarters, or the enemy has figured out a way to send seemingly legitimate orders to distant posts. Some of our people may be compromised."

The admiral swore angrily, fixing Maddox with a steely gaze. "What do you mean specifically?"

Maddox gave him a quick rundown of what had just happened by the Pluto Laumer-Point.

Cook laughed bitterly. "You're a troublemaker, son. It follows you like a flock of vultures. But enough of that. I'll look into those false orders soon enough. Tell me what happened out there on the rim of 'C' Quadrant. Did we beat the enemy fleet? What happened to Fletcher? Is he still alive?"

Maddox highlighted the important details as quickly as he could.

During the speech, Valerie piloted the starship closer to Earth.

"Thank God Admiral Fletcher is still alive," Cook said with relief. "I congratulate you, Captain. You succeeded marvelously. Half the Fifth Fleet is coming home. This is wonderful news, simply wonderful. You beat the New Men. I'm amazed, sir. It seems that Brigadier O'Hara was right about you all along."

"There's more, sir," Maddox said. In a broad outline, he spoke about the doomsday machine and its magnetic-storm method of transfer.

"Hold it, Captain," the admiral said. The older man had leathery features. They'd grimly fixed onto Maddox. "I want you down here on the double. This is a face-to-face conversation. By the way, how is Professor Ludendorff? You brought him with you, yes?"

Maddox hesitated. That seemed like an odd question to ask at a moment like this. "I have him in stasis, sir. He mutinied against us—"

"What?" Cook asked, with worry in his eyes. "Professor Ludendorff is in stasis?"

"Yes, sir," Maddox said.

Cook appeared shocked.

"Sir, once you hear—"

"No more," Cook said, raising a big hand. "I don't want... I want you in Geneva on the double, Captain. Bring the professor with you."

"What about the rest of the professor's team, sir?"

"They're in—never mind. They must be. Yes, bring them down, too. I can't believe this."

"I'm going to let—"

"That will be all, Captain. Not another word, do you understand me?"

The admiral's look told Maddox the other finally understood what it meant with Pluto Command receiving false instructions. If the enemy could send manufactured orders, could he also tap into regular communications?

Maddox wondered about that. Earth must still be rife with enemy espionage attacks. The New Men had a long-distance transfer pyramid. The star cruisers appearing in the Xerxes System had proven that. Even though Star Watch had *Victory*, the enemy had a faster method of travel. The New Men would exploit whatever advantages they possessed.

"Yes, sir," Maddox said, "I understand."

"I imagine you've already written a full report of all these activities."

"No, sir, I have not." Maddox hated writing reports, always putting them off until the last minute.

Cook eyed him. "Get here on the double, Captain. I'm giving you emergency clearance. If this—blast it! Get down here now, Maddox. Cook out."

***

Sergeant Riker helped Maddox load the stasis tubes into the shuttle's cargo hold, the tubes holding Ludendorff, Villars and the archeologists. Maddox did not intend to thaw them out first. There wasn't time, and he wasn't going to risk it.

"You're in charge of *Victory* while I'm gone," Maddox told Valerie in the hangar bay. "I'd like to let you have some leave on Earth before we're on the clock again, but I'm not sure that's an option."

"I'm fine, sir," Valerie said. "I doubt this is a time for a vacation anyway. The doomsday machine could turn up any minute. I'll be ready, sir."

"You're staying up here, too," Maddox told Riker.

The sergeant nodded reluctantly. He was probably the most homesick of the crew.

"Ready?" Maddox asked Keith.

"Aye-aye, sir," the ace said.

The two boarded the shuttle and strapped in. Riker and Valerie hurried out of the hangar bay. Soon, the giant bay doors opened. The shuttle lifted off the deck and drifted toward space.

"The Earth looks lovely, doesn't she, sir?" Keith said from the pilot seat.

Maddox sat beside the ace, staring at the blue-green planet.

The shuttle began the plunge. Maddox spied Australia and New Zealand. Neither landmass had much cloud cover. There was a big storm brewing over Tasmania, though.

"Feels as if I've been gone forever," Maddox said, surprised at the pang in his chest upon seeing Earth.

"Aye," Keith said. He manipulated his panel. The shuttle began its flight for Europe and the Geneva Spaceport.

They passed Star Watch laser satellites, spied big battleships in low orbit and saw heavy lifters heading to space haulers waiting at a Lagrange point.

Maddox's fingertips tingled in anticipation of the coming meeting. Should he have said anything about Strand? Maybe it was better to have kept quiet about that. If the chief of Nerva Security could slip back and forth, Strand or his proxy could probably intercept laser messages from *Victory* to Star Watch Headquarters.

The shuttle began to shake as it entered the stratosphere. Maddox glanced at the pilot. That shouldn't be happening.

"Not to worry, sir," Keith said. He tapped the board.

Instead of eliminating the shaking, it got worse. Suddenly, an explosion in one of the rear engine ports caused the shuttle to plummet even faster.

"What just happened?" Maddox shouted.

260

"Damned if I know, sir," Keith said between clenched teeth. "Hang on. This could get rough." Keith swerved sharply and aimed them almost straight down. At the same time, the shuttle twisted and began to buck and heave.

"What are you doing?" Maddox shouted.

"Saving our lives, sir! Now kindly shut up and let me pilot. We're under attack."

Maddox was thrust forward, to the side and back, but finally managed to grip the straps crisscrossing his body. "How do you know this isn't an engine malfunction?"

"Because I checked those babies myself, sir, before we left the starship. They were dandy." The ace cursed profoundly then.

Maddox saw it on the pilot's board. The heat on the skin of the shuttle rose dramatically.

"We're going down too fast," the captain said.

Keith snarled something about a microwave beam striking the craft. He twisted the shuttle. The bulkheads shook. Screaming sounds from outside added to the confusion.

"Need some missiles," Keith said. "Okay. This is going to get really rough now, sir. Get ready. Three, two, one…here we go."

Maddox gritted his teeth as the ace took the shuttle through even more intense maneuvers. They corkscrewed, flipped, slid sideways and burned through the thickening atmosphere.

Then, Star Watch interceptors joined them. They were sleek, ultra-fast atmospheric fighters that looked like giant wasps. Keith flipped on the radio and garbled something to the pilots. Seconds later, missiles blasted from the interceptor under-bays, disappearing as they zoomed down to the surface.

It told Maddox Star Watch was still on his side, just as the microwave beam attack told him the enemy was definitely up to something sinister.

Soon, Keith leveled out. The shaking stopped, so did the sounds of shrieking wind. They were over the Pacific Ocean, heading northeast toward Hawaii.

Maddox released his death grip on the straps, finding his fingers stiff from the intensity of the strain.

"You said microwave beams?" the captain asked.

261

"Aye, sir," Keith said. "That's my best bet. We should be okay now, I think."

"Someone on Earth—"

"That's right," Keith said, as he adjusted their flight path. "Someone down there wanted to make our deaths look accidental. They beamed a microwave ray at the engine port, burning it out. They tried to do the same thing to the other one, but I wouldn't let them."

"That's why you committed that insanity?" Maddox asked.

Keith laughed. "Any time they can hit a fighter I'm flying, when I know what's going on, I deserve to die. They didn't realize who piloted our shuttle. You're lucky I came, sir," the ace said with a grin. "Without me beside you, you'd be a goner."

"Indeed, and I'm grateful for it," Maddox said. "And the interceptor missiles…?"

"I was tracking the enemy as he tried to beam us. I gave the coordinates to the interceptors."

Maddox found it amazing Keith had been doing all that while he—the captain—had been hanging on for his life.

The rest of the flight proved uneventful. Keith took them over Central America, the Atlantic Ocean and brought the shuttle down in Geneva Spaceport in the Alps Mountain Range.

Maddox watched several hovers rush out of a terminal building. There was something off about them. He wasn't sure what, but he felt it in his gut.

"Let's not go over there," Maddox said, pointing at the hovers. "Head to the terminal over there," he said, pointing at a large, square building in the distance.

Keith glanced at the captain, giving him a look that said the others were expecting them at the first location.

"Something feels wrong about this," Maddox said. He'd been doing some heavy thinking during the flight. The enemy wasn't going to let them reach the Lord High Admiral so easily. The Pluto Command quarantine and the microwave attack showed that.

"Got it, sir," Keith said. He turned the shuttle, using repeller rays to float them to the new destination.

In seconds, a hard-faced man in space marine greens appeared on the screen. "Where are you headed?" the marine asked.

"You can send the hovers away," Maddox said. "We don't need them."

The grim-faced marine hesitated just a moment. Then, he shook his head. "Sorry, Captain, I can't do that. You're under emergency orders. I have to take you in myself. I'm supposed to guard you and your packages."

Maddox tapped his board, making the man's image disappear. He called Cook's office. A secretary answered. Before she could speak, the screen went blank.

"What the heck?" Keith asked. He'd been watching the exchange.

Maddox made a quick check. Someone used ultra-advanced jamming equipment against the shuttle.

"It appears the attack against us isn't over," Maddox said. "The enemy must want us dead pretty badly if they're willing to burn an asset embedded in Star Watch space marines."

The captain unbuckled. In three strides, he reached the weapons locker, opening it.

"The hovers have speeded up," Keith said. "They're not going to let us get away, sir."

Maddox turned toward the ace. A premonition of greater danger touched the captain. The marines coming to escort them weren't going to stop in the face of a grenade launcher. If he simply took them all out, though, without the enemy first showing his hand, there might be hell to pay.

He was playing with the end of the world at stake. Who was his hidden foe? It couldn't be Strand himself, right? The man was far away in space. It might be Strand's second-in-command then. It was possible Kane had returned to Earth. Or had some other New Man gotten here, sent by the space pyramid in New Men territory?

A hard knot of certainty filled Maddox. "Turn the shuttle around," he told Keith. "Then use a missile. Take out the hovers."

For once, Keith looked surprised. "Are you sure, sir? They'll court martial us for doing that."

"Turn the shuttle," Maddox ordered, leaving the grenade launcher in the locker. He sat back in his seat as Keith caused the shuttle to rotate on its repellers.

The three hovers flew across the tarmac toward them.

"Could you be wrong about them, sir?" Keith asked.

Maddox didn't answer. Instead, the captain leaned forward, engaging a missile. The space weapon wasn't meant to use like this, on the ground, but it should work.

Tapping the screen a second time launched the missile. The shuttle shook as the missile ignited its engine. Through the blast window, Maddox watched the streaking thing. It struck the lead hover and exploded into a giant fireball. One hover flew into the air, its dome a splintered shell as it tumbled end-over-end. There was no sign of the other two hovers. Heat and debris smashed against the shuttle, causing the craft to tremble as hard as it had during the flight down.

Seconds later, the shuttle stopped shaking. The airborne hover smashed against the tarmac. Pieces went everywhere, some rattling against the shuttle. The other hovers were smoking debris.

Maddox slouched in his seat. At the same moment, sirens began to blare. Just how many more attempts was the enemy going to make against him?

-30-

"Sir," Keith said. "Look over there. Combat cars are coming."

The ace pointed out the blast window. Three dots in the sky floated down, rapidly gaining size.

Maddox stood and drew his gun.

Keith tried the radio. It worked. The ace asked for confirmation regarding the air-cars. He told Maddox, "They're from Intelligence, straight from headquarters."

Maddox eyed the growing combat cars, finally putting the gun into its holster. He waited until they landed, dust puffing outward from their armored skirts.

Opening a hatch, the captain watched soldiers bound out of the cars, racing into a circular formation around the shuttle, facing outward with rifles leveled. A major exited the lead combat car. He marched near the shuttle, studying Maddox.

It was Major Stokes, one of O'Hara's chief aides. Maddox was relieved to recognize someone.

Stokes glanced at the smoking hover wreckages before shaking his head. "Never can leave things as they are, can you, Captain? You went and ruined the welcoming committee."

"The more things change," Maddox said, dryly.

"You have a knack," Stokes said. "There's no denying it. Wherever you go, people learn to love you."

"What's the next step?" Maddox asked.

"In a hurry, are you?"

"As a matter of fact, I am."

265

"Good," Stokes said. "You're to come with me."

"To see the admiral?"

"In time," Stokes said. "First, The Iron Lady wants an explanation for all this mayhem."

Stokes had never been a fan of his, but the man was solid. The enemy wouldn't have been able to corrupt him, and the major was too logical to fall easily for a trick.

In three minutes, Maddox found himself secure in a combat-car, flying nape-of-the-earth to headquarters. They landed on the roof of a squat fortress-style building. Stokes marched them through every security check. Underground, Keith left them, no doubt heading to a different debriefing.

"Why the silent treatment?" Maddox asked.

Stokes cocked an eyebrow. "Orders, my fine fellow. The brigadier doesn't want you tainted before she sinks her claws into you. This time—well, never mind. We're almost there."

Several minutes later, Stokes escorted Maddox into Brigadier Mary O'Hara's office.

The Iron Lady sat behind a large synthi-wood desk, with her hands folded beside a thick and ancient book. The brigadier of Star Watch Intelligence had gray hair, a matronly image and a reputation for never losing her temper.

"Here he is, Ma'am," Stokes said. "I found him as delightful as ever. The man stayed in his shuttle like a turtle, eyeing me as if I were the Devil himself come to hang him."

"Thank you, Major," O'Hara said, quietly.

Stokes cocked another eyebrow, coming to ramrod attention, giving a perfectly crisp salute.

"None of that now," O'Hara said. "You did your chore. I'm appreciative of it, I assure you."

The major turned around.

"There's something wrong here, quite wrong," the brigadier told Stokes. "I wanted someone to go that the captain would trust and who could also sniff out trouble. This isn't over, Major. In fact, I think it has just begun." O'Hara glanced at Maddox.

The captain nodded.

"See to the postings outside the building, Major. Then ready a combat team."

266

Stokes turned back around to face her. "You think someone is going to try to storm the building, Ma'am?"

"I wouldn't be surprised if our hidden enemy launched an attack on us. I can't explain it, but there is a nefarious presence on Earth. I'm beginning to wonder if it has something to do with Captain Maddox's return."

"Ah," Stokes said. "I shall redouble my efforts then."

"That is most appreciated."

With a final nod, Stokes took his leave, quietly shutting the door behind him.

For a moment, Maddox didn't know what to do. It was strange. He almost felt like a young lad again, coming home after a year away from his...his...

"Captain," O'Hara exclaimed. She almost jumped to her feet as she rose. The brigadier came around the desk and gave Maddox an uncharacteristic hug.

He held out his arms, finally patting her back. She was so much smaller than he was.

Abruptly, the brigadier released him, returning to her desk, sitting down and folding her hands back beside the dusty tome. She regarded him solemnly, now seeming more like a superior officer.

"Please, Captain, sit down. Tell me what you've done with Starship *Victory* while you've been away."

"Yes," he said, moving to the chair before her desk. Maddox sat, crossed his legs and began to relate his and the crew's exploits.

O'Hara didn't ask questions. She let the captain explain things his own way. Halfway through his talk, a small red light on her desk blinked on. She pressed a switch and the light disappeared. Afterward, the brigadier watched him more closely than he recalled from previous debriefings.

He gave her a look. She chose to ignore it. Maddox filed that away. He spoke at length, trying to include everything of note.

Finally, he came to recent events. "After the microwave-beam attack, Ma'am, I knew the enemy wouldn't stop there. My instincts told me the space marines in the hovers were the enemy's next play—at least this round, before I spoke with you."

"The comm-blanketing at the spaceport suggests you're correct about the marines," O'Hara said. "But what if you're wrong?"

"Then I killed innocent men, for which I'm sorry. However, I believe the stakes involved mean I should err on the side of Earth's survival."

O'Hara studied him.

Maddox wondered about the red light and the book on her desk that didn't seem to serve any purpose. The book was positioned so if a recording device were up there in the display case….the recorder's on-light wouldn't show because the book would have blocked it.

Maddox found that interesting and telling.

"We're still making inquiries about the marines," the brigadier was saying. "The Lord High Admiral didn't order them there. We know that much, which would seem to substantiate your instincts." O'Hara touched the book on her desk. "We are to meet with the Lord High Admiral. In fact, he is waiting for us. Are you ready, Captain?"

"I'm surprised," Maddox said. "I would have thought you had questions for me."

"Oh, I have questions. Your tale is…*miraculous*. By your account, the Adok starship is proving successful beyond our wildest fantasies. Ludendorff's actions since the Battle of the Tannish System…I find them odd. Can he really have done all those things you say? Your discovery about Strand…" The brigadier shook her head. "If true, your discoveries have unpleasant implications concerning the Methuselah People. That personally troubles me, as I've taken the preliminary treatments, which you well know."

"Yes, Ma'am," the captain said. Her answers seemed strange.

"I'm sure there's even more you haven't told me. It's difficult to absorb so much in such a short amount of time, but—"

O'Hara stood. Maddox followed her example.

268

"If you're correct about this doomsday machine..." the brigadier grew quiet. "Come, we must speak with the Lord High Admiral. We're wasting time with this chitchat."

The brigadier headed for a secret door, opening it with a wave of her hand. O'Hara led the way down a corridor. Maddox followed close behind. This wasn't how he'd expected it to go. They should storm Nerva Tower at once and arrest Octavian and whomever Strand had put in his place.

O'Hara turned abruptly, staring up into the captain's eyes. "Security personnel will be at the meeting."

Maddox absorbed the information in silence.

"In the past few days we have uncovered evidence that suggests you're a traitor in the pay of the New Men."

Slapping his face would have surprised Maddox less. First, there had been Commodore Kinshasa at the Pluto Laumer-Point and now this. "What is the nature of the evidence?" he asked quietly.

"That doesn't matter at the moment. I should tell you that scanners have checked you while you were in my office. You're clean, devoid of hidden assassination devices on or in your person. We were advised it would be otherwise."

Had that been the reason for the red light?

"If I had these devices," Maddox said, "and you only found I was clean while in your office, why did you risk meeting me by yourself first?"

"Never mind that," the brigadier said. "It's time to proceed to the next phase."

"If you will allow me one more question, Ma'am," Maddox said.

O'Hara regarded him.

The next words were difficult. *This is ridiculous. Just ask her.* "Ma'am," he said, with the slightest catch in his voice. "Do you believe I'm guilty of traitorous intent?"

"Don't be absurd," she said in a soft voice. "And Captain," she added, speaking louder. "Our conversations have been recorded throughout."

Maddox ingested the information.

The brigadier faced forward again, continuing to move down the corridor.

269

Soon, they entered a large, circular room. Five guards lined the walls. Each of them tracked Maddox with their eyes.

The brigadier indicated Maddox's chair. After he sat down, she walked around the table, sitting across and slightly to the left of him.

Seconds later, another door opened, and the Lord High Admiral entered. He sat beside O'Hara.

Now, a third door opened. Guards brought Professor Ludendorff into the room. The leathery-faced man with his bald dome and gold chain around his neck looked small beside the marines escorting him into the chamber. To Maddox's amazement, the professor had magnetic cuffs on his wrists.

Maddox watched as the marines pushed Ludendorff to a location between Cook and him at the table. Then the marines put Ludendorff's wrists over magnetic receivers embedded in the table, testing to assure a secure connection. Afterward, the marines left.

Ludendorff lifted each arm, discovering the range of motion the magnetic cuffs were going to give him. "This is splendidly melodramatic," he said, glancing at Cook. "Yet I wonder if it's necessary?"

"Quite," Cook said in his deep voice. The big man shifted in his seat and seemed to shift topics in his mind. "We've desired to speak with you for some time, as you know. For years now, you've rejected our requests to come to Earth or any suitable place in the Commonwealth. The captain's information regarding you has added to our worst fears. Clearly, you are even more dangerous than any of us thought."

"Nonsense," Ludendorff said.

"Please, professor," Cook said. "None of that is going to work here. You are a mystery wrapped in an enigma. We intend to learn why, and the sooner we do, the better it will be for you."

"You know, that's what they used to say about Russia in the twentieth century," Ludendorff told the admiral—"the enigma part."

No one responded to that.

"This is a fine mess you've put me in," Ludendorff told Maddox. "If you would have revived me on the starship, we

270

could have forgone this silliness and gone straight to solving the problem."

"That the captain had the foresight to put you in stasis speaks to his uncommon wisdom," O'Hara said.

"It has little to do with wisdom," the professor told her, "but everything to do with his suspicious hybrid nature."

O'Hara's mouth tightened. "I do not appreciate the comment. You will desist from making more in that vein."

Ludendorff glanced from the brigadier to Maddox. "Ah, I see. This is interesting, quite interesting. I hadn't foreseen that."

The Lord High Admiral cleared his throat. "We don't have time for your games, Professor. If Maddox is correct..." Cook glanced at O'Hara.

"I do not believe the allegations against the captain," O'Hara told Cook. "In my opinion, we can trust him implicitly. I believe the new information against him came from tainted sources. We should put those sources under the microscope."

Cook appeared thoughtful. "If the captain is correct," the admiral continued, "an ancient doomsday machine is headed for Earth even as we speak."

"The captain is indeed correct," Ludendorff said. "The doomsday machine is on its way here."

"According to the captain," Cook said, "the evidence suggests the machine is a Builder vessel."

"That's a ridiculous notion," Ludendorff said. "I'm surprised you could utter such an idea."

"According to the captain, the Builders used the machine in the distant past."

"Oh, the Builders most assuredly did use it," Ludendorff said, "but they didn't construct the machine. Frankly, I don't know who did. So let's avoid the subject as it's a waste of time."

The admiral studied Ludendorff. "I find it hard to believe you don't know the creator of the planet-killer."

"Believe what you wish," Ludendorff said, "just as long as you don't pester me with stupid questions."

"Here, now," O'Hara said. "This is the Lord High Admiral of Star Watch you're addressing. You will keep a respectful tone when speaking to him."

"Do you know what I find disrespectful?" the professor asked O'Hara. "These magnetic cuffs. Even more to the point, the ill effects of stasis have finally begun to wear off. Stasis shock is many times worse than Jump Lag, in case you didn't know. It's a fine thing to sit back here on Earth like a spider and quite another to run around in space, engaging in life and all its ills as I do. But I suppose that's neither here nor there. The important thing is that it's time to put the shoe on the other foot, as the old saying goes."

The admiral looked annoyed.

Ludendorff noticed, sighed and sat back in his chair. "Don't you understand the gravity of the situation? The doomsday machine could show up at any hour. There is only one way for us to deal with it. We must gain entrance—"

"Professor," Cook said, sternly, interrupting the man. "I know you delight in verbal games, and you believe yourself the smartest man in the universe."

"Guilty on both counts," Ludendorff said.

"But I don't enjoy frivolity when everything I hold dear is at stake," Cook said. "According to the captain, you suggest the total destruction of the New Arabia System has occurred, the complete annihilation of the heart of the Wahhabi Caliphate."

"I don't suggest that," Ludendorff said. "It is a truth, a fact of grim reality. Not only that, but the bulk of the Wahhabi Fleet is gone. The caliphate will not be joining humanity in its war against the New Men, which is a pity, as we're going to miss their ships as the war begins in earnest. So far, the Commonwealth has merely faced an enemy probe attack. Heavier assaults are coming, although nothing more like the doomsday machine."

"Your words suggest that you don't believe the planet-killer can destroy Earth," Cook said.

"Nonsense," Ludendorff said. "The doomsday machine can easily demolish the planet and the protecting Home Fleet. But I expect yours truly"—he pointed at himself—"will save you

272

from it. Well…That isn't precise. I'm not setting foot on the terrible machine. But I'm going to give you the game-winning plan. The actual hero will be the captain here and several others I've yet to choose."

Cook glanced at Maddox. "In your opinion, is the professor mad?"

"No, sir," Maddox said. "He's a Methuselah Man of considerable age. His ways are not our ways."

"I should inform you that I feel myself giddy," the professor told Cook, "which could account for my seemingly odd behavior. Coming out of stasis does that to me. I really wish you hadn't put me under, Captain." Ludendorff sat forward, concentrating on the Lord High Admiral. "We have to get on with it, though. Time's a-wasting, yes?"

"Now see here," Cook said.

"No!" Ludendorff said, in a voice suddenly devoid of humor. There seemed something menacing about the man now. "I am announcing the Armageddon Protocol. You will find it in the secret Gilgamesh Covenant of the Star Watch Constitution, section three."

Cook glanced at the brigadier before staring at Ludendorff again.

The professor's intensity vanished as quickly as it had appeared. He told them, "I can wait while you look that up."

"What are you talking about, man?" Cook asked in exasperation.

"Come, come," Ludendorff said. "Don't tell me you've never read the Gilgamesh Covenant."

Cook slapped the table in seeming outrage. "There is no such covenant and no…*Armageddon Protocol.*"

"Sir," O'Hara said, softly.

Cook turned to the brigadier in surprise. "You've heard of this nonsense?"

"Yes, sir," O'Hara said. "It's in the Secret Orders Nine section."

"I don't seem to recall…" Cook frowned. "Yes, now that you mention Secret Orders Nine, I think I do remember something about an ancient covenant. Aren't there control words attached to its reading?"

273

"Very good," Ludendorff said. "Brigadier, if you would take your tablet, look up Secret Orders Nine, we could get started."

Hesitantly, O'Hara reached for a tablet on the table.

"Check paragraph five," Ludendorff suggested.

"Go ahead," Cook said. "Let's see how crazy the professor really is."

The brigadier picked up the tablet, tapping the screen until she read script. Afterward, she stared at Ludendorff.

"You're wanting the controls words, I take it," the professor said.

She nodded.

"Better a poor but wise youth than an old but foolish king who no longer knows how to take warning," Ludendorff quoted.

Cook's deepening scowl put lines in his face. "Is that right? Are those the control words?"

The brigadier nodded mutely.

"You have a few control words for me," Ludendorff told her.

"He just quoted from the Book of Ecclesiastes," O'Hara told the Lord High Admiral. "My response comes from the Book of Daniel." The brigadier cleared her throat, reading from the tablet. "Do not be afraid, Daniel. Since the first day that you set your mind to gain understanding and to humble yourself before your God, your words were heard, and I have come in response to them."

"Wonderful, wonderful," Ludendorff said in a cheery voice. "And here is my final response to you from Daniel chapter twelve. Then I, Daniel, looked, and there before me stood two others, one on this bank of the river and one on the opposite bank. One of them said to the man clothed in linen who was above the waters of the river, 'How long will it be before these astonishing things are fulfilled.'"

"Well?" Cook asked O'Hara. "Was that also correct?"

"To the word," the brigadier said in a soft voice.

"What are the instructions of this Armageddon Protocol?" the Lord High Admiral asked.

"It doesn't say," O'Hara told Cook. "Instead, I'm to open a safe in an underground vault here in the building. The vault is in Room Twenty-seven. I've never heard of that room, sir."

Cook's eyes grew large. He stared at Ludendorff in astonishment. The Lord High Admiral stood abruptly. "How do you know about Room Twenty-seven? Only a few in High Command are told about it."

"Yes, yes, I'm sure that's true," Ludendorff said. "I don't care to divulge just yet how I know. Go and check the vault. Then come back and tell us what you've found."

Cook hesitated before standing and marching for the door.

After the admiral left, Maddox studied Ludendorff. Despite the man's seemingly cheery manner, Ludendorff struck him as strained, maybe even worried.

"You chose well with him," Ludendorff told O'Hara, as the professor indicated Maddox. "I'm impressed with the both of you. That was well thought out on your part."

The brigadier said nothing, although she pressed her lips together as if she worked to keep from talking.

Ludendorff slouched in his chair, letting his chin drop to his chest. It seemed as if he fell instantly asleep.

Time lengthened as the brigadier watched Ludendorff. Not once did she take her eyes from him. Maddox was content to sit quietly and wait. He was thinking about Strand, Ludendorff, Octavian Nerva and the Methuselah People. He also reconsidered the microwave-beam attack against the shuttle, and the information someone had given High Command that suggested he was in the pay of the New Men. It felt to Maddox as if many secret threads were pulling together. The situation with the approaching doomsday machine was like a hurricane over a sea, but with just as many deadly underwater currents in play. The planet-killer was bad, but the hidden things held danger, too.

Perhaps fifteen minutes after Cook's disappearance, the big man strode back into the room. He held an old yellowed folder.

Ludendorff opened his eyes, sitting up. O'Hara tore her gaze from him and turned to Cook. The big man stared at the professor. The admiral seemed stunned.

275

Slowly, Cook went to his spot at the table and slapped the folder onto it. Then, he tapped a spot on the table.

The magnetic cuffs opened and dropped from Ludendorff's wrists and onto the table. The professor rubbed his wrists afterward.

"What does the Armageddon Protocol say?" O'Hara asked.

Cook took his time answering, "We're supposed to do everything the person who gives the correct coded responses says to do."

"Who are you?" O'Hara asked Ludendorff.

Maddox nodded in agreement with the question.

"The admiral told you a few minutes earlier," the professor told her. "I'm a mystery wrapped in an enigma. We'll leave it at that for now."

The brigadier blinked several times before she put her hands on the table as if exhausted. "Do we follow the protocol?" she asked Cook.

"We've sworn to obey all lawful commands," Cook said. "This is lawful."

"Yes," the brigadier agreed, "but to just cede control to him like this…"

"I know," Cook said. "It seems wrong. Yet, I've followed Star Watch all my life. I intend to finish what I started." The Lord High Admiral faced Ludendorff. "What are your orders?"

The professor smiled. "That was hard, wasn't it? I can't say I blame you." The smile vanished as Ludendorff looked at Maddox. "This little incident has caught you by surprise, I'd warrant."

Maddox said nothing. Among other things, he was thinking about Villars and Meta. What would the professor do with his newly acquired power? How had the man set up a situation where old protocols gave him the power to do as he liked at a time like this?

"Very well," Ludendorff said. "I've had my fun. It's time to get to work." He pointed at Maddox. "Here's my first order."

Before the professor could finish, one of the guards drew his gun and pulled the trigger.

-31-

Slugs tore into Ludendorff, knocking him off the chair, hurling him onto the floor. The gunman took two steps to the left, pumping another two rounds into the professor's head, shattering it.

Seconds earlier, when the guard first reached for his gun, Maddox noticed the motion. There had been too many surprise attacks against him today for him to sit comfortably with that. The gunman had caught everyone flatfooted except for Maddox. He thought the guard intended to kill him, though, not the professor.

The first *boom* caused several fellow guardsmen to flinch in surprise.

By that time, Maddox had already made his decision. He'd analyzed his options, deciding against quivering in fear as he tried to hide for his last few seconds in life. Crouching behind the table wouldn't save him. Therefore, the captain chose to attack.

At the second *boom*—with the second bullet riddling the professor like the first—Maddox leaped onto the table. By the third *boom*, he crossed the table and leaped airborne.

The professor tumbled to the floor. The gunman shifted position and managed two headshots. At that point, Maddox finally reached the man.

Incredibly, the gunman didn't pay Maddox any heed. There was hypnotic determination in the man's eyes. Thus, the gunman didn't dodge or turn the weapon against Maddox.

Instead, the gunman fired at the professor's broken head once again.

Maddox hit the killer in the face as hard as he could. It catapulted the gunman backward so he slammed against the nearby wall. The assassin slid down the wall, letting the smoking gun drop out of his quivering hand. The shooter's eyes fluttered. Then, his head slumped to the side.

Two other guards finally drew their weapons, aiming at Maddox. A second later, the rest drew their sidearms to do likewise.

Carefully, slowly, Maddox backed away from them. He turned to the admiral. "Better put the shooter on ice, sir, keep him unconscious."

"What?" Cook asked in bewilderment. "Why? What are you talking about? That bastard just killed the professor."

"Of course," O'Hara said, as if figuring things out. "The shooter is a kamikaze. Yes, no doubt he is supposed to die after killing the target. Good work, Captain. Instead of letting him commit suicide, you've rendered him unconscious for us."

"Do you mind if I check on Professor Ludendorff?" Maddox asked the Lord High Admiral.

"What?" the old man asked. "He killed the professor. He—"

"Sir," Maddox said, interrupting the admiral. "May I check on Ludendorff? I want your permission so your guards don't gun me down for approaching the professor."

The white-haired, old admiral stared in shock at the remaining guards, each of them with a drawn gun. "I don't understand this. You're, you're an elite group, the best in security. No one could have infiltrated your ranks."

A first sergeant holstered his gun and stepped up to Cook. The sergeant saluted crisply. "I don't understand this any better than you do, sir. That was Hicks. He's...I've been in tight places with Hicks before. There's no one better, sir. This makes no sense to me."

Cook scowled at the first sergeant.

"B-But it happened, sir," the sergeant said. "I can't explain it."

"Outside, all of you," Cook said. "No. Belay that. You stay right here. But I want all of you to put your guns on the table."

"I don't suggest that, sir," Maddox said. "Keep your guards armed."

"*You* don't suggest it?" Cook asked explosively. "Do you realize—?"

"Sir," O'Hara said, softly, interrupting him. "Do you think I could have a quick word with you?"

"What about Ludendorff, Ma'am?" Maddox asked.

"He's dead," O'Hara said. "Forget about the professor for a moment. We have more pressing worries."

"Let me check him please," Maddox said.

"Go, do it then," O'Hara said, as she tugged at the admiral's sleeve.

"Yes, check," Cook said absently. He bent his head afterward, listening to the brigadier whisper to him.

Maddox moved to Ludendorff, telling himself to examine the evidence and subdue his thumping heart. This called for cool concentration. Yet, he found himself shaking.

The first thing Maddox noticed was the lack of blood. There was some, but considering the number of slugs that had torn into the body, it was a pitiful amount. Maddox knew about head wounds. Anything above the nose bled copiously. The professor's braincase was shattered. There should be blood and gore everywhere, but there was not.

The second thing Maddox noticed as he closed the distance were small, blue, electrical discharges from inside the body. The third something was the smell of ozone in the room combined with the burnt gunpowder odor.

Maddox knelt on one knee, staring at the wreckage of Professor Ludendorff. The sight shocked him, but not in the manner that he'd expected it would.

It was clear that the outer layer was composed of skin and blood. But that was it: the epidermis was just a layer. Underneath was something else entirely that had nothing to do with humanity.

Maddox leaned lower, put his fingers into the worst wound and pulled to get a better look.

One of the guards at his back vomited. That caused a commotion among the others.

"What's going on over there?" Cook called out. Someone must have pointed at Maddox. The admiral swore in disbelief.

Maddox continued to tug and pull at the wound. He saw steely-colored bones and circuits of a kind he'd never seen before.

"What are you doing?" the Lord High Admiral asked in disgust.

Maddox did not answer. He continued to search.

"Captain Maddox, have you gone mad?" the admiral asked.

The captain glanced over his shoulder. Everyone stared at him. A few of the guards had become pale-faced. One man looked as if he was going to faint. Only the brigadier seemed halfway normal. She looked at him curiously.

"Sir," Maddox said. "You might want to order the guards out of the room."

Cook opened his mouth. It seemed he might reprimand Maddox. Instead, after a moment's contemplation, the admiral shut his mouth with the click of his teeth. Motioning with his head, he silently ordered the guards to leave.

"We'll be outside if you need us, sir," the first sergeant said.

"Good," O'Hara told him.

The Lord High Admiral seemed unable to speak.

The guards began to file out.

"Wait," O'Hara said. "First Sergeant, take the assassin to medical. Inform Major Stokes that the gunman isn't to wake up until the doctors have thoroughly scanned him for suicide procedures."

The first sergeant glanced at Cook. The admiral was staring at Ludendorff.

"Yes, Ma'am," the first sergeant said. He snapped his fingers, giving his men orders. They hoisted the unconscious assassin, carrying him out of the chamber.

When the door closed behind them, Cook woodenly moved to the body. "Why are there blue sparks in his wounds?" the admiral asked.

280

"This thing is an android, a *cybernetic organism*," Maddox said. He blinked and looked up at Cook. "He wasn't human."

The admiral turned to O'Hara. She nodded.

"Am I missing something?" Maddox asked.

"I have to see this," Cook said, ignoring the captain's question. The old man grunted, and his joints creaked as he bent beside the carcass.

Maddox pulled flesh and wiped away blood. It allowed the admiral a better look inside.

"He was a machine," Cook said. "But—"

"But like nothing we might have constructed," Maddox said.

The Lord High Admiral lost his balance, or maybe the strength went out of him. Cook sat down heavily on his butt. Like a big kid, he sat there stunned.

"What do you make of this, Captain?" O'Hara asked.

"I'm not sure yet," Maddox said, hedging.

"I don't believe that for a minute," O'Hara said. "Your quick action rendered the assassin unconscious. We might actually be able to trace his source because of that."

Cook's head snapped up. A fierce light glowed in his eyes. He pushed off from the floor, grunting again, staggering to a chair. He sat down heavily, with his elbows on the table.

O'Hara followed his example sitting down.

With a shrug, Maddox did likewise. The dead android would keep as it was. The captain studied the thing. That had been Ludendorff? It didn't make sense. Had Doctor Rich fallen in love with a cybernetic organism?

Maddox slapped the table.

Both Cook and O'Hara looked up.

"Who made Ludendorff?" Maddox asked.

"Yes," O'Hara said. "That is the question. Do you have any ideas?"

"The Builders," Maddox said. "Given the professor's actions, I doubt the New Men constructed him."

The admiral groaned in dismay as he massaged his forehead. "This is all too much, too bewildering. A doomsday machine races to Earth, New Men attack out of the Beyond, what appeared to be a Methuselah Man recited an old code

281

sequence that gave him unlimited emergency authority over Star Watch. How did this-this *Builder android* learn about the Armageddon Protocol in the first place? Just how deeply are we compromised?"

O'Hara studied the admiral before turning to Maddox. "What do you know about the Builders?"

Maddox nodded. That was a good place to begin. "I happen to know more than you might expect. We had a breakthrough on *Victory*." He began to explain what he'd learned from Galyan, their latest experiences in the Xerxes System and the egg with the cybernetic Swarm creature inside."

"It seems these Builders have some expertise in modifying what would be to them alien creatures," O'Hara said.

"There's that," Maddox said. "But we have another problem. If Ludendorff was a Builder android...I take that back. He can't—*it* can't—be anything else. That means we're not only contending with the New Men, but with these hidden Builders."

"No," O'Hara said. "By your tale, it's worse than that."

Maddox frowned at her. "Oh, yes. The New Men transferred to the Builder pyramid. Our enemy uses fusion beams and has what must be Builder electromagnetic shields. Ma'am, if the New Men have all these things... Maybe the New Men do know how to construct androids."

"Then why did Ludendorff fix your disruptor cannon?" O'Hara said. "More to the point, how did an android have the expertise to fix it?"

"How did an android know to search for *Victory*?" Maddox asked.

During their talk, Cook had continued to massage his forehead. He sighed now, letting his hands drop to the table. "Those are interesting topics, but not germane to our immediate problem. An assassin hid among my most trusted security personnel. The killer slew Ludendorff. This was after the professor gained our trust and pointed to you, Captain. What was Ludendorff going to tell us?"

"I have no idea," Maddox said. "Am I under suspicion again?"

"Yes!" Cook said.

"I see," Maddox said.

"No you don't," the Lord High Admiral said. "This *thing* just recited the code words to initiate the Armageddon Protocol. Whoever built Ludendorff knows how to gain total control of Star Watch."

"Interesting," O'Hara said.

"No," Cook said. "It's frightening, nightmarish. Whom can we trust? No one. That means we're finished. Without trust, we can't operate as a military force. Of course, I doubt you, Captain. You've been traveling with this thing—"

"Ludendorff took control of my starship," Maddox said, sharply. "I…" The captain glanced at the dead construct on the floor.

"Go on," O'Hara said.

"Ludendorff had control of *Victory*," Maddox said, quietly. "He had full control of the starship until he left for the Builder base in the Xerxes System. We retrieved him from the wreckage of the asteroid base. He had been neatly wrapped and was unconscious."

"What is your point?" O'Hara asked.

"I don't have a point, yet."

"Don't try that on me, Captain. What are you suggesting?"

"Before I attempt to answer," Maddox said. "What does Star Watch know about Ludendorff? I mean, what was in his file?"

"He was old," O'Hara said.

"Do you have a number?"

"Octavian Nerva is often proclaimed as the oldest living Methuselah Man," O'Hara said. "Our records indicate he isn't. Until a few moments ago, the title belonged to Professor Ludendorff."

That didn't surprise Maddox. "How old was the professor supposed to be?"

"I can't answer that with any precision," O'Hara said. "We don't have any record of his birth. Now, we know why. He wasn't ever born, he was made."

"Do you have any number at all?"

"We don't," Cook said. "But we do have records that go back four hundred years. In them appears a man—what looked like a man—that matches what we know about Ludendorff."

"You're saying Ludendorff was four hundred years old?" Maddox asked.

"I'm saying there were people in history, in the shadows, that match Ludendorff," Cook said. "We can find obvious references to him that go back four hundred years. After that—" the Lord High Admiral shrugged.

"What's your point?" O'Hara asked Maddox.

"I still don't have one," the captain said. "I merely find it odd that Ludendorff had control of *Victory* before he left for the Builder base."

"And, you obviously have an 'and' to your thought," O'Hara said.

"What happened inside the asteroid base?" Maddox asked.

"I'm not following you," O'Hara said. "At great risk to himself, the professor collected this egg, which is supposed to save Earth against the doomsday machine."

"Surely Star Watch has tried to capture Ludendorff before this," Maddox said.

"We have," Cook said. "There are some strange stories that go with several of those incidents. But until now, we've never gotten hold of him."

"Let's get back to your point," O'Hara told the captain. "Is the Builder asteroid base important?"

Maddox drummed his fingers on the table. What happened inside the asteroid base? Why did Strand and Ludendorff program people? Maddox squinted suspiciously.

"You just thought of something," O'Hara said.

"Yes," Maddox said. "I'm recalling Wolf Prime when I was down in the Swarm dig. Kane grabbed Professor Ludendorff, shoving him into a shuttle and fleeing to the New Men."

"Wait, what?" Cook asked.

Maddox told them how Ludendorff had used his friend Lank Meyers as a decoy professor, the one Kane had grabbed before fleeing.

"What are you suggesting?" O'Hara asked.

284

Drumming his fingers on the table, Maddox stared at the android professor. "Not a suggestion but a point," he said. "Ludendorff was a master of deception."

"I see where you're going with this," O'Hara said. "You're suggesting Ludendorff might have made a switch in the Builder base."

"It's a theory, nothing more."

"You think there is a real Ludendorff," O'Hara said.

"I find it difficult to believe that Doctor Dana Rich fell hopelessly in love with an android," Maddox said.

"Your theory strikes me as too complicated," O'Hara said.

"Which makes me more suspicious than ever," Maddox said. "The professor loved complicated. He positively thrived on it."

"Why send an android of himself to Earth?" Cook asked.

"Because our planet is doomed and Ludendorff—the oldest Methuselah Man on record—practiced caution," Maddox said.

"I don't accept that," O'Hara said. "Besides, it still wouldn't explain the technology that produced something like that." She pointed at the carcass—or wreckage—lying on the floor.

"We have to interrogate the gunman," Maddox said. "We must find out who sent him. That might help us understand what we're dealing with."

Cook and O'Hara exchanged glances. The admiral nodded minutely.

"That is excellent advice, Captain," O'Hara said. "I think it's time we see to that."

-32-

"Commander," Kane said. "It looks as if they're getting ready to try again."

Oran Rva sat in front of a primary console in the most ultra-secret hideaway Strand owned. The console had electronic links to backdoors everywhere, even into the heart of Star Watch's main computers. The dominant adjusted controls, concentrating on his latest operation.

Kane watched an underground scope. The Rouen Colony man wore a silver suit like a New Man. He looked incongruous in it, as he was much blockier than any of the dominants. Kane wore a blaster at his side, with a silver ball in a special holster dangling from his belt.

He glanced back at Strand.

The sick old human sat in a chair, with his legs and wrists secured. A cap sat on his head, with leads attached to the wrinkled facial skin. The Methuselah Man trembled from time to time. He had been through a painful ordeal these past days, in time answering all of Oran Rva's questions.

The three of them waited in an underground chamber far beneath Nerva Tower. Several shafts led to the room. On Kane's scope, three railway cars eased on magnetic tracks toward them. Soon, the cars would reach other wrecked vehicles blocking the tunnel, with corpses festering inside the twisted metal.

Kane had witnessed Oran Rva's work. The commander awed him. With Strand's incredible knowledge, Oran Rva had spread chaos throughout Earth and even to Pluto Command. The process was consuming every embedded espionage agent, however. The dominants would have to start from scratch in rebuilding a new secret service once this mission was over.

"Kane," the old man whispered.

The Rouen Colony man looked up at the prisoner.

Strand glanced sidelong at Oran Rva, who continued to hunch over the primary console. Afterward, the Methuselah Man concentrated on Kane.

"This is a mistake," Strand whispered. "My assets will win through to me in the end. I have too many schemes within schemes for the commander to survive them all."

It galled Kane that the other thought of him as weak-willed. Strand couldn't offer him anything real. No one could beat Oran Rva. Ignoring the old man, Kane pressed his face against the pads of the scope.

He saw that the three-car train slowed in the tunnel. The conductor must see the wreckage ahead. Soon, the railway cars came to a halt, sinking down onto the magnetic rails. Hatches opened. Power-armored troopers jumped down.

Adjusting the scope, Kane zoomed in on them. The troopers carried heavy weapons. It was likely they meant to batter their way in or to destroy the armored chamber, one or the other.

He debated telling Oran Rva about the development. Kane had just tried to speak to him. The commander had ignored the warning. That meant the dominant did not want to be disturbed.

Am I supposed to take care of this myself?

"Kane," Strand whispered.

The Rouen Colony man raised his head.

"I am the master here," Strand whispered. The blue eyes had a crazy shine to them. "This is my doing. You realize that, yes?"

Kane had learned incredible information these past days. It both awed and troubled him. He had listened to the interrogation and listened as Strand had tried to bargain and then reason with Oran Rva.

"Why did the commander demand my key?" Strand whispered. "There's one purpose only: to gain entrance into the ancient doomsday machine. Surely, the Throne World has released it. That's a terrible mistake."

Kane said nothing as he watched Strand.

"Do you suppose anyone can overcome the cybernetic organism inside the planet-killer?" Strand whispered. "That's madness, lunacy of the worst order. They're like gods, Kane, gods. Their power is unimaginable."

"This doomsday machine," Kane said, "the Builders constructed it?"

Out of the corner of his eye, Kane saw Oran Rva stiffen.

Strand noticed it, too. He cackled like a madman. "That got your attention, did it not?" he told the commander. "I know more than you, Oran Rva. I am old beyond your reckoning. I fashioned the Thomas Moore Society colonists into the New Men. I have used Cestus Haulers from time to time, bringing desperately needed supplies to the Throne World."

The faintest of smiles appeared on the commander's face.

"Do you doubt me?" Strand asked. "Don't you realize the Methuselah People are layered into tiers of understanding? At the top are the Old Ones like me."

The commander went back to work at the console.

Taking his cue from Oran Rva, Kane once more pressed his face against the pads. He watched as the power-armored troopers cautiously approached the wrecked cars blocking the tunnel.

"At the beginning of the Space Age," Strand droned from his chair, "with the discovery of the Laumer Drive, we Old Ones found evidence of aliens. You know them, yes. There were the Swarm, the Adoks and the Builders. The aliens were gone, though. It took time to realize that. Even so, what had been there once could be there again. Besides, there was evidence that some of the aliens had gone into hiding. We Methuselah People—the first few—decided humanity needed an ace card. We also realized that humans are notoriously thin-skinned, easily upset and far too prone to letting others do their work for them. If the human race trusted the ace card to take care of them, they would never develop in their own right. Thus, we decided to make the weapon secret in the extreme."

Kane watched a team of power-armored troopers lower their shoulders against a car and heave. Slowly, the crumpled train-car eased off the tracks.

"The Thomas Moore Society colonists were the perfect front," Strand droned from his chair. "They traveled deep into the Beyond. There, we began to fashion the colonists into the Defenders. If the Swarm appeared, for instance, in overwhelming force, we could bring the Defenders—bring you and your ilk, Commander—onto the scene to save the human race."

Kane watched the troopers push aside another car. Why did they bother? There wouldn't be enough room on the tracks for the three good railway cars to approach the underground chamber.

"I'm an Old One," Strand said. "You are my children, the offspring of my vast intellect."

"You are a fool," Oran Rva said.

Kane listened keenly as he continued to watch on the scope.

"I am the master here," Strand said.

"Of course," the commander said. "That is why you are strapped to a chair."

"My people come to rescue me," Strand said. "You have no idea how many hidden layers I have."

"I know the precise number," Oran Rva said. "That is why I have waited for this team to appear. I need something from them."

"You lie," Strand said.

"I have created turmoil on Earth," Oran Rva said. "It should keep Star Watch busy long enough for me to gather the final item. Then, it will be time to win lasting glory. I will win such a coup as to gain the throne itself."

On the scope, Kane watched the power-armored troopers push aside the last car. As they did, others struggled with a large platform. On it was a unique cannon. It looked like a sonic gun. Several troopers struggled to carry it toward the underground chamber at the end of the line.

"Commander," Kane said, looking up.

Oran Rva swiveled his head to regard him. "They have brought a sonic cannon?" he asked.

"Yes, Commander," Kane said, surprised.

"Guard our talkative prisoner. I must attend to business." Oran Rva stood, drawing a blaster from its holster. He strode to the hatch. Opening it, the commander slipped through. Just before it clanged shut, Kane heard the buzz of an enabler from the commander.

Without regard for Strand, Kane put his face against the pads. He wanted to see this.

In moments, the commander appeared on the scope. He strode toward the power-armored troopers like a man possessed. Suddenly, one of the enemies saw Oran Rva. The metallic gorilla pointed. Those carrying the sonic cannon halted. A second later, the troopers lowered the big weapon.

The troopers brought up their heavy rifles, beginning to fire.

At that, Oran Rva burst into action. It was uncanny. The commander fired with beautiful precision. Each shot downed a trooper, with a smoking hole in his armor. The enemy projectiles and laser beams missed the dominant in the silver suit. Oran Rva moved too fast, and he wore a miniaturized magnetic repeller for additional protection.

Kane realized he witnessed one of the supreme soldiers of the Throne World in action. Few could have matched this performance.

Then, it was over. All the enemy power-armored troopers lay dead in the tunnel.

The commander charged the sonic gun. It hadn't fired in the melee, which was likely a good thing for Oran Rva. He didn't have a defense against it.

The dominant clambered onto the platform. He opened a compartment and withdrew a fist-sized object. This, Oran Rva dropped into a pouch at his side. The commander thereupon sprinted back at high speed for the chamber.

"Don't move," Strand whispered.

Kane felt the end of a barrel pressed against his temple.

A sick feeling of failure washed over the Rouen Colony man. He remembered now that he was supposed to have kept his eyes on Strand. How had the wasted old man escaped from the chair?

"What is the New Man doing now?" Strand whispered into Kane's ear.

"He attacks the others," Kane said.

Strand chuckled. "I am much more than you realize, and I understand that you're lying to me. For that, you shall die."

"Wait," Kane said, pulling away from the scope.

Strand held Kane's own blaster against his head. This was even worse than he had expected.

Something vile glittered in Strand's eyes. His unnatural vitality disturbed Kane.

"There is to be a change in plans," the old man said. "I—"

The hatch began to open.

Strand swore, shoved Kane's head, which did nothing to move the square thing. Then Oran Rva came through the hatch.

Strand fired at him, producing a click but nothing more from the blaster. The old man stared at the blaster before looking up at the commander.

"For once," Oran Rva said, "I would like to meet an opponent who wasn't so wearily predictable. Kane lusted for knowledge and you, clone, didn't think I would understand your guile."

"What do you mean, clone?" Strand asked.

"Do you truly think you are the great Strand?" Oran Rva sneered. "Do you think he would allow himself to be on Earth with the coming of the doomsday machine?"

"I am Strand."

"You are a pale replica of the real thing," Oran Rva said. "I know, for I have trained under Strand. He thought to use me to supplant the Great One on the throne. The real Strand finds it bitter indeed to have lost the role of chief puppeteer. The real Strand taught me more than was wise on his part. Because of that knowledge, I am here to win the greatest prize imaginable."

"You have no means to defeat the driver of the doomsday machine," Strand said.

"Clone, do not attempt to understand what is beyond your pay grade."

"I am Strand, me."

"You have served your usefulness, clone. Now—"

"Wait," Strand said. "There are things I can show you. In my office—"

Oran Rva pulled the trigger. The blaster fired, and Strand, or the clone of Strand, fell down dead.

Kane watched with icy detachment. Whatever the dead thing was, it had stolen his blaster from him.

"I have failed," Kane said.

"I knew you would," Oran Rva told him. "However, I still have need of your abilities. I am the supreme soldier. You are much better than the sub-men, and we still have much to do before the doomsday machine arrives."

"We're going to stop it, Commander?"

"No. It will destroy the Earth. That is the plan, and it is a wise one. The Great One has decreed the origin point's destruction."

"Then…?"

"I have a plan within a plan," Oran Rva said. "I have discovered that I am the best-suited to rule. For others to understand my greatness as I do, I must have the greatest ship in the universe."

"The component to the sonic cannon is the critical element?" Kane asked.

"The second-to-last critical element," the commander said. "I need one more item. Gaining it will be our most dangerous task. You must concentrate, Kane, as I will accept no more buffoonery on your part."

"Yes, Commander," Kane said.

"First, though, we shall leave a little something for Star Watch Intelligence. I believe my latest gift to them will motivate the brigadier's people to furious action against us. That is how I wish it to be."

Oran Rva sat down at the console, tapping the screen, implementing the next step in his master plan.

292

-33-

Dana stared at a small comm-screen on the desk in her quarters. Maddox spoke to her on it, explaining how guards had shot and slain Ludendorff, and that he had been an android.

"Say that again," Dana whispered.

Maddox seemed to choose his words with care. He went through the situation a second time. He spoke about metal bones, circuits—a cybernetic organism like the Builders were supposed to be. That's what Ludendorff was, had been, according to the captain.

Dizziness threatened Dana. She had to clutch the edge of her desk in order to steady herself. She found herself trembling.

"Ludendorff is dead?" she whispered.

"Is that even the right way to say it?" Maddox asked. "He was a machine."

"No. I cannot accept that."

The captain tilted his head. "Do you want to see footage of the cybernetic—?"

"That isn't what I'm saying." Dana spoke slowly but deliberately, interrupting the awful words. Her grip on the edge of the desk tightened until her fingers began to ache. Her breathing accelerated until she was almost hyperventilating. Fortunately, she understood what was happening and carefully brought her breathing under control.

Dana found the captain staring at her. How long had she been silent?

"You should talk to Meta," Maddox said.

"I will talk to no one. I do not need to. The professor was a living person, not some freakish android, some *machine*, as you put it."

"This must be difficult for you, Doctor. It's why I called right away. I wanted you to hear it from me before you picked it up somewhere else."

"Listen to me, Captain. I did not leave Brahma Tech, did not leave my home and planet to wander the stars for years with some mechanical man. Ludendorff was fully human in every conceivable way. I can assure you of that."

"I believe you, Doctor, which poses an interesting question. Could Ludendorff have made a switch?"

"What do you mean?"

"It's simple, really. We have an android down here, a dead one, if that's the correct way to say it. If Ludendorff was—is human. Then, somewhere along the line the professor made a switch. The most likely location was the Builder base in the Xerxes System."

Dana hardly heard the man's words. Finally, though, they penetrated her thinking. "What? The asteroid base, a switch? Yes. That's possible, I suppose." Her eyes widened. "Not only possible. It is the only conclusion."

"Who was he really?" Maddox asked.

Dana's head swayed. "You're asking that as if I should know. I don't know."

"But you just said—"

"Captain, if you will excuse me, I must, I must..." Tears welled in Dana's eyes. She angrily wiped them away.

"I'm sorry," Maddox said. "I can't understand how this happened. Ludendorff—"

"Yes, thank you," Dana said, interrupting him again. "Thank you for telling me, and thank you for your concern."

Maddox studied her once more, finally saying, "I wish you would talk to Meta."

"I don't see how that will help. I must go. I must think this through."

A concerned look swept over the captain. Dana found she hated that. How could Ludendorff be a mechanical man? The way they had intertwined with each other during their lovemaking years ago…the passion… No machine had done those things to her. That was impossible.

Dana turned off the comm-screen. Let the captain continue his espionage games down on Earth. She had to…

Dana rose, wandering aimlessly in her quarters. Finally, she threw herself onto the bed. Tears welled until they wet her cheeks. How could the professor have done this to her? Had he really not been human?

Angrily, she got up and ran into the corridor. She banged against a bulkhead and wept quietly. The tears kept coming. Finally, she wiped them away with her sleeve. If Ludendorff had switched places with a machine in the Builder base…

Was the man that clever? Yes. Ludendorff was old with knowledge. How much knowledge, though? What had the professor learned concerning the Builders? It would seem much more than he had ever told anyone. Just how old of a Methuselah Man was he? He had secrets and—

Dana's features hardened with resolve as a possibility dawned on her. Soon, a fierce recklessness came over her. With purpose she strode down the corridor, heading for the professor's quarters.

Ludendorff had his secrets and his games, did he? Well, she wasn't going to let him get away with them anymore. She knew him better than anyone did, certainly better than anyone else on the crew. He'd let slip too much during their time together. Who did Ludendorff ultimately serve? She simply couldn't accept that the thing down there in Geneva had been the real professor. He loved trickery and used guile the ways other breathed.

That wasn't the point now. She wasn't going to stand for any more of his tricks. She would use her intellect and figure out a thing or two, and she would do it this very moment.

Dana entered his quarters. She searched until she pulled out a chain with a small metal ball on the end. Sitting down, Dana examined it in minute detail. This thing had generated a small force field around his person.

I'm going to figure out how this works. I'm going to pierce his greatest tech. Maybe it's booby trapped to kill whoever tampers with it. Well, you know what? I don't care anymore.

Dana discovered the tiniest of protrusions. She put the chain over her head and let it rest against her neck.

She took a deep breath and pressed the protrusion. She felt a vibration, while the smell of ozone became noticeable. She moved her arm, and she felt a slight difference.

How could one tell if the force field had activated? She needed to test it.

Opening a drawer, she found a small tack and threw it at her arm. The thing deflected away, sliding around just before touching her skin.

It works. Then how am I able to breathe? Does the force field only stop speeding objects?

Because she knew so little about the personal force field, she turned it off and slipped the chain from her neck. Clearly, the professor hadn't worn it when he went to the Builder base. There must have been a reason for that. Perhaps it didn't work while one wore a vacc-suit.

Setting aside the tiny item, she searched for the flat device. Some of the fire had departed her by then, but she wanted to see if she could figure that out too. If she waited, she'd get scared and wouldn't search for it. It had been a strange but powerful device.

Dana found the flat device hidden in a cache in his desk. She examined it for some time. It had fifteen various knobs.

What had he done to enmesh them in a force web? Would the device explode as Maddox had wondered if she tried to use it?

Dana laughed a moment later. She retrieved the chain and force field emitter, slipping it back onto her neck. After turning it on, she began to experiment with the flat device.

It took her a half hour to activate it. Then, it took her three hours before she figured out the combination that webbed an object in the force field.

There wasn't a booby trap. That was interesting. Hadn't the professor been worried this would fall into the wrong hands? It would appear not.

Suddenly, as she realized what she had done, Dana's knees became weak. Pulling out a chair, she sat down, resting her elbows on the table.

She'd just risked her life in a foolish experiment. Maddox hadn't tried these objects because he'd been convinced the professor had rigged them to explode. Why, then, would she have done this?

Wearily, Dana folded her arms on the table and lay her head on her arms. She shut her eyes.

Ludendorff was gone again. Either he had always been a machine man, or he had switched the android for himself, and the likeliest spot had been in the now-destroyed asteroid base. Where in the galaxy had Ludendorff discovered that sort of technology?

Are there more machine men out there?

It was a chilling thought. But soon, emotionally exhausted, Dana fell asleep.

-34-

Maddox woke up feeling refreshed. He hadn't slept this well for some time. He presumed it was because he'd slept on Earth for the first time in a long while.

Since he was already at Star Watch Intelligence Headquarters, he soon found O'Hara.

"You're just in time, Captain," she said.

He followed her into a medical theater. It reminded him of the time he'd been with Nerva Security agents in the mid-Atlantic Ocean. O'Hara, Major Stokes and he looked down on the technicians.

The android's killer lay on a medical cot, with many wires attached to his head and body.

"This is a ghastly business at times," O'Hara said. "I dislike this end of it."

Maddox looked on as the technicians went to work, questioning the shooter, watching the mind probe screens as he mumbled answers.

An inspiration struck the captain. Maddox leaned near the brigadier. "I just thought of something, Ma'am. It seems incredible I've overlooked it until now."

"Yes?" she said.

"I suggest we use the best teams and begin searching orbital Cestus Haulers from top to bottom. Begin with those that came to Earth…three days ago and work backward in time from there. I'd also search any haulers leaving Earth and those near any Laumer-Points."

"We've already been doing that," the brigadier said.

"Oh?"

"Captain, I *listened* to your story. It was a treasure trove of information, believe me."

For the next thirty minutes, the experts worked on Hicks. He had many mental blocks and went into cardiac arrest three different times. The doctors brought him back each time for further questions.

Finally, the technicians received a vital clue. It was one word: Strand.

O'Hara turned to Maddox. "I thought Strand was far away in space."

"Meta saw him on an enemy star cruiser," Maddox said. "That was several months ago now."

"You're certain about what she saw?"

"I am," Maddox said.

"Perhaps Strand returned the same way he left," O'Hara said, "using that silver pyramid of theirs."

Maddox digested the idea. "Why would a Methuselah Man come back to a world doomed to die?"

"That is an excellent question," O'Hara said. "Captain, I believe you should head to Nerva Tower. On second thought, we should storm it with space marines. After the building is secure our best snatch team can grab Strand, if he's there, and Octavian Nerva."

"Do you think Octavian is guilty of espionage against Earth?" Major Stokes asked.

"Whether Octavian has orchestrated anything or not, I don't know," O'Hara said. "Clearly, Strand ran the murder operation against Ludendorff. Likely, Strand sent the signal to Pluto Command and engineered the microwave beam attack against the captain. I'd like to know if Octavian knows who and what Strand really is."

"Ma'am, I'd like to lead the snatch team that grabs Strand," Maddox said.

"Really," Stokes said. "I think that's a bad idea."

"Why's that?" the brigadier asked the major.

"Too many people are suspicious about Maddox," Stokes said.

299

"I beginning to think that Strand planted the evidence that compromised the captain," O'Hara said.

"Perhaps you're right," Stokes said. "Still, the agents will feel distrustful toward him until his name is officially cleared."

"There it is again," O'Hara said, "a constant lack of trust among us. Our enemy is stymieing Star Watch with it."

"If it's all the same," Maddox said, "I'd still like to go."

"Of course," O'Hara said.

"Before I go, though," Maddox said. "I'd like to make a call to *Victory.*"

"Why is that?"

"Before I enter Nerva Tower, I want someone with me who trusts my decisions, which means I'd like Sergeant Riker with me on this one."

It took O'Hara three seconds to decide. "Make your call, Captain. The sooner we attack the nest of vipers, the better I'll like it."

✳✳✳

Despite a great deal of hurrying, Maddox delayed joining the assault force against Nerva Tower. He stood outside a grounded air-car on a grassy hill. From his vantage, he spied the city in the distance. With a pair of binoculars, he studied the giant Nerva Conglomerate Building, which towered over the rest of the city.

Riker was racing down from *Victory* and should arrive in another few minutes. Until then, Maddox was content to wait by the air-car.

Checking his watch, Maddox realized the initial assault teams would be reaching the tower in another few minutes. Space marines in power armor would lead the assault. The Lord High Admiral had decided Star Watch wasn't going to worry about constitutional niceties at a time like this.

Of course, Octavian had some of the Commonwealth's best lawyers on his payroll. What would any of that matter once the Earth was a smoldering lake of lava, though? The doomsday machine had struck the Wahhabi Caliphate. Earth was—in Maddox's opinion—likely the next target.

The entire Solar System hurried to get ready for the planet-killer as the Lord High Admiral gave his orders. More space marines and Intelligence sweep-teams rocketed for orbital Cestus Haulers and those heading for various Laumer-Points.

Had Kane returned to Earth that way? Had New Men come this time?

A beep sounded from Maddox's air-car. He lowered the binoculars and saw a red light on the dash. The light meant the space marines were going in.

Leaving the door open, Maddox sat in the driver's seat. He tapped the screen, seeing through a recording camera on a space marine lieutenant's helmet. The woman was charged with finding Octavian Nerva. According to the latest data, he was in the tower. No one had seen Strand.

Maddox watched the scene. The lieutenant made huge leaps as her team charged the glass tower. Combat-cars would be zooming like wasps for the higher floors. This was a smash-and-grab assault. Octavian was the richest, most powerful man on Earth. Nerva Tower was like a fortress.

Gunfire hammered the space marines. The team was inside the tower, in a lobby. One of the armored troopers went down, smashing a glass table.

"The Nerva personnel have exo-piercing bullets," the lieutenant radioed.

Maddox checked his watch. Where was Riker? Couldn't they bring the sergeant down any faster? Maddox wanted to be there when they grabbed Strand, if the man was there.

On the air-car's screen, the lieutenant's marines downed three Nerva Conglomerate guards. The company personnel wore body armor, but it wasn't as good as the marines had.

Maddox stared at the screen. The lieutenant's team moved in over-watch bounds through a large corridor. The Nerva combat team had pulled back.

A noise alerted Maddox. He looked up. A combat-car descended. Finally. He called up with his comm-unit to check if it brought Riker.

The combat-car pilot said, "I'm bringing your man down, sir."

301

Maddox acknowledged that, stepping outside, watching the combat-car thud onto the grass twenty meters away. A portal opened. Sergeant Riker hurried down a ramp and jogged toward the air-car.

Seconds later, the combat vehicle lifted.

Riker breathed deeply of the air of Earth. Some of the tension he'd had aboard the starship had already eased from his features. He gave a sloppy salute. "It's good to be home, sir. Thanks for asking for me."

"It is good to be on Terra Firma once again," Maddox agreed.

The combat vehicle above headed for Monte Carlo.

"Get in," Maddox said. "We're going to follow them."

Riker headed for his side of the car, opening the door, climbing into the bubble dome.

Maddox slammed his door shut, tapped the ignition and listened to the engine purr. "Strapped in?" he asked.

Riker grunted acknowledgement.

The flash on the tiny screen alerted Maddox. He stared at it. The screen turned blinding white. That shocked him. A second later, blankness showed on the dash screen.

What had happened over there? Before he could worry about it too long, the entire horizon exploded into a giant ball of light. A vast mushroom cloud billowed into existence.

Maddox reacted without thinking. He engaged the engine, turned the air-car and accelerated away from the devastation. He wasn't going to try to outrun the thermonuclear blast that must be killing nearly everyone in Monte Carlo. Instead, he raced down the hill for the bottom of the ravine, hoping to reach it before the blast wave and heat rolled against them.

"Hang on," Maddox shouted. He dropped the air-car. They bounced in their seats as dry gravel rolled underneath them. The car slewed one way and another. Finally, as dust billowed, the car screeched to a stop. Maddox and Riker curled as tightly as possible.

Soon, thermonuclear-powered winds howled over the hill. Trees on the highest part of the slope bent low. Then, heat struck, igniting grass at the top of the hill and some leaves. Fortunately, the air-car was far enough away from ground zero and tucked down out of direct line-of-sight. The two Intelligence officers endured the worst in the car.

Finally, the winds died down and the heat passed, although the grass fire grew.

Maddox tried the ignition. The engine purred once more. He lifted the car and zoomed away. Devastation and raging fires radiated back to Monte Carlo. The captain didn't bother with communications. He was sure they wouldn't work.

"Who set the bomb?" Riker asked gruffly.

The answer blossomed in the captain's thoughts. The enemy must have known they were coming. If the enemy had attacked the shuttle on its way down, had unleashed a gunman against the android Ludendorff, they would have known about the snatch-teams sent to grab Octavian and Strand.

"What do you think the bomb means, sir?" Riker asked.

"That's the question," Maddox agreed. He flew for Geneva, thinking hard.

Riker stared silently out the window.

"I wonder if the bomb is meant to paralyze Star Watch from reacting properly," Maddox said.

Riker nodded.

"We don't know enough at this point, but I'm thinking we can guess. What is the enemy's greatest power against us?"

Riker looked thoughtful.

"Knowledge," Maddox said. "Our enemy knows more than we do. The New Men also have access to greater technology. Did Ludendorff have a long-distance communicator or not?"

"We never found one, sir."

"No, we didn't. Ludendorff must have broken it down into its component parts and hidden them." Maddox raised an eyebrow. "The New Men appear to have the power of faster communication. Either they have a long-distance receiver on Earth, or they used the silver pyramid to send someone back here before we arrived."

"Who did they send?" Riker asked.

"I doubt that matters as much as whether they did send someone. That person knows the doomsday machine is coming. Yes, of course. The enemy has been burning up his espionage assets at a prodigious rate. If the Earth is going to

303

end, none of that matters. So, the fact our enemy is using up his espionage assets—maybe ones gathered over thirty years—means he's after something."

"That makes sense, sir."

Maddox tapped his thumbs against the controls. What would the enemy want? Why had the enemy gone to such lengths to stop him personally? The secret foe had used every trick to dump false data, and to gain access to impossible places, to—

Maddox tried the comm, getting harsh static. Had the thermonuclear blast fused the radio or just played havoc with the radio waves? He tried the comm again. The static sputtered, and then the comm quit altogether.

"Right," Maddox said. "Hang on, Sergeant." With a quick manipulation, the captain aimed the air-car upward.

"Where are we going, sir?"

"Upstairs, Sergeant, back to *Victory.*"

"Why there, sir?" Riker asked.

"I know what the enemy is trying to do."

"Do you care to let me in on that, sir?"

"Yes," Maddox said. "Here's their plan…"

-35-

Meta pushed a portable-floater to the main hatch of *Victory's* hangar bay. At the closed entrance, she grounded the floater as worry seethed through her.

Taking out her comm-unit, Meta called the bridge. "What's happening now?" she asked.

"Nothing new other than confirming the worst," Valerie said in a quiet voice. "A nuclear device definitely went off in Monte Carlo. I haven't had word about Maddox or Riker yet."

Meta bit her lower lip. Riker had left *Victory* on Maddox's orders. The sergeant was going to Nerva Tower, which was in Monte Carlo. Could the nuclear explosion be a coincidence? She didn't believe that for a minute. Maddox's life was in terrible danger. In fact, he could be dead.

Squeezing her eyes closed, Meta shook her head. She couldn't accept Maddox's death. It wouldn't happen like that.

How will it happen?

Until this moment, Maddox had seemed to lead a charmed life. That was pure deception, though. The captain lived dangerously. At times, Meta wondered if he sought such assignments because of the demon riding in his soul. The captain loathed his dual nature. The idea of being part of an experiment, a hybrid—

"The shuttle has landed and oxygen has returned," Valerie said. "You can enter the hangar bay."

Meta opened her eyes, staring at the comm-unit. "You'll tell me the minute you hear something, good or bad, okay?"

305

"I'll do that," Valerie said.

"You promise?"

"Meta, this is me. I keep my word. I'll tell you the minute I know something about the captain. I'm sure he's all right."

"Don't lie to me," Meta said. "You're not sure."

"Okay," Valerie said, in a softer voice than before. "I'm worried just like you."

Meta closed her eyes again. There it was. Just like her, Valerie must realize Maddox had died in the nuclear blast. He'd headed for Nerva Tower, and that had been where the heart of the explosion had occurred.

Meta opened her eyes as she slid the comm-unit into a pocket. Putting her hands on the floater, she activated it. The thing lifted off the floor. Meta opened the hatch, pushing the floater into the vast hangar bay.

A Star Watch hauler shuttle rested in the center of the chamber. It was bigger than the shuttle Maddox and Keith had left in. The haulers were the workhorses of the fleet.

Meta frowned to herself. If Maddox was dead...*what will I do now?*

The captain had loved her...hadn't he?

Don't think of him as dead until you know for sure.

Meta nodded. Sometimes, she didn't think the captain loved her enough. He liked her, certainly. The man loved to lay with her. But she didn't feel as if Maddox needed her, couldn't function without her. His work engaged him too heavily. He was always thinking about his mission, always plotting, planning...

He could be dead. You're supposed to think well of the dead, not complain about them.

Maybe she was seeing Maddox as he really was for the first time. Kane had been like ice, but there had been a secret need in his eyes. The Rouen Colony man had pretended not to need her, to be impervious to her charms, but she could tell it had been otherwise.

Why didn't I see this before?

Meta shook her head. Because the brute Kane had kidnapped her and hauled her halfway across the galaxy, that's why. He had been a pig, always knocking her down. There hadn't been any love in Kane, but lust, greedy desire to use her body.

I love Maddox, and he's dead. He must be dead. No one survives a nuclear blast.

She would have to move on.

Meta sneered at herself. She was moving fast. Was it a survival mechanism? She had to protect her heart, right? She had been through so much in her life. Besides, Maddox had blown hot and cold with her. He—

The rear entry hatch lowered on the hauler-shuttle. The crew must want her to take the item back there for them. What a bunch of lazy shirkers.

Meta almost pulled out the comm-unit to ask Valerie if she'd learned anything more. What would *Victory* do now, what would Galyan do with Maddox dead? Would the Adok AI remain loyal to Star Watch, or had the alien computer been loyal to the person of Captain Maddox?

We're going to need Galyan against the doomsday machine.

Meta glanced at the silver egg on the floater. Star Watch HQ had called up after the blast. They wanted the Builder egg in order to get ready for the doomsday machine. Maddox had spoken at length with Brigadier O'Hara and the Lord High Admiral. With Ludendorff's help, Star Watch would use the egg to defeat the ancient planet-killer. At least Maddox's last mission would have helped to save the Earth.

The former assassin peered at the object, shivering with dread. Inside the egg was a bionic Swarm creature. Was it anything like the horrible medical creature they had fought just before boarding *Victory* for the first time? That seemed like a lifetime ago. Now, Builder pyramids transferred her a hundred light-years in a jump, ancient drones used fusion beams just like the enemy's star cruisers and—

Meta bit back a sob. She wasn't going to cry yet. She didn't even know whether Maddox was dead or not. He could have pulled off another of his miracle finishes. The microwave-beam attack hadn't killed him. Maddox had fired a missile at treacherous space marines in the Geneva Spaceport—

307

How many secret assaults could Maddox fight off? He must have died in Monte Carlo. How did one dodge a nuclear blast?

"I want to go home," Meta whispered to herself. She was already sick of Earth with Maddox gone.

Embroiled in her thoughts, Meta pushed the floater up the ramp into the nearly empty cargo hold. She didn't stop to call out. Instead, she kept walking.

Poor Maddox had played his last card. He had been good, one of the best. But in the end, he had fallen to the Methuselah People or one of the clever agents of the New Men. How was Star Watch supposed to beat a superior foe that had access to better tech?

Meta heard a whirring noise. She blinked and looked back. The ramp she'd walked up was closing.

"Hey," she said. "I'm still in here."

Meta looked around. The cargo hold was empty except for several big crates. The deck plate under her feet shivered. The engine had come online.

"Hey, can anyone hear me?" she shouted. "I'm still in here. You're supposed to wait until I'm gone before you lift off."

There was no answer.

"All right, enough of this," Meta said to herself, scowling. She pulled out her comm-unit, using her thumb to press the 'on' switch. It didn't matter because nothing happened.

Meta shook the comm-unit. "Don't tell me the battery is dead." She adjusted a dial.

"Hello, Meta," a deep-voiced man said.

Meta looked up, and her jaw dropped. This couldn't be happening.

"Kane?" she asked.

The man wore a silver suit like a blasted New Man. He had the same bulk as before with his square head and gray hair. The man was massive. She knew the futility of fighting against him hand-to-hand.

"How are you here? You're supposed to be—" Meta spun around, sprinting for the still closing ramp. If Kane was here, the enemy was pulling a fast one. She couldn't believe this.

A stunner purred behind her. Meta felt the bolt slam against her back. It propelled her off her feet. She thudded onto the vibrating deck plates. From on the floor, Meta watched the ramp seal shut.

"This is a delightful surprise," Kane said in his deep voice. "I had no idea you, personally, would bring the egg."

"What...?" she whispered. Vaguely, Meta was aware that Kane knelt beside her.

"When I saw you walking across the hangar bay floor, I asked the dominant if I could keep you. He shrugged, which means yes."

"Kane," she whispered. It was hard to think past the stun effect.

"The Earth is doomed," Kane said. "Leaving with me gives you life. You have the genes of a Rouen Colony worker. We are the beginning process, Meta. For thirty years already, the Throne World has taken the weak clay of humanity and molded it into a superior form. I've just learned that soon, throughout Human Space, there will be more Rouen Colonies, turning out better people like you and me."

"I don't understand," she whispered.

"I want you, Meta. I will have you. Oran Rva has consented to it."

With seemingly rusted muscles, Meta turned her head. Her vision was blurry, but she could make out Kane's square head.

"The commander of the invasion armada—"

"Is here in the shuttle," Kane said. "You've brought the last component for a glorious task. If you had been an inferior, I couldn't have kept you. Now, as my reward, I will keep you for my own. I have wanted to make love to you for some time."

Meta made out his white teeth. The pig was grinning at her. Make love to her? She would stick a knife between his ribs.

"I should have done this a long time ago," he said.

Meta felt his hands touching her, groping, squeezing. "Kane," she whispered. "What..."

"We have no more time," he said, pushing her over onto her back. "This is our one chance—"

"Are you going to rape me while I'm stunned and immobile?"

"You're so beautiful. I must—we won't—you're trying to confuse me."

Meta heard a new note in Kane's voice that hadn't been there before. He didn't sound as aloof as last time. How had the enemy agent gotten back to Earth before *Victory*? The answer was obvious. The New Men had sent him through the Nexus. Had repeated long-distance jumps worn him down?

"I am ice," Kane said, as he squeezed her flesh.

"What's that supposed to mean?"

He was silent, and his hands no longer roved over her body. One hand lingered on her shoulder. His breathing became heavier.

Beneath her, Meta felt the shuttle lifting. This couldn't be happening. Had Valerie opened the hangar bay doors already? How could the lieutenant do that without first checking in with her? Had the enemy tricked Valerie?

Yes. That must be it. Horrible Oran Rva was here in the Solar System and had tricked them into giving him the Builder egg—because the commander had pretended to be a Star Watch hauling team. This was a disaster. Now, Kane was kidnapping her all over again. Worse, he planned to rape her to fulfill his own base appetites.

"When I was a boy," Kane rumbled. "The trainer took us out to Rollo Glacier."

What was he talking about now?

"On the Rouen Colony?" Meta asked.

"Yes," Kane said. "You know Rollo Glacier is as large as some continents. We trekked across it for days, enduring, as the trainer hardened us into gang-leaders. We were the chosen, but first we had to show him we had the desire to survive. It was so cold, Meta. The iciness seeped up through the soles of my boots. The winds came, and still the trainer forced us to march. We had to endure. We had to prove we were tougher than the ice."

Through a porthole, Meta saw the darkness of space. Was the shuttle outside the starship? She wanted to weep with frustration.

"Some of the lads sank down in exhaustion," Kane said, absorbed with his stupid tale. "I hauled up my friend. The trainer struck me. 'Let the weakling die,' the trainer told me. I did not listen. The trainer beat me that day until finally I collapsed beside my dying friend."

Meta tore her gaze from the porthole to stare at the fuzzy-imaged face before her.

"I remember seeing the trainer's boot before my eyes," Kane said. "I lay on the ice, shivering, freezing to death. He laughed at me. He asked if I, too, was a weakling like my dead friend. When I didn't answer, the trainer knelt before me, staring me in the eye. 'You have grit, Kane,' he told me. 'You dared to endure my wrath. Let me tell you the secret of life. Be the ice. Rid yourself of useless emotion. Let your cold freeze others into submission as you beat yourself into a superior being.' I stared into his eyes, hating the man for what he had done to me and for letting my best friend die. Finally, he shrugged, climbing to his feet. He left with the rest of the lads."

"What did you do?" Meta asked. She didn't understand why he was telling her all this, but she found herself wanting to know more, to understand more about the New Men's mysterious agent.

Kane inhaled deeply. "I lay on the ice, absorbing its power. It grew in me that day. It entered my soul and filled me with the resolve to live. I would endure until I had the opportunity to kill the trainer because he had beaten me for helping my friend. I became the ice, and I climbed to my feet. That night, I staggered into camp. The trainer let me eat hot food, even though I was late. That was weakness on his part. Five years later, I showed him the foolishness of his moment of weakness by beating him to death with my fists."

A little more of Kane's blocky features came into focus. Meta shivered at the hard stare in his eyes.

"I am ice," Kane said. "I will destroy those who hurt me." He turned his head, staring at the hatch that led to the corridor that must lead to the shuttle's flight compartment.

"Where are we going?" Meta asked.

Kane focused on her, and he glanced at the hand on her shoulder. Slowly, he removed the hand. "You are mine, Meta."

She said nothing, but a plan began to form in her mind.

311

"This time you will stay with me." Kane stared into her eyes. Finally, he held out a hand.

Meta forced herself to move until her fingers touched his. Kane hauled her to her feet.

"Come," he said. "Let us see Oran Rva. He will wish to examine you, perhaps test your fitness for the mission."

One more time, Meta glanced at the porthole. It showed Starship *Victory* outside. Behind it was the Earth. Both the vessel and the planet grew smaller. Where was the New Man taking the shuttle?

-36-

Maddox pushed the air-car higher into the atmosphere. The blue had begun to fade away into darkness.

Riker stared out of the bubble canopy. "Makes a man feel insignificant. Can't say that I like this in the slightest."

The captain hardly heard the sergeant's words. He focused on the task. The enemy kept one or even two steps ahead of them. It seemed clear they would try for the Builder egg. The nuclear blast in Monte Carlo had been a diversion. Now would be the perfect moment to stage—what would the enemy do? It seemed to him they would try what they had in the past.

Per Lomax had led a boarding team against *Victory*. With Star Watch codes, how many troopers would the enemy use to try to grab the starship?

"This is going to be hard without any communication," Riker said. "Where is the starship in orbit exactly?"

"One thing at a time, Sergeant," Maddox said.

Riker turned to him in wonder, aghast. "Don't tell me you don't know, sir."

"Try the radio again," Maddox suggested.

Riker stared at him another second. Then, the sergeant tried the radio. It was still dead. "That's no good, sir."

"Try your communicator."

"Don't have one on me, sir."

"I have one," Maddox said. He pulled it out and tried it. Nothing happened. "Hmm. That's not good, as you say."

"We have to go back down, sir," Riker said.

"I don't think so."

"Begging your pardon—"

"Kindly shut up, Sergeant, and let me think."

Riker nodded. "That's it, sir. Take it out on me, why don't you? I'm just the hapless enlisted man—"

"Sergeant," Maddox warned.

Riker fell silent, once more staring out of the bubble canopy.

"I have an idea," Maddox said in a bit. "It presupposes greater intelligence on Galyan's part. I have to believe the AI is busy monitoring everything. That's what the hyper-intelligent do."

Riker kept quiet, fixedly staring at the now appearing stars.

"Yes, I understand, Sergeant. I'm a difficult taskmaster." Maddox began to fiddle with the controls. He shut the engine on and off in exact sequences.

The fuel gauge showed the air-car had just enough to get back to Earth if they started down now. Maddox had no intention of doing that, though. If the enemy had made his move for the egg, the doomsday machine was likely going to show up soon. The enemy must be able to track the planet-killer—if they truly possessed long-distance communicators.

"We need communication," the captain said. "I want Keith to bring up a jumpfighter."

Riker glanced at him. "Can I ask what you're doing, sir?"

"It's a simple enough expedient. I'm turning the engine on and off in Morse code sequences."

"That's it?"

"If my guess is correct," Maddox said, "it should be enough."

"I'm afraid I don't understand, sir."

"Galyan must be monitoring everything around him," Maddox said. "With his greater intelligence, I expect he's gotten more curious about things."

"He has machine intelligence," the sergeant pointed out. "I imagine that's quite different from human intelligence."

"Perhaps," Maddox said. "We'll find out soon enough."

As the air-car zoomed upward under its initial velocity, the captain continued to turn the engine on and off. The last atmospheric blue faded away. The stars shined around them. Soon, the Earth's curvature took his breath away. It was beautiful up here. What had the sergeant said? It made a man feel small. Why should that be? What was there inherent in the human soul that felt insignificance at such grand beauty?

The minutes ticked away, five, ten and finally fifteen.

"It's not working," Riker declared.

"Then what is that out there?" Maddox asked, pointing at a bright spot in the starry distance.

"I don't see anything, sir."

"It's growing."

Riker glanced at him. "You're imagining it."

"I hope you're wrong."

Another five minutes proved Maddox right. Both of them could tell the outsized shape of Starship *Victory*. Galyan must be coming to get them.

"Sir, I don't mean any disrespect saying this. But what you just did was a cockamamie piece of lunacy. We should both be doomed, waiting to fall to Earth like a shooting star. Sometimes, you push your luck too far."

"It had nothing to do with luck," Maddox said, "but heightened reasoning. I correctly estimated Galyan's intelligence and his curiosity. I played the probabilities and—"

"Got lucky as can be, sir," Riker said. "If you can't see that...well, then you aren't as smart as you like to believe yourself to be."

"That will be all, Sergeant."

"Yes, sir," Riker said.

The two then waited in silence as the starship approached the drifting air-car.

***

Maddox stood on *Victory's* bridge, speaking to Brigadier O'Hara in Geneva.

The captain had already learned the worst from a crestfallen Valerie. In order to function—*they've kidnapped Meta*—he concentrated on what he had to do to defeat them. He put his emotions in cold storage and icily decided what step to take first.

"Ma'am, I have bad news," the captain said. His face felt numb, but he ignored that. A volcano of force bubbled beneath his calm exterior. "The enemy has acquired the Builder egg, I'm afraid."

The brigadier blinked at him in shock. She sat at her desk in her office. Her eyes seemed like bright gems in a ghostly face. Maddox had never seen her like this before. She looked old. Her shoulders sagged as she stared at him.

"They came in a Star Watch shuttle with orders from the Lord High Admiral's office," Maddox said. "It was all quite correct, verified, I assure you."

How...how can this be?" the brigadier asked. "They're baffling us at every turn." She scowled. "How is it you're up in the starship and not in Geneva?"

Maddox explained what had happened and how he correctly guessed that the enemy would go for the egg.

"You should have raced straight here, Captain. I could have radioed *Victory*. We might have stopped their latest ploy if you'd done so."

Maddox hesitated for just a moment. "Recriminations aren't going to help us now." He shifted his stance, as a shadow seemed to pass across his face. "They kidnapped Meta, poor girl. She brought them the egg." For just a moment, Maddox lost focus. An animal in his heart snarled silently. Outwardly, he kept it chained. "It seems the shuttle vanished around the other side of the planet before I could board and warn my crew about the situation."

O'Hara stared at him a little longer before saying, "I don't know what to do. I'm baffled. What are our options?"

"Ma'am, I believe we're operating against a New Man. They've sent their best person to Earth. He moves with bewildering speed. Because they grabbed the egg, it seems obvious they're going to try to board the planet-killer."

"To what purpose?" the brigadier asked.

"Why, to own the doomsday machine," Maddox said.

"Yes..." the brigadier said, staring at her hands. She looked up. "Do you think it's possible this...New Man can succeed?"

"If anyone can, he will. Yes, I believe it's possible."

"Normally, I would order you to stop him. But if he fails to board the doomsday machine, it will annihilate the Earth."

"I request that you send me Keith Maker in a jumpfighter. Then, I will take care of the situation."

"Just you by yourself, Captain?" O'Hara asked. "You can succeed where all of Star Watch has failed?"

"No," Maddox said, "not just by myself. I'll have my team with me. Galyan is sharper than ever. He is busy scouring the starship, fixing all the inoperative systems."

"Do you mean the alien AI?"

"Yes."

"It is an 'it,' not a 'he,'" the brigadier said.

"Driving Force Galyan disagrees with you, Ma'am."

The brigadier looked as if she wanted to argue. Finally, her shoulders deflated a little more "I'll have to ask the admiral about this."

"We don't have time, Ma'am."

"You see the doomsday machine?"

"If the enemy has snatched the egg, it must be because the planet-killer is near. I should leave Earth orbit immediately. The enemy has to reach the doomsday machine in order to implement his goal. Perhaps I can stop him before he does that."

O'Hara studied Maddox. Did she see the ramrod stiffness in his stance, the glint in his eyes that spoke of steely determination?

"This is a disaster, Captain. The enemy truly is better, smarter and quicker than we regular mortals are. You, your alien ship and your crew are going to have to deliver us from death. The Home Fleet will fight, but if you're right about what happened to the Wahhabi Fleet in New Arabia—God help humanity."

"I think He is," Maddox said, softly. "We have a fighting chance with this ship."

"What is your plan?" O'Hara asked. "You lack the egg. You lack a key such as the one Ludendorff gave Per Lomax. I don't see that you can board the doomsday machine. Even if you could, how could you succeed where Per Lomax failed?"

317

"Do you really want me to divulge my plan?" Maddox asked. "It's quite possible enemy ears are listening to our conversation."

O'Hara searched his face and smiled sadly. "This is why you went into the Beyond, searching for the impossible. This is why I took a gamble with you from the beginning. No, Captain, do not tell me your plan. As to your request, I will send your ace with the required fighter. Godspeed, Captain. Defeat our foe. We'll do everything we can to help you. Brigadier O'Hara out."

Maddox faced Valerie. The lieutenant continued to scowl at her board. She'd been sullen ever since she told him the terrible news.

"It wasn't your fault," Maddox told her for the tenth time. He wasn't sure if he was saying it to convince her or to convince himself.

Valerie looked up. "Then whose fault was it, sir?" she asked in a bitter voice.

"It was all of ours."

The lieutenant shook her head. "Sorry, I don't accept that line of bull crap, Captain."

He raised his eyebrows.

"Excuse me, sir," Valerie said. "I mean to say that I don't accept your line of reasoning. I made the decision to send Meta to get the egg. I was in charge. I gave the enemy what they came for. It was my fault and no one else's. Worse, I let them kidnap Meta. I am sick inside. I'm so sorry, sir."

Maddox focused on the lieutenant. Her wellbeing was his responsibility. Valerie was part of his crew. They were going to need everyone in top form soon. They were going up against the enemy's A team. The lieutenant was badly in need of encouragement. But Valerie Noonan wasn't just anyone. She was the welfare kid who had fought against the elitists and won. The captain believed he knew the right angle to take with her.

Taking his own sorrow in hand, Maddox concentrated on the next step with Valerie.

"I see," he said. "You're going to wallow in your defeat, are you?"

Valerie sat up with her features stiffening.

"You lost me my woman, Lieutenant. I do not appreciate, then, this defeatist manner. If you cannot remain at your post because you want to sulk, tell me now so I can find someone who can do her duty."

Valerie's face turned red.

"I want people who fight through to the bitter end. I don't want quitters, Lieutenant. Which are you, I'd like to know now?"

Lieutenant Noonan's eyes burned with outrage even as tears glistened in them.

Maddox nodded. "I like that much better, Lieutenant. You're angry. Good. Now you listen to me. One of the most dangerous men in the world tricked you. That man has run circles around Star Watch Intelligence. That man slipped an assassin into the highest levels of command. He even reached out to Pluto and ordered my arrest. We're not dealing with a few uppity cadets at the Space Academy. We're dealing with the most ruthless man alive. You're frustrated for being beaten. Worse, he pulled your trousers down around your ankles, as it were."

Valerie looked away.

Maddox stopped. It was time to let her reason it out for herself.

Soon, the lieutenant shook her head. She squared her shoulders. Without facing him, Valerie said, "You're right, sir. I was acting like a spoiled, rich-kid cadet just now. But I'm a Star Watch line officer. It's time to fight."

"It's time to outthink our enemy," Maddox added.

Valerie faced him with fire in her eyes. "That's *your* task, sir. You think like the New Men much better than any of us can because you're like them."

Maddox felt a stab of annoyance at her words.

Valerie smiled grimly. "You have their blood, sir. You're quicker and smarter—"

"That's quite enough, Lieutenant."

She stared him in the eyes. "I'm just saying, sir. You don't like being the hybrid, the one who's different from everyone else. But I'm glad you are different. You're my big brother. I

319

trust you with my life. We all do, sir. You have to accept who you are. Now, you have to use the New Man side of you, sir. You have to beat their A team by being ours."

Maddox looked away, thinking. Then he looked back at her. "I suppose I deserved that."

"Yes sir, you did. But then so did I."

"We're two wounded tigers, Lieutenant. Maybe this is the mission where we finally get our licks in."

"I hope you're right, sir. It's time."

Maddox said nothing more as he studied orbital space. The enemy had kidnapped Meta right out from under his nose. That enraged him, but he refused to let it color his thinking. For this, he would need his coolest concentration yet.

Who had taken the egg? Was it a New Man? It had been breathtakingly bold. He both hated whoever had done it and admired him greatly.

All I ask is that I get the chance to return him the favor.

-37-

Twenty-four hours brought little change to the overall situation. The biggest difference was *Victory's* location, half a million kilometers from Earth.

Luna Defense was off the port bow one hundred thousand kilometers away. Various Star Watch destroyers and frigates orbited Earth at the Moon's distance from the planet. Their sensors searched everywhere for a sign of the shuttle that had stolen the egg. Every Cestus hauler, every merchant ship near Earth had been ordered to stop and await another round of space marine and SW Intelligence search parties. Unfortunately, it took time to board and search each vessel from top to bottom a second time.

Downstairs on the planet, relief efforts were underway for the nuclear bomb victims who had survived the terrible tragedy.

The battleships in the Outer System were accelerating as fast as they could for Earth. Every warship in the Solar System gathered into one hard nucleus. The Lord High Admiral had already taken a shuttle and headed for his flagship.

Maddox had told Star Watch Command about the New Arabia System. That didn't mean humanity was going to let an alien doomsday machine destroy Earth without a titanic fight. The best scenario had Star Watch defeating the neutroium-hulled planet-killer. Even if they did that, though, how many Star Watch warships would drift as wrecks afterward?

Admiral Fletcher's Fifth Fleet was coming. Together with the Home Fleet, that represented seventy percent of Star Watch's warship strength. To beat the doomsday machine but lose half the Home Fleet would be a disaster for the continuing war against the New Men.

Humanity had finally beaten the enemy in the battles of the Tannish and Markus Systems. If they lost too many warships now against the doomsday machine…the greater war might be lost before they got a chance to turn the tables on the arrogant enemy.

"I cannot believe I haven't found them yet," Galyan said.

Maddox sat in the command chair. How much longer did they have? When would the doomsday—

"Captain," Valerie said. "I'm picking up ionic magnetic signals."

The captain's stomach clenched. This was too soon. Earth needed more time. "Where is the location?" he asked in a quiet voice.

"Approximately three million kilometers beyond Mars' orbital path," the lieutenant said.

Maddox peered up at the main screen.

Valerie put a hand to her right ear. "Signals are coming in from Mars Command. They're reporting a magnetic storm. Sir, I think the doomsday machine is already coming through."

The lieutenant referred to the time delay from three million kilometers beyond Mars' orbital path to Earth. Because of the speed of light—which affected both messages and sensor signals—the delay was only a matter of minutes, but it was still there.

The captain stood, staring at the main screen. He remembered Ludendorff's holoimage video from the Wahhabi Caliphate capital system.

"It's definitely getting bigger," Valerie said, referring to the magnetic storm.

"There!" Galyan said. "I have spotted an anomaly."

Maddox glanced at the holoimage. Galyan pointed at the screen that showed orbital Earth. On the screen, he produced a red circle around an object out there.

"What is that?" Maddox asked. It was a red-circled dot on the screen, showing something in Earth orbit.

"I am highlighting a jumpfighter," Galyan said. "Ah, it is jumping."

The dot on the screen winked out of sight.

"Where did the jumpfighter come from?" Maddox asked. "Can you trace that?"

Galyan stared at the screen. "There. The jumpfighter originated from that orbital ship." Another red circle encompassed a different vessel. The holoimage's eyelids fluttered. "That is Cestus Hauler five," the AI said, "in near Earth orbit."

"That's the hauler's official designation?" Maddox asked.

"No," Galyan said. "That is the Star Watch search number."

"I'll inform headquarters of the Cestus hauler," Valerie said.

"Head out for the magnetic storm," Maddox told Galyan.

"Should I engage the star drive?" Galyan asked.

"Negative," the captain said. "Strain every sensor you have. Watch the ion storm, and tell me everything of note that happens to the doomsday machine. Have you seen it yet, by the way?"

"Negative," Galyan said. "I have—wait. I see the planet-killer now. I am giving you full magnification."

A new image leapt into view on the screen. It was that of a magnetic storm out beyond Mars' orbital path. The storm looked just like the one he'd seen weeks ago. Long strands of purple lightning flickered from it.

"Do you notice the greater darkness within the storm?" Galyan asked.

"I do," Maddox said softly.

Then it appeared—the giant, teardrop-shaped doomsday machine.

"Do you see the jumpfighter?" Maddox asked.

"How could I?" Galyan said. "The jumpfighter just left Earth orbit. I need more time to see what just happened out there."

Yes, of course. Maddox waited. They all did as the minutes passed away.

"There," the AI said. "I have spotted the jumpfighter. I will highlight it for you."

A red circle appeared, but Maddox couldn't see any dot of a jumpfighter within the circle that was in the ion storm. The red circle touched the hull of the doomsday machine, though. That was cutting it mighty fine to appear practically on the planet-killer's outer skin. Was there a reason for making such a risky jump?

"Are you sure the jumpfighter is there?" the captain asked.

"Utterly certain," Galyan said.

"Do you find it odd the jumpfighter appeared so close to the machine's hull?"

"It does not seem odd at all," Galyan said. "I suspect the jumpfighter appeared so near for a reason. The likeliest explanation is that it needed to appear close enough so it didn't trigger the planet-killer's defensive mechanisms."

"Right," Maddox said. That made sense. The ancient destroyer must have an inner zone where it would annihilate anything that got so close. Then, there must be an even nearer safe area where it would assume something that close was friendly. But that would call for tight jump control to get within the safe zone. Who but a New Man could pilot like that over such a long distance?

"What's the enemy jumpfighter doing now?" Maddox asked.

"I can give you a computer-generated approximation," Galyan said. "But know that it will not be one hundred percent accurate. The ion storm is interfering with the clarity of my long-range scanners."

"Yes, do it," Maddox said, without hesitation. "Show me a computer-generated graphic."

The stars and the magnetic storm disappeared from the screen. In its place was a realistic computer graphic of the giant vessel with its neutroium hull.

"I am using my probability processors to guide me in this," Galyan said.

Maddox nodded absently.

The hull looked smooth. Then, a jumpfighter appeared. It looked just like the one Maddox had used to journey to Wolf Prime with Dana and Keith. The jumpfighter maneuvered expertly, gliding beside the ancient wrecking-machine. A port opened on the jumpfighter. The people inside must have used the latest experimental drug to hinder Jump Lag to be able to exit the jumpfighter so quickly. Three people in vacc-suits and maneuver packs left the tiny craft. How could they survive in the ion storm? It must be more Builder tech that allowed it. The visors were silver-colored, hiding the people's features. A trail of hydrogen spray spewed from the thruster-packs.

Soon, the three suited voyagers landed on the neutroium hull. The disjointed way they walked indicated that they used magnetic boots—boots that worked in the magnetic storm!

"Why doesn't the planet-killer destroy them?" Valerie said.

"I cannot answer that," Galyan said. "Perhaps the original builders did not envision anyone appearing so close near the hull. The others out there must have understood the particular design feature. Ah, this is difficult, but I am sensing a faint signal from one of them. It comes from a small object that the prime person carries."

"Two questions," Maddox said. "How can you sense all this through the ion storm? And how can you tell which one is the prime person?"

"My sensors are vastly superior now, able to pierce the magnetic interference," Galyan said. "I sense the prime individual from the manner of his locomotion. Due to my heightened senses, it is an easy thing to decipher."

Maddox and Valerie traded glances.

"The magnetic storm is beginning to dissipate," Valerie said.

"The lieutenant is correct," Galyan said. "The ionic particles are vanishing into the portal. This will aid me in my analysis. Ah, let me correct the image into a truer picture."

The main screen wavered. Now, the neutroium hull showed pitted marks, obvious wear and tear.

"Is that a hatch in the machine's hull?" Maddox asked.

"You are correct," Galyan said. "The three walk to the closed hatch."

"I can't believe we're seeing something so detailed that is happening well beyond Mars' orbital path," Valerie said.

"Starship *Victory* is an Adok marvel," Galyan said with pride. "Now that I am beginning to operate at maximum efficacy, you will soon become used to greater things than this."

"I'm glad to hear it," Valerie said.

Maddox wondered if the AI caught the sarcasm. The AI likely would learn about it in time. *If we have more time to live, that is.*

"No," Valerie said.

Maddox's throat tightened. The hatch on the neutroium hull slid open. The three space-suited people entered the doomsday machine. After the last one vanished within, the hatch slid shut.

For several seconds, no one said a word.

"At least we know it's possible to enter the doomsday machine," Maddox said, softy.

"Fat lot of good that does us," Valerie said. "You said Ludendorff had a key. I imagine so did they out there. But we're left hanging to rot out here without one."

"Ah," Galyan said. "A key—that is most interesting. Yes, I suppose that was the wave frequencies I detected a moment ago."

"Explain that," Maddox said.

"There is little to tell," Galyan said. "I picked up signals. They were faint, as I said. Soon after the wave sequence emitted, the hatch opened."

"Could you duplicate those signals?" Maddox asked.

"They were a complicated series of hard-to-reach frequencies—"

"Can you do it?" Maddox asked.

Galyan glanced at him. "It would take time to build such an emitter. You would have to take the device along with you to the vessel."

"How long would it take you build this emitter?" the captain asked.

"Two, maybe three days," Galyan said.

Valerie swore softly under her breath.

Maddox began to pace. Because a pilot had brought a jumpfighter to precisely the right spot, three people had entered the doomsday machine. Could one of those people have been Meta? Hopefully, he would know more in an hour. Star Watch raced smash-and-grab teams to the selected Cestus hauler. Soon, everyone on that ship would enter interrogation. Someone there might have seen Meta.

"The planet-killer is accelerating," Valerie said. "It's headed in-system."

"Given its trajectory what's its probable destination?" Maddox asked. Would it attack Mars first or head straight for Earth? Just maybe, they could sacrifice Mars in order to gain time for Galyan to construct the emitter. But if—

"It looks as if the machine is heading for Earth," Valerie said. "It's going to bypass Mars, which is quite a ways out from the machine's initial appearance point."

"I wish I could remember the range of its beam," Maddox said. "I wasn't paying attention to that when Ludendorff showed me his recording. How long do we have until it begins the attack sequence?"

"Star Watch battleships and heavy cruisers are already leaving Earth orbit," Valerie said. "According to their headings, they appear to be on an intercept course with the machine." The lieutenant shook her head. "It's too bad the Home Fleet doesn't already have the ten battleships coming in from Pluto. The readings from that thing—the doomsday machine has vastly more mass than our combined Home Fleet, sir."

"I doubt we're going to beat it in a head-to-head battle," Maddox said.

"What other option is there?" Valerie asked. "Can we delay the planet-killer for three days while Galyan fashions his emitter?"

Maddox watched the giant machine. How could a spaceship be fifty kilometer's long? Who had built it anyway? If the New Men gained control of the doomsday machine—

The captain whirled around to stare at Galyan. "Question," Maddox said, "could you beam the wave frequencies from *Victory* in order to unlock the hatch?"

Galyan's eyelids fluttered. "Theoretically, it is possible."

"I'm not asking that. Can you *do* it?"

"If I came in close enough, I should be able to," Galyan said.

"How close would *Victory* need to be?" Maddox asked.

"Four hundred thousand kilometers," the AI said.

"I'd imagine our starship would be in range of the enemy beam at four hundred thousand kilometers range," Valerie said.

"Which means it would be suicidal to use the star drive to get that close," Maddox said. "Unfortunately, by the time we flew out there the normal way to meet it... Galyan, you're going to have to do better than that. You have to reach farther with your special beam."

"One cannot wish expert marksmanship into existence," the AI said.

Maddox wasn't interested in excuses. "You said the key device emitted a wave frequency."

"In an extremely narrow band and beam," Galyan said. "That is correct."

"Did you see where exactly the beam struck?"

"That is one of the variables," the AI said. "That is why I must be in such near proximity."

"What's your plan, sir?" Valerie asked the captain.

"Ludendorff sent Per Lomax in a jumpfighter to board the doomsday machine," Maddox said. "The enemy just did that again, now. We'll have to do the same thing."

"Who could pilot..." Valerie said, her words dwindling away.

"You understand, as I do, that Keith will have to pilot our jumpfighter," Maddox said. "The ace is always telling us how good he is. Here's a chance to see if he's as good as a New Man."

"Can any of us doubt that?" Valerie asked. "But that's not all, is it, sir?"

"No," Maddox said. "Galyan has to strike the lock with a tight and correct wave frequency beam to open the hatch for us."

"Open it for whom, sir?" Valerie asked.

Maddox considered that for two seconds. "Riker and me," the captain said. "I'll take the sergeant along."

"The two of you against the three of them?" asked Valerie.

"It will be three of us against two of them," Maddox corrected. "I think one of those people is Meta."

"What makes you think that, sir?"

"Per Lomax wanted Meta to join him," Maddox said. "Why not whoever kidnapped her? It's just a guess, though." The captain shook his head. "This talk is pissing in the wind so far. Galyan, you're going to have to fire a long-distance beam at precisely the right spot. Otherwise, humanity dies. I don't care if you think you can't do it, you're going to give it your best shot."

"When do you envision this attempt?" the AI asked.

"In less than an hour," Maddox said. "Speed is of the essence. Who knows how fast the doomsday machine will accelerate into range of Earth? Once we enter the thing, if we can, we're going to have to figure out how to stop it. That's all going to take time. Lieutenant Noonan, you have the bridge. Alert the sergeant and the second lieutenant of their assignments. Then call the brigadier in Geneva and tell her what we're doing. I'm heading to the armory to collect what I need."

***

Dana halted the captain in a corridor. He seemed preoccupied, and for good reason.

"Just a minute," she said.

Maddox halted, but he seemed antsy. "I have no time, Doctor. I'm—"

"I know very well what you're doing. I've been listening. Captain...I want to give you something. But you must promise to give these objects back to me when you're finished."

"What are you talking about?" Maddox asked.

"These," Dana said, holding out the small chain and force-field-emitting ball, along with the flat device.

The captain looked startled. "What are you doing with those?"

"I can use them," Dana said.

Understanding lit the captain's eyes. "You tested them?"

"I did," Dana admitted. "When you first told me about Ludendorff—I became so wrought-up inside, I had to do something. I decided to figure out some of the professor's secrets."

"That took courage."

"No. I was foolhardy. Sometimes, however, fools succeed where angels fear to tread. This was one of those times. Take them."

"I don't know how to use them," Maddox said.

"I'm going to show you. This seems like the final confrontation. You may need an equalizer aboard the doomsday machine, especially if there are New Men involved."

"Yes, good thinking," Maddox said. "How long will it take for you to explain how to use them?"

"Not long," Dana said. "Now pay attention. You have to use these items correctly. The force-field emitter could be the most dangerous to you. You cannot wear it while wearing a vacc-suit."

"Then what good is it?"

"You'll have it," Dana said, "just in case you find yourself in that sort of situation."

Maddox grinned. "Doctor, thank you. This is most welcome. We need an edge."

Dana wasn't sure what to feel. She allowed herself a small smile. "I suppose I want to do my part."

"You already have, but this doubles it."

"Good. I wish you luck, Captain. The human race may well be resting on your shoulders."

"Then we'd better get started."

"Yes," Dana said. "Now, notice this protrusion…"

-38-

Ninety minutes later, Maddox and Riker wore vacc-suits inside a jumpfighter drifting near the starship. The ace piloted them to the doomsday machine.

Instead of regular space-marine weaponry or even the Intelligence tools of the trade, both operatives wore New Men blasters on their hips. Each of them had two, and all were at full battery power.

Maddox had picked these up from the enemy when the New Men had stormed the starship in Wolf Prime orbit several months ago. The failed attempt had left enemy weapons scattered throughout the vessel's corridors, and the captain had stored them in *Victory's* armory.

The more esoteric New Men weapons he'd left in the armory. Both he and Riker had shot the blasters before. The weapons fired bolts of deadly energy able to pierce the best body armor. A simple selector switch allowed one to change the intensity of the beam. The narrowest setting produced a needle-thin ray. The widest could act like a giant shotgun blast.

Just in case the enemy had defensive equipment that could render a blaster ineffective, both men brought their personal guns with extra magazines. Maddox also had a slarn knife, Villars' old blade. The sergeant had a smaller knife attached to a set of tungsten knuckles. He would slip that over his bionic hand to aid his blows if the need arose.

"Valerie is ready, mate. I mean, sir," Keith said. The ace had been flipping switches and tapping controls. The

331

jumpfighter now vibrated: with the engine ready to perform its miracle.

Maddox tested his straps once again.

"Hold on," Keith said. "Sir, the brigadier is on the line."

"Patch her through," Maddox said, looking up.

"Aye, Captain," Keith said.

A moment later, the brigadier appeared on the jumpfighter's screen.

Maddox had his visor open. "News, Ma'am?" he asked.

"I've just received a report from Major Stokes," O'Hara said. "He led the Intelligence team onto the designated Cestus hauler. The major, ah, persuaded the right person to speak. Meta definitely left on the enemy jumpfighter. So did an enemy agent named Kane."

Maddox nodded. "That explains why they kidnapped her."

"Captain, I have further bad news. You were correct about a New Man having come to Earth. I can hardly fathom the major's data. Yet, it appears that Oran Rva is in the Solar System."

The captain's lips tightened.

"That makes little sense to me, though," the brigadier said. "If Star Watch had an important Intelligence mission, we wouldn't send the Lord High Admiral to do it."

"No, we wouldn't," Maddox said. "But we don't think like the New Men. They view themselves—they are—highly competent at whatever they choose to do. I imagine it might be more than that, Ma'am."

"What do you mean?" O'Hara asked.

"Oran Rva's goal must be to gain control of the doomsday machine. Might that control give him greater authority among the New Men?"

"You mean that this could be a power play among them," O'Hara said.

"It's just a guess, Ma'am."

"That's an interesting point, though," the brigadier said. She grew quiet before asking, "Can you truly defeat Oran Rva and Kane? They are exceptional soldiers, I'd warrant."

"We've all seen the Odin video," Maddox said. "I doubt you think I can best them. But I've faced the New Men before and beaten them. What else do you suggest we try?"

"I suggest we wait a few more hours," the brigadier said. "Let's send teams of space marines in power armor against them."

"I'm done waiting," Maddox said. "Besides, we don't have time. The doomsday machine is racing toward Earth. If we begin too late, it won't matter if we win against the planet-killer or not."

"I'm sending space marine backups," the brigadier said.

"Fine," Maddox said. "We'll be the tip of the spear. My pilot is signaling me. I have to go. I have to let Second Lieutenant Maker concentrate so he makes the perfect jump."

"I wish you well, Captain."

"Right," Maddox said. "I appreciate that."

The brigadier's image vanished. In its place appeared a visual of outer space.

"Ready?" Maddox asked Keith.

"Not yet, Captain," the ace said "Galyan doesn't have the wave frequencies down just right."

Maddox exhaled impatiently. Then, he nodded. "Right, we're likely only going to get this one shot at doing it."

The minutes ticked away until a half hour had passed and then forty-five minutes.

Keith sat up. "Got some news, sir," he said. "The doomsday machine has increased acceleration again. The Lord High Admiral has given the word. The Home Fleet is accelerating on its intercept course."

"What's taking Galyan so long?" Maddox asked, impatiently.

"Should I call him, sir?" Keith asked.

"Yes," Maddox said.

A moment later, the deified AI stared at them from the screen.

"Galyan," Maddox said, "how long until you're ready?"

"In several hours I should be able to try the first—"

"Listen to me," Maddox said, interrupting Galyan. "We've run out of time. I don't remember the range of the planet-killer's beam. I'm sure it badly outranges our vessels. If we defeat the machine but our Home Fleet is destroyed, that just means a slower death for Earth when the New Men renew their invasion."

"I recognize the situation for what it is," Galyan said. "A premature attempt will not aid us. I have already begun to suspect that failed attempts will freeze the doomsday machine's entry lock."

"How can you tell?" Maddox asked.

"It seems like a logical safety feature."

Maddox shook his head. "That doesn't change the fact that I have to stop the machine before it destroys Cook's fleet. It's time to act."

"Perhaps you could persuade the Lord High Admiral to delay his present effort," the AI said.

"I doubt I'm going to have any luck with that," Maddox said. "If I fail, the admiral will want to fight it out with the doomsday machine. Earth isn't going to die without a struggle."

"That is a noble sentiment. However—"

"We're jumping, Galyan. You're going to have to fire that wave frequency beam as best you can."

"I cannot guarantee success."

"I'm not asking for that. I just want you to give it your best shot. We have to go now before the doomsday machine builds up too great of a velocity. We're going to be hard pressed to match it as it is."

"Reasonable," Galyan said. "Yes, let us begin the attempt then." The AI paused.

"What now?" Maddox asked.

"I do not have any meaningful last words for you, Captain. My probability processors tell me you will fail, which means you will die. I doubt I shall ever speak to you again, Captain. I should give you meaningful parting words. But I can think of nothing proper, as I still do not sufficiently understand human motivations."

"I appreciate that, Galyan. Thank you for the thought. You've been a good friend."

"What did I say, sir?" Galyan said. "It wasn't meaningful."

"You're wrong. It was very meaningful. You gave it your best shot, which means more than the actual words you didn't say."

"That is not logical," Galyan said.

Maddox gave the AI a wintery grin. "Let's beat the enemy, my friend. We've done it before. Now, you and I and the rest of the crew are going to do it again."

"You hope," Galyan said.

"Yes. That I do. Captain Maddox out." Before he could motion the pilot, Keith cut the connection.

"Better start building up greater velocity," Maddox told the pilot.

"Aye-aye, sir," Keith said, opening channels with Valerie.

Since the small jumpfighter didn't have giant engines like the planet-killer, or anything like the needed amount of fuel, *Victory* had been accelerating, using the tractor beam to pull the tiny fighter with it. Now, they were going to match the correct speed and heading of the doomsday machine. Soon now, Keith would engage the jump mechanism and try to put them beside the distant alien doomsday device at just the right location.

As the old saying went, the balloon was about to go up.

***

"I'll have to do this in two jumps," Keith said. "I can't give you the pinpoint accuracy you're asking for from this far out."

"The enemy did it," Maddox said.

"I'm good," Keith said, "but I'm not that good."

"How close do you plan to appear in front of the doomsday machine with the first jump?"

"The closer we can get, the better chance we have of arriving in its magic radius," the ace said.

"That isn't an answer."

"I'm thinking of appearing three hundred thousand kilometers before it with the first jump. The second jump will put us in the magic zone."

Maddox considered that. "Three hundred thousand kilometers from it will put us in the machine's proximity zone. The planet-killer will be sure to fire at us."

335

"I've been thinking about that, sir. The doomsday machine has its giant orifice. Will it warm up the killing ray to swat a tiny jumpfighter like us?"

"I have no idea. Maybe it has secondary weapons."

"With a three hundred thousand kilometer range," Keith said. "No, I don't think so."

"We lack sufficient data to know for sure," Maddox said.

"For a fact, we do lack data, sir. But we made it onto Starship *Victory* the first time without enough information."

Maddox didn't say anything to that. Keith was wrong, though. Ludendorff had collected the needed data for them. "Yes," the captain said. "Do it your way."

Maddox believed in trusting each person to do his or her specialty. Keith was the master pilot. If he suggested this was the best way to do it, then they would do it the ace's way.

Keith passed out hypos with the Baxter-Locke shots. Injecting that into himself left Maddox feeling ill. Five minutes later, the ace said it was go time.

Maddox gripped the arms of his padded chair. He noticed that Riker did likewise.

"Round one," Keith said. "*Victory*, you can release the tractor beam."

"One moment," Galyan said. "The two-jump sequence is going to make matching my firing of the wave frequency beam that much trickier."

"You're the hyper-intelligent AI," Maddox said. "You can't let us down, Galyan. You promised to show us miracles with your Adok starship. This is your chance to shine."

Galyan didn't respond to that.

"The tractor beam is gone," Keith said thirty seconds later. "Here we go." He tapped the controls.

The grim sensations of jump slammed upon Maddox. Time lost meaning until he felt disoriented and sick, wanting to vomit. The Baxter-Locke shot seemed not to have taken effect for him this time.

Keith garbled something and repeated it a few moments later. Neither time made any sense.

"What?" Maddox finally managed to mutter.

336

"We've hit a glitch, sir," Keith said. "My sequencer is off by several degrees. I wouldn't have noticed, but we're not exactly where I'd predicted we'd be. I wanted a perfect jump, sir. This is definitely going to throw off Galyan's timing."

Maddox's gut seethed as the sickness hit him. He clamped his jaws so he wouldn't vomit.

"I need to recalibrate the sequencer," Keith said.

"Do it," Maddox whispered.

"Are you all right, sir?"

"I'm fine," Maddox wheezed. "Now fix the sequencer."

The ace unstrapped, pushing past them as he floated weightless. He tore open a panel, using a magnetic tapper to try to fix the sequencer.

"What's that light mean on the controls, sir?" Riker asked.

"What?" Maddox asked. He felt more horrible by the minute. With splotchy vision, the captain noticed a red light on the pilot's board.

Keith swore at them. "Why didn't someone tell me about that?" He shot past Maddox, floating to his seat, sinking into it and strapping in. His fingers fairly flew across his board.

Sudden acceleration slammed Maddox against his chair. The back of his helmeted head struck hard, making him groan. What was wrong with him?

Then something glowing hot erupted from the bulkhead, hissing past Maddox's head and striking the opposite bulkhead. The lights in the craft began flashing on and off.

Maddox's visor whirred shut and oxygen began to pump into his vacc-suit.

"The doomsday machine is using a rail-gun to fire at us," Keith said. "Must be using proximity shells, grenades, as munitions. Looks like the machine got lucky with us. That was a pellet smashing through our systems. We can't stay here, sir. I'm going to have to jump now."

"Go for the hull," Maddox said. "Get us into its safe zone."

"The odds of doing that now—"

"Don't argue," Maddox said. "You have to trust your instincts, son. Just do it."

"Do or die, sir, right you are. Hang on, mates. The death ride has just begun."

The acceleration worsened, pushing Maddox deeper against his seat. Then the craft must have zipped to the left. The G forces shoved against the captain, making him want to vomit again.

"Three, two, one…zero," Keith said.

Once more, the disorienting process caught Maddox off-guard. The world spun. Noises garbled in his ears. The next thing Maddox knew, Riker stood over him, clicking off the straps and yanking him to his feet.

"What's wrong with you, sir?" Riker asked. "You have to snap out of it. We're here. The damned pilot pulled off a miracle. Now, we have to hope the AI can do the same thing."

-39-

Maddox stopped inside the tiny jumpfighter twice, dry heaving. He felt awful.

Someone gripped his elbow painfully. "What's wrong, sir? Why are you acting so strangely?"

"Feel...sick," Maddox whispered.

"How, sir?"

"My gut...want to vomit...feel achy."

Seconds passed into an eternity of dull-eyed apathy. A new person in a vacc-suit floated before him.

"It's me, mate, Keith. Did you feel this way after the Baxter-Locke shot?"

"Yes..." Maddox slurred. "Is that important?"

"It's an Apollo reaction, they call it. Happens every seventh or eighth shot. I should have warned you about it, I suppose. It's one of the reasons they don't hand the shots out like candy to everyone."

"What do we do now?" Maddox whispered.

"You hope the effect wears off. There were a few people... Well, never mind about that. We have to get out, sir. We're practically on the hull, but we're drifting. Our window of opportunity is small. Galyan will be firing his unlocking beam soon. If we're not at the hatch in time..."

"What's the best remedy for the Apollo effect?" Maddox asked.

"Simple old mulishness, sir. Get mad. Sometimes that seems to burn out the nausea. Don't know why, but that was the scuttlebutt I heard."

Maddox tried to focus on his hatred against the New Men. They planned to select the winners and losers in the universe, choosing who lived and who died. The odds were bad for everyone. One out of five chances of living in the New Order. No. That wasn't going to get him angry. He had to make this personal.

The captain smiled bitterly. He should focus on Kane grabbing Meta. But the agent for the New Men was a cipher. Maddox wanted the head honcho. Oran Rva had come to Earth. The commander had tugged the webs of the enemy's espionage net. Likely, Oran Rva had coordinated the various assassination attempts against him. Maddox had always wanted a face-to-face with one of the leaders, one of his mother's killers.

"I'm not going to get angry," Maddox whispered to himself. "I'm going to get even. I'm going to do this my way. For that, I refuse to let this nausea stop me."

"What's that you're saying, sir?" Riker asked.

Maddox realized his radio link had been on the entire time. That was fine.

With the greater concentration came a realization that Riker and Maker had hooked him into a thruster-pack. Now, each of them floated to theirs.

"You have to go back with the jumpfighter," Maddox radioed Keith.

"I'd love to do that, sir," the ace said. "But the sequencer burned out with the last jump. The fighter's finished. I'm coming along, going to add my two credits to the fight."

Maddox didn't say a word. He concentrated, forcing his mind to burn through the drug-induced haze. He had made it to the doomsday machine, the outer hull, anyway. Had Per Lomax gotten this far? Was the New Man inside the planet-killer helping the others?

"Let's go," Keith shouted. "We're drifting and will be out of range soon."

"Here goes," Riker said. "I hope you're ready, sir."

"Do it," Maddox whispered.

The sergeant slapped a switch. The hatch blew away.

Maddox forced himself to shove off, drifting through the opening. Before him was a wall of pitted neutroium armor. Looking at it made his eyes water. Seen from this close, the hull seemed primordial. It made *Victory* seem new.

Maddox stared at the pitted surface. As he did, there stirred in him a feeling of... *evil*. It made him shudder. Here was something truly alien. If they went inside—

"We have over ten kilometers to go," Keith radioed, the transmission scratchy-sounding.

The words startled Maddox out of his reverie.

"Ten klicks is near the limit of our hydrogen tanks," Keith added.

"Lead the way," Maddox muttered. "I'll follow behind."

"Sergeant," Keith said, with a same ring of authority in his voice as when he piloted. "You bring up the rear. Make sure the captain keeps up."

Several seconds passed before Riker said, "Yes, sir."

White hydrogen spray spewed from the thruster-pack ahead of Maddox. That must be Keith. The pilot lurched forward as he went lower toward the gigantic, pitted hull.

"Get going, sir," Riker radioed. "We can't split up or we'll never get back together soon enough."

"Right," Maddox said. He had the feeling of something old and vile watching him, waiting to devour him like a bloated spider. It lived inside the ancient machine, wanting him to enter the lair of evil.

"Get a grip," the captain muttered. He squeezed the trigger and aimed the throttle down. In seconds, he zoomed toward the giant, pitted hull.

The fuzziness in his mind refused to go away, though. The sense of danger continued to radiate from the armor, making his fingers sweaty.

"You're going down too sharply, sir," Riker radioed. "Ease off."

Maddox squeezed his eyes closed and opened them wide. What was wrong with him? As he licked his lips, he eased off the throttle. If he wasn't careful, he'd slam against the hull.

341

Soon, his booted feet were less than ten meters from the hull. It felt as if he flew over something older than the stones of Earth. Maddox shook his head to rid himself of the feeling, but that just hurt his eyes. He looked up at the stars, but that made him dizzy. Once more, he peered past his feet at the neutroium. How many encounters had this ancient machine survived? How many times had its beam destroyed life on a planetary surface? What chance did he have against something so…immortal?

"No," Maddox whispered. He refused to despair. They may be three specks flying over the neutroium monster, but they were going to defeat this thing. The three men from Earth would go inside and defeat whatever waited for them no matter how ancient and vile it was.

"Galyan should be firing his wave frequency about now," Keith radioed. "But we're still too far away from the hatch."

The words helped focus the captain's thoughts. "Can you…can you see it?"

"It's a little over a kilometer from here," Keith said. "We're going to have to start braking."

Some of the regular Maddox returned. Galyan and he had gone over the sequence of the commando raid in exquisite detail. He knew the timing of this.

"No," Maddox said. "If we begin braking from this far out, we won't make it in."

"You're right," Keith said a second later. "Okay then, mates. Follow me. Our only chance is to shoot like a bullet through the hatch before it closes."

The pilot pulled away from the ancient hull.

Maddox tilted his throttle and added thrust. He was feeling better, his head clearing. The aura of evil faded, but not enough that he grinned at this former foolishness. There was something alien in the worst sense about this machine. But it wouldn't get the better of him.

The seconds ticked away, with the thruster-packs spewing their remaining fuel. The three specks had picked up speed.

"I see it!" Keith shouted, the words blaring in Maddox's headphones. "The hatch is still open. I don't know how much longer it's going to stay that way."

Even though the hatch seemed like the maw of a deadly beast, Maddox shouted, "Full throttle! We have to get on board." He squeezed the trigger, focusing as he aimed at the tiny entrance.

Keith laughed recklessly, sounding as if he enjoyed the moment.

Surprisingly, Maddox zipped passed the ace as the captain shot at full throttle for the opening. None of them was going to have time to slow down. They had to beat the clock or remain out here until the fleet made its attack run.

Maddox concentrated. For a second, he felt sibilant laughter in his mind. *Come to me, yes, come into my lair.* The captain's lips hardened, and his eyes become like flint. He was coming all right. The way into the doomsday machine was before him. Galyan had successfully copied the wave frequency. The Adok starship had done its job. Now, it was time for the three of them to do theirs.

"We're almost there, sir," Riker shouted.

Coolly, telling himself he wanted to meet the ancient evil, Maddox began to undo the buckles of the thruster-pack. Seconds later, he pushed off the pack. Then, he folded himself into a cannonball as if launching off a diving board.

"I'm squeezing myself into a fetal position," Maddox radioed. "If I hit too hard, I'm hoping this will keep me from breaking any bones."

"Good idea," Keith said. "I'm doing the same thing. Be careful you don't push your pack off too hard, Sergeant. You don't want to spoil your aim."

That was the last comment. Then, Maddox shot through the hatch and into the corridor. He struck a bulkhead, ricocheted and struck another. He tightened his muscles as he kept himself like a cannonball, enduring blow after blow.

"The door's closing," Riker radioed. "I'm still outside."

Maddox slammed against another bulkhead. It jarred his head so stars blossomed before him. That loosened his cannonball position. Then he struck even harder, feeling as if a sledgehammer banged his chest. Air gushed away as he faded into semi-conscious. Had he stopped? A final bone-jarring hit put him out cold inside the ancient doomsday machine.

Maddox's eyelids fluttered. With a groan, he attempted to sit up. Vertigo struck. He sagged back onto the deck, panting, his head pounding with gongs.

"Hello," he whispered a minute later. The words reverberated inside his helmet. There was no answer. Did his helmet radio work? Or had his caroming descent down the corridor broken it?

The captain gathered his resolve. Slowly, he brought a hand to his helmet. At least his arm worked. He tried the other one. It was sore but functional.

Maddox unglued his eyes. A dim diffused glow let him see the ceiling. Weird, polygonal shapes fit together like a jigsaw puzzle. There were several colors. The pieces did not seem metallic but like hardened or lacquered growths or the secretions of alien bees. Yes, the polygonal shapes felt as if once they had been soft and later hardened into their present state.

Maddox felt revulsion, which gave him greater energy. He wanted to get out of here. Trying to bolt upright, dizziness stole his vision. His muscles relaxed as if a boxer had hit him on the chin.

As he lay there, he felt a thrum, a vibration. Then, eerie noises like whales make deep in the ocean managed to leak past his helmet.

What was that?

It came to Maddox the ship itself must be making the noise. The ancient death machine groaned as its systems pumped, cycled and did whatever else they must do to keep the vessel running.

I have a mission. The planet-killer is heading for Earth to kill all life there. If I don't stop it...who will?

Opening his eyes once more, Maddox eased onto his elbows and raised his head. The sides of the corridor had the same bizarre, polygonal patterns. No two were the same. The jigsaw pieces had the same colors and the feel of being hardened resin instead of metal. More than ever, it felt as if alien bees had constructed the ship's interior.

344

Maddox inspected his vacc-suit next. He found plenty of abrasions with smears of resin but no tears. The jigsaw pieces must have more give than metal. He appeared to be in one piece. Did his legs work, or had he broken bones?

Gingerly, the captain levered himself to a sitting position. He twisted around, noting that he'd cannonballed around a corner. There was no sign of Riker or Keith.

Could something alive in the ship have dragged them away?

Maddox's shoulders twitched. He had to get a grip. His imagination was running wild. Where was his coolness under fire?

"Time to test my legs," he whispered. The sound of his voice helped his nerves.

Maddox brought his knees to his chest. It encouraged him that they worked. He began the arduous process of standing. Too many muscles complained, having taken a battering. He found himself panting from the strain. The process took far too long and he winced from endlessly painful jolts. Finally, however, he swayed as he stood.

He tasted saltiness on his lips. Time was ticking against him. He had to get going, do the job he came here to do. Lurching, he took a step, a second and a third. It left him panting harder than before, with sweat prickling his skin.

Why is this so difficult?

Then it came to him. Grav-plates were at work. This felt more than regular 1 G. Maybe it was 1.5 Gs. He didn't think it was two. Whoever had built the doomsday machine seemed to have originated on a heavier planet than Earth.

Maddox had no idea if that was useful information or not, but he filed it away.

I'm not going to discover anything standing here. I have to move, explore—and fight the enemy when I run into him.

Star Watch marines were supposed to show up soon. He had to figure out the specifics of how to win before their arrival.

Shuffling around, Maddox began searching for the other two. He headed for the bend, the one he was sure he'd bounced past coming in. Each footfall seemed to go down too fast and

345

too hard. He didn't like the increased gravities. It was going to make the assignment harder.

Not for Kane and Meta, though. They're used to 2 Gs.

The movement began to loosen some of his muscles. The painful jolts and pulls lessened, and he brought his breathing under control. Finally, Maddox worked around the corner.

He exhaled with relief, seeing the other two. One of them knelt beside the other, who was prone on the spongy deck. Worse, something moved on its own. It was a piece of arm. The twitching thing gave off a spark.

"What the..."

Maddox got it then. The twitchy thing must be part of Riker's bionic arm. Apparently, it had broken off during his violent entry.

"Riker!" Maddox said, hurrying. He lost his balance and crashed down onto his knees. He could feel the deck matting give just a little. Nevertheless, the fall caused his teeth to click together painfully. He panted for a moment.

If Riker had lost part of his bionic arm, it necessarily meant a tear in the vacc-suit. Was the sergeant dead?

Climbing to his feet, walking carefully, Maddox reached them.

Keith repaired the sergeant's torn sleeve with a seal kit. Riker's suit over his chest rose and fell. It appeared the sergeant was still alive for the moment.

The ace looked up sharply, the visor aimed at Maddox.

The captain tapped his head.

Keith nodded in understanding.

On inspiration, Maddox knelt before the pilot and lowered his head. He felt it as Keith made an adjustment. Whatever the ace did, it caused the headphones to crackle.

"Can you hear me now?" Keith asked, the words coming past static.

"I can," Maddox said with relief. "Can you hear me?"

"I can, sir."

"Is Riker alive?"

"I'm alive all right," the sergeant said, gruffly. "My bionic arm is frozen, though. I won't be any good in a fight."

"You can still shoot a blaster," Maddox said. "Can you walk? Or are you too beat up?"

"I'm sore, sir," Riker said. "My bones ache. I have no idea if I can stand. That was a crazy idea shooting through the hatch."

"We can't stay here," Maddox said. "You'll have to stand, Sergeant."

"Why don't the two of you give me a hand," Riker suggested.

Maddox listened to both of them strain and wheeze. Soon, the sergeant swayed on his feet.

"How do you feel?" Maddox asked the ace.

"Like I played a week of rugby," Keith said. "I want to lie down and sleep a year."

"It must be 1.5 Gs in here," Maddox said.

"At least that," Keith said. "It's dragging me down. What's with the weird walls?"

"Don't know," Maddox said.

"Sir..." Keith said. "Does it...does it feel freaky to you in here?"

"Can you explain that?" Maddox asked.

"This place feels haunted. It gives me the creeps."

"I feel it," Maddox admitted.

"I feel it, too," Riker said. "The sooner we're done here, the better. It feels like slime is coating my skin, maybe even my mind."

"I suggest we concentrate on the mission," Maddox said. "Whatever is bothering us, we'll either defeat or—we're here to win. So, we'll concentrate on that. Sergeant, are your blasters still in one piece?"

"I guess I'd better check," Riker said. "Yes, sir. They look good."

Maddox's blasters didn't. They were crushed, useless. "Better give me one of yours. Do you have any personal weapons?" he asked Keith.

"I don't," Keith said. "Didn't know I'd be coming along."

"That was an oversight on my part," Maddox said. "I won't let it happen again."

"So what's the plan?" Keith asked.

347

Maddox nodded. "We're not leaving until we succeed. So we're not going that way." He pointed toward the hatch, however far away it was. "Instead, we're heading the other way."

"Could be a long time before we find anyone in this monster ship," Keith said. "It's fifty kilometers long."

"We have to keep pushing ourselves," Maddox said. "We're down two blasters, and missing a bionic arm, but we have a third member to our party. If you think about it, this part of the mission is a near total success."

Keith examined the weird walls. "It sure doesn't feel like success to me."

"It is," Maddox said. "Now, let's go. It's time to finish this."

-40-

Valerie sat in the command chair aboard *Victory* as the starship accelerated to join the main fleet under Admiral Cook.

Meta was gone. Maddox, Keith and Riker were aboard the doomsday machine. That left Dana and her with a few technicians, and Galyan and his single combat robot. In other words, the Adok starship was emptier than it had been for quite some time.

The AI ran everything. That gave Valerie a queasy feeling. She had never been able to trust Galyan fully. Who really knew the ancient computer's thoughts, if one could even say it that way? With its extra, experimental computing power...

Valerie shifted in the command chair.

"I have been analyzing the doomsday machine," Galyan announced.

The lieutenant jerked with a start.

"Is there a problem with that?" Galyan asked.

"Ah, no," Valerie said, "no problem. You startled me. That's all."

"I am sorry," Galyan said. "I did not mean to do so." The holoimage paused. "What did I do specifically that caused surprise?"

"It wasn't you. It was me. I was thinking."

Galyan seemed to absorb the information. "I do hope that Captain Maddox is well. His odds for success are extremely low to nonexistent. But, then, so are our odds terrible if we chose to engage the doomsday machine in direct conflict. It is

349

likely that I will cease to exist if I go through with the present attack."

Here it was. Valerie wasn't surprised in the least to hear the AI talking about letting everyone down. "Are you suggesting that the starship pull out of the Solar System?"

The holoimage studied her.

"I have gained new observation abilities," the AI said. "It has allowed me to run personality profiles on each of you. With these programs, I am beginning to build up a profile for humans in general and each of you specifically."

"Oh," Valerie said. That didn't sound good.

"There," Galyan said. "I have detected it again. You evidence a lack of trust in my words. Have I done something that causes you to feel I'm untrustworthy?"

Valerie shifted uncomfortably.

"I can understand your squeamishness regarding me," Galyan said. "Once, I held you captive. I should point out that that was in the past, when the virus infected me still. Surely, you realize I am indebted to Captain Maddox. The actions he committed in my favor, especially turning me on again when I suspect others suggested otherwise…I will not forget that."

"Will you fight your hardest to protect Earth?" Valerie asked.

"That is not your real question," Galyan said. "You are asking if I will sacrifice myself in a futile endeavor to prove how grateful I am. Captain Maddox saved my life. Now you desire me to sacrifice myself as a gesture of goodwill."

"I'm not saying that."

"But you are, Lieutenant. That is what I was trying to tell you before your mannerisms halted me. I have run through one hundred thousand simulations regarding the coming battle. Star Watch cannot win even with my help."

"So you're going to run away?" Valerie asked.

"You attempt to wound with words. Consider this then: self-immolation does nothing to fulfill my wish to honor Captain Maddox. I must survive so his name lives on into the ages through me."

"Do you consider him dead?" Valerie asked.

"If Captain Maddox is not dead yet, he will be shortly."

"I don't agree."

"You work through faith," Galyan said. "I operate in the realm of facts."

"You have to at least *try*," Valerie said. "If you run away, you lose. If you fight, maybe we'll get lucky."

Galyan's holographic features twisted into an approximation of a grimace. "Firstly, I am not suggesting that I 'run away'. I am saying that headlong attacks against the machine are futile. I must survive. Star Watch must maintain its fleet for later battles. Sacrifice to no purpose lacks sense. The doomsday machine does not operate on faith. It is an ultimate killing machine designed for remorseless action. It will destroy the Home Fleet and then your homeworld. I am sad, as this is too much like my last days as flesh and blood against the Swarm. I do not wish to relive such a horrible event."

"If you're not going to help us fight, then let Dana and me off. We plan to attack the planet-killer with everything in us."

"No!" Galyan said.

"You're making us prisoners again?" Valerie asked, surprised at his vehemence.

"No, no, you misunderstand me. I..." Galyan looked away, silent for a time. Finally, the AI said, "I have been alone for six thousand years. With my former intellect, I could maintain computing balance. With my new, heightened awareness, I cannot bear another six thousand years all alone with only my thoughts."

"So you want to keep Dana and me as pets?" Valerie asked.

"You continue to attempt to wound with words. I recognize the tactic. I have seen you humans practice it on each other. I dearly wish you would not do that to me. You are my friend, Valerie. I have so few friends in this cold universe. I do not want to lose those I have. Maddox, Meta, Keith and Riker are gone. You cannot leave me now. You must keep my company for as many years as you have left."

The lieutenant blinked in shock. Valerie hadn't expected this. She knew what it meant only having a handful of friends. Sometimes, she hadn't even had that many. Instead of being angry with Galyan's talk of running out, she began to feel sorry for the ancient intelligence.

"This is interesting," Galyan said. "My words have a struck a chord."

"Are you a mind-reader?"

"That power is beyond me. No. I observe your mannerisms and match them against my known parameters concerning you. Your present posture and facial expressions tell me you are feeling sympathy toward me. That is fading as I explain this. Why is that, Valerie?"

She shrugged. "I supposed I don't like a soulless machine cataloging me so carefully and accurately. It gives me the creeps."

"I see. You are not like Captain Maddox, who prefers strict truth. You wish to hold certain illusions. I find that interesting, these differences among humans."

The lieutenant didn't care for alien psychoanalysis. "How about we help the fleet, huh? That's what we came to Earth to do."

Galyan faced the main screen. "You have misunderstood me. I will fight the planet-killer by staying alive and looking for ways to defeat it. However, for your sake, I will remain with the fleet for the first round. As we've talked, I have been listening to the comm-chatter around me. You humans lack comm-security as we Adoks practiced against the Swarm. The Lord High Admiral is about to attempt an interesting tactic. It is revolutionary, to say the least. He had hoped to save this as a surprise for the next encounter with the New Men's invasion armada. But now he will use it against the doomsday machine."

"What are we going to do?" Valerie asked.

"I have stoked your interest, yes?"

"Will you quit bragging already? Are you going to tell me what's going on or not?"

"Let us observe the tactic as it occurs. I find it is more enjoyable to communicate than remain alone with my thoughts. I have many thoughts, Valerie. They never cease except when I communicate with one of my friends. Then a process from the engrams of Driving Force Galyan takes hold of me. Don't you think that is interesting?"

Valerie *did* figure that was interesting. There was something else, too. Galyan needed her, genuinely needed her. The lieutenant smiled, liking that.

"You're something else, Galyan. Do you know that?"

"I am unique. I am the last of the Adoks."

"That you are. Now, it's time to go to work. Let's join the main fleet as they begin their maneuvers against the doomsday machine."

"Affirmative," Galyan said.

***

Sometime later, Valerie studied the screen. Starship *Victory* sped toward Cook's main concentration of battleships, which had already left the Moon far behind.

The doomsday machine still hadn't reached Mars' orbital path, but it was rapidly building velocity.

A mothership among the fleet's most forward warships launched two special jumpfighters. Instead of missiles, those two held space marines, the ones O'Hara had told Maddox were coming as reinforcements.

"Special ops," Valerie said. "I hope the pilots are as good as Keith."

As she watched, both jumpfighters folded space, disappearing from view.

"I will use full magnification so we can witness their success," Galyan said.

Valerie waited. It would take several minutes for the images of what happened out there to reach here at light speed. Finally, the lieutenant saw them again.

The first jumpfighter appeared too near the neutroium hull. The tiny craft had forward momentum and crashed against the doomsday machine. Debris scattered and drifted away like flotsam, including slowly squirming bodies. The second jumpfighter appeared much farther out. It would take the craft time to reach the planet-killer.

"Notice to your left on the machine," Galyan said. The AI used a red circle to highlight a tiny area of the hull. A plate slid aside on the neutroium armor. A gleaming cannon poked out. It expelled small rounds of matter.

"What are those?" Valerie asked.

"According to my sensors," Galyan said, "the cannon is a rail-gun. Those must be proximity shells."

The second jumpfighter exploded under the quick barrage of doomsday rounds. The debris scattered more slowly, but this time included pieces of armored space marines.

Valerie felt a hollow pit in her stomach. Keith had once again proven himself the better pilot. Maddox wasn't going to get any reinforcements. He'd have to do this on his own.

The lieutenant waited for Galyan to make one of his soulless comments. Instead, the holoimage remained silent.

"Well?" she finally asked.

"I am observing a moment of sadness for the dead," Galyan said. "They gambled their lives for their world. It is a pity they died so uselessly."

"War is Hell," Valerie said.

The AI turned to her. "That is an apt phrase. I will catalog it for future reference. I did not realize you had a gift for phraseology."

"I didn't coin the term."

"Coin?"

"As in mint," Valerie said. "In the old days, people minted or stamped coins. It means that I didn't come up with the phrase you like so much."

"Who did?"

"An old-time Yankee general named Sherman."

"Let us observe the next tactical attempt," Galyan said. "It might help to take your mind off the death of the brave marines. Notice, the Lord High Admiral is positioning the next wave of jumpfighters for the assault."

"I'm surprised he's going to throw them away after witnessing what just happened."

"War is Hell," the AI said. "I remember my last days as Driving Force Galyan. I imagine the Lord High Admiral is making difficult choices. He must do something, or it is possible the Earth will die soon."

***

Lord High Admiral Cook stood on the bridge of the Flagship *Bull Run*. The *Gettysburg*-class battleship accelerated for the doomsday machine. The white-haired admiral had watched the destruction of the two jumpfighters. Even now, he continued to keep his leathery face impassive.

He, the Home Fleet, Earth itself; all were in a terrible predicament. This wasn't the time to get emotional or let himself rage. He had to think and then act in the right way. If he failed, Earth died. Billions died, and the Commonwealth would perish under this alien machine and later to the New Men with their infernal ideas of guided selection.

The Home Fleet was presently diminished, with ten priceless battleships far away in the outer system. What could he do with his part? Could he even defeat the doomsday machine with the *entire* Home Fleet intact? Few of his tactical officers believed it possible. That meant he certainly couldn't defeat the fifty-kilometer vessel with only part of the Home Fleet. Under those conditions, he had listened to the pleading of the Jumpfighter Commodore from the experimental school on Titan.

"Let us show you what we can do," the commodore had said an hour ago.

"No," Cook had told him. "I will not send pilots on a suicide mission."

The commodore had laughed. "Are you kidding me, sir? The entire program is one giant suicide mission. We chose reckless fools as jumpfighter pilots for a reason. Their craft don't have armor or shields for survival, but velocity, trickery and the ability to fold space."

"Folded space? No, no, they'll just sit around after jumping, stunned by Jump Lag for too long."

"That's why we have the Baxter-Locke shots, sir."

"Which don't always work," Cook had said.

The commodore had glowered. "Sir—"

"No! We must all coordinate as one, the jumpfighters with the battleships with the heavy cruisers and destroyers. A mass assault will allow us the greatest opportunity for success."

"Begging your pardon, Admiral, but we no longer have that luxury. If everyone bores into firing range against that thing, it will annihilate half to all the battleships at the very beginning of the fight. That way, even if we beat the death machine, we'll lose to the New Men nine months later."

"Damn it, man—"

"Admiral, you have to risk the jumpfighters now—or if you don't like that, let me use half of them on a trial run. Let's see if we can touch that big bastard."

Cook had shaken his head. "Half measures are always worse than picking one way or another."

"I don't think that's right today, sir. We're talking about human survival. We're going to have to take some terrible risks. Everything we've learned about the doomsday machine shows us that the antimatter torpedoes are our only hope."

Cook had turned crimson with anger. "Jumpfighter pilots aren't kamikazes, Commodore."

"No, they're *not*. But I will tell you what they are, *sir*. They are egotists, solipsists, a band of psychos that may just give us the edge we need to defeat this thing. If they didn't have the experimental antimatter torpedoes, well, we do have them. That gives us a fighting chance. Begging your pardon, sir, but you don't have any choice. Let my boys do their job to possibly save the Earth."

"They're our secret against the New Men."

"That doesn't matter anymore, sir. This is their hour, and you know it. The question is only whether we use half now or all now. Personally, I'd use half of them. Save the others for the death ride if the first wave fails."

For a full minute, Cook had stared at the commodore. Feeling one hundred years older, the Lord High Admiral had finally nodded.

"I'm going to make one change to the operation, though," Cook had said.

"Sir?"

"You'll see. It's something the tactical officers thought up. After watching the last two jumpfighters, well, maybe it will help."

As Cook stood on the bridge of Flagship *Bull Run* in the here and now, he watched the final preparations taking place outside in space.

Three motherships disgorged the special group of jumpfighters. The tin cans congregated, the comm-chatter growing thick among them.

Cook's nostrils flared. One hundred and seventeen jumpfighters were about to attempt the first mass fold-attack. Likely, the pilots were injecting themselves with the Baxter-Locke shots this very moment. Some of those brave men would undoubtedly die from the drug.

The Lord High Admiral began hardening his heart. Sending men to their deaths had always been hard for him. This was like the ancient battle during World War Two, the Battle of Britain. There, a few brave Spitfire pilots had taken on the German Luftwaffe, staving off defeat.

Could the experimental jumpfighters together with antimatter torpedoes stop the doomsday machine?

"Sir," a comm-officer said. "The thermonuclear missiles are ready. The launch officers are waiting for your signal."

This was it. Once he gave the word....

"Begin," Cook said, in a voice that sounded far too much like the toll of Death.

**

Several large missiles with fold capability disappeared from view. They were set with Laumer-Point timers and big thermonuclear warheads.

Each missile appeared in the path of the doomsday machine. The closest was a kilometer from the hull, the farthest nineteen kilometers. Each timer clicked, and each thermonuclear warhead ignited.

Brilliant flashes of light, heat, billowing electromagnetic pulses and hard radiation flared outward.

None was meant to hurt the neutroium hull. They had gone ahead of the jumpfighters in order to blind the doomsday machine's sensors. The warheads were supposed to give the jumpfighters an extra margin.

As the white flares died away, as the EMPs traveled toward the ancient machine, time passed. The officers coordinating the attack had timed this to the second. Finally, from a little

357

beyond Luna, they pulsed the signals to the waiting jumpfighters.

One hundred and seventeen jumpfighters disappeared from near the three motherships. Folding space, one hundred and thirteen jumpfighters moved from a little beyond the Moon to past Mars' orbital path in front of the doomsday machine. They made the journey faster than light could travel the distance, popping back into reality.

Four jumpfighters never reappeared in normal space. No one knew what had happened to them or where they had gone. In terms of the space battle, they no longer mattered.

One hundred and thirteen jumpfighters appeared, using their initial velocity. Ninety-nine of them began to jink. Fourteen of the pilots had negative Baxter-Locke reactions. Of those fourteen, seven died immediately. The rest were fated to die within six minutes.

If the doomsday machine had felt any bad reactions to the thermonuclear warheads, none of the pilots perceived it. Twenty plates slid aside on the planet-killer and cannons poked out of each one. They began to chug proximity shells.

At first, nothing happened. The shells had to fly out. Soon, though, jumpfighters began to explode.

The survivors jinked harder. Two-thirds armed their torpedoes and launched. The planet-killer's targeting AI fixed on the hotly burning streaks. The next proximity shell salvos blew apart every one of them.

"This ain't working," Lieutenant Hawks radioed. "I'm folding right next to the bastard. Let's see if he can stop that."

Hawks' jumpfighter disappeared, shells bursting where it had been. It reappeared five hundred meters from the hull. He launched the antimatter torpedo. Two seconds later, a proximity shell destroyed his fighter.

Then, the antimatter warhead struck the ancient hull and ignited. A terrific explosion shattered the integrity of the armor, blowing off neutroium pieces. Incredibly, it opened a breach. Alien atmosphere blew second after second into space. Something that glimmered sealed the hull thirty seconds later.

By that time, another antimatter torpedo ignited against the alien neutroium. It blew off a plate but failed to rupture the hull into the interior.

The rail-guns fired a blizzard of proximity shells. Amidst that, five more jumpfighters closed the distance, launching their torpedoes. Only two hit, blowing away more neutroium. The other three torpedoes disintegrated under the hail of proximity shells.

Then the last jumpfighter near the doomsday machine died, more debris in space.

Twenty-three of the tin cans returned to their respective motherships. The rest would never come home, having sacrificed themselves in the hope of stopping Earth's doom.

The giant planet-killer soon passed the last of the debris. It bore four wounds, but continued remorselessly for Earth just the same.

On *Bull Run*, Admiral Cook despaired. The Jumpfighter Commodore had other ideas, sitting down with his tactical heads to figure out how to make the next run more efficient.

***

Aboard Starship *Victory*, Galyan showed a close-up of the damage.

"I don't believe this," Valerie said. "The admiral actually wounded the ancient monster."

"I am duly impressed," Galyan said. "I did not think such a thing was possible."

"It hasn't stopped the planet-killer, though."

"Indeed not," Galyan said. "But I submit to you that now the admiral has a location to fire his beams. If he can target one of the four hull breaches, he can pour fire into the ancient killer and possibly chew up the insides."

Valerie clapped her hands. "In other words, we have a fighting chance."

"Correction," the AI said. "Star Watch's Home Fleet now has a miniscule chance of damaging the great machine. But that is better than none at all."

359

"Let me ask you, Galyan. Now that Earth has a chance, as miniscule as it is, are you joining the fleet with a frontal assault?"

Galyan took his time answering. "The Lord High Admiral pulled off a miracle. Maybe there are more to come. Maybe faith has its place in the world of hard reality. I will most certainly join the assault to save my friends' homeworld."

Valerie nodded, excited by the success. She wondered, though, if the four antimatter torpedoes had hurt or helped Captain Maddox and the others inside the doomsday machine.

-41-

Meta stumbled after Kane and Oran Rva. She was exhausted, the sound of her panting reverberating in her helmet. She hated this place with its eerie walls, spongy deck and crystalline architecture. The interior of the doomsday machine didn't feel like a technological device, but like an alien place filled with crystalline fungus. Normal fungus would be wet. These substances felt as if they didn't belong to the same natural universe that Meta did.

I shouldn't be here. It's watching, waiting for me to weaken.

Meta hurried. She'd fallen behind again. The closer she was to Oran Rva, the less these feelings invaded her thoughts.

She passed spires, and heaps of what looked like massed coral. Mechanisms whirred in the crystal spires, and odd patterns of lights flickered in the coral like firing neurons in a brain.

The excess Gs weighed down her muscles. Meta wasn't used to that anymore. Her chest was actually sore from breathing.

Finally, she came within the magic radius. Oran Rva held up a silver ball. Every so often, it pulsed, sending out flickering blue lines of radiance. The length of those lines had lessened. They used to flicker beyond the dim lighting into the shadows. Now, they didn't go as far.

The New Man inspected the silver ball. "This is more draining than I thought it would be."

361

What did that mean?

She tightened her grip on a spring-driven rifle, brought along expressly for the doomsday machine. It shot thumbnail-sized, razor-sharp metal cones, each magazine holding twenty rounds. There could hardly be a simpler weapon except for the knife at her side, perhaps.

A small part of the Rouen Colony assassin would have liked to aim the rifle at Oran Rva's back and cut him down. A mental block kept her from lifting the weapon against him. Instead, she waited for the New Man to give his next order.

Just then, the deck shivered, and Meta stumbled, pressing a knee into the spongy substance. An eerie groan from the doomsday machine penetrated her helmet.

What was that? What had just happened? She hated those noises.

Oran Rva halted and looked up. The sound repeated three more times. Each time, Meta flinched, expecting something even more terrible to happen.

After a while, the groaning stopped. Finally, Oran Rva shrugged. Once more, he led the way. The New Man strode with purpose. Like them, he wore an armored vacc-suit.

They moved through a vast chamber. A dim, diffused light provided illumination. It seemed to come from the polygonal shapes on the walls. At random locations, huge pits glowed darkly, seeming to suck away light. Heat billowed from the pits. Some kind of force field must have kept the… What was the blackness, anti-energy? Something kept the heat from consuming them.

"Why is this place so strange?" Meta whispered to Kane via a shortwave helmet hookup.

The big man looked back at her. Kane's eyes were wide and staring. Oran Rva had done something to Kane's mind. Meta had begun to resent that.

"Halt," Oran Rva said.

Meta looked up.

"My stressor is nearly drained," the New Man said. "I must let it recharge a moment." With a deft move, he clicked the silver ball and put it into something metallic in his pouch.

An unseen force seemed to rush in and push against Meta's mind, causing greater unease. What did the commander's stressor do? Why couldn't he explain for once what was going on?

As if complying with her wish, the New Man said, "Many of the interior sequences are automatic." He paused, perhaps rethinking his statement. "They're more accurately called responses. I don't know if the ship will release a defense now or come to inspect and analyze us with a monitor."

Meta found herself trembling as the oppressive force made her eyelids heavy. How did the ship do that to her? What had the stressor done to combat it?

"Kane, Meta, ready your rifles."

Meta stared at the New Man, marveling at his composure. Oran Rva glanced back at her. Through his visor, his lean features showed a placid, golden face, although the eyes were like inky fires. How could he remain so calm in the belly of the beast?

She determined to do likewise, refusing to let fear overcome her.

"Excellent," the New Man said. "You show rare courage in a dreadful place. Clearly, you are superior to the cattle of Earth and a tribute to our initial breeding program."

Odd croaking sounds floated through the air.

Oran Rva turned, staring into the chamber's depths. "Something comes."

Fear loomed in Meta. She ignored it, raising her rifle. Beside her, Kane did likewise with his.

"Look far into the darkness," Oran Rva said.

Meta squinted. She didn't see—wait. Her breath escaped her. In the gloom were three glowing red dots in a small isosceles triangle. They seemed like eyes and were several meters off the deck.

"Do you see?" Oran Rva asked.

"Yes," Meta said.

The New Man clicked on his helmet lamp. A beam speared into the darkness, falling onto a strange creature.

It had eight spindly spike-like legs that jabbed into the deck. Atop that was a wet carapace like a giant cockroach. It

363

had five metallic spikes for arms. The spikes flowed like whips of living metal. An insect-like head regarded them. It did so with the glowing, triangle-positioned red dots. Below the eyes were clackers.

"What is that?" Meta whispered.

"It would appear to be part organic and part robot," Oran Rva said in his maddeningly-calm voice. "I would imagine the brains and bio-matter are tank-grown."

Meta gave the New Man a horrified look. "Do you understand any of this?"

"Do not seek to question me," the New Man said in a reproving voice.

"There are more," Kane said dully.

Oran Rva washed his lamplight from side to side, revealing three of the creatures. They scuttled across the deck in swift, jerky movements.

"Kill them," the New Man said. "Aim for the braincases."

Meta tightened her jaw, sighted the first creature and pulled the trigger. A cone hissed through the alien atmosphere. The round missed, as the thing shifted its head impossibly fast.

Kane seemed to have similar bad luck.

"Three shots to judge its reactions," Oran Rva said. "Use the fourth and fifth to kill."

The calm voice did more than anything else could to belay the jitters. Meta shot, cataloging the way the creature dodged. How was it even possible for it to do so? Its reactions were quicker than she could blink.

She pulled the trigger in quick succession, laying down a pattern, watching, judging and finally firing in a place the head should weave into.

"Hit!" Meta shouted. To her dismay, the razor-sharp cone didn't do anything to stop or even slow down the creature.

"They're invulnerable to our cone rifles," Kane said.

"No," Oran Rva said, softly. "Keep firing. You'll take them down."

Meta saw that the creatures were close. Those spikes would jab her chest and end everything. She fired again, again, again until the rifle clicked empty. Frantically, she tore out the

364

magazine and tried to slap in another. The magazine jammed, and she fumbled at it.

In her headphones, Oran Rva sighed. He lifted the silvery ball and must have pressed a stud. Blue lines of radiance flashed outward. In the New Man's other hand was a blaster. Hot energy in a pencil-thin beam burned the first head.

Meta watched transfixed.

Oil, she swore it was oil, gushed out of the first creature's neck trunk. The thing took several more spiky steps before it collapsed. In the meantime, the New Man burned off the other heads.

Each creature or robot collapsed onto the spongy deck. They froze in seconds as a machine would. An incredible volume of oil gushed out of them, soaking onto the spongy floor.

As Meta continued to observe, the oil began to disappear, draining somewhere. Did it go back into the ship or into oil reservoirs? Seeing this made her chest heave. She loathed this place more than ever.

"Will more...will more of the things appear?" she asked.

"Strand did not give specifics," Oran Rva said.

Meta struggled to understand what that meant.

"It doesn't matter," Oran Rva said. "To the victor goes the spoils. Once I own the doomsday machine, I will dictate terms. I will unite humanity under my crown. I will find Strand and make him kneel before me, or I will kill him."

Kane raised his head. "You did kill Strand, dominant."

Oran Rva sighed once more. "Soon, Kane, I will return you your intellect. I slew a clone. Don't you remember? The real Strand is still out there. He is a clever Methuselah Man, as difficult to kill as Professor Ludendorff. The two are different sides to the same coin."

Meta wondered what that meant.

"Come," Oran Rva said, as he raised the silver ball. I cannot wait any longer." He shut off the helmet lamp and bypassed the three fallen machine creatures.

At last, they exited the vast chamber, coming to another corridor. This one was huge like everything else here. After three hundred meters, Meta looked into a smaller chamber. It had three torn cocoons with tubes dangling from them.

"The creatures obviously came from here," Oran Rva said.

"Dominant," Kane said. "Notice. More cocoons. Intact. They squirm. A spike, I see a spike punching through one."

Meta stepped back. Thirty or more black silky cocoons shivered, with more wet spikes punching through.

"Quick," Oran Rva said. "Give me a pulse grenade. It's time to use one."

Kane pulled out a heavy ball from a pouch at his side.

Oran Rva flicked a button on the pulse grenade. Red numbers flashed along the side. He bowled the grenade so it rolled between shivering cocoons. Already, one of the things emerged, its three red eye-dots shining evilly.

"Run!" Oran Rva shouted. "I set the grenade for maximum blast."

Meta clutched her cone rifle against her chest. She ran in the excess Gs. The New Man easily outdistanced the two of them. He reminded Meta of Maddox doing that.

Kane lumbered beside her. She wondered if he could go faster. Probably. Even so, he stayed with her.

A terrific explosion shook the resin-like walls.

"Down," Kane roared.

Meta threw herself onto her stomach. Seconds later, heat billowed over her. Static burst in her headphones.

Slowly, she turned her head, peering at Kane. He looked at her as he lay on the deck. She wanted to ask him if he would serve Oran Rva willingly for the rest of his life.

"Come," the New Man radioed. "Why are you waiting? The pulse grenade worked, and those things are dead. We have many more kilometers to go to reach the driver."

Wearily, Meta rose. The doomsday machine seemed to be a horrible mixture of incredible technology and eerie, bio-matter robots with alien insect walls. She had begun to suspect that something dark beamed fear at them. This was unlike anything she was used to.

With sweat trickling in her eyes, Meta climbed to her feet, hurrying to catch up to Oran Rva and his stressor.

-42-

Maddox led the way through the strange corridors of the doomsday machine. A growing fear had slowed his step. The sensation was oppressive and malignant.

He'd drawn his blaster some time ago and had to work to keep from firing blindly into the darkness. Someone or something watched him. Yet no matter which way he turned, he couldn't spy the watcher.

The captain hissed between his teeth. Did something truly watch, or did he feel an aura of death from a machine that had slain billions maybe trillions of living beings? How old was the doomsday machine? Could massed death through endless ages have soaked the ship with a feeling of doom?

Maddox silently sneered at the thought. He was a Star Watch Intelligence officer. He had a task to perform. Therefore, he needed to concentrate on that and burn away extraneous ideas or feelings of dread. This was a ship like any other. Age didn't matter. Ambiance good or bad made not a whit of difference. He had to reach the controls before Oran Rva did. That was going to be difficult, though. The planet-killer was huge, with endless paths.

Behind him, Keith helped the sergeant. Riker stumbled from time to time, clutching the ruined bionic arm against his chest.

Maddox had felt the four shivers earlier and heard the eerie groans as if the machine was alive. Maybe Star Watch had found a way to attack the planet-killer. The process hadn't repeated. Maybe it had been a one-time attack. If that was true, the machine yet moved against Earth and the assault had failed to stop the ancient destroyer.

How much time did they have left? Had he chosen the right paths? A man could wander these corridors—

Maddox halted, staring at a wall.

"Is something wrong, sir?" Riker radioed.

Ignoring the sergeant, Maddox approached the wall. A black line a meter long marked two polygonal shapes.

With his heart beating faster, Maddox looked around, searching for other lines. He didn't see any. With his blaster drawn, Maddox increased the pace. The malignant oppression still weighed down his mind, but now, he felt a stir of curiosity.

Then he spied a second line. Twenty-six steps later, he saw a third.

"What is it?" Keith asked. "What are you looking at?"

"Stay alert," Maddox said.

"Alert? I'm sick to my stomach with fear, mate. My eyes feel like they're going to pop out of my head. This place is worse than any Halloween barn I've been to, worse than any horror show I've seen."

"Ignore the feeling," Maddox said.

"Are you daft?" Keith asked. "You don't ignore something like that. I've been praying ever since I entered here. I can hardly—"

"Quiet," Maddox said. "We have company." He stood at an intersection of corridors, peering around a corner. Down the length of the dim hall with its resin-coated walls approached a hideous monstrosity.

It had eight spindly spikes that moved in sharp jerks up and down, propelling the body. Over that was a platform of crystal that glowed eerily, providing the extra illumination. Attached to the crystal were separate cockroach-like carapaces. Each of the bio-matter forms supported an odd-shaped crystal with mechanisms whirling within.

Maddox realized his sense of fear came from the thing. It radiated off the crystals. That made no sense to him.

Darting back, Maddox motioned to the sergeant. Riker pulled away from Keith, staggering to the captain.

"Grenades," Maddox said in a choked voice. "Give me three."

Wordlessly, Riker used his good hand, digging out three grenades, handing them one at a time to Maddox.

The captain didn't trust his blaster against the crystal thing. He also didn't want to expose himself any more than he had to. There was something extra-sinister about the robot, plant, insect, whatever the approaching thing was.

Holstering the blaster, Maddox activated the first grenade, moved to the corner and slung the grenade underhanded at the thing. He quickly did the same with the other two grenades before shifting himself to safety.

Seconds later, explosions shook the corridor. They were ordinary grenades, not the pulse type Oran Rva had used.

Drawing the blaster, taking a deep breath, Maddox peered around the corner.

The thing had canted onto its side. Oil gushed from the torn carapaces. Some of the mechanisms in the crystals still moved.

"Give me one more," Maddox said.

"It's my last grenade, sir."

"Do it," Maddox hissed.

Wordlessly, Riker gave the captain the last grenade.

Maddox steeled himself. Then, he dashed around the corner. Immediately, waves of fear billowed against him. The captain knew the machine or thing saw him and went into overdrive. It radiated the raw emotions at him.

Maddox felt as if he drove himself against a hurricane. Wheezing gasps hiccupped past his throat. Tears sprang to his eyes. He didn't care. He had a job to do. This thing tried to stop him. It used—

A raw sound of anguish tore past Maddox's lips. He activated the grenade, setting it among the crystals. Then, Maddox sprinted for the intersection.

He dove around the corner, landing on the spongy deck. He wasn't sure he heard the explosion. The immediate cession of the fear told him the last grenade had done its job, though.

"What just happened, mate? I feel ten times better."

"It's gone," Maddox said, climbing to his feet "That's what matters. Maybe it has more of them, though."

369

"Who has more?" Keith asked.

"The doomsday machine," Maddox said.

"Is it alive?" the ace asked.

"Is Galyan alive?" the captain rebutted.

Keith's helmet tilted as if he thought about it. "Sure seems like it to me."

"Same thing with the planet-killer," Maddox said. "I can think like myself again, and I can finally tell you. I've seen evidence of Per Lomax."

"What?" Keith and Riker asked together.

"Blaster burn marks on the walls," Maddox said. "The New Man must have made it this far. I'm betting that thing I just broke had something to do with Per Lomax's death."

"How do you know the New Man died?" Keith asked.

"Because he didn't stop the doomsday machine, now did he?" Maddox said. "In any case, we're going that way." He pointed down the corridor with the broken crystal thing.

"Any special reason why?" the sergeant asked.

"Yes," Maddox said, although he didn't elaborate.

***

They found Per Lomax's corpse twenty minutes later. The carcass lay in a large chamber, crumpled forward on a dim, spongy deck.

"What killed him?" Riker asked.

Maddox knelt, gently turning the corpse onto its back. Three stab wounds had opened the vacc-suit many weeks ago.

"Nasty," Riker said. "Looks like whatever did this got close."

"Yes," Maddox agreed. He didn't have to search the body long. The corpse's gloves gripped two items. One was a blaster. A quick check showed Maddox the battery was drained. The other item looked like a recorder with a small screen.

"What's that?" Keith asked, as Maddox picked up the recorder.

"I'm betting it's something Ludendorff gave the New Man, something to help Per Lomax while he was in here."

"Ah," Keith said.

Maddox examined the recorder and screen, finally pressing what looked like an activation switch. Nothing happened. Did it have any power left or not? He studied the small device longer, finally opening a slot on the bottom. A ball dropped out of it. He'd seen a ball like this before, but where...

"I remember," the captain said. Opening a pouch on his vacc-suit, he pulled out the force field ball Dana had given him. Removing the chain, he fit the ball into the empty socket.

Closing the slot, Maddox tried the switch a second time. A grin split his features as the screen activated.

"It works," Keith said.

"So it would appear."

"You're a clever man, Captain," the ace said.

Maddox didn't have time to bask in the compliment. He examined the device again.

"Say," the ace said. "When you turned it on, I felt even better."

Maddox nodded.

"You know why?" the ace asked.

"Likely, there are more fear-producing machines wandering the corridors," Maddox said. "Maybe they have to be near for the full effect. Maybe you were feeling one that's headed our way."

"I don't like the sound of that."

"No," the captain agreed. "Ah, I think I may have something." He showed the others. What appeared to be a schematic of the vessel showed their position and the location of what Maddox surmised must be the control room.

"Does it give any distances?" Riker asked.

"No."

"How about—"

"Just a minute," Maddox said. "I think..." He adjusted the controls. Tiny blue dots appeared on the screen. The dots were near the control room. "I think I may have found Oran Rva. Look." He showed the others.

"It seems we're going to have to increase our pace. It should help that we know where we're going now. Are you two ready?"

"Let's do this," Riker said.

The ace nodded his agreement.

***

Maddox could feel Riker trembling through the vacc-suit. The sergeant struggled to maintain the hard pace. Clearly, the man's injury pained him.

Keith also dragged. No doubt, the wearying Gs took their toll.

The sense of urgency grew in Maddox. He wanted to sprint ahead and attack the others. There was another problem. Every second longer they took, the doomsday machine flew that much closer to Earth. If they took too long, Star Watch wouldn't have a fleet left.

Finally, the urgency boiled up in the captain's chest. It forced him to say, "We have to run."

"How long do you think we can run under these conditions?" Keith asked.

"We're about to find out."

"Sergeant?" Keith asked. "How do you feel about that?"

"This isn't a debating society," Maddox said. "Ready, Sergeant?"

"No," Riker said, wearily. "But that never stopped me, sir. This is like Loki Prime all over again. Instead of the infected prisoners chasing me, we're chasing the end of our world."

"Correct," Maddox said.

The captain gripped Riker around the waist and began to run. Riker stumbled, but found his footing. Together, the two Intelligence operatives lumbered down the corridor. Keith struggled to keep up.

Soon, Maddox heard the harsh sound of Riker and Keith's breathing in his headphones. He kept pulling the sergeant with him. Every time he glanced back, the ace doggedly remained a few steps behind them.

In time, their breathing worsened, becoming ragged.

"We're running out of time," Maddox told the other two.

"Yeah," Keith wheezed. Likely, it was all he could say.

They hit a ramp, and Riker stumbled. Maddox held the sergeant up until the man found his footing again. When the captain looked back, Keith had lost several meters.

"Need…rest," Keith wheezed.

"Not yet," Maddox said. "We have to push. Think of it this way, nothing else you've ever done in all your life matters as much as this. We have to reach them in time to save the human race."

They ran through massive corridors and crossed bigger chambers. There were dark pits, crystal machines emitting loud clicking noises and another room that was thick with a cloudy atmosphere. In there, discs of varying sizes changed position like long-ago dancers, with electrical discharges zigzagging between them. Motes shimmered in the cloudy haze.

Maddox tried to encourage Keith. The captain discovered that the shortwave radios didn't work in here. He had no idea what kind of alien technology the discs represented.

Riker stumbled more and more often. The man's strained features looked old and weary. Sweat stained his leathery skin, and his eyes stared straight ahead. The sergeant didn't complain, though. Maybe he couldn't anymore. He seemed to be on autopilot.

Keith had dropped even farther behind by the time they left the floating disc chamber. The ace now limped noticeably. Maddox also felt the strain, but what he felt even more was a terrible sense of urgency.

They turned a corner, and it felt as if someone slugged Maddox in the chest.

He saw thirty bio-matter robotic creatures. They had spikes for legs, three dots in a triangle for eyes and five spikey waving arms. In swift, jerky movements, the thirty robots headed in the direction of Oran Rva's party.

Keith made a strangled noise over the headphones.

Maddox glanced back. The ace fell onto his chest, having tripped or given up. The next moment, Maddox drew a blaster. He didn't have time to hide or figure out a different way to reach Oran Rva. Thirty alien machines blocked the way and he had to get rid of them now.

"Are you ready, Sergeant?" Maddox asked.

"I'm no good shooting left-handed, sir. I'll give you my blaster."

"The two of you go back around the corner and hide," Maddox said.

"No," Keith said.

"Don't be stupid," Riker said. "Do as the captain tells you. If he's worrying about us, he won't do his job as well."

Maddox didn't wait to see if they obeyed him. Out of the corner of his eye, he saw the sergeant set his blaster down on the spongy deck by his feet and back away.

Maddox picked up the second blaster. He had no idea how much of a charge these weapons had. Today, he would find out one way or another. Aiming at the first head, Maddox pulled the trigger.

A pencil-thin beam gushed out and burned the first head. He shot a second and a third. Oil gushed from neck trunks. Each of the machines collapsed and froze. More oil pumped onto the floor, soon sinking out of sight.

The seconds passed and Maddox continued to burn them down. He waited for the other bio-robots to turn around and attack. They never did. Each surviving creature continued to spike-step forward, following their programming without deviation.

Maddox felt a tug at his shoulder. He turned, staring at Riker.

"Stop, sir," the sergeant radioed.

Maddox lowered the blasters.

"I'm thinking you don't have to kill them," Riker said. "They're going after the others, right?"

"Right," Maddox said. He should have already figured that out. He was tired and getting sloppy. "Where's Keith?"

"I'm coming," the ace said.

As the three men spoke, the remaining bio-robots continued to jerk down the corridor, ignoring the broken machines behind them.

"How much of a cushion should we keep between them and us?" Keith asked.

"We'll hang back a little," Maddox said. "I want to keep them in sight, though."

The three men walked past the frozen robots. There was no sight of the spilled oil.

374

Ahead of them, the other bio-robots moved faster than the critters appeared to be going. Soon, the three men broke into a jog. Even so, the alien constructs gained separation.

Finally, the men ran after the machines to keep up.

More of the bio-robots joined the others until sixty or more seethed down the corridors.

Behind the machines, the three men staggered, barely able to see the robots anymore.

"We're close to the control room," Maddox said, glancing at the recorder.

"What's that?" Keith shouted.

"What?" Maddox asked, hearing the worry in the ace's voice.

"See that little ball sailing over the robots?"

Maddox looked up. As usual, Keith was the first to spot a flying object. Then, the captain realized what he'd spied.

"Down," Maddox shouted. "It's a pulse grenade."

The captain hit the deck. An instant later, so did Riker and Keith.

The small object landed and ignited, blowing away bio-robots, raining body parts and oil. Another grenade sailed and a third, fourth and fifth. Heat billowed in waves down the corridor, concussions washing against Maddox's vacc-suit as he lay on the deck.

Then, a thick man in an armored vacc-suit appeared down the hall. He held a blaster, and he burned the surviving robots. Afterward, the man seemed to inspect the destroyed constructs. Satisfied, or so it would appear, the man holstered the blaster and disappeared around the farther corner.

Keith turned to Maddox as they lay on the floor. "We've reached the others."

"Yes," Maddox said, climbing to his feet. "It's finally time to finish this."

-43-

Meta was bewildered by everything that had happened but most especially by what *was* happening. Deep in her mind, she tried to free herself from her immobility.

She stood in a small chamber, at least small in relation to things inside the doomsday machine. Crystal machines hummed around her, seven of them. They were tall, like spires, with mechanisms visible inside. At the top, flows of energy went from point to point. The energy lines continually changed color. It made her skin feel itchy.

In the very center of the chamber was a crystal-cube machine. It was ten meters by ten by ten. Swirling colors moved at random on the surfaces. If Meta looked at the colors too long, her thoughts faded away. It was like watching flames flicker but even more so.

At the top of the cube was an odd mechanical construction that seemed different in nature from everything else in here. It was shaped like an octopus, with a bulbous section and eight cable arms. The ends of the arms were embedded in the cube.

At the moment, Oran Rva balanced on top of the cube. He manipulated the giant octopus machine, opening panels as if searching for something.

Just then, slots opened on the bulbous section. That part was bigger than Oran Rva. The bulbous section must have had five times the New Man's mass. Those opening slots seemed to be vision ports. They focused on the New Man.

If Meta hadn't been frozen in place at Oran Rva's command, she would have shrieked. The octopus thing up there seemed alive as it began to click and whistle in precise sequences that implied a language.

"Meta," Oran Rva said, with a catch to his voice. "Throw me the square device. Make sure you pitch it high enough."

Freed from immobility, Meta dug in the sling-pouch Oran Rva had given her before he'd climbed up the cube. She found the square device, a box with many controls. Gripping it with both hands, she judged his position and heaved upward.

It was hard to throw in the greater Gs. The box sailed up but not quite high enough. Meta readied herself, grunting as she caught it, nearly tearing off her fingers.

"Foolish woman," the New Man said. "What's wrong with you?"

"I lack sufficient strength," she called up.

Oran Rva muttered something to himself before saying, "Gather your strength. Heave as hard as you can. The gravities in this chamber are greater than elsewhere on the vessel. It is part of the driving mechanism, a safety feature, I believe."

Earlier, the New Man had worked, harder than he should have needed to, to climb the cube. Now, Meta knew why.

Taking several deep breaths, she hurled the box upward, straining her muscles.

This time, it reached high enough. Oran Rva caught the box. For a second, it appeared he might lose his balance. Would the New Man break bones falling from that height in the higher Gs?

Meta hoped so.

Then, he regained his balance. Oran Rva looped a cord from the box around his neck. Studying the square device, he began to manipulate controls. Soon, clicks and whistles emitted from the box.

Incredibly, and surreally to Meta, the eight cables of the octopus machine shifted as if uncomfortable. The bulbous section emitted more clicks and whistles in a faster sequence.

Oran Rva had plugged a cord from the box to his helmet. For just a moment, Meta heard mechanical sounds through her headphones. Then words came through.

377

"It has been many cycles since I spoke the true tongue. You are from Rexes Seven from the Curator?"

The New Man must have shut off the radio link between them then, because Meta didn't hear the strange words anymore.

An involuntary shudder swept through her. Did Oran Rva communicate with the mechanical octopus up on the cube? Was that a Builder construct? Is that what drove the doomsday machine?

After that, Meta's thoughts drifted. In time, the radio link crackled back into life.

"Meta," Oran Rva said. "Toss me the egg. It's time."

She dug the Builder egg out of the pouch, the one Ludendorff had brought back from the asteroid base in the Xerxes System. With a heave and a grunt, she threw the egg up to the New Man.

Oran Rva caught it, keeping his balance better this time.

Meta kept her head craned to watch the proceedings.

Oran Rva tapped the egg with his fingers as if playing a musical device. The metal egg split open, one part falling away to strike the floor.

Meta groaned in revulsion. A giant mechanical centipede crawled out of the other half of the egg, almost flowing as it crossed Oran Rva's vacc-suited arm.

The octopus machine squirmed too, the cables beginning to thrash, although the ends remained embedded in the cube. The clicks and whistles were louder than ever.

The New Man must have forgotten to turn the radio link with Meta back to off.

"Please, do not do this thing to me. I have served the Curator faithfully for many cycles of existence. This is—" A weird scream came through the headphones.

The mobile Swarm virus launcher flowed onto the octopus's bulbous head. The centipede forced a slot to open and chewed into the machine. Then, the centipede thing quivered.

"It is attacking my processors. It is changing…changing…changing code. P-P-Please…"

Oran Rva slapped the bulbous head. "I am about to give you new instructions. You will listen to the instructions and implement them at once."

"I am linked to the ancient machine. It is not as easy as you think to change protocols."

"You will listen to my new instructions," Oran Rva said. "I will not countenance any rebellion on your part."

"You are failing to understand the ancient machine."

"I will succeed at this," Oran Rva said.

"The machine has safeguards. It will break the conditioning we installed long ago. You have injected a Swarm virus into me. It is too crude to use in conjunction with the machine."

"You will do as I command," Oran Rva said.

"Obedience is not the issue. Yes, I will certainly obey. What I am trying to warm you—" The octopus-shaped thing screamed once more.

Meta heard the agony as she watched the cables writhe. The Swarm virus centipede no longer quivered.

"I am losing coherence. There is danger here, grave danger."

"You are about to receive your new instructions," Oran Rva said.

"No, no, the ancient machine is growing aware of me. There is grave danger here for Rexes Seven and the Curator. If the doomsday machine should fully wake up again—"

"You will not change my mind," Oran Rva said. "I am fixed upon my goal. You will be my steed in achieving greatness."

"I will try. But I am losing coherence. Soon, I will not be able to subdue the ancient protocols. The Swarm virus is creating confusion in my processors. Danger, there is danger for Rexes Seven and the Curator. I implore you to listen to me."

"No," Oran Rva said. "You will listen to me."

As Meta stood listening on the floor, she shuddered with revulsion. She hated standing here waiting for…for…

Meta looked around. Why hadn't Kane returned yet? Wasn't he supposed to be back by now? What was keeping him?

***

Maddox stared down at the force-webbed enemy. The blocky man couldn't move, and it appeared he hadn't been able to radio Oran Rva.

Going to one knee, shining a ray on the visor, Maddox saw Kane straining inside the vacc-suit. He should have known it would be the Rouen Colony agent.

"Let's do this," the captain said.

Keith knelt and manipulated Kane's helmet, shutting down the shortwave radio link with the others. With a change in setting, the ace linked the enemy agent to their net.

"Kane, I presume," Maddox said.

The other stared balefully at him.

"I'm Maddox," the captain said.

There was a slight tightening of Kane's eyes, but that was it.

"Has Oran Rva made it into the control room?" Maddox asked.

Kane said nothing.

"Should I just shoot you and get it over with?" Maddox asked.

Again, the enemy agent didn't say a word. Kane kept staring with deadly intent.

"He's hypnotized," Riker declared.

"What?" Maddox asked.

"Look deep into his eyes," Riker said. "He's been programmed."

Maddox studied the square-faced Kane. "Yes, I see it now," the captain said. "What do you think about that, my friend? Your masters trust you so much they program you for obedience. Yes, I trust that side. Programming masters are the best people to serve. They treat you like chattel and toss you aside when they're finished. You've clearly chosen well, Kane."

Slowly, as the rest of Kane lay frozen on the deck, the big man shook his head. "You don't understand. No one can defeat the dominants. Their victory is inevitable."

380

"By dominants I take it you mean the New Men?" Maddox asked.

Kane said nothing more, although his glare became more baleful.

"Right," Maddox said. "I'm not yet ready to kill you. I don't know enough, but it's time we moved on. Sergeant?"

"Here, sir," Riker said.

"Hold the web-gun," Maddox said. "I want to shackle him."

Riker took the flat device, keeping it trained on Kane.

Maddox pulled out shackles. "Let's do the legs first."

Tucking the web-gun under an arm, Riker pressed a tab.

Kane's feet rose minutely as he attempted to kick them, but the feet remained force-webbed. As the Rouen Colony man attempted to thrash his legs, Maddox shackled Kane's wrists, securing them.

"You really do fall for the most elementary ploys," the captain said. "Now stay still this time so we can get this done."

Kane struggled, but it wasn't fast or hard enough. Soon, the Rouen Colony agent lay on the deck, squirming in the shackles.

Maddox retrieved Ludendorff's flat device from the sergeant. He was going to need it to trap Oran Rva. How lucky was it that Dana Rich had figured out how to use the professor's high-tech gadgets?

"Oran Rva isn't going to fall as easily as Kane did," Riker said.

"I have no doubt you're right," Maddox said. "But we don't have a choice. This is the moment, gentlemen. Are you ready?"

"I am," Keith said.

Riker grunted his reply.

"Here we go," Maddox said, leading the way to the control room.

-44-

Kane lay on the deck, staring up at the bizarre ceiling. He'd retreated into his mind for much of the trek through the freaky doomsday machine.

Part of him recognized what Oran Rva had done to him. The dominant had stolen much of his wits. That was wrong, just wrong. They had marched through horror, killing alien bio-robots. Kane hadn't even been able to make love to Meta before the dash into this eerie planet-killer.

Would Oran Rva ever let him enjoy the fruits of his struggle? Kane had begun to suspect not. Instead, Oran Rva was like the trainer long ago on Rollo Glacier. Oran Rva thought to train him into a guard, a killer, an obedient slave of the dominants.

The one named Maddox had just sneered at Kane. That galvanized part of his persona. Maddox owned Meta, had used the beautiful woman. Kane resented that. Maddox was not better than Kane.

How can I regain my wits? How do I break the conditioning? The dominants have programmed me like a machine. That is a crime against my person.

"I am Kane," he rumbled. "I am ice."

Yes, the ice, Rollo Glacier, he remembered long ago as he'd lain on the ice. The trainer had beaten his best friend to death. Kane had watched. That had been an evil spectacle. Hatred had burned in him that day. The ice had numbed his skin and finally his heart. The words *I am ice* had thrummed in his skull. Kane had risen from the ice and endured. He had returned to the world of heat. He had eaten and rebuilt his strength. In time, he had slain the trainer.

No one hurts me and gets away with it. I am Kane. I am ice. These shackles...

As he lay on the deck in the alien doomsday machine, Kane turned his head, staring at the locks on his wrists. His lips twisted with a snarl. Was he a beast? Did others think to master him?

Yes, Oran Rva believes that he is better than Kane. No one is better than me. I will survive.

"Really?" Kane asked himself in mockery. "You're too stupid to know what to do. You're a lout, a fool and a dupe. Captain Maddox has beaten you, chained you to the floor and gone to the control room to claim Meta for his own."

Kane shook his head. "Meta is mine, mine. No one will have her body but me."

Kane began to thrash on the floor. He roared inside his helmet, struggling to free himself from the chains. Nothing helped. He was too weak to burst them as he desired.

Finally, Kane lay panting on the spongy deck.

"You have to think. You have to use your wits as you did once on Rollo Glacier. The dominant thinks he can keep you stupid. No. I will regain my mind, and I am going to do it *now*."

Kane closed his eyes. He thought back to the room in the star cruiser. That is where the dominants had begun to program his mind.

As he lay in the doomsday machine, Kane groaned like a wounded beast. Then, he clamped his teeth together. He strove to think, to break the mind conditioning through force of will. He used hatred, stubbornness and finally sheer grit. By remembering what he had been like, he tried to lever himself back into that frame of mind.

Try as he might, though, Kane remained dull-witted.

I have to do something else, something new. What do I have that might work?

Kane struggled for a new concept. The old ways weren't going to smash through the dominant technology and processes. To do that, he must, must, do what…?

Futility began to eat at him. This was impossible.

Kane sighed, thinking of Meta and the delightful curves of her body, the beauty of her features. He even liked her voice. It did something to him; stirred emotions he hadn't realized existed.

It dawned on Kane then. Maybe there was a way out of the trap of the programming. If he did nothing, Meta would die. He would never see her again.

Why should I care?

Kane wrestled with the thought, finally concluding it didn't matter why he should or shouldn't care. He did. Was that friendship? He had gotten off the glacier for the sake of a friend. No. This was more than mere friendship. Could this be the thing called love?

Kane almost sneered at himself. Instead, he lay utterly still. *Maybe that's the key. Think what it means that Meta dies.*

He did, concentrating on the subject. It bothered him deeply, stirred emotions Kane had no idea existed in him. Sure, love existed for others, but not for him, the man who was ice.

Love is real.

Something strange settled on Kane's features. He felt peace in his heart.

I will die having loved.

"No," he said aloud. "I will break free because I must save the one I love."

Gritting his teeth, Kane strove for mastery of his mind. He pushed, teased and began to see new possibilities. Finally, a gleam of the old Kane appeared in his eyes.

Once more, he studied the shackles on his wrists and ankles. Just maybe, he could escape from them, but not by brute force.

Oh…yes, he would have to do it like this…

-45-

Maddox peered around an entrance into a strange chamber. He had no doubt this must be the doomsday machine's control room.

Along the walls appeared bursts of light in odd sequencing. In a circle were seven crystal spires with mechanisms whirling inside. Lines of energy thrashed from one pinnacle to the next. In the center was a large cube with swirling, hypnotic colors. An octagonal machine sat on top of the cube. Attached to the bulky part of the silvery machine was an inert centipede, the Swarm-Builder mobile virus carrier.

A vacc-suited person backed away from the cube, staring upward. Maddox noticed another suited person, one who hung from the cube by his fingers. Yes, that must be Oran Rva. The tall New Man released his hold. His feet struck the deck, the knees bent and the New Man toppled onto the spongy substance.

"This is it," the captain told the others. "If I fail to hold him, fire at the taller one."

Maddox walked into the room with Ludendorff's flat device in his gloves. Oran Rva stood up. Something must have alerted the New Man to Maddox's presence. The enemy turned.

Aiming the flat device at the man, Maddox manipulated the controls of the web-force. The New Man froze in place.

"Now," Maddox told Keith. "Adjust the frequency so we can talk." He heard static in his headphones as the ace switched their helmets' setting.

In a second, Maddox heard new breathing. "Meta," he said.

"M-Maddox?" she asked. "How did you get here? What happened to Kane? Where is he?"

Maddox grinned until Oran Rva drew a knife and came at him. That shouldn't have been possible. How had the New Man short-circuited Ludendorff's web-field?

"Shoot him," Maddox said.

Keith raised a blaster and pulled the trigger, but nothing happened. Maddox dropped the flat device, drew his own blaster and tried to fire. Absolutely nothing happened.

Oran Rva chuckled as he said, "I'm impressed, hybrid. You've done much better than I would have believed. You are a testament to our breeding program."

"Fan out," Maddox said. "We're going to have to do this the hard way."

"Meta," Oran Rva said, "to me."

She didn't move.

The New Man glanced at her. "Did you hear my command?"

Meta said nothing.

The New Man turned faster than Maddox would have believed possible. Oran Rva's knife sank through Meta's armored vacc-suit into her belly. She moaned painfully. With his other hand, Oran Rva shoved her.

Meta stumbled backward, striking a crystal spire and sliding down, sinking onto the spongy floor.

Oran Rva faced Maddox, with Meta's blood dripping from his blade.

Maddox wanted to howl with rage, lower his head and charge the fiend from the Throne World. An icy part of him told the captain he would certainly lose if he did that. That was exactly what Oran Rva wanted him to do. He'd never faced a deadlier opponent.

Feeling surreal, Maddox took a viper-stick stance. This was awkward in a vacc-suit. Instead of a whippy instrument, he gripped a slarn knife, a length of deadly tri-steel.

"That was a mistake," Maddox said, his voice hyper-calm.

"Does the pup seek to instruct the wolf?" Oran Rva sneered. "That is poor form, hybrid. I am your better."

"Which is why you're trying to eliminate us one by one, right?" Maddox said.

"Why yes, because that is the best tactic."

Maddox's eyes narrowed, as did his focus. "I will kill you, Oran Rva."

"Boasts, Captain?"

"A statement of my intent, rather," Maddox said.

Out of the corner of his visor, the captain saw Keith. The ace gripped the sergeant's trench knife with its tungsten knuckles over the vacc-gloves. The pilot stepped hesitantly like someone afraid of knives.

Where was Riker? The sergeant wouldn't stay out of this. Was Meta alive or bleeding to death?

No. I must remove her from my thoughts.

Maddox refused to dwell on the doomsday machine either. This was the moment of supreme concentration. This would be the duel of his life.

Maddox narrowed his focus onto Oran Rva and the New Man's blade. It was shorter than the slarn knife. Why had the blaster failed to fire? Why hadn't the flat device worked for long in this room? There had to be some sort of dampener field in place.

The captain felt it then. The greater Gs. He swished his knife-arm back and forth. There was resistance in the air, and he moved too sluggishly.

"I beat you in the Tannish System," Maddox said, hoping to goad Oran Rva into making a mistake.

"All is forgiven, hybrid," the New Man said. "You see, it showed me a greater path. I am taking control of the only war machine that matters now. I am about to become king."

Maddox emptied himself of emotion, of extraneous thoughts. In the viper-stick stance, he began to approach the other. He concentrated on the tip of his knife. The goal of these next few minutes would be to bury it in his opponent's heart. First, he must test the other. He must gauge the reflexes and cunning.

Oran Rva closed in a similar manner, with the shorter knife thrust low and outward.

Maddox noted the lean features. They were like his, more so than anyone else's he'd seen to date. He caught the golden hue of the skin, the intense eyes blacker than sin. He wondered for a second if Oran Rva could have been his father.

"You desire to ask me questions," the New Man said. "But I say to you: surrender or die, hybrid."

"You will allow me to surrender?" Maddox asked.

"Put the knife on the deck and—"

"No!" Keith shouted. The ace launched himself at the New Man, moving in slow motion. Keith held the trench knife before him like a shield.

Maddox had hoped to lull Oran Rva. Instead, the captain had demoralized one of his own men into attacking prematurely.

To save Keith, the captain began his attack approach while maintaining the viper-stick stance.

Oran Rva spun, moving at Keith and then leaning, thrusting with his long reach. The ace stopped short and slashed down, no doubt attempting to block the enemy knife. Stopping short did more than the blocking move to help save Keith's life. Oran Rva's knife-tip touched the armored vacc-suit instead of sinking into it.

Maddox strove to reach Oran Rva in time. The New Man stepped toward Keith. The ace already twisted away, diving for the floor. The tactic led Maddox to believe that Keith hadn't been blindly charging the enemy, but pretending to be a fool.

Oran Rva came up out of his knife-fighting stance, standing tall. He made a short run at Keith and lashed out with his foot. The boot connected with Keith's chest. That would have cracked some ribs. The kick propelled the fallen pilot several meters. Worse, Keith went limp, groaning through Maddox's headphones.

Maddox lunged. Oran Rva spun around impossibly fast in this alien environment. The New Man's blade clinked against the captain's, blocking the thrust.

Maddox tried a quick, slashing cut. The New Man blocked that, too. In five seconds, the captain practiced another three attacks. Each time, Oran Rva produced a spark and a notch in the blades as the knives clashed against each other.

Finally, the captain retreated. He saw the gleam in Oran Rva's dark eyes. A triumphant, cool smile appeared on the New Man's face.

"I am much better than you are, Captain."

"Why didn't you kill me then?" Maddox taunted.

"You figure it out."

No. Maddox wasn't going to fall for that gambit. He would not try to overthink this. Knife dueling against a superior opponent was a time for reflexes and swift ploys. To that end, the captain controlled his breathing, watching for an opening. He refused to dwell on the very real possibility that Oran Rva was going to murder the lot of them and take control of the doomsday machine.

A feeling of futility swept through Maddox. Whom was he fooling? The New Man's strength and speed—the captain shook his head. He could win this. He just had to figure out how.

"Your woman is dying," Oran Rva said. "I crushed your friend's chest. Your last companion is a coward, hiding. I suspect he is bewildered."

"Fine," Maddox said. "That just leaves you and me. It will make my victory sweeter by winning it alone."

"Yes," Oran Rva said. "We are all alone. The weaklings bleat to each other, seeking comfort in this cold universe. We of the Throne World realize that each man is an island unto himself. We strive against each other, seeking honor. I am the dominant here. You are the inferior. Goodbye, Captain Maddox, I thank you for this brief moment of sport."

The New Man advanced.

Maddox retreated.

Oran Rva chuckled. "Do you think I do not know your tactic? But go ahead, proceed with it."

Maddox did just that, concentrating on trying to get ready for the right moment to attack.

Suddenly, Oran Rva surprised him. The New Man straightened once more and dashed for a spire. A second later,

Riker tried to run away from behind that spire. The enemy strained to reach the sergeant.

Maddox shouted, and he, too, ran, but after the New Man. He knew what Riker had been going to do. Why was he so slow?

Oran Rva closed the distance. At the last moment, Riker stopped and turned, hurling the length of his broken bionic forearm and hand at the New Man, the burden Riker had been carrying. The tall man reached out, catching the forearm by the hand. He swung the bionic piece at Riker.

After hurling his forearm, the sergeant had used his left hand to draw a knife, a short one. As he did, Riker looked up. Oran Rva swung the forearm like a sap, hitting the sergeant's stomach.

Maddox heard the *oomph*. Riker doubled over the forearm. In his other hand, Oran Rva raised his blade.

"Here, Dominant!" Kane roared.

The Rouen Colony man sprinted around another spire. The blocky man now wore regular clothes and an emergency rebreather and goggles. Where was Kane's armored vacc-suit? The man's hands and feet were stark red.

It took Maddox a moment to comprehend what he saw. Had Kane wriggled out of his vacc-suit? Yes. That had to be it. How else had the man escaped the restraints, which had been over the suit? It would appear Kane had used an emergency rebreather, letting his skin resist the alien atmosphere inside the ship.

In those brief seconds of thought, several things occurred at once. Oran Rva pivoted and lowered himself into a knife-fighting stance. That allowed Riker to roll out of the way. Then, Kane was airborne, with his fingers hooked like claws.

Oran Rva stabbed upward, the knife sinking into Kane's chest. Instead of roaring with pain, Kane crashed against the New Man, his weight bearing the golden-skinned man onto the deck.

"Strike, Maddox, while I hold him," Kane roared.

Incredibly, Kane clutched onto Oran Rva's knife-arm, keeping the blade buried in his body. The New Man struggled to withdraw the blade. He was doing so centimeter by centimeter.

The New Man let go of the knife-handle, beginning to turn on the floor.

Maddox laid a palm on Oran Rva's helmet. Then the captain stabbed the slarn knife into the New Man's throat. The blade sank, with the tip pushing into the spongy deck. Maddox twisted the knife. Their eyes met then. Oran Rva's became wide and staring, shocked with agony.

"I killed you," Kane rumbled. "I killed you because you hurt the one I loved. No one hurts me because I am ice."

Maddox removed the blade, staring at the bright blood along the length.

Oran Rva began to thrash, gurgling in the captain's headphones.

"Kane," Maddox said. "You can let go. I'll look at your wound."

The big man moved his head, staring up at Maddox through the goggles as he kept hold of Oran Rva's knife-hand. "I'm dead, Earthman. Save Meta. She's why I did this. Save her, Captain. Tell her…"

Maddox stared at the big man. What was Kane trying to say?

The Rouen Colony man's skin paled. His reddened eyes became haunted and frightened. "Tell her I loved her. You'll do that…won't you?"

Shock numbed the captain's lips. What was this? Kane loved Meta. Anger boiled in Maddox's heart. Yet, the big man had just acted heroically, saving their lives with his selflessness. It *had* come from love.

Kane kept staring at him, waiting.

The words seemed to force themselves out of Maddox's mouth. "I'll tell her," he said.

Relief flooded over Kane. Then a sad smile spread across his features. "That was the secret to breaking the conditioning. I did it because of love. I loved her, but I learned that too late. Don't…don't be the same kind of fool, Maddox."

The captain opened his mouth to speak. He wasn't sure what he would have said. He didn't have the chance to tell

Kane anything more. The enemy agent, servant of the New Men, closed his eyes for the last time.

At that point, the hyper-focus left Maddox. The world seemed to expand. The room was shaking, with riotous colors swirling along the sides of the center cube. One of the machine cables—the thing on top of the cube—whipped out and began to thrash. Blue smoke began to trickle from the main housing of the octagonal-shaped Builder device.

-46-

With his fists clenched, Maddox knelt over Meta. A resilient, plastic-type substance had already auto-sealed the cut in her vacc-suit. He wished the same had happened for the wound in her gut.

Through her visor, Meta's eyelids fluttered.

She's still alive. "Can you hear me?" Maddox asked.

Her features were drawn and much too white. Lines pulled at her mouth. "Maddox," she whispered.

"Oran Rva is dead. So is Kane. This place—"

Meta feebly raised an arm and latched onto a vacc-suit sleeve. Weakly, she pressed her fingers against the armored fabric.

"Are you trying to tell me something?" Maddox asked.

"Yes," she whispered. "Listen."

"We don't have much time." Not that Maddox had any idea what he should do next.

"Bring me...the translator," Meta whispered.

Maddox looked around. Yes. They must have had a device to speak with the Builder thing controlling the planet-killer. Getting up, Maddox retrieved a box. It was near the center cube. Oran Rva might have set it there.

"That's it," Meta whispered. In a few words, she told Maddox what the New Man had done with the box, the translator.

Noticing the looping cord, Maddox slung it over his neck. Another cord dangled from the box, one that would fit in a comm-slot on his helmet. Maddox plugged it in.

He heard the translator's words: "I am losing coherence. The virus—"

"Hello," Maddox said, looking up at the silvery, octopus-shaped machine on the cube.

"You must listen to reason," the octopus thing told him.

"I will," Maddox said.

"You will?" it asked.

"Yes."

"Then why did you insert the Swarm virus into me?"

"That doesn't matter now," Maddox said. "Tell me the problem."

"I will be succinct. I am losing control of the machine. The old intellect is taking over. It has lain dormant longer than I can understand. Soon—"

"Never mind about that," Maddox said. "How do we stop the doomsday machine?"

"Reference your meaning of doomsday machine."

"This machine, this ship," Maddox said.

"I perceive your meaning. There is no solution. No warships in this sector of the galaxy can harm the machine."

"Do you sense the warships outside?" Maddox asked.

"Yes. They are engaging in a futile attack run. The machine will soon destroy the bulk of them and render the rest harmless."

"Transfer somewhere else then," Maddox said.

"How does that change the final outcome of the situation? The scourge will have awakened. It will return here. Then—"

"I have the answer," Maddox said, seeing it in a flash. "But it will mean sacrificing your life."

"I am not wedded to existence like a biological life form. I exist to serve my programming. If I cannot control the machine, I must render it harmless. But I have less than three *tarns* to achieve anything. Then, my control will forever disappear, and it will be in control."

"How long does it take you to transfer?"

"Two tarns," it said.

"Do you see the local star nearby?" Maddox asked.

"Of course," it said.

"You must transfer the machine into the center of the star."

It took three long seconds. Then the thing said, "That is a brilliant solution. Do you wish to eject before I begin?"

"Can we?" Maddox asked. He hadn't expected to survive this.

"If you can reach an exit in a tarn's time," the thing said.

"Are there any escape pods?" Maddox asked.

"The concept is alien to the machine, as it never envisioned defeat or destruction. Go—"

"Give me the nearest exist."

"I will not, as that will be too far. I can give you the location of a hull breach. The local life forms of this star broke through with an antimatter device. If you can reach there in time—"

"Tell me the route to the nearest breach," Maddox said.

"Can you commit it to memory?"

"Yes."

The Builder creation began to explain the torturous route to Maddox.

"That's not going to work," Maddox said. "We won't reach the hull opening in time."

"I suggest you begin praying to the Deity then and making your peace with Him."

"Question," Maddox said. "Can you switch the gravity settings in the corridors?"

"Of course," the Builder thing said.

"Make everything weightless."

"Would that help you escape?"

"Yes," Maddox said.

The Builder thing paused before saying, "There. It is finished. Now, you must stop communicating with me. I will need to use my last moments to concentrate on control and transfer."

Maddox stopped talking to the Builder computer. He tore off the translator's loop and plugin, and realized he was weightless. "Listen to me," he radioed the others. "This is what we're going to do…"

***

Maddox gripped Meta's belt with one hand and propelled them down the corridors with his legs, using his free hand to guide them. She was groggy, going in and out of consciousness.

Despite the broken ribs, Keith practiced zero-G maneuvering like a monkey. The ace shot ahead of them. Riker did his best to keep up.

So far, they hadn't run into any more bio-robots.

"Even if we get outside," Riker said, "won't we get sucked into the transfer node?"

"You ask the cheeriest questions," Maddox said. "I have no idea. First, we have to get out of the doomsday machine. Then, we can listen to you croak despair."

One thing helped Maddox remember the route. The feeling of evil had departed. Was that due to the Builder octopus?

As the captain gained speed, negotiating the intersections with cool concentration, he thought about the ancient machine. Who had built it? Did it even belong to this galaxy? Clearly, it destroyed planets. Why, though? What had been the reasoning behind the decision to make something like that?

We'll probably never know. Oran Rva might have told us, but he's dead. What about the other New Men, do they know?

"I see stars," Keith radioed from ahead.

"Is the breach big enough for us?" Maddox asked.

"Oh yeah it is, mate. It's the loveliest exit I've ever seen in my life. I never thought we were going to be able to do it, sir."

"We're not done yet," Riker grumbled.

"No, not yet," Maddox said. He didn't want to think about Meta. She hadn't said anything for some time. Was she dying?

You can't think about that yet. Get everyone out of here first.

Then, Maddox saw the stars. There was a breach through the neutroium hull. He couldn't believe it.

"It's not an opening," Keith radioed. "There's hard...something like clear plastic, I think. It sealed the opening."

Maddox drew his blaster. Then, he holstered it. As best he could, he slowed his momentum. Soon, he reached Keith by the jagged breach and its seal. Putting the blaster nozzle a centimeter from the clear substance, he began to burn it. Maddox worked fast. He had no idea how much time they had left.

Finally, he burned a circle, creating a man-sized hole. Anchoring himself, he shoved the substance with his shoulder. The clear plastic-like stuff popped out into space, tumbling away. Some ship atmosphere blew out, but not as hard as the captain would have expected.

"Now," Maddox said. He pushed Meta through the opening, joining her outside a second later.

Soon, Keith and Riker floated with them. They had each shoved as hard as they could off the hull, Maddox taking hold of Meta while Keith and Riker grabbed onto him. They drifted a few meters per second away from the ancient pitted neutroium. It wouldn't be far enough, though, when the ionic storm appeared for transfer.

The giant craft slowly began to rotate. At first, none of them was aware of what happened.

"Do you sense that?" Keith asked.

"What?" Maddox asked.

Keith told them about the hull drawing away from them.

Maddox watched the pitted neutroium. The bad feelings had begun again. Was the ancient intelligence waking up for good and engaging the fear machines?

Then, the giant doomsday machine began to move away from them faster and faster.

"There," Keith said. "I see the exhaust."

Maddox saw it too, a hot plume. The exhaust stopped suddenly as the giant craft rotated again.

"Why's it doing that?" Keith asked.

"I think I know why," Maddox said. "The Builder is making sure the exhaust doesn't kill or radiate us. Now, the port should spew exhaust again."

Ten seconds later, it did just that. The plume extended as the planet-killer increased separation from them. Soon, Maddox could no longer see the machine, just its hot exhaust.

Quicker than he would have expected, the plume shrank until it was no brighter than a star.

At that point, the magnetic storm appeared, growing rapidly to its regular planet-circumference. Maddox spied purple flashes of lightning. None of the bolts threatened to reach him and his companions. Even so, increasingly heavy static made it difficult to communicate with each other.

"I'm still alive," Riker grumbled. "Now, we can suffocate once we run out of air."

"Yes," Maddox said. "But that's better than starving to death, right?"

"Are you serious, sir?" Riker asked.

"Not in the slightest," Maddox said. "I have no intention of dying, not after we've won the greatest victory in human history."

"How do you plan on getting us out of here, sir?"

"At the moment, I have no idea. But until I'm out of air, I'm not giving up."

∗∗∗

On *Victory's* bridge, Galyan said, "Look. The doomsday machine is transferring."

"Do you know to where?" Valerie asked.

"According to my calculations, it appears to be heading into the core of the Sun."

"Are you kidding?"

"No. I am being factual."

Valerie wanted to howl with laughter. "Could Maddox have convinced the planet-killer to commit suicide?"

"I give that a high probability," Galyan said. "Ah, this is remarkable. I will record the event."

∗∗∗

As had happened many times before, a portal appeared in the magnetic storm. Unlike others of its kind, this portal was highly unstable due to the target. Nevertheless, the great doomsday machine shot into the portal and disappeared.

A second later, the primordial planet-killer transferred into the core of the Sun.

The G2V spectral-class yellow dwarf—a ball of hot plasma—had a mass 330,000 times that of Earth. While the surface of the Sun was a mere 5,800 Kelvin, the core had an infernal temperature of 15,700,000 Kelvin.

The core, with a density 150 times that of water, extended outward from the center to twenty to twenty-five percent of the solar radius. That was the only region of the Sun that produced an appreciable amount of thermal energy through fusion. That happened to be a proton-proton chain reaction, which turned hydrogen into helium.

The neutroium armor was massively denser than the surrounding plasma. The doomsday machine slid through the Sun's core, withstanding the heat and thermonuclear fusion far longer than seemed possible. The traveling distance was simply too far, however, especially at the planet-killer's present velocity.

In the end, the core's fantastic heat and energy output blasted through the neutroium. The ancient machine with its terrible secrets disappeared into the hot plasma, adding its molecules to the nuclear fusion reaction. The deadly menace to the Commonwealth, to all of humanity, had become a smear of atoms.

Long before the doomsday machine's alien intelligence perished, the Sun caused the unstable portal to collapse. That left the magnetic storm on the other side of the transfer point.

-47-

On *Victory's* bridge, Valerie continued to watch the main screen even after the doomsday machine's disappearance. The lieutenant observed the transfer point inside the magnetic storm. Unlike previous times, this one closed suddenly before the ionic particles drained away.

"I can hardly believe we've won," Valerie said. "It's fantastic. But the magnetic storm isn't going anywhere soon. We have to save our friends before it drifts toward them or their air runs out."

"A sterling suggestion," Galyan said. The holoimage stiffened then.

"What's wrong?"

"My incredibly refined sensors are detecting a cloaked vessel."

"What?" Valerie asked. "Where is it?"

Galyan paused before saying, "The vessel is approaching the drifting survivors."

The lieutenant glanced at the holoimage. "Can you tell what kind of cloaked vessel it is?"

"I am attempting to do just—yes, I recognize the type. It is a star cruiser.

"The vessel belongs to the New Men?" Valerie asked in disbelief.

"That is the most logical conclusion. I wonder if they wish to capture the survivors."

"Of course they do," Valerie said. "It's time to engage the star drive *now*. We have to rescue our friends."

"Affirmative," Galyan said. "I suggest you communicate with the Lord High Admiral and tell him what I am about to do."

"Roger," Valerie said, as she manipulated her board.

***

Victory used its star drive, transferring from the Home Fleet onto the other side of the planet-sized magnetic storm between Mars and Earth.

As soon as Valerie recovered from Jump Lag, she launched an automated shuttle. It headed toward the people drifting in space. The lieutenant hadn't been able to make a radio connection with them yet due to the nearby ion storm, but she continued to try.

Finally, Galyan reappeared on the bridge. The AI always seemed the hardest hit by Jump Lag.

"Do you still see the cloaked vessel?" Valerie asked.

"I do not."

"Is it gone?"

"No. I see them now, Valerie. They deviated from their course, although the star cruiser is still heading for the survivors. Now, it is doing so from a different direction. They are practicing guile for a reason."

"We should open channels with them."

"This near the storm?" Galyan asked. "I do not believe you will prove successful in the endeavor. Instead, I will give them a neutron beam shot across the bow. That will undoubtedly gain their attention in the quickest manner possible."

"Good idea," Valerie said.

The lieutenant continued trying for a radio connection, first with the survivors and then with the star cruiser.

Finally, after warming up the neutron cannon, Galyan fired a purple beam into space. It was twenty thousand kilometers from the drifting survivors and five hundred kilometers from the cloaked vessel.

A moment later, Valerie gasped. The enemy commander over there must have received the neutron-beam message loud and clear.

A star cruiser appeared on the main screen as it dropped its cloak.

"You were right about it being there," the lieutenant said.

"Did you doubt me?" Galyan asked.

"Maybe just a little," Valerie admitted.

"What is this?" Galyan said. "I am detecting life forms. The New Men are ejecting them from the star cruiser."

"Who are they?" Valerie asked.

"I have no idea."

The lieutenant monitored the shuttle. It had already begun to brake, slowing down as it inched toward the doomsday-machine survivors.

"The star cruiser is reengaging its cloak," Galyan said.

Valerie looked up at the main screen. The star cruiser vanished from regular sensor sight.

"They are in for a surprise," Galyan said, "as I am not through with them." The AI fired the neutron cannon a second time. A purple beam struck near the enemy vessel. The craft shimmered for a moment, reappearing before going invisible again.

"Does the enemy commander think I cannot target him?" Galyan asked.

"How come I'm not detecting a shield?" Valerie asked.

"Because the star cruiser does not have one up," Galyan said. "I do not think they could maintain the cloak if they raised a powerful shield."

"That gives them something of a dilemma."

"Yes," Galyan said. "My next shot will strike the star cruiser and end this farce."

As if understanding their perilous situation, Valerie's comm-screen came alive. The magnetic storm behind *Victory* made the image fuzzy. Even so, the lieutenant recognized the Methuselah Man on the screen. It was Strand.

His wizened features stared balefully at her. Finally, Strand smiled, although the warmth didn't reach his eyes.

"Is this Starship *Victory*?" Strand asked.

"You know it is," Valerie told him.

"I have given you a peace offering," Strand said. "Accept it, and let us depart in peace. Otherwise, I will kill the two Patrol officers and your Captain Maddox."

"What two Patrol officers?" Valerie asked.

"Commander Kris Guderian and Lieutenant Betty Artemis," Strand said. "I ejected them from my vessel. They have gained new insights under my brief tutelage. I rescued them from disaster in the Karachi System. You may not know it yet, but the doomsday machine struck there before coming to the Solar System."

"Why would you have rescued them?" Valerie asked.

"I have my reasons for doing so," Strand said. "It should be sufficient for you that I'm returning them to Star Watch."

"Sorry," Valerie said, who didn't feel sorry at all. "I can't let your star cruiser leave. I'm placing you under arrest."

"If you are serious," Strand said, "then your Captain Maddox dies. My vessel has targeted the survivors. I will kill them before you are able to destroy my augmented star cruiser. Are you willing for that to happen, hmm?"

Valerie licked her lips. This Strand was a bastard. "What do you think, Galyan?" she whispered.

"We have won the engagement with the doomsday machine," the AI said. "There will be time enough for Strand and his secret star cruiser. Let us rescue our friends."

"Rescue our family," Valerie said.

"You are correct," Galyan said.

"If I agree to your terms," Valerie said, peering at Strand again, "where will you go?"

"That is no concern of yours," Strand said.

"I think it is. You're in our Solar System, our home territory."

"If that is the problem, know that I will leave the Solar System within the hour."

"There isn't a Laumer-Point that close," Valerie said.

"Nevertheless," Strand said, "I will leave. What is it to be, Lieutenant? You must choose quickly."

"How do you know my rank?"

Strand smiled. "I know far more than you could possibly realize."

"Why have you sided with the New Men?" Valerie asked.

Strand continued to smile.

Valerie loathed the man. "Go," she said, thickly. "But if you've harmed the Patrol officers—"

"Please," Strand said. "Do not threaten me. It will gain you nothing but my enmity. You truly do not want that."

Valerie tried to think of a good retort, but failed. Maybe she was too worried about the others. "Go," she said, "while you are able."

Strand nodded in a mocking way. Then, the Methuselah Man cut the connection. Once more, the star cruiser faded from visible view.

"Should I warm up my disruptor cannon?" Galyan asked.

"No," Valerie said. "That risks Maddox and the others' lives. I don't think we could destroy the star cruiser before he kills those drifting in their vacc-suits. Besides, as you said, we've already won this round."

"I wonder what he was doing in the Solar System."

"Trying to get control of the doomsday machine would be my guess."

"How?" Galyan asked.

"I have no idea,' Valerie said. "Frankly, I'm not interested right now. We should head for the shuttle. It possible some of them could need medical attention."

***

In space, Maddox eased Meta through the open shuttle bay. Gently, he floated her toward the emergency medical cot.

"I'm in the control room," Keith radioed.

"Give me a few more minutes," Maddox said.

"Aye, Captain," Keith said.

Maddox hated this feeling of helplessness. He was safe, the doomsday machine was gone, but Meta could be failing. He increased speed.

Finally, Maddox pushed Meta onto the cot. Behind him, Riker sealed the hatch.

"I'm pumping atmosphere into the chamber," Riker radioed.

Maddox nodded, waiting impatiently.

"Okay," the sergeant said.

Maddox peeled off Meta's vacc-suit. When he saw the blood, his hands began to tremble.

If ever I needed my calm, now's the time. Detach. Don't think of it as Meta.

Such was the captain's concentration that his hands stopped trembling. He hooked Meta to the cot and began fastening the life-support systems onto her.

Finally, he radioed Keith. "I'm done. Let's head for the starship."

"Aye-aye, Captain, easy does it."

The gravity generators came online. Then, the shuttle accelerated for the starship looming in the near distance.

***

An hour and a half later, Dana came out of the medical station aboard *Victory*.

Maddox looked up from where he had been pacing.

The doctor smiled. "She's going to be all right. She's lost a lot of blood, but I've given her enough transfusions to last until we reach Earth." Dana paused. "She's asking for you."

Maddox headed for the hatch.

Dana stopped him by grabbing a forearm. "Captain, she's been through a lot. Don't excite her too much."

"I understand," he said. "And doctor?"

Dana raised her eyebrows.

"Thank you for everything you've done."

Dana nodded.

Maddox glanced at the hatch, and it seemed he would hurry through it. Instead, he paused, looking at Dana again.

"If it's any consolation," Maddox said, "I think he's still alive."

Dana didn't ask whom he meant.

"I don't know how Ludendorff did it," Maddox said. "But if anyone could have made a switch like that during a battle in the Xerxes System, it would be the professor."

"I think you're right," Dana said, softly. "I wonder, though, if I'll ever see him again."

"Do you have any doubt?"

Dana stared at Maddox. "Right now, I'm filled with endless doubts." She smiled sadly. "Go see Meta. We can worry about those things later."

Maddox looked as if he would say more. Then, he headed for the hatch, going through, closing it behind him.

Meta lay on a medical cot, with tubes hooked to her. She looked pale and withdrawn. Then, she turned her head, seeing him. The smile—

Maddox grinned back in turn, striding to her and taking one of her hands. He bent down and kissed her. Her lips were chilly.

"How are you feeling?" Maddox asked.

"Tired," she whispered.

"You have to quit leaving me like that," he said.

"I know." Her features clouded. "What happened to Kane?"

Maddox frowned for just a moment. He never should have made the promise. Yet, Kane had saved their lives by sacrificing his. He had to tell Meta. Was this the wrong moment?

"What is it?" Meta asked. "Did you kill him?"

Maddox shook his head. "No. Kane...Kane told me to tell you something."

"He did?"

This was hard, but Maddox said, "Kane saved our lives."

"You're kidding? How?"

The captain told Meta what had happened. He told her how he'd captured Kane with the professor's web-field generator. The captain also explained how Kane had escaped from the shackles and armored vacc-suit.

"He sacrificed himself," Maddox said. "He purposely took Oran Rva's blade into his body in order to hold the enemy down long enough for me to kill the New Man."

"Amazing," Meta said.

"It reminds me of an old saying," Maddox said.

"What's that?"

"Greater love has no man than this, that he lays down his life for another."

"That's beautiful," Meta said. "Who said that?"

"An ancient carpenter named Jesus," Maddox said.

Meta stared into the captain's eyes.

That's when Maddox realized he would fulfill his promise. "Meta," he said. "Kane had a message for you. He said he did those things because...because he loved you."

"What?" she whispered. "You're kidding me?"

Maddox shook his head.

"Kane loved me?"

The words coming from Meta shocked Maddox. He recalled what Kane had told him at the end. They had been the man's last words, heavy with meaning. Kane had told him to stop being a fool. Did the dying see things others couldn't?

Maddox squeezed Meta's fingers. "So do..." He was going to say, "So do I." But that didn't sound right. "Meta," he said. "I..." The words stuck in the captain's throat although he couldn't figure out why.

Maybe Meta could see his dilemma. "You silly fool," she said. "I love *you*. Do you know that?"

Maddox stared into her eyes.

"I've loved you for a long time, Captain, but do you hold it against me for having traveled with Kane for so long?"

Maddox shook his head.

Meta smiled, and tears welled in her eyes. It made her features look even more drawn.

She was so beautiful, and he had almost lost her.

"Meta," he whispered.

Her eyes became bright.

"I love you," Maddox said.

She beamed up at him while squeezing his hand.

He leaned low and kissed her. She clutched his head, whispering, "Maddox, Maddox."

Finally, he disengaged from her. "You should sleep," he said.

"Will you stay and watch over me?"

"Of course."

Meta closed her eyes. "Thank you," she whispered. "Thank you…" Before she could finish her thought, she was asleep.

Maddox gazed down at her for a time. It was crazy that it had taken the admonishment from an agent for the New Men to push Maddox to say the words he felt in his heart. Love. It was a strange emotion. But once one had tasted it, nothing else compared.

-48-

Several days later, Maddox found himself back in Geneva, in the brigadier's office.

Meta was healing rapidly. One of the world's best surgeons had already operated to repair Oran Rva's damage. The captain had been surprised to learn how much wreckage a single knife-thrust had been able to achieve. Thank God for modern medicine.

Dana was planning a surprise party for Meta. Maddox was supposed to drive Meta there in a few hours. He hoped he could get out of Geneva in time.

Behind the desk, O'Hara lowered a tablet she'd been scanning. The Iron Lady looked tired. It showed in her eyes and the hunch of her shoulders.

"That was far too close, Captain," O'Hara said. "Another half hour and the Lord High Admiral would have engaged the doomsday machine. According to Commander Guderian's report, that would have ended the Home Fleet."

"How is the commander?" Maddox asked.

O'Hara's tired eyes became haunted. "It's too soon to say. Strand...I wonder if Lieutenant Noonan spoke with the original."

"I suspect she did," Maddox said.

"Do you care to elaborate on that?"

"Certainly," the captain said. "These past few days, I've been sorting through what everyone knew. I've come to believe that the original Strand manipulated Oran Rva."

"Is that possible?"

Maddox smiled wryly.

"Come now, Captain, none of that. What are you suggesting and why?"

"According to Oran Rva, Strand and Ludendorff are two sides of the same coin. It's clear the New Man knew more about those two than we do. It almost seems as if those two have been manipulating events behind the magic curtain, so to speak."

"When did you become poetic?" O'Hara asked.

Maddox shook his head. "I believe that Ludendorff and Strand are privy to knowledge the rest of us lack. Strand created or helped to create the New Men, but he lost control of them."

"Meaning what?" O'Hara asked.

"In this instance, that a group of Methuselah People created a society that went its own way. The New Men rebelled, deciding for themselves what the good life consisted of. They rejected the idea that they would be humanity's defenders, deciding to be its rulers and remodelers instead. I've spoken with Dana. She told me that such things have happened before."

"Really?" O'Hara asked.

"History is replete with military organizations forged to defend a society, but instead they decided to take over the reins of power. The Mamelukes or slave soldiers did it in Medieval Egypt. The Muslim rulers bought horse-archer slaves to fight for them. After a time, the Mamelukes began to rule Egypt. To a lesser extent, the Praetorian Guard of ancient Rome did that too. They made and unmade many an emperor. The German barbarians in the Roman legions, brought in to fill the places the peaceful citizens refused to take, took over in the end. I could go on and on."

"That does nothing to solve the problem of Strand and Ludendorff."

"We know about them now," Maddox said. "That will go a long way to solving the problem. We also know more about the New Men."

"True," O'Hara said. "We also know that the doomsday machine greatly aided them. The Wahhabi Caliphate is a shattered remnant of their former selves. Their navy isn't going to help us in any appreciable way in the ongoing war with the New Men."

"That's true, Ma'am, but I think you're overlooking a critical factor that is going to help us."

O'Hara studied the captain with her tired eyes. "I'd like to hear this. Yes, we dodged a bullet, as the saying goes. But how does defeating the doomsday machine help us in the greater war against the New Men?"

"I'm surprised you don't see it," Maddox said.

The Iron Lady drummed her fingers on the desk.

"Even now," the captain said, "Intelligence is combing the various estates and industries of the Methuselah People. The nuclear detonation in Monte Carlo has created an outcry for it."

"I'm quite aware of that, Captain. The increased workload has given me many a sleepless night."

"In his grab for the doomsday machine, Oran Rva used up some—many, I believe—of the New Men's most deeply embedded agents on Earth. We're sweeping up more enemy espionage people by the day. Their secret service is shattered here, a broken reed."

"That's true," O'Hara said. "Yes, I see your point. We're consolidating our position."

"It's more than that," Maddox said. "The Earth and the Commonwealth are uniting. We're hardening our resolve. The enemy is losing his ability to learn about our plans. Given our espionage breakthroughs, it's possible we'll soon discover the location of the Throne World."

"Are you suggesting we go onto the offensive?"

"Absolutely I am," Maddox said. "I'm also suggesting that *Victory* spearhead the assault."

"Without the help of the Wahhabi Navy?" O'Hara asked.

"It's time we gathered the Windsor League warships and the Spacers under our command."

"Such a thing will take time," the brigadier said thoughtfully.

"If I might make another suggestion, Ma'am, I think we should rush a flotilla to the Xerxes System."

O'Hara smiled tiredly. "The Lord High Admiral is already planning just that. As I said, we dodged a bullet, and our fleets are intact. The idea, though, of Builder drones still working after all these centuries, and transferal pyramids in space... It leads us to a frightful question. Are more of those aliens out there?"

"More?"

"What would you call the doomsday machine but an alien vessel?" O'Hara asked.

"That's a good point," Maddox said.

O'Hara drummed her fingers on the desk until she sighed deeply. "We've uncovered some critical plots against us, only to discover that there are even more mysteries out there. Who built the doomsday machine? What happened to the Swarm?"

"I suggest we worry about these things one at a time," Maddox said.

"Then I have a question for you. Do you believe we're going to be given that luxury?"

"Only the future will tell us that, Ma'am. I'm still elated at our present victory. I want time to soak it in."

"I can understand the feeling, Captain. But you must know the ancient saying, 'There is no rest for the wicked.'"

"Is that us, Ma'am?"

"What else would you call the people of the Intelligence Service?"

Maddox didn't answer the question, but turned away, staring at a glass case of model starships. He'd been wondering about something ever since the fight in the doomsday machine. He hadn't told anyone his thoughts about it. More than ever, he wanted to know his father's identity. Could it have been Oran Rva? He didn't like to think so. As much as he disliked the New Men, he wasn't sure he wanted to be his father's killer.

O'Hara sighed. "Captain, I'm tired. The constant worry, the latest espionage war with the host of enemy agents...I need a rest. I plan to take a week off and recuperate. I suggest you do likewise."

"Is Star Watch content to let Galyan orbit Earth alone?"

412

"We are in constant communication with the AI," O'Hara said. "The Adok intelligence has made it quite clear that it will allow no other commander aboard *Victory* but you. Like it or not, you're going to remain a starship captain for the foreseeable future."

"I'm going to want my crew with me."

O'Hara nodded as if that was obvious. "Now, if there's nothing else, I believe you have a lady to escort to a surprise party."

"How do you know about that?" Maddox asked.

"Please, Captain, I am the head of Star Watch Intelligence for a reason."

"Yes indeed, Ma'am. I can see that."

O'Hara smiled. "You did excellent work, Captain. You must realize that I'm proud of you."

Maddox nodded ever so slightly, feeling a flush creep up his neck.

"Now you must go before I say something I'll regret later," O'Hara told him, "Goodbye for now, Captain."

***

Maddox flew to the hospital in an air-car. He picked up Meta, pushing her wheelchair out of the building.

"This is ridiculous," she said.

"It's an old custom, I hear."

"An Earth custom," Meta said. "I'm a Rouen Colony woman, much stronger than the natives of this backwater planet."

"Much prettier, you mean," the captain said.

Meta smiled up at him.

Maddox stopped by the air-car, opening the passenger-side door. Then he held out a hand, helping Meta into the vehicle.

He folded the chair and put it in the trunk of the air-car. Soon he lifted, heading for a Normandy beach.

"Is Galyan in orbit?" Meta asked.

"Keeping watch," Maddox said.

"I can't imagine being him. In fact..." Meta faced the captain. "I've begun to feel sorry for Galyan."

413

"Just a minute," Maddox said. He turned on the radio. "Galyan?"

"Here, Captain Maddox," the AI said.

"Are you feeling lonely?"

"That is a preposterous notion," Galyan said. "I am in constant communication with the Earth's greatest chess master. So far, I have beaten him three times. I have also configured a new probability process that will—"

"Galyan," Maddox said, interrupting.

"Yes, Captain?"

"I just wanted to check in to make sure you're doing all right."

"Thank you, Captain. That was thoughtful of you. Is Meta in the air-car with you?"

"Do you really need to ask?"

"No," Galyan said. "I have been monitoring you since you left the hospital. If the air-car should falter, I have devised a method to use my tractor beam to—"

"Galyan," Maddox said, interrupting once more.

"Yes, sir," the AI said.

"Thanks for all you've done. I, personally, appreciate it."

"Thank you, sir. And Captain?"

"Yes?" Maddox asked.

"Nothing," Galyan said a moment later, as if reconsidering. "Enjoy your time with Meta."

Maddox glanced at Meta. She shrugged. "I plan to," he said.

"This I know," the AI said.

"Okay," Maddox said. "I'll see you soon." Then, he turned off the comm.

Meta smiled, stroking one of the captain's arms. "Thanks for showing me that Galyan is doing fine. He's enjoying himself."

Maddox grinned at her.

She leaned near and they kissed. Afterward, Meta peered out of the bubble canopy. "So, where are we going?"

"Hang on," Maddox said, increasing speed. "I'll show you."

414

***

Later that evening, on a beach in Normandy, a fire blazed. Six people sat around it in beach chairs.

Dana Rich sipped a glass of wine. No doubt, she thought about Professor Ludendorff. Whenever someone spoke her name, Dana smiled. From time to time, she stared at the flames, lost in thought.

Keith Maker ate a polish dog. The ace had been grinning all night. He laughed a lot, and his hair was tousled. None of the others seemed to get tired as he retold various flying exploits.

Treggason Riker flexed his new bionic hand. He said little, one side of his face puffed out from holding so many sunflower seeds. There was a mass of shells at his feet. He seemed content, occasionally guzzling from a beer bottle and spitting more shells.

Valerie Noonan added wood to the fire, keeping it a hot blaze. Often, when a log popped, throwing up a shower of sparks, she laughed with delight. Her father had taken her on a camping trip once. The same good feeling filled her tonight. She was with her family, and she was happy to be alive.

Meta held the captain's hand. She kept thinking about Kane. The Rouen Colony man had saved them because he'd loved her. Life had been hard for Kane. The New Men had misused him. In the end, Kane had helped the old-style humans over the so-called dominants. Meta was determined to beat the enemy. Such a noble sacrifice shouldn't go to waste.

Captain Maddox glanced at his crewmembers. They were his responsibility. He had to make sure to use their talents to the best of his ability and then he had to make sure to bring them back alive. Meta's near death, and watching Ludendorff's android die, had brought that home more than ever.

The war had been ugly, and it would likely get worse. Tonight, though, they celebrated another victory. Who knew how many more surprises were in store for them? Who knew whether they were going to pierce the many secrets swirling around them? The origin of the doomsday machine, the reasons for Strand and Ludendorff's differences—

415

Maddox released Meta's hand. He stood, and he held his arms wide as if encompassing his crew. "You people are the best in the universe," he said. "And let's be honest, we have the greatest starship there is. I'm proud of each one of you. We saved the Earth and..."

The captain lowered his arms. He gazed into each face, finally nodding. "I don't have the words to say anything other than this: thank you."

"If I had a drink, I'd toast you, Captain," Keith shouted. "Instead, I salute you, sir." The ace stood up and saluted crisply.

The others cheered, clapping their hands.

Maddox grinned, nodding in appreciation. Afterward, he sat down, as did Keith.

The party continued as the fire blazed on the Normandy shore.

***

High in stationary Earth orbit, Galyan kept his best sensors trained on the crew. He watched them, with several weapons systems ready in case anyone should try to harm his friends. Without them—

Galyan shied away from the thought, content to know that his people were safe and happy for this moment in time.

The End

SF Books by Vaughn Heppner

DOOM STAR SERIES:
Star Soldier
Bio Weapon
Battle Pod
Cyborg Assault
Planet Wrecker
Star Fortress
Task Force 7 (Novella)

EXTINCTION WARS SERIES:
Assault Troopers
Planet Strike
Star Viking
Fortress Earth

LOST STARSHIP SERIES:
The Lost Starship
The Lost Command
The Lost Destroyer
The Lost Colony
The Lost Patrol

Visit VaughnHeppner.com for more information

Made in the USA
Monee, IL
30 January 2020